MURDER IN CENTRAL PARK

MURDER IN
CENTRAL PARK

A BILL DONOVAN MYSTERY

MICHAEL JAHN

ST. MARTIN'S MINOTAUR ✠ NEW YORK

THOMAS DUNNE BOOKS.
An imprint of St. Martin's Press.

Library of Congress Cataloging-in-Publication Data

Jahn, Michael.
    Murder in Central Park : a Bill Donovan mystery / Michael Jahn.
      p. cm.
    ISBN 0-312-24222-0
    1. Donovan, Bill (Fictitious character)—Fiction. 2. Police—New York (State)—New York—Fiction. 3. Central Park (New York, N.Y.)—Fiction. 4. New York (N.Y.)—Fiction. I. Title.

PS3560.A35 M874 2000
813'.54—dc21

                          99-086191

First Edition: March 2000

10   9   8   7   6   5   4   3   2   1

For my son, Evan Jahn, of whom I'm so very proud

New York City is fun to write about. Almost anything you can imagine short of an Antarctic expedition or a trip over Niagara Falls in a barrel is likely to happen. Whenever I think I am wrong about that I am proven, well, wrong.

For example, when beginning a yarn set in Central Park I wanted to show how wild the place can be and so cast about for wild animals I could place there. I thought, a resident falcon or two, some exotic migratory birds, a large murder of crows, perhaps I would take a chance and install a beaver in one of the ponds. Then Amy Eddings of WNYC, the city's Public Radio station, broadcast a report about the plan, cooked up with extreme seriousness—and taken exactly that way by some community groups—to introduce wolves into Central Park. That was just as I was beginning to write *Murder in Central Park*. Two months after I finished, still wondering if I had gone too far in using the wolf thing, a coyote was captured in Central Park. I have this image of him trotting down from upstate New York, along the Grand Concourse through the Bronx, past Yankee Stadium, over the 155th Street Bridge, and down Fifth Avenue through Harlem, with no one noticing, or if someone did, perhaps wondering how in hell he knew where he was going. There are some cab drivers, recently arrived from a far corner of the world and speaking almost no English, who can't find Central Park. Finally, as I worried over my depiction of the high rocks at the north end of the Park, *The New York Times* ran a story about rock climbing there.

And so I would like to thank the city of New York for providing constant material and continual astonishment. Care to discuss the city that never bores, Donovan, or anything else? Write to me c/o St. Martin's Press, 175 Fifth Avenue, New York, N.Y. 10010, or electronically at medj@worldnet. att.net. or donovanbooks@hotmail.com. I also anticipate having a Web site up by the time *Murder in Central Park* is published. The planned URL (Web address) is http:// www.home.att.net/medj/ but, should that fail, a trip to www.clueless.com or one of the other mystery sites should turn me up.

I also would like to thank one New Yorker in particular, my firstborn son, Evan Jahn, who lives in Greenwich Village with his wonderful wife, Denise Pizzini. He is the city's biggest fan and a source of constant pride to me, and hopefully will keep on taking me on tours of New York's exotic nooks as long as I am able to keep up with him. It is to Evan that this book is lovingly dedicated.

Michael Jahn
August 15, 1999

1. ROCK-A-BYE, CAPTAIN, IN THE TREETOPS

The clouds skittered like wary spectators past a full moon that glistened in the water and gave knife edges to the shadows of the weeping willows, ferns, and skunk cabbage that lined the isolated and largely abandoned pond not far from Central Park Lake. There was no wind on that midnight late in April when the bright lights of Central Park West, the nearest boulevard, were less than a memory, and the sounds of the occasional ambulance rushing a survivor to an emergency room were as weak and faraway as the heartbeat of the victim.

When Captain Bill Donovan, chief of special investigations for the City of New York, pushed open the passenger's side door of the forest green Range Rover he stepped into a world few native New Yorkers and no visitors knew. His old black Keds broke through the wild blueberry underbrush and crushed the dried twigs that lay atop an inch or two of rotting leaves, left from the previous autumn, that formed the bed of this old forest that surrounded a small pond that existed, wild and largely unknown, amidst the Big Apple.

The trees were old-growth maples and oaks, with a solitary elm pushing the limits of its lifespan not far from the little-used dirt path that wound into the woods. The path finally became overgrown and impassable a hundred yards before the muddy bank of what the sole history book to remember it called Fiddler's Pond. That same book, published in a solitary edition in 1937 and currently falling apart in the archives of the New-York Historical Society, never mentioned the path. No one recalled who cleared it or when, and all that kept the path from being reclaimed by the forest was the sometime passage of a scientist's vehicle.

Gently opening the driver's side door and quietly closing it, Lauriat stage-whispered across the top of the Range Rover, saying "Don't slam the door. You'll startle the crows. They get jumpy when someone they don't know is around."

Donovan whispered back, "Okay," and did as he was told, pulling his well-traveled, old canvas L. L. Bean tote bag from the vehicle and inching with it to the front, squeezing between the fender and the brush, which scratched the back of his head and his old suede jacket.

Lauriat did likewise. Then he pulled a small flashlight from his hunter's vest, from one of the loops that in another usage was given to shotgun shells, and shone it on the ground. Someone long ago had tried to pretty up the path by strewing it with broken oyster shells. They crunched vaguely beneath Donovan's feet, but not loudly enough, he was glad to note, to wake up the crows.

Lauriat said, "The road ends here. We have to walk a hundred yards through the brush. But the workmen who put up the scaffolding cut a path. Follow me."

Donovan did that, following not so much his friend and neighbor in the Federalist brick apartment building on Riverside Drive, but the sandwich-plate-sized patch of light just ahead of his logger's boots.

Lauriat had exaggerated the success of the workmen in cutting a path. The track had been cut in winter and was subsequently overgrown, and new leaves licked Donovan's cheeks and supple, just-grown branches brushed his shoulders. Still, soon the patch of light shone on the floor of a dining room–sized clearing nestled at the feet of three mature oaks. Behind a gated and locked green chain-link fence was steel construction scaffolding—also painted green in an attempt at camouflage.

"I forgot to ask if you're afraid of heights," the scientist said, grasping a shoulder-high rung of a metal ladder that went straight up, rising from the blueberry brush to parallel the scaffolding and the immense tree trunk and finally disappear into the canopy of newly grown leaves. Lauriat aimed his beam up the ladder, as if it could reach to the treetops. Only the moon, serendipitously out from behind a cloud, allowed Donovan to detect that *something* was up there: the Crow's Nest, Lauriat called it. All Donovan could see was a mass of some sort hidden in the leaves. Nearly impossible to make out at night if you weren't looking for it; difficult during the day, Donovan imagined. But he wondered how much the crows were fooled.

"I actually *am* afraid of heights," he admitted. "But I'll be okay if I don't look down. Are you sure that your high-tech tree house is safe?"

"Absolutely safe. This is construction-grade scaffolding, city certified."

"And no inspectors were paid off?"

"Not by me," Lauriat replied.

"Well, *that's* reassuring," Donovan replied, thinking of the other possible culprits within the construction crew.

Lauriat began up the ladder, holding the small flashlight, Tarzan-like, in his teeth.

"What do the crows think of this?" Donovan called after him.

"You'll hear them rustling around, but overall they're

used to me," the scientist replied, his boots now above Donovan's head and receding into the dark, tiny chips of soil flaking off the soles and falling down the ladder.

Donovan took a breath and followed, knowing that if he made the climb fast enough—and didn't look down—the height wouldn't bother him. He carried the Bean bag in one hand, hoisting it up, rung after rung, as he went.

The sound of Lauriat's boots was reassuring as the two men climbed through the lower branches and into a dark realm thick with slumbering creatures. The full moon was gone; Donovan assumed because of the trees, but maybe it ducked back behind a cloud. Halfway up the ladder, he felt disconnected . . . from earth and from sky . . . nowhere. He could see nothing in any direction, and he tried them all, even down. All light was extinguished. He could see none, not the moon, nor the street lamps of Central Park West, nor the famous lights of Broadway (admittedly dimmed that night by a power outage that affected ten nearby blocks), or any of the lights of the Manhattan skyline, though he knew it rose famously around him on all sides, and even Lauriat's flashlight beam was lost in the black of the midnight canopy.

"You're still with me?" Lauriat called down.

Donovan responded with a grunt.

"Almost there."

Donovan heard Lauriat's boots stop climbing, then step onto a metal platform of some sort. Next came the sound of keys being plucked from a pocket and put into a lock. Then a door swung open, noisily compressing a mass of leaves invisible to the captain.

"The crows . . ." Lauriat began to say something, but his words were obscured by loud squawking, not from a lot of birds—perhaps half a dozen—but nearby and loud. The cries didn't sound frightened, either, Donovan thought; but Lauriat was the crow expert. More like irritated. Woken up. But just

4

the closeness of those angry black beaks, each one big and sharp enough to pluck out a man's eye in the dark, startled Donovan.

"Pipe down," Lauriat said, his voice part commanding, part reassuring. "It's just me. And a friend."

The birds piped down, of a sort. The cries of irritation gave way to a few parting caws of complaint, following by a rustling of wings. They were settling back down, Donovan sensed. He was reminded of how Marcy *umph*ed and rolled from one side to the other after being awakened by a passing siren.

"They listen to you," Donovan said.

"I know it seems that way. But they really just know the sound of my voice and the time I get here every night. And that I've never been a threat to them. These crows are like that. If they know you, no problem. But if you're a stranger, they raise the roof. You're with me, so you're okay."

Lauriat stepped inside the hut and a light clicked on. It was from a small bulb, maybe forty watts, set in a ceiling fixture. But it sent a rectangle of light out into the canopy. Leaves were everywhere, Donovan could see then. Previously engulfed by black, Donovan found himself engulfed by green. Oak leaves came to within a foot of his face. But he could spot no birds. Not one. Even though he knew they were there.

"Where'd they go?" he asked.

"Where'd who go?"

Lauriat was inside the shack, switching things on.

"The *boids*," Donovan responded, affecting the accent frequently heard tripping from the lips of his associate at the NYPD, Sergeant Brian Moskowitz of the Canarsie section of Brooklyn.

"The *boids* are there, even though you can't see them. Be careful. Don't stick your hands in those leaves. Crows can be nasty . . . protective of their nests and young."

Donovan heard those words just as he was about to push away a branch that was rubbing against his neck. He let it stay there.

"Come on up," Lauriat said.

The scientist knelt and reached down a hand to take Donovan's bag, which Donovan handed over. Then the captain took a final, wary look at the deceptively peaceful green around him before climbing up the final rungs of the ladder and letting Lauriat give him a hand up into the hut.

"Welcome to the Crow's Nest," Lauriat said as Donovan got to his feet and saw what looked like a small studio apartment. It was perfectly rectangular, with an unfinished wooden floor and fake wood paneling, the thin metal kind, broken on all four sides by medium-sized windows. The room was furnished, in a sense. One entire wall was taken up by an equipment bench that was loaded with technical gewgaws—two laptop computers, audio and video recording decks, several cameras of varying types, a small TV, a radio, and an ominous-looking black box that may have been a power supply. Another wall held an armchair battered enough to have been scavenged during the Tuesday night sweeps, the weekly West Side ritual wherein the young and less fortunate competed for those bearable bits of furniture put out on collection night by the older and quite successful. Donovan still owned several pieces—a freestanding brass ashtray, a wrought iron umbrella stand, and a marble-topped end table—found on Tuesday nights in front of the wealthy apartment buildings along Central Park West and the main crosstown boulevards. The armchair's brocade was worn through in half a dozen spots and bore cat scratches along both sides. Next to it, an orange crate, set on one end, served as a table. In addition to those pieces, a watercooler sat next to a small refrigerator. Against another wall was a folding army cot and a small white bookcase of the cheap, build-it-yourself Swedish type sold by Ikea.

The wall was decorated, of a sort, with photographs of crows—dozens of crows—each labeled with a number and some with names. Donovan noticed that, in naming his birds, Lauriat favored the classics—Heckle, Jeckle, Edgar, Allan, Poe and an especially old and grizzly bird that had a look of pure evil in its one eye—the other had been put out; Donovan made a mental note to ask why. That ghastly black apparition was named Nevermore; his photo was central to all the others, a kind of hub, which showed that he mattered.

"This guy looks like the straw boss," Donovan said, pointing at Nevermore.

Lauriat snickered. "He's a tough one, all right, smart as a fox and mean, too. Lost his left eye in a fight with a peregrine falcon that came too close to the rookery."

"Let me get this straight," Donovan said, "Crows will *fight* with hawks?"

"You bet. One time five crows chased a peregrine falcon down Forty-seventh Street and finally cornered him behind a store marquee sign and damn near ripped him apart, diving and pecking at him, until he was rescued by the Humane Society."

"What happened to the falcon?" Donovan asked.

"They took him up to Duchess County and let him go out on a hilltop. I tell you, Bill, New York is a rough town."

"The crows here carry semiautomatics," Donovan said as he put his Bean bag down by one end of the cot. Then he sat on the cot, patted its olive-drab surface, and said, "I get the cot, by reason of age, rank, and the fact that, within the memory of my spinal column, I spent the last six weeks of Marcy's pregnancy sleeping in a chair in her hospital room."

"I figured the cot for you," Lauriat said. "Working in the rain forest I got used to a sleeping bag on the ground. Here,

I put my bag on top of an inflatable mattress."

Donovan looked around, and Lauriat directed his attention to a pile of clothes, blankets and other apparent debris that the captain now could see included an inflatable mattress.

As the scientist deployed the latter and then fussed with one of the cameras, Donovan sat on the cot and unpacked. He changed from his jeans and sneakers into sweatpants and socks, and hung his old and tattered black sweater on a nail. He pulled on a huge and loose polo shirt, one comfortably worn and good for sleeping, and, finally, commandeered a patch of benchtop for the cell phone and laptop that connected him to his family at home and his computer at the office.

He heard the sound of bottles being opened. Lauriat came over bearing two bottles of beer—a Harp for himself and a nonalcoholic Kaliber for Donovan. The latter was the treat that the captain allowed himself after giving up drinking and changing his life around ten years ago.

"It seems vaguely masochistic to drink beer in a tree house," Donovan said, nodding in the direction of what looked to him like a low-capacity portable potty.

"You'd think that," Lauriat responded. "But this is an isolated area and the downstairs neighbors—tree roots—like to be sprinkled with nitrogen."

He walked over to where a rag was draped over an accommodation that the captain hadn't noticed—a funnel stuck into a length of black rubber hose that disappeared through a hole in the wall.

"I used to know a guy who had one of those in his toolshed," Donovan said. "All the guys thought he was pretty neat. Had it together, you know? Then one night he went around giving away his tools . . ."

"Uh oh."

". . . then sat down and ate a shotgun shell."

Lauriat shrugged. "In my case, it indicates only practicality. And I don't get that many women guests."

"This isn't exactly the ideal 'come up and see me sometime' situation," Donovan said.

"In fact, I don't get guests at all. You're the first."

"I needed to get out of the house and into the fresh air," Donovan said. "We had the pregnancy from hell. Marcy had every complication on the left side of the menu. Then came five months of crying and diaper changing."

"Too much parenthood isn't always a good thing," Lauriat said.

Donovan didn't agree, but left the subject alone. "And I came up here because I'm interested in your research."

Lauriat smiled. "I find it hard to believe that a New York City police detective, even one of your eminence, would find much of interest in canopy research."

"Why not? You study life in the treetops. I study life on the fire escapes. Explain to me the difference."

Lauriat nodded. "Not much, when you put it that way."

"So why crows?" Donovan asked.

"You mean, why do I study crows?"

"Because they're smart?"

"I study them because they study back," Lauriat said, bobbing his head up and down. "They're *the* smartest birds. I watch them. They watch me. They want to know why I'm here. I mean, they seem to be convinced that I'm harmless . . . no threat to *them*, anyway . . . and they're curious. Crows are among the few bird species that use tools. Did you know that?"

Donovan knew. "Twigs, you mean."

"There's a tropical species, *corvus moneduloides*, which lives in the South Pacific, in New Caledonia," Lauriat said. "The researcher who reported on them calls them the most intelligent nonhuman animal species. His crows make three types of tools . . . standardized, too, which is amazing for a bird . . . including hooks. They use them to pry insects out of holes."

"Your crows don't do that?"

"Not that I've seen . . . yet. I can tell you this, though. My guys can get a garbage can open faster than any animal except a raccoon."

"Possibly including some winos," Donovan said.

"They also play."

"Play, as in games?"

"Yeah. They play tug-of-war, for example. Two crows will play with a stick that way. And they do things that are just *weird*."

"Such as?" Donovan asked.

"Well, now you cut to the reason why I'm here, stuck in a tree six or seven nights a week for the better part of a year." Lauriat sat down on the mattress and, cross-legged, began to pull off his boots. "I haven't observed toolmaking behavior among my crows, but I think they're doing it. And here's why. A crow—Nevermore is a good example—will fly up carrying a stick, leave it atop a pole or wedged in the fork of a tree, fly off, then come back an hour or a day later to get it."

"Why, do you think?"

"When a New Caledonia crow makes a tool, he often will leave it in a secure spot and come back for it when he needs it," Lauriat said.

"And you think that's what Nevermore is doing," Donovan said.

"Yeah, I think the old cutthroat has made himself a fine tool . . ."

"Maybe a crowbar," Donovan said.

"For digging worms out of the ground," Lauriat said with a smile. "Or for picking a pocket, or plucking the marrow from the bones of a dead animal. Who the hell knows what these very clever birds will do."

"And he's sticking it places for safekeeping."

"Not that he needs to. *No one* would steal from Nevermore. I'll point him out to you tomorrow."

Lauriat stripped down to his shorts and a T-shirt, then relaxed to regale the captain with an hour's worth of bird stories, not wilderness adventures so much as tales of grants fought for and research topics accepted or rejected. At one in the morning Donovan was beginning to nod off; noticing such, Lauriat pulled his pants and boots back on and opened the door. So doing roused the captain from his twilight sleep.

"What's happening?" he asked, propping himself up on his elbows.

"I have trouble sleeping. I usually go for a walk at two in the morning. But having you here is throwing me off, and I'm going to go now."

When Lauriat opened the door, more came in than fresh air. Donovan heard the sounds of kids . . . teenagers, he supposed . . . talking and playing the radio.

"Are you going to join the party?" Donovan asked.

"The party?"

"The one that's going on downstairs."

"Oh, the two teenagers. They show up every night almost, drinking beer in a clearing not far from here."

"I thought this whole section of woods was pretty impenetrable," Donovan said.

"There's another trail like the one we walked up . . . twenty or thirty yards to the north, leading right up to the water. There used to be a gazebo, but it fell down years ago and is overgrown with weeds. The kids don't mind the moss."

"A lot of people spend nights in this park," Donovan said. "Most of them are harmless. That said, do you want a police escort?"

Lauriat shook his head. "They're harmless. Besides, I'm only going to walk back to the Range Rover to stretch my legs. I won't come anywhere near them. Look, it's a bit cold out tonight. Do you mind if I borrow your sweater?"

"Be my guest."

"My jacket is in the cleaners," Lauriat said, taking Donovan's black sweater and pulling it over his head.

"See you later," Donovan said, and lay back down as Lauriat closed the door behind him and started down the ladder.

After a moment, Donovan got up and went to the workbench. He got his cell phone and called Marcy, waking her up long enough to exchange a few air kisses and I-love-you's. Then he sat the phone back on the workbench. At quarter to two, with Lauriat still out, Donovan took a look out the window at the moon, by then well to the west and dipping toward the western skyline, then stretched out on the cot once again and pulled a plain white sheet up to his chin.

His heels pressed against the crossbar that stretched the bottom of the canvas web beneath him. This set off a memory, one of those falling asleep memories. Donovan was twelve again and on the last of the camping trips he used to take with his parents before childhood faded into the confluence of his coming of age, the sixties, and the loud and angry arguments with his father over Vietnam. And then the elder Donovan, a respected old-school police sergeant, was shot dead—by a Harlem junkie, the file on the still-unsolved murder read—and that was it for sleeping on cots and the idylls of youth. For a few moments fading into twilight sleep, however, Donovan was a boy again and back stretched out on the old army cot, his feet so proudly reaching all the way down to the bottom crossbar, listening to the roar of the surf at Hither Hills State Park near Montauk.

A while later . . . around two, according to the captain's

watch . . . he was aware of Lauriat returning. The two men exchanged grunts and the scientist settled onto the air mattress, which squeaked like an old rocking chair on a bare wood floor for a minute or two until Lauriat fell asleep. There was no sound after that, not the wind, not the treetops, not the hundreds of clever black birds scant inches away, not the City of New York.

All changed with dawn's early light. Donovan sat bolt upright, awakened by a racket that sounded like the old number 1 local clattering into the 110th Street subway station. It came from all directions.

"What the hell is that?" Donovan asked, rubbing his eyes.

Lauriat too sat up, a bit groggily, and looked around. "The crows," he said.

"Do they always get up on the wrong side of the nest? Are they *angry* or what?"

The scientist looked alarmed. "Not angry," he said. "Frightened."

"I thought they fought hawks," Donovan insisted, lowering his feet to the floor.

"Something is wrong."

Both men scrambled to their feet, the fiftyish Donovan feeling the ache of the morning cold in his joints a bit more keenly, he was sure, than the forty-something Lauriat. That notwithstanding, Donovan beat the man to a window.

The gray of dawn pounded into the Crow's Nest, a blue sky about to emerge, a hint of a wind coming from the north. Donovan was amazed at how near he was to the sky. Climbing up into the canopy in the pitch black of midnight, he would have sworn the sky was gone forever, lost in a mat of little green leaves and big black birds. Now the sky seemed at arm's reach, gray turning blue, with the living canopy swarming below.

The little breeze from the north rippled the water of Fiddler's Pond, visible between the trees below. And there was the source of the commotion, plain as day, a few yards from where the billowing leaves of the skunk cabbage and the drooping branches of a weeping willow concealed most of the shoreline. A few yards from shore, an Eastern painted turtle had climbed out of to the water onto a forked log. A man's body lay on its back, half submerged, a white shirt ripped open to reveal a distended, disemboweled torso. Blood stained the water in a slick around the man, spreading from water's edge to midstream. And there was more. Perched on the corpse's chest, blood running down its beak and spattered across the black feathers of its chest, was a triumphant-looking, proud, old one-eyed crow.

As it looked up—Donovan swore it was looking at him—it opened its beak and let out a piercing cry that stirred the rest of the flock to an even higher level of racket. Donovan thought he saw the crow smile.

Lauriat said, "Nevermore."

2. That's Why They Call It a "Murder" of Crows

Lauriat became speechless, literally so. He gripped the windowsill tightly, his knuckles white. After a horrified silence, he said, "That's a body down there."

"A tasty one, apparently," Donovan replied, fetching his cell phone and making a quick call.

"Who . . . who were you calling?"

"My office. The boys and girls will start arriving soon. I'd better get down there. Want to come?"

Lauriat turned away from the window, but stiffly, as if he

had to think out the motions before making them. "You mean . . . to see the body?"

"Why not? You never saw bodies in the rain forest?"

"Not bodies of *people*. Of carrion . . . of animals that were killed and being eaten."

"Look out the window again and explain to me the difference," Donovan said.

"Oh, my God," Lauriat stammered, fumbling his way across the room to sit on the cot.

The captain had moved down the wall and was using the portable potty. When he was done, he reached into a storage compartment on the side of the device and plucked from it a spare plastic liner bag.

"You may as well come with me," Donovan said. "I guarantee you there will be no bird-watching today."

"I . . . I don't think I can."

"Why not? You didn't kill that man, did you?"

"What! Me! A murderer? Of course not. How could you even ask?"

"It's my job," Donovan replied.

"I don't know how you could bring yourself to ask that question. I was with you all night."

"With the exception of the hour between one and two in the morning," Donovan replied.

Lauriat said, "I thought you were my friend."

"I am your friend, and that's why I'm asking. 'Cause if I don't, some other cop will, and whoever you get will be a lot less friendly. Now that you've gotten used to the idea of being a murder suspect . . ."

"A . . . murder . . . suspect," the scientist said slowly. He shook his head, then laughed bitterly. "There goes my grant," he said.

"Not if Nevermore was using a tool to pry out that guy's spleen," Donovan replied.

Lauriat buried his head in his hands. "I can't believe this has happened."

"If you didn't kill that man, do you know who did?"

"No," Lauriat said, this time flatly. Donovan sensed that he was getting accustomed, and fairly quickly, to being involved in a police investigation.

"Not those kids last night?" Donovan asked.

"Kids . . . oh, the ones over by the old gazebo. I never saw them. I did what I said I was going to do. I walked out to the Range Rover and stretched my legs."

"For an hour?"

"I listened to the radio and heard some music. A Chopin nocturne, if you must know. To help myself fall asleep. On the way back to the ladder, I noticed that the music the kids were playing had stopped. I assumed they went home."

"More likely down to Times Square to mug tourists. So, are you coming with me or not?"

"Oh, *okay*," Lauriat said, walking across the room and reaching for his boots.

"Hold on a second," Donovan said, reaching out for the boots. "I'll take those." He got them from the scientist and put them into the plastic bag he had just appropriated.

"What's this about?" Lauriat asked.

"And the clothes you wore when you went on that walk. Your pants and shirt."

"That's all I have to wear," he objected.

"Then I guess you better stay up here after all," Donovan said. "I'll send someone to get you a change of clothes."

Traumatized once again, Lauriat got back into his sleeping bag and rolled into the fetal position atop his air mattress.

Donovan returned to the window and looked down at the body. It was still there, with the old black bird still atop it. Donovan opened the window, and the bird turned to give the captain a sharp look.

"Shove off," Donovan said, but not, apparently, loud enough to be heard. So he aimed his Smith & Wesson at the bird, who responded with a loud caw and a languorous fluttering of wings as he rose into the day and flew off.

Donovan put the gun back in its holster and shut the window just as the sounds of sirens approaching were drifting across Fiddler's Pond.

Sergeant Brian Moskowitz handed his boss a brown paper bag with a baseball-sized lump in the bottom as well as a paper cup—the sort that diners give out, printed with ersatz Greek columns and amphoras—that steamed in the morning air. As Donovan peered into the bag suspiciously, his aide said, "They didn't have everything bagels. I got you poppy."

Donovan scowled. "There's no bagel shop in the city that doesn't have everything bagels at this time of day."

"I swear on my mother's grave," Moskowitz said, pressing his fist to his chest in a devout sort of way.

"Your mother's not dead."

"A technicality."

Fishing out the bagel, Donovan said, "You've been going behind my back again, talking to my wife."

"This would be about the health thing?" Mosko said.

Donovan nodded, unwrapping his breakfast and taking a bite before mumbling, "At least it's fresh."

"And the coffee's hot. Really hot. Try it."

"Admit it. She got to you. It was that gyro that she thought had goat meat in it."

"We didn't discuss that."

"So you *have* been talking to her."

"Come on, boss, the woman wants you to live forever. Can I help it if she calls me now and then and asks me to watch what you eat? No everything bagels. Too much salt.

Marcy is my boss's wife. And very persuasive. Not to mention a black belt in kung fu."

"Practice has lapsed since the baby came," Donovan said.

"So *you* argue with her, then." Mosko's tone of voice indicated that he felt he had won the argument. He said, "What happened here last night? I thought you were taking time off. Bird-watching or whatever."

"It wasn't *bird-watching*. It was science, son. Canopy research."

Mosko imitated Chico Marx. He did it badly, saying, "I don't see no can o' peas."

Two hours had passed since dawn and the discovery of the body. In that time, the area surrounding Fiddler's Pond had undergone a transformation. Emergency vehicles were everywhere, in each open space. Yellow crime-scene tape—maybe a half mile of it—extended from Park Drive West all the way around Fiddler's Pond to the Ramble on the far end of Central Park Lake. At least a hundred law enforcement personnel—uniformed cops, detectives, and forensic technicians—swarmed around the pond, out of the water and in it, both in hip boots and in rowboats. Some were dragging the bottom of the pond, looking for the murder weapon. The body had been removed from the water and laid out on a rubber mat that itself was placed on a patch of shoreline newly swept for evidence.

"Where are these birds I keep hearing about?" Mosko asked, looking up into the treetops, around.

"They ate and ran," Donovan responded. "You should nag *them* about the cuisine. I heard you found a wallet while I was back up in the Crow's Nest checking on Lauriat."

Moskowitz bent over and squinted at his laptop, which was perched, precariously, on a tree trunk in a clearing a distance from the body.

"Yeah, wallet, a lid to a can of Sterno, and some beer

bottle caps. The I.D. in the wallet reads Harvey Cozzens," Mosko said, spelling out the surname. "He was forty-seven and lived on First Avenue near Eighty-fifth Street. An employee identity badge in one pocket lists Tamarisk Software."

"A computer guy? Do we know what, exactly, he did?"

Mosko shook his head. "It's too soon to get anything but the barest details."

"Such as how he died. By the knife, I presume."

"You got it. The field coroner says it was a large one, maybe a foot long. We're dragging the bottom of the pond now, looking for it."

Donovan said, "I got a close-up look of the body when we dragged the victim out. Did you?"

Mosko shook his head. "You got a stronger stomach than I do, boss. All that scotch over all those years, I guess."

"The late Mr. Cozzens was sliced more times than a smoked salmon, both in the back through his jacket and in front," Donovan said. "The throat was cut. The tummy was cut open and left to become crow food. Whoever did it wanted to make sure the bum was dead. And went to a *lot* of trouble. What does that suggest to you?"

"Amateur night," Mosko replied.

"Yeah, an amateur . . . and one who was incredibly pissed off at the victim. This was *personal* and not just some random killing. What else was in the wallet?"

"A stub from a dry cleaner. A MasterCard and a Visa. A Cost Plus membership card with his picture on it."

"The deceased was fond of a bargain," Donovan said.

"A library card," Mosko said, reading further down a list. "From where?"

"The Mid-Manhattan Branch."

"My old library," Donovan said. "Go on."

"A card from Jack LaLanne. But I don't think the guy

went often enough. He was five-foot-eight and at least two hundred pounds."

"One hundred and ninety-*nine* after Nevermore got through with him," Donovan said.

"There also were four coupons for Big Macs. But the coupons expired before their owner did. There also was a ShopRite card and a bookstore receipt."

"From what bookstore?"

"Black Orchid Books on East Eighty-first, a few blocks from where he lived."

"What did he buy?"

"Doesn't say. But I'll find out. That's it for the contents of the wallet."

"No driver's license?" Donovan asked.

"The guy lived in Manhattan. Who needs a car? The only reason that *you* have one is that you can park anywhere you damn well feel like. There was something else in Cozzens's wallet, though . . . some white powder."

Donovan was interested. His aide noted it.

"What kind?" Donovan asked.

"We've having it tested. It looks like a pill that crumbled when he sat on it. There still are a few tiny chunks."

"I want to know right away about this powder," Donovan said.

Mosko made a note on his laptop. To do so, he had to bend over considerably. Donovan found the image of his muscle-bound sergeant bending over to peck away at a laptop computer perched on a tree trunk slightly ridiculous.

"All the same, I don't think that Cozzens was the drug-using type," Mosko said. "Did you see *Jurassic Park*?"

Donovan had. "I had to sit through half a dozen tear-jerkers to pay Marcy back for watching that movie with me."

"You remember the computer nerd who ate Hershey bars all day? Cozzens reminds me of him."

Donovan stuck his hands in his pockets and looked around. He could make out the boxy frame of the Crow's Nest high above in its oak tree, the base of which was forty or fifty yards away. He wondered how Lauriat was making out, sitting alone in his cabin, awaiting further instruction.

"What in hell did Cozzens do to get himself disemboweled and tossed into the pond . . . presumably in the middle of the night," Donovan wondered out loud.

Moskowitz said, "You got the 'middle of the night' part right, boss. The preliminary estimate by forensics says that Cozzens shuffled off this mortal coil about six hours ago."

Donovan looked at his watch. "Two A.M.," he said.

"About that."

"Just as Lauriat was getting back from his walk," Donovan said.

Mosko asked, "What about the kids you heard?"

"Lauriat thought they split before two."

"Do you believe him?"

Donovan replied, "I'll tell you when we get the results back from his clothes. Did you send them downtown?"

"They're on their way now. That was quick of you to have thought to snatch Lauriat's duds before he could ruin any evidence."

"That's what they pay me for," Donovan said, patting his associate on the back. "To be thorough and on top of everything."

Mosko shook his head. "No, that's what they pay Bonaci and me to do."

Howard Bonaci was Donovan's scrupulous crime-scene chief.

"They pay *you* to be smart and think of stuff for us to do. Like having an idea what we're looking for on Lauriat's clothes."

"Moss," Donovan said. "There was none on the trail him

and me walked last night to get from the Range Rover to the tree house. But the ground is said to be covered with the stuff where the kids were sitting. Did you send someone out to buy Lauriat a change of clothes?"

"Yeah," Mosko said with a nod. "I got a guy standing on the corner of Broadway and Eighty-sixth waiting for the Gap to open right now. Like you said, we'll get him a pair of khakis and a red polo shirt. Kind of like the stuff you wear when the commissioner doesn't force you to put on a suit."

Moskowitz, who favored off-the-rack suits that fit snugly enough to show off his hard-won muscles, glanced at Donovan's jeans and baggy sweater. Then he gestured at the Crow's Nest. He said, "What's it like to sleep in a tree, anyway?"

"They don't have trees in Canarsie?"

"Sure, little bitty ones the city planted along the street years ago. Somehow they never grew up. Too small to climb up and fall asleep in."

"I feel your pain," Donovan said.

"And if you *could* fall asleep in one, the guys in the white suits would come and haul you off," Mosko said.

"The hard part was getting up and down the ladder. I'm telling you, even a man who isn't afraid of heights would be scared going four or five stories up that ladder in the dead of night surrounded by big, nasty birds. But going up at midnight was nothing compared with climbing down at dawn."

"When you could see how far up you were," Mosko added.

Donovan used the back of his hand to wipe imaginary sweat from his brow. "Which leads me to believe that no one, no matter how much of an insomniac, would voluntarily go down that ladder—an hour after going up—to take a walk."

"Not me. If I was on top of a tree and couldn't sleep I'd

do what any red-blooded, modern American would do."

"Take a pill," Donovan said.

"You bet. So that's why you suspected Lauriat right away?"

"It just seemed weird what he was doing. And even if he didn't, Lauriat is the only person who I am absolutely sure was in the vicinity of the crime scene at the time the murder took place."

"What about the kids?"

"What about them? I heard a radio and voices and Lauriat said they come there at night. He's still the only one I know was there. So I put him under tree-house arrest. I took away his clothes."

"I'm surprised that having nothing on but underwear stops anyone from going out in public anymore," Mosko said. "Did you ever notice how many women walk down the street in T-shirts and panty hose?"

"They're called 'tights,' " Donovan said.

"Is this a great country or what?" Mosko replied. His cell phone beeped then, and he brought the instrument to his ear. After a few seconds, he grunted "yeah," then asked his boss, "Are you ready for another close-up of the corpse? This one after the terrain was swept for evidence?"

Donovan nodded as he finished the last of his bagel. Leaving the computer on the tree trunk, Mosko led the way along a tortuous path that led almost all the way to Park Drive West before curling around and, plunging into increasingly thicker brush, winding up by the Range Rover. In the morning light, it seemed as if the front end had been planted in the trees; even more difficult to get around than it had seemed the night before.

Bonaci had pulled his crime-scene van in behind it and was standing by its hood, peering at his own laptop. This was a new development, one that Donovan greeted with amazement.

"Hi, Cap," Bonaci said, tapping the fingers of one hand on the shiny skin of his increasingly bald pate.

"What's this?" Donovan asked, pointing at the laptop.

"I caved in to the inevitable, as you would say."

"No more spiral notepads? No more notes scribbled in the margins of the *Daily News*?"

"I got a bargain from Uncle Stanley. I still haven't figured out how to initialize the cellular modem, though, so any time you got a moment . . ."

"I'm proud of you," Donovan said. "Tell me about Harvey Cozzens."

"Dead for between six and seven hours," Bonaci said.

"That puts the time of death between one and two in the morning. What changed?"

"Well, we looked at this and we looked at that. Do you need to know every detail?"

Donovan shook his head.

"Meaning Lauriat could have done it when he went for his walk," Mosko said.

"I suppose," Donovan replied, casting a glance up at the Crow's Nest, visible as a dense blob far up in the greenery to the east.

"You *suppose*?" Mosko said. "Two hours ago you were confiscating his clothes as evidence. Ten minutes ago you were wondering if there was moss on his boots."

"Now I'm thinking that a scientist who devotes his life to sitting in the treetops studying birds is not very likely to turn homicidal," Donovan said.

"And guys who do nothing but sort mail all day never go postal," Bonaci said. "There's tons of moss by the murder scene, by the way."

"Which is where? By the old gazebo?"

"You got it. Look at this." Bonaci opened a pad on which he had sketched the crime scene. It showed an arc of shoreline on that side of Fiddler's Pond, the oak in which sat the tree house, the trail in from the road, and the rundown gazebo twenty or thirty yards away. In the water, a body's length from shore, was a stick-figure body. But on the shoreline, amidst the ruins of the gazebo, was another stick figure.

"Cozzens was killed in the gazebo, sliced up there, then dragged into the water," Bonaci said.

Donovan nodded. "He must have been dragged right over the skunk cabbage. They were beaten down and broken, which if you've been anywhere near skunk cabbage . . ."

He looked at Moskowitz, who shrugged.

"No, of course not—not in Canarsie. Stupid of me."

"But *you* used to spend summers at your aunt's house out on the Island," Mosko said.

"Funny, I was thinking about the Island last night," Donovan said. "You're right . . . there's plenty of skunk cabbage by the stream that runs through my aunt's place. When you break the stems they truly stink. I could smell these ones a mile off this morning."

Bonaci tapped a pencil eraser on the drawing of the gazebo, especially a tiny rectangle. "From a preliminary look at the blood-spatter evidence, I would say that the victim was sitting on this bench . . . an old wrought-iron one with no back . . . when he got his throat slit. He fell forward . . ." Bonaci tapped the stick figure. ". . . to here, at first on his face, judging from a contusion on the forehead and a banged-up nose as well as by a big pool of blood about where you figure the neck would land. Then he rolled—*or was rolled*—onto his back. That's when his stomach was cut open."

"Weird," Mosko said.

"We'll know better tomorrow, but it looks like a combination of stab and slash wounds and maybe, like after death, some deliberate incisions."

"Deliberate incisions," Donovan said. "You're not suggesting that the early ones were accidental?"

"No," Bonaci said. "What I mean is, the guy was dead." Bonaci spelled out the word: "D.E.A.D. There was no need to cut him open. Unless . . ."

"Unless what?" Donovan asked.

"Unless they were . . ." He tossed his hands up. "I don't know. I can't think of a good reason."

"Were they looking for gold or what?" Mosko asked.

"I think that the answer is simple rage," Donovan replied. "Has forensics finished with the murder scene yet?"

"About ten minutes ago," Bonaci replied, after glancing at his watch.

"I want to see it."

"Follow me." Bonaci left the laptop, but closed the sketch pad and tucked it under his arm. He turned to walk to the back of the Range Rover and past to the paved road. Donovan and Mosko followed, the latter humming, not quite to himself. *Volare*, Donovan thought.

Donovan was fascinated with the route, which led back to Park Drive West and north to a raggedy patch of green between the road and the woods. "How did you find the murder scene?" Donovan asked.

"I've been to worse," Bonaci replied.

Donovan scowled, but no one saw it. "Allow me to rephrase: How do you know this is the way to the old gazebo?"

"It seemed the shortest route from the start. If you begin at Park Drive West and walk east . . ."

He pointed the way as they walked in the direction he was describing. "And find the spot where pedestrians can cross the drive to get to this lawn. This way . . ." He led them onto a rough, poorly tended patch of green, a city parks mixture of Kentucky bluegrass, dandelion, and wild chives. The latter stuck above the rest in clumps that made Donovan think of barrel cacti poking their stubby bodies from the desert floor.

"People sunbathe on this grass," Bonaci said. "We found a cap from a tanning lotion tube ground into one of the bare spots."

"I wouldn't," Mosko said, watching where he stepped. "Too many dogs like it here."

"If you go across the grass you find two places where you can get into the woods without being a squirrel. One is the old, one-lane trail that your scientist friend drove his fancy Jeep up. The other is down a ways and really hard to see if you're not looking. Here . . ."

Bonaci pointed at what looked to all the world like two stripling maples, the lower branches of which were locked in springtime embrace. Beneath and between them, Donovan saw the faint remains of a long-abandoned footpath. Bits of oyster shell were not quite overgrown by wild grass and weeds. Wear by occasional feet was evident—flattened leaves, broken stems, and a squished toadstool, the latter with a bit of crime-scene marking near it.

"Did you check all this stuff?" Donovan asked, stooping to look at the toadstool. "These things are very fragile . . . pop up overnight and are gone the next day."

"Yeah. If that mushroom . . ."

"Toadstool."

"Whatever. If it was stepped on by Lauriat, we'll find out. Walk around it, Cap." Bonaci parted the maple branches and pointed down what someone or something, maybe a raccoon, would recognize as being a path.

Donovan followed his two aides, who led the way down a trail so narrow he had to hold his hands up to keep the branches out of his face.

"How did those kids find their way to the gazebo at

night?" Donovan asked, to no one in particular.

"How did the dead guy?" Mosko replied.

"God still must smile on drunks and children. I've got to come back here at night and find out. How those kids did it."

"You're gonna come back here at night?" Mosko asked, absent-mindedly letting a branch snap back into Donovan's face.

That earned him a mild epithet.

"Sorry, boss," he said.

"Look at it this way. A couple of teenagers come down here in the dead of night to do what?"

"The usual," Mosko said.

"That they can do anywhere these days. Under a blanket on the Great Lawn. In a stairwell in their parents' apartment building. On the floor behind the bar at their friendly neighborhood saloon."

"People have sex in bars?" Bonaci said, using a voice that didn't feign all that much surprise.

"I once heard of such a thing happening," Donovan responded. "My point is that you can have sex anywhere. The kids who went to the gazebo last night—and, maybe, the late Harvey Cozzens—came here for a very specific reason."

"Like what?" Mosko asked.

"Sex, drugs, and something else. Murder, maybe," Donovan said. "Let's look at the body and see if we can figure it out."

The three men got to the murder scene a lot faster than Donovan expected. However overgrown, the trail was short. And marked every so often by crime-scene markers that his men had put where they found something of interest. Looking south from the trail through a stand of trees not yet fully foliated, Donovan could see the approximate outline of the Crow's Nest. *Not so far away*, he thought.

The crows had gone. He wondered where. He knew that they had followed Nevermore, flapping off noisily when Donovan went down the ladder to take a first look at the body.

The trail widened suddenly into a clearing that Donovan could see had once been an idyllic setting. He could imagine the gazebo as it had been a century before: a proud, even cocky Victorian sun shade made of oak beams and hand-cut cedar shakes, with facing, wrought iron benches each perfectly fit for a gentleman and his lady—hoop skirt, petticoat, and all—to sit in while enjoying the view across Fiddler's Pond. Perhaps there had even been a fiddler at that time, standing on a rise playing "Heather's Lullaby" for the entertainment of Sunday strollers.

But over the years the gazebo had fallen down. What was left of its beams were termite-eaten stubs that rose but a foot or two above the garbage-strewn ground. The wrought iron benches had rusted in place, still facing one another and, amazingly, still strong enough to sit on. They were the sole reminders of onetime glory, now relegated to the roles of sentinels watching over the moss, cigarette packages, and skunk cabbage. The view was largely gone, for the weeping willow had branches that dipped, like the long and slender fingers of a concert pianist, into the water.

Cozzens's body was laid out on its back on a black vinyl sheet. It was dressed in a cheap blue-green, zip-up jacket, a white nylon business shirt, also inexpensive, cotton-poly blend pleated trousers, a black vinyl belt, and black wingtips constructed, in China, of all man-made materials. Water from the pond soaked the body and the area, long since swept for evidence, between the two benches. Two field coroners were still fussing over the remains. Bonaci cleared his throat by way of alerting them to the arrival of brass. And upon seeing Donovan they straightened up and stepped back respectfully from the corpse.

"Anything new on the time of death?" Donovan asked.

"About the time we thought, Captain," was the response from one of them. "Between two and three. And we think that the first blow was struck from behind. The killer cut his throat."

"Which would explain why I didn't hear anything," Donovan said.

"That's all we know right now."

Mosko was looking down at the sliced-open chest and the dozens of claw and peck marks around it.

"I see now why they call it a 'murder' of crows," Donovan said.

"We found this over here," Bonaci said from off to one side.

The captain turned around to find his colleague squatting right at the tree line, behind the southernmost of the benches, pointing to a spot two or three feet into what looked like a vacant spot among the underbrush.

"What did you find?"

Donovan walked over and squatted beside Bonaci.

"There's this little spot in the bushes where it looks like someone may have been hiding last night. If you look close, you can see that the little straggly grass is squashed down." He pointed to show it. "And over there, some pebbles are displaced and if you look real close at that soft spot where the dirt is dark and squishy . . ."

"Loam," Donovan said.

"If you say so. Look, Captain, and you can see a shoe print. A partial. Actually, the impression of the toe of a man's right shoe." Bonaci stood, complaining about bad knees as he did so, and pointed over the bench to the corpse. "That shoe," Bonaci said.

"The dead man was squatting in the bushes," Donovan said.

"Watching the kids," Bonaci added.

3. "You Man-eatin' Son of a Bitch, I'm Gonna Have Your Ass Before I'm Done"

Donovan always thought he had a soft voice. Marcy swore she couldn't hear him from one room to the next unless he absolutely bellowed. But Mosko and the rest of his men were forever telling him he was yelling at them. The discrepancy, Donovan imagined, could be explained by who was reporting to whom.

Considering that he was in his policeman mode that day, Donovan was sure his voice carried for miles—or at least far enough to reach Lauriat who, presumably, was still crouching in his skivvies atop the old oak tree. Holding a Gap shopping bag in one hand, Donovan looked up the ladder and yelled, "You better come down, Francois. I'm not climbing this ladder again."

There was no response.

He yelled again, "Do you hear me? Come down! It really doesn't bother me that your crows were eating my corpse!"

Still nothing.

Donovan turned to Moskowitz and said, "Could he have taken off on us?"

"You mean, like, scrammed back to the rain forest to hide? Not a chance, Cap. I had a man watching this tree the whole time you were away from it. Unless Lauriat flew off with the crows, he's still up there."

Mosko beckoned to a very young, very newly minted uniformed officer who had faded, at the approach of the captain, into a spot where the bushes parted. "You! Patrolman Rodriguez."

The young man stepped into the clearing, the leaves crushing beneath rough steps delivered by heavy black brogans.

"Yeah, Sergeant?" he asked, averting his eyes, as if so doing made him invisible. But Donovan looked around at the sound of the voice. A look of surprise and a slight smile appeared on his face.

"Did anybody come down from that tree house?" Mosko asked.

"No," the young man said, addressing the ground.

"You sure?"

Having his word questioned got the patrolman's attention. His temper flared and he snapped, "I worked my ass off to get this badge and practically my first assignment is watching a fucking tree house."

Moskowitz rapped the kid on the chest using the back of his knuckles. "Hey, you watch your mouth in front of the captain."

"Leave him alone," Donovan said with a smile, then turned his attention back to the Crow's Nest. He looked up, cupping one hand alongside his mouth, and truly bellowed, "Lauriat!"

That got a reply. A few seconds later the door to the Crow's Nest swung open and Lauriat stuck his head out.

"What?"

"Didn't you hear me before?" Donovan called back up the ladder.

"No. You have a soft voice."

"You have to come down to get your clothes. I'm not going up this ladder again."

Lauriat said, "I'm not coming down in my underwear."

"Come on, Francois," Donovan argued. "There's nobody here but cops."

"There could be newspaper photographers in the bushes. For the past week now I've felt that someone was watching me."

"We're keeping the reporters far away. None of them can see us."

"You can't be sure. I may be able to save my career, but not if there's a photo in the paper of me running around Central Park in my underwear."

"I got to admit the man has a point," Mosko said to his boss.

"So take the man his clothes," Donovan said, shoving the Gap bag into the sergeant's hands.

"Oh no, not me. I don't climb no trees. A fire escape now and then, but no trees."

"We have a problem here," Donovan called up to Lauriat.

It was then that the young patrolman said, "Jesus . . . let me do it. Gimme the bag," and snatched the bag away from Moskowitz.

And he started up the ladder.

"Be careful," Donovan said, and that time his voice *was* soft.

When the patrolman was twenty feet up the ladder and out of earshot, Mosko said, "What about the mouth on that kid?"

"What about the mouth on *you?*" Donovan replied.

"Hey . . . I'm a sergeant. I got the right to be a bastard. Throughout history, sergeants have been bastards. I got the weight of human history on my side."

Ten minutes later, Lauriat descended the ladder, dressed in spanking new khakis, sneakers, and a brown sweater. Behind him came the young officer, who no sooner hit the ground than he said to Moskowitz, "I got to go. Okay?"

"Take off," Mosko growled.

"Thanks," Donovan said to the blue-clad figure as he disappeared in the direction of Park Drive West, shaking his head.

Lauriat said, "Who is that poor man who was killed? Did you learn anything about him?"

"His name is Harvey Cozzens," Donovan said. "Does that mean anything to you?"

Donovan introduced his sergeant to Lauriat. The scientist shook his head and replied, "Who was he?"

"A computer something who lived on Eighty-fifth Street," Donovan replied.

"I don't know him. Why should I?"

"I'm just checking. And those kids who were partying at the gazebo. Tell me about them."

"I don't know who they are," Lauriat insisted.

"You never met them?" Mosko asked.

"Never."

"You never laid eyes on them?" Mosko asked.

"Never."

"Then how did you know they drink beer?" Donovan asked.

"Did I say that?" Lauriat asked.

Donovan nodded.

"I guess I sort of guessed. That's what kids do in parks, isn't it?"

Mosko shrugged. "I drank beer at Canarsie Pier. But I had friends who liked to fish."

"Did you ever see this brand?" Donovan asked, dangling an evidence bag in front of the scientist's face. Within it was a reddish brown bottle the label of which bore a faux lithograph of a six-story brick building standing below the Brooklyn Bridge. Nearby, steam puffed from the twin stacks of a sidewheel ferry boat.

"Steamboat Ferry Inn Ale," Lauriat said, reading the label.

"A boutique microbrewery located on Fulton Landing in Brooklyn," Donovan said. "Very pricey. This six-pack costs nine dollars."

"Nine bucks for a six-pack of beer," Mosko said.

"Where was this stuff during my pub-crawling days? Answer: It didn't exist. None of these highfalutin microbreweries existed ten years ago. In those days a six-pack cost two twenty-nine. Now it's nine and ten bucks."

"What teenagers can afford to pay that much?" Mosko asked.

"Rich ones," Donovan said. "Rich kids who are educated, maybe, and concerned about the environment, curiously."

"Why do you say that?" Lauriat asked.

"Because they carefully deposited all the bottles as well as a can of Sterno in a trash container over there." Donovan nodded in the direction of Park Drive West.

"Which are emptied at seven every morning," Mosko said. "And would have been today if the area hadn't been roped off as a crime scene."

"But . . . perhaps in their haste to depart the murder scene . . . they left behind a few bottle caps."

Donovan displayed a second evidence bag. Two Steamboat Ferry Inn Ale bottle caps were suspended in it.

"Now, when we connect these caps to these bottles . . ." Donovan said.

". . . and we will," Mosko added.

"We'll establish that the people—kids or otherwise—who drank this beer did so at the gazebo," Donovan said.

"Sometime before dawn, when you guys woke up," Mosko added. "And after five yesterday afternoon, when the second daily garbage pickup is made."

"In other words, around the time you and I heard those kids over there," Lauriat added, seeing in the sequence of events at least partial verification of his yarn.

"As we speak, my men are trying to find out which stores in Manhattan sell this brand," Donovan said.

"And maybe there are fingerprints on the bottles?" Lauriat asked hopefully.

"And maybe there are," Donovan responded.

"Bill, I'm impressed. You make it sound easy."

"It sometimes seems that way," Donovan said.

"For a minute and a half, maybe," Mosko added.

Lauriat shuffled his feet around, saying, "Am I . . . am I . . . ?"

"Still a suspect?" Donovan asked.

"Yes . . . yes. Am I still a suspect?"

"Not if you didn't kill anybody."

"You know I couldn't kill anyone," Lauriat insisted.

"I know that you're my friend and neighbor and that no other of my friends and neighbors are murderers that I know of," Donovan said. "If you want to connect those two facts and draw a conclusion, be my guest."

"You're practicing the scientific method," Lauriat said with a smile.

"Who needs to practice?" Donovan asked.

"I think I've just been let off the hook."

"There is just one other thing."

"There often is," Mosko added.

"And what is that?" Lauriat asked.

"You're off the hook if your boots come back from the lab without moss on the soles," Donovan said.

"Moss? Why moss?"

"There's none here," Donovan said, pointing at the ground. "There's none between here and the Range Rover. But there's a ton of it around the gazebo."

Lauriat seemed to be considering the matter.

"Will I find any on your boots?" Donovan asked.

"No," he replied.

"Then you're off the hook."

Lauriat expelled a cloud of air, then smiled and touched Donovan's arm. "Thank you. Can I go home now? I need to lay down in my own bed."

"Go ahead. I know where to find you." Donovan looked at his watch, then at Moskowitz, and then said, "I think I'm going to go home for lunch. Can you handle things here?"

"Is the Pope a Catholic?" Mosko asked.

"I feel the need to spend some time with my son."

"I'll give you a ride," Lauriat offered.

"I was hoping you would offer," Donovan replied.

When Donovan got home, he found the baby lying on his tummy on a blanket that had been spread in the middle of the living room floor. Seeing his dad, the boy raised himself on his pudgy arms, offered a toothless grin, and said, "Eh."

"Eh yourself," Donovan replied, lying flat out to face him and poking him on his buttery cheeks with a fingertip.

"Are you home for the day, Captain?" Mary asked. The Irish nanny, all of twenty-three and with a storm cloud of red curls that framed a round, freckled face, sat on the floor nearby.

"Just for lunch and to visit Himself," Donovan replied, using the term that the Irish commonly applied to one of high importance. "How is he this morning?"

"He's grand. What an appetite there is in the child. He was at the breast all morning and also had some peaches and bananas."

"My luck. A vegetarian. But at least he likes to drink, so not all of the Donovan family values have gone out the window." Slipping into a forced brogue, Donovan asked, "Where's me wife?"

"Finishing her workout. She'll be out soon."

"Amazing woman. A month after having a C-section she was lifting weights. Five months after, she's doing a full workout."

"Soon she'll be back into her kung fu," Mary said, uncurling her legs from beneath her and springing to her feet.

"I think that the martial arts have gone the way of the badge and the gun," Donovan replied. "My sense is that from now on she'll be happy just to stay in shape."

"Do you ever miss those days? My uncle thinks that you must."

Her uncle was John Finney, a politician in Ireland and Donovan's cousin. That made him Mary O'Connor's third cousin by marriage, as nearly as he could reckon. What was important was that he would only trust his son to the care of a relative, and Mary was the only one in the family who did that sort of work (and needed a respectable American to co-sign the immigration papers). No one in Marcy's family—either in the Jewish or the African-American sides—was a nanny.

"Your uncle would do well to mind his own business and stick to watching the polls . . . or else he's going to lose another election and have to go to work for a living," Donovan said.

She smiled. "You don't miss having a glamorous police-woman for a wife?" Mary asked, smiling.

"I like knowing that my family is home safe," Donovan said. "Besides, she's still glamorous."

"She is that," Mary said. "Would you mind watching the baby while I run to the store?"

"I think I can manage." With that he rolled onto his back with the baby on his stomach; the child smiled and made noises while pounding his dad on the chest.

Donovan listened to his son gurgle for ten minutes until Marcy came into the room, sweat pouring from her face and neck and into a white bath towel that she had draped over her shoulders.

"Hi honey, you're home," she said, kneeling next to him and giving him a peck on the cheek.

"You'll make me lunch?"

"Sure. Where's Mary?"

"Gone to the store."

"We're out of milk, eggs, and bread. And half the stuff in my freezers at the restaurant melted last night when the electricity went off. Can you deal with leftover meat loaf and potatoes?"

He said that he could.

The baby had begun squealing in a higher-pitched tone when his mother walked into the room and now was reaching out for her, rocking back and forth on his round tummy and approaching tears.

"Your turn," Donovan said, handing the boy to her and moving to the couch. She joined him there, slipping off her sweatshirt and giving her son a breast.

"How often can you do that?" Donovan asked.

"As often as I need to. Daniel has your appetite. Which reminds me . . . I think I'm going to start taking him to work with me."

Following her retirement as a police sergeant a few years back, Marcy opened a restaurant on Broadway not far from their apartment. Marcy's Home Cooking was a success, enough so that it could stand the business lost when one table was taken out and replaced with a playpen.

"Is that a good idea?"

"Sure it is. Mary can bring him over for the afternoon. I *miss* the little guy. And you don't?"

"It shows?" he asked.

"Just a little. So . . . why are you? I heard you had a busy morning. It was on the news. Did you get any sleep last night?"

"Four or five hours."

"Don't go back to work today. Stay home with your wife and child."

"I can't," he replied. "I'm needed at the murder scene, if only as a scarecrow. What were they saying on the news?"

"That police are looking for a gang of teenagers in connection with the brutal murder of a computer software designer in a remote corner of Central Park."

"Now it's a *gang* of teenagers? Well, it must be a slow news day."

"No gang?" Marcy asked.

He shook his head. "Two . . . maybe three."

"Were you the one who found the body?"

"One of the crows found it. Or dozens did. It's hard to tell."

Marcy winced, and said, "If this is a gruesome story, I'm not in the mood. How is Francois?"

"He didn't get any work done today. And he's worried about his grant. Lewis was there."

Marcy gave her husband a pointed look, one in which her face turned a bit hard. Then she returned her gaze to her child, and within a few seconds the proud-mommy glow was back. Without looking up again, she said, "He just showed up?"

"Materialized out of the bushes, literally," Donovan replied.

"Was he friendly?"

"No."

"This is the second time he's turned up at one of your crime scenes," Marcy said.

"Third."

"Interesting."

"Yeah," Donovan said, getting up and stretching. "My back is a wreck after sleeping on that cot."

"Army cots were meant for nineteen-year-old bodies."

"Which can do things that older bodies can't . . . like drive tanks and climb tall ladders."

"Get yourself a cup of tea and two ibuprofen."

"And some meat loaf," Donovan said, ambling off toward the kitchen.

After the sun set and Central Park became a bed of solitude given soft illumination by the street lamps that dotted the drives and pedestrian paths, Donovan and Moskowitz drove down Park Drive West in the captain's Buick and pulled into the grassy area across which they had followed Howard Bonaci early in the day. The patrolmen guarding the scene held up the yellow tape to admit the two detectives, dressed in jeans and sweaters and doing a passable imitation of ordinary citizens.

It was just after nine. The sun was solidly down; no hint of twilight lingered. The wooded section of park that hid both Crow's Nest and crime scene was as black . . . well, as black as night. By focusing his attention Donovan could see landmarks beyond the woods, though; the light of certain tall buildings on the far side of the grass, woods, Fiddler's Pond and nearby parts of Central Park Lake, all of them nearly invisible in the dark, shined from several tall buildings on the Upper East Side.

Donovan peered at them, then looked behind him at the lights of Central Park West on the Upper West Side. Then he alternated between the two views until Mosko said,

"You're gonna screw your head off doing that."

"I got it figured out," Donovan replied.

"What?"

"How those kids found their way to the old gazebo in the dark. Look."

Donovan pointed to the west. "See the Greek Orthodox church over there . . . the cross atop it is floodlit."

"Got it."

Donovan then pointed to the east. "See the modern apartment building over there?" He watched his associate looking too far to the south and corrected him, saying "No . . . the narrow one . . . it's called a 'sliver building.' You know, the type that gave the *Times* architecture critic fits years ago."

Mosko said, "I knew there was something missing in my life and you just showed me what it is—architectural criticism."

"Down Park Drive West is the spot where the Rollerbladers hold their all-night competitions and smoke pot," Donovan continued. "The kids we're looking for enter the park along with the rest of the regulars at Seventy-second Street or through Strawberry Fields. They hang a left on Park Drive West. You know that the park drives are closed all night, don't you?"

Mosko knew. He said, "So the kids walk north past the roller derby. A lot of kids, and some grownups, hang out around there, smoking pot or whatever."

"But the Rollerblading crowd is like the bicycle messenger crowd," Donovan went on. "They're kids who are in great shape but who smoke a lot of dope with the Walkmen on."

"I've caught their act," Mosko said.

"They can take the high moral ground—of a sort—on their peers on several scores. One, they're not fit. Two, they don't know how to party. This breed of fit young guys who do a lot of dope is new on me. In my day, the kids who did drugs hung out at the Laundromat watching the clothes go around in the dryer."

"Today's kids are intense," Mosko said.

"Yeah, the Rollerbladers can get a little intense for the rest of us. So let's say that the kids we're looking for watched them for a while. But our suspects wanted to be alone."

"You sound like you know them," Mosko said.

"I know what it's like to want to be with your girl and watching the moonlight glint off the pond in the park," Donovan said.

Moskowitz smiled. "I heard some of the stories about you and the rest of the guys while you were off-duty and in Riverside Park."

"Those were the days, my friend. My liver thought they would never end. So yes, I believe that you and I are looking for two young lovers who went to the gazebo to exchange body fluids and wound up in a homicide. Whether they were the perps or merely innocent bystanders . . ."

"Or know nothing about it."

". . . is something we will figure out once we lay our hands on the horny little bastards," Donovan allowed.

"How'd they find the gazebo in this dark?"

"Simple. Walk north on Park Drive West until you line up with the Greek Orthodox church. There." He pointed at it. "Then hang a right and walk toward the sliver building. This way."

Donovan led Mosko across the grass, walking toward the mass of black that was the woods at night.

"Watch out for yourself, Captain," one of the uniformed cops called.

After taking a few steps into the darkness Donovan pulled a Mag Lite from his pocket and flicked it on. The beam illuminated a patch of grass, dirt, stones, and wild chives and then the wild brush at the base of the twin stripling maples that hid the trail to the gazebo. The crime scene marker that, early in the day, pointed to the crushed toadstool was gone.

"You're something else," Mosko said.

"I've spent most of my adult life in the dark," Donovan replied.

With Donovan in the lead, the two detectives made their way to the crime scene. The old gazebo had been searched and cleaned up, though the evidence of trampling by dozens of feet remained. At least the crushed skunk cabbage had lost its odor and the ground glistened in a clean sort of way thanks to the washing that also removed most of the blood. Some crimson—now turned reddish brown—remained around the edges of the mossy cobblestones that formed the floor of the gazebo.

"Have a seat," Donovan said, and took one.

Mosko complied, but not before looking behind, trying futilely as it turned out, to see if he would be sitting in dried blood.

"Creepy," Mosko said.

Donovan reached into a pocket, pulled out a small tin of Sterno, used a pocket knife to pop off the lid, and lit the contents. Soon the old gazebo was awash in faint blue light . . . just enough to see the other person.

"Maybe it's a *little* romantic when you light it like this," Mosko allowed.

"Add a full moon and a bottle or two of Steamboat Ferry Inn Ale . . . forget about it." Donovan pronounced that *fahgeddabowdit*, as he did every so often in recognition of Mosko's Brooklyn accent.

"You *can* see the moon in the water if you look past the—whaddya call that stuff?"

"Skunk cabbage."

"Yeah, if you look past that."

"Add some music . . . hey, I know it's only rock and roll, but . . ."

Mosko grunted and pulled his laptop from his leather shoulder bag and set in on his lap. As the yellow glow from the screen mingled with the blue light from the Sterno flame, Donovan looked up at the trees framed against the sky, which had fast moving and puffy clouds like the night before. He said, "I guess the crows are back up there in the branches, sleeping."

"Where else would you expect them to sleep?" Mosko replied, flipping through the screens. "Motel Six?"

Donovan addressed the birds, saying, "Nevermore, I know you're up there. You man-eatin' son of a bitch, I'm gonna have your ass before I'm done here."

"Read him his rights first," Mosko replied. "Okay, here's what I wanted to share with you. It was your theory that the kids we're looking for came from the West Side."

"They had to have. It's half a mile at most, coming straight from Central Park West. But if you come from the East Side, you have to walk around the reservoir, around the lake, through the Ramble where the gay guys hang out, and around a lot of other stuff before you get here."

"I hear you," Mosko said.

"No teenage lovers are going to wait that long . . . trust me. So, what did we find?"

Summarizing what he saw on the screen, Mosko said, "There are seventeen joints that sell Steamboat Ferry Inn Ale in Manhattan."

"Do you want a beer?" Donovan asked, pulling two frosty bottles from a bag and clinking them together.

"Am I on duty?"

"Nah. I gave you the evening off."

"You're the kind of boss a guy dreams about. Tell you what, you take the evening off, too."

Donovan handed his friend a Steamboat Ferry Inn Ale and opened a Kaliber for himself. "Go on," he said.

Mosko took a sip and said, "Well, this ain't bad. Brewed in Brooklyn, eh? That ought to be their slogan. As I was saying, ten of the places that sell this stuff are below Fifty-seventh Street."

"Forget about them."

"Four are on the Upper East Side."

"Them, too."

"Wait. One of them . . . an upscale food market on Third Avenue in the Seventies . . ."

"Too far away," Donovan said.

"Hear me out. Sold a six-pack to a pair of kids. The boy had I.D. that said twenty-one, but the kid looked . . . you know, fishy. And the girl looked like fifteen."

"About what time?"

"Between nine and ten. The both of them carried Rollerblades."

"Okay," Donovan said, warming to the chase, "Let's keep them on the list. Did the storeowner know them?"

"He said the boy was someone he'd seen before," Mosko replied. "The girl was new to him."

"May God and a few thousand of my friends forgive me for assuming that teenage murderers have to hail from the West Side. What else?"

"Three stores on the West Side sell this brew," Mosko reported, taking another swig and adding, "which *really* ain't bad, I got to say."

"Where are they?"

"Broadway and One-fifteen."

"The Columbia place. Killer hero sandwiches; used to

come with warning labels. Who bought the ale there last night?"

"They sold four six-packs to two kids, both of 'em presenting with Columbia I.D."

"They're a long shot, but check 'em out."

"We're working on it," Mosko replied.

"And the second place?" Donovan asked.

"Broadway and Eighty-seventh."

"What place?" Donovan asked, a trace of indignation in his voice. "That's my neighborhood and not far from Marcy's restaurant. How come I don't know about it?"

"You stopped drinking, not counting that nonalcoholic stuff you swig," Mosko said, pointing at the bottle of Kaliber in his boss's hand. "The name of the place is Maximal Sandwich."

"Oh, yeah. Know it. Four-dollar cappuccino served in plastic cups."

"They sold a six-pack of Steamboat Ferry Inn Ale last night, but it was to . . . are you ready for this?"

"Go ahead . . . tell me . . . Mary O'Connor, Daniel's nanny."

"No, and your wife didn't buy it, either. It was bought by Gabriel Allen Cohen."

Donovan's eyes widened. "Not *the* Gabriel Allen Cohen?"

"How many of them are there?" Mosko asked. "When a poet gets famous enough to become a household word even in Canarsie, he's got it made."

The most reclusive of the Beat generation writers was known to live along Central Park West, but was so rarely seen in public that no one quite knew what he looked like anymore. Various rumors abounded: He was dying of cancer, he was a senile old fool who no longer could tell his left foot from his right—the result of a storied heroin habit that followed him throughout the 1940s, 1950s, and 1960s. Admirers said, nonsense, he was secretly working on his long-awaited free-verse history of America. This was the work sure to get him that Pulitzer Prize. Not counting his publishing career, the facts about Cohen were scanty. There were two ex-wives and a new, young spouse who also was rarely seen. A son died a decade earlier, under mysterious circumstances. And there was a young daughter about whom *nothing* was known. Cohen and his family had become like Garbo during her final years—much speculated about but seldom seen on the streets.

"I read all his poems when I was in high school," Donovan said. "I even was fascinated by his Buddhist thing for a while."

"So go ask him for his autograph," Mosko replied. "Now you got the excuse."

"I don't want to embarrass the man. He is supposed to be a teetotaler these days. How can I just go and ask him if he bought a six-pack of beer."

"This shy streak of yours leaves me speechless," Mosko replied. "Anyway, he can't be *that* reclusive; the shopkeeper knew him. And it looks like you won't have to pester the old junkie. The third Upper West Side store that sold a six-pack of your nine-dollar beer last night? A deli on Seventy-second and Columbus."

"That's the one," Donovan said. "That's where the kids bought the beer."

"Last night at eleven, to be exact."

"Just when you would pick up beer on your way into the park for an all-nighter."

"The shopkeeper sold a six to a couple of kids. Like what happened at the place on the East Side, the boy had I.D. for twenty-one but looked seventeen."

"And probably was," Donovan said. "My nephew? First

thing he did when he got his new PC was make up a fake I.D."

"The girl looked fifteen or sixteen," Mosko said.

"White kids?"

"Yeah, again like the ones on the East Side. And get this . . . the girl bought a chunk of cheddar cheese and a paring knife."

"Like you use to cut apples."

"Or throats. The storekeeper said she looked scary. The deli owner thought the boy was her stooge."

"At such a tender age, already stepping into the role life carves out for us all," Donovan said.

"Do I hear a hint of dissatisfaction with the idyllic life of sober husband and mature father?" Mosko asked.

"No," Donovan said sharply. "I was just running off at the mouth. I adore my family and am never willingly apart from them."

"So what are you doing drinking beer on a park bench at night?" Mosko asked.

"I'm working," Donovan replied.

"Oh, my mistake. Well anyway, that's all I got to tell you about the search for the beer buyers. Did I mention that the lab connected the bottle caps we found at the site to the bottles in the trash can?"

"You told me."

"And that there are two sets of readable prints on the bottles?" Mosko added.

"That you didn't tell me. Is there anything on file?"

"We haven't found anything yet, but there are a couple of databases that we haven't been able to get into."

"Juvenile courts," Donovan said.

"Those are the ones. I heard late today that we need a special dispensation from the youth offender authorities. You'll have to pull some strings."

"First thing in the morning," Donovan said. "Did we interview the beat cops who patrol this sector of park at night?"

Mosko nodded. "There are six guys—four guys and two gals, actually—who the Central Park precinct assigns to this section of park. We talked to five of them. One thought she saw the kids we're looking for but didn't have names to attach to them."

"They *were* regulars, then."

"Yeah, and her feeling also is that they're lovers. But she—she being Patrolwoman Ebby, Jonelle Ebby. She's a two-year veteran of this park, and she said we ought to talk to her patrol partner, Patrolman Rodriguez."

Donovan looked up from his beer and made eye contact with Mosko in the faint blue and yellow light.

"She says he knows who the girl is. We were going to talk to him tonight. He's supposed to work the midnight-to-eight shift in the Central Park precinct. But he called in sick," Mosko said. "You remember Rodriguez? The cop who climbed the ladder this morning? The kid with the mouth."

"Lewis Rodriguez," Donovan said.

"Yeah, that's the one. Do you know him?"

"Not really at all," Donovan said.

"Didn't he also turn up when we were working that homicide over on East Eighty-first, in Yorkville?" Mosko asked.

"As I recall, he did. So . . . is there anything else?"

Mosko scrolled down even more screens, then switched programs from his case files to e-mail. Within seconds, the cellular modem was downloading messages from headquarters.

"Did I mention that we got prints off the Sterno can?" Mosko said.

He hadn't.

"They matched one of the sets on the beer bottles. Probably the boy's."

"Why do you say that?"

"They're bigger."

"Hey, the girl could be a longshoreman," Donovan said. "What makes her automatically smaller?"

"Probability," Mosko said.

Donovan grunted.

Something in the incoming messages caught Mosko's eye, a change that Donovan dutifully noted. The sergeant fell silent as he read.

"What?" Donovan asked.

"We got a garbled transmission here. The satellite must have been hit by an asteroid."

"You know, there's an asteroid coming that could destroy the world in thirty years," Donovan said, looking up into the moonlit and off-and-on cloudy night as if in search of it.

"I heard. Well, it looks like we got a match for the boy. No need to wait for approval from juvenile courts. He's eighteen."

"Still a boy," Donovan said.

"Officially an adult," Mosko replied. "In any case, he's old enough to have gotten himself busted for shoplifting."

"What did the kid steal?"

" 'Computer parts,' it says here."

"Do we have his name and address?" Donovan asked.

"Yeah . . . the message is coming through again and it looks readable this time."

"You can always count on American technology," Donovan said. "Maybe not always on the first pass, but eventually."

"Here it comes . . . whoa!"

"Whoa what?" Donovan asked, his eyes widening once again, though not yet to owl-like dimensions.

"How does your bird-watching friend spell his name?" Mosko asked.

Donovan said, "L . . . A . . . you got to be kidding me."

"I swear on my mother's grave."

"I keep telling you, your mother ain't dead."

"No," Mosko said, shaking his head, "but your friend is gonna be."

"Let me see that," Donovan said, and waved Mosko to move over so he could sit next to him. The sergeant complied, and the two men huddled over the laptop like touts over a tip sheet.

Donovan read, "Frank Lauriat, born eighteen November, nineteen eighty-one, in Antipixapi, Brazil. Francois had his base camp there. I remember having to endure the slide show. I'm gonna kill the sonofabitch."

"Told you," Mosko said.

"Junior has joint U.S.-Brazilian citizenship. Oh, *man* . . . why didn't Francois just *tell* me?"

"Tell you what, that his kid killed a man in Central Park?"

"In the wee hours of the morning while his dad just happened to be taking a walk nearby," Donovan said.

"And New York's most decorated detective was slumbering in a tree house up alongside the crows," Mosko said.

"I *am* pissed," Donovan said.

"Junior lives at nine twenty-eight west One-oh-six Street. The entrance is on Columbus Avenue."

"The last neighborhood on the Upper West Side to escape gentrification," Donovan said. "It's still possible to get a coffee and donut for a buck in a bodega or buy grass from a kid who brings it to your car. Or look out the living room window and watch an old-fashioned gunfight between drug lords."

"As an old rabble rouser, you probably find that refreshing," Mosko said, shutting down his computer, perhaps feeling the adrenaline level start to rise.

"It takes all sorts," Donovan said.

"Let's go get him."

Donovan drained the last bit of nonalcoholic beer from his bottle and said, grandly, "My work here is done."

"And dad?" Mosko asked. "What about him?"

"Yeah. Send someone out to pick him up." Then, repeating a favorite, if never exactly meant, phrase from his rowdy old days, said, "Kick the shit out of him and cuff him to the radiator in my office."

4. "I Ate Fish. I Ate Cheese. I Saw the Virgin Mary"

The bodega was tiny and tomb-shaped, a slender rectangle wedged between a takeout *comidas y criollas* joint and the local off-track-betting parlor. The sidewalk outside was littered with discarded betting slips, tip sheets, and copies of *The Racing Form* that were folded over and creased so they could be read with one hand while the other was holding a paper coffee cup. The local retirees and cigar-chomping municipal workers who packed the parlor during working hours had long since shuffled back to their railroad flats and corner bars. Donovan stood inside the shop leaning against the Twinkie rack and dividing his attention between the building across the street and Madame Rosa's Dream Book and Lottery Picker. That was one of a dozen cheaply printed guides to hitting the daily number or another illegal or legal drawing. A display of them was appended to the Twinkie rack, just to one side of the roach spray, as if to suggest that junk food and inner city easy dreams went together. Stuck for a three-digit number to play when the friendly local numbers runner comes round? Remember what you dreamed last night? Look up the dream and get your answer.

Moskowitz was listening to his cell phone. Donovan swatted him on the arm and read, "I ate fish. I ate cheese. I saw the Virgin Mary standing beneath a tree."

"Add a green vegetable," Mosko replied.

"Three twenty-seven," Donovan told him.

"Three twenty-seven what?" Mosko replied, without taking his eyes off the street or his ear from the cell phone.

"That's the number to play if you have that dream."

"I could have sworn it should have been four thirty-five for fish, cheese, and virgin."

Donovan flipped through some more pages, finally stopping on one that bore a drawing of a candle. He read, "I lit a candle. I switched on a light bulb . . ."

"I saw the roaches run back under the sink," Mosko said.

Donovan shook his head. "I filled a bowl with water. Six eleven."

"Here's the scoop, boss," Mosko said. "We know the kid ain't home. I had a guy knock on the door, pretending to be the roach exterminator. There's no one home."

Donovan hefted a can of Black Flag roach spray. "Too bad. That place across the street looks like it could use it."

Mosko said, "Not true. The facade of that building . . ."

" 'Facade,' " Donovan said, smiling. "You used the word 'facade.' I am so proud of how well you've been doing with your English lessons."

"They *do* speak English in Brooklyn, bro'," Mosko replied.

"Prove it."

"I be tryin'. So, while the *front* of that building looks like a slum, the inside has been renovated. The guts have been torn out and new condos put in."

"Condos?" Donovan said. "On One hundred and sixth Street and Columbus Avenue? This neighborhood is being gentrified, too?"

"Sorry."

"Jesus Christ, is no corner of Manhattan safe from the creeping hand of gentrification? You!"

He called to the shopkeeper.

"Yes, officer?" replied the sixtyish, Spanish proprietor.

"What do you pay in rent here?"

"Six thousand."

"Six thousand dollars a month in rent for a postage-stamp sized bodega?"

"It just went up from fifteen hundred," the man replied, a mix of sorrow and resignation in his voice. "I'm going to have to close. The landlord wants me out so he can put in a Starbuck's."

"A Starbuck's? Four dollars for a cappuccino? On One hundred and sixth Street? How much do those *condos* across the street go for?"

"I hear, one hundred thousand for the studio, one hundred and fifty thousand for the one-bedroom. Two hundred and twenty-five for the two-bedroom."

Donovan rolled his eyes, then asked his associate, "Which does Frank Lauriat live in?"

"A two-bedroom," Mosko replied.

"How does this kid afford an apartment that costs nearly a quarter million? Does he live with his mom?"

Mosko nodded. "Eleanor Lauriat. She teaches botany at Bronx Community College. You don't know her?"

Donovan shook his head. "They broke up before Francois moved into my building. I never met the woman. Heard the usual horror stories . . . you know, trapped in the Amazon jungle with the wicked witch of Endor. And God knows what she was telling *her* friends about him."

"When you got an ex-husband who works up in a tree you don't have to devote that much energy to explaining the divorce," Mosko said.

"How does a woman who teaches botany at a community college afford . . . oh, never mind. Maybe there's family money. So, Mr.—what's your name again?"

"Correra," the older man responded.

"Do you know Frank Lauriat?"

"The boy? He's good. I can't imagine what you want him for? There are still some bad boys in this neighborhood—no matter how high they raise the rents—but he's not one of them."

"What do you know about him?" Donovan asked.

"Just that he's studying computers—like all kids these days."

"Where?"

"In the Bronx, where his mother works."

"Cozzens was a computer guy," Mosko reminded his boss. "But I'm not sure if that means anything anymore. What is it, forty percent of American families have computers?"

" 'Having' is different from 'studying,' " Donovan responded.

The two detectives fell silent for a while as Mosko answered a call that came in on his cell phone and the storeowner shuffled off to the cash register to ring up a Lotto ticket and a pack of generic cigarettes for an elderly woman who asked for them in Spanish.

After listening to the phone and nodding as if the caller could see him over the airwaves and through the fly-specked window of the bodega, Mosko said, "We have him in sight, boss. He got out of a downtown train and is walking east on One hundred and sixth."

"Duke Ellington Boulevard," Donovan corrected. "They changed the name a full twenty years before the rents went up. Which goes to show you that the real estate market can be fickle."

"Or that jazz doesn't sell."

"Whatever. We'll nab him on the corner—whatever the street may be called. But go easy on the kid unless he tries something."

"Go easy?" Mosko asked. "The kid is prime suspect in a vicious murder."

"He's my neighbor's son," Donovan explained.

"And all is forgiven, right? Hold on, time has come."

Donovan followed Mosko out of the bodega and down the block, past a crumbling Laundromat and a suspiciously dark-looking bar that seemed to have no one in it to hear the old Donna Summer disco tune throbbing away on the jukebox. Two figures, nineteenish blacks wearing immense coats that covered most of their bodies and, no doubt, a variety of firearms, stepped out of the shadows that hid a crevice, big enough for two garbage cans and a rusted old Key Foods shopping cart, between two buildings. The men moved forward eagerly, sensing customers for drugs but finding two men who were unmistakably cops, and ducking back into the dark.

"Easy, guys," Donovan said, in a friendly sort of way but fingering his revolver nonetheless. "It's not you, not tonight."

There was no reply beyond a weary grunt from a drug dealer who had grown accustomed to treating the local police mainly as annoyances.

When Donovan and Moskowitz got to the corner they looked west down 106th Street, which on the West Side was, by and large, a broad boulevard of once stately older apartment buildings now gone considerably to seed, suffering from a no-man's-land location halfway between the sparkling clean university community surrounding Columbia and the now-upscale West Side below 96th Street. The buildings along

106th were, nonetheless, an improvement over those on adjacent side streets.

At ten in the evening, the sidewalk ranging toward Amsterdam Avenue was deserted save for a lone teenager loping along, looking preoccupied, Donovan thought, lost in the shadows of deep thought. The boy was handsome, thin, with close-cropped black hair and his hands jammed into the pockets of a somewhat garish, navy blue and orange Tommy Hilfiger down jacket worn over a gigantic gray sweatshirt. He was looking down and paid no more attention to the two men waiting for him on the corner than he did to the pair that had been shadowing him from the subway stop.

Mosko moved up to him, saying, "Frank Lauriat?" and taking the boy's arm.

"Hey!" the boy said, snapped out of his thoughts, someone having broken New York street life's no-touch tradition. He stared down at the hand on his arm. "Yeah . . . that's me."

"Police officers, son," Donovan said, showing his gold badge.

"I . . . hey," the boy said again as he was pushed against the red-painted steel door of the corner building's service entrance and searched.

"He's clean, Captain," Mosko said, releasing young Lauriat.

"What'd I do?" he asked, his voice cracking slightly.

"Murdered Harvey Cozzens, maybe?" Mosko suggested.

The boy sucked in his breath as if to speak, but said nothing, looking back down at the pavement and shaking his head.

"I didn't hear you," Mosko said.

"Who's he?" the boy asked.

"The man who was stabbed to death in Central Park last night," Donovan said. "It was in the papers today."

"I don't read the papers," the boy said. To Donovan, the teenager's head seemed as if it were spinning. He looked overwhelmed—but not entirely surprised—to be asked if he had killed someone.

"You were in Central Park last night," Donovan continued.

"No," the boy said, his eyes still fixed downward.

Mosko said, "You bought a six-pack of Steamboat Ferry Inn Ale, then you met your girlfriend and walked to a secluded spot near Strawberry Fields."

"I don't have a girl."

"Read him his rights," Donovan said.

Mosko did as he was told. Being given the Miranda warning seemed to get to the boy. He didn't exactly look up, but he began to shift his weight from side to side and breathe more rapidly. He said, at last, "I . . . well . . . I . . . don't . . . wow!"

"I'm a friend of your father," Donovan said.

The boy looked up. "You know my dad?"

For the first time in the encounter, suggestions of life came to his face.

"I was with him last night. I heard someone playing a radio by the pond—at the old gazebo—you and the girl drank beer there. At some point, you cleared up after yourselves and dropped the bottles in a trash basket by the drive."

"You were with my dad? Up in the tree?" The younger Lauriat's tone was a little amused, a little bitter.

"He's my neighbor. He's told me about his research. I was interested. So I went to the Crow's Nest with him and heard you and the girl."

"I told you, I don't have a girl."

"Don't want to talk about her, eh?" Mosko said. "That's funny, 'cause she told us all about you."

"Natasha wouldn't do that," the boy snapped.

"Wouldn't she?" Mosko said. "You better start looking for friends, kid. You don't have too many."

"Your father went to see you at about one in the morning," Donovan said, guessing.

That got a response. "No!" the boy said, nearly shouting. "He didn't come to see me last night! He didn't come to see me any night! He left my mom and me when I was ten. And I don't talk to him ever!"

"Emotional kid," Mosko said to Donovan.

"So you *were* there last night," Donovan said. "And you *do* have a girl."

Flustered by his mistaken admission, the boy stammered, "If you're a friend of my dad's, you're no friend of mine."

Then he turned to Mosko and said, "I don't have to talk to him, do I?"

"Eventually you have to talk to one of us," Mosko said. "And like I just told you, it's time to look for friends. The captain here likes you. I can tell that. So stop lying to him. That only pisses him off. But like I also told you, you're entitled to have a lawyer present."

"I want one," the teenager said, crossing his arms and trying to appear resolute.

"In that case, I'll have to handcuff you and take you downtown," Mosko said.

Lauriat Junior stuck his hands in front of him to be cuffed.

"In back," Mosko said and, directing the boy, completed the action.

Donovan said, "So you say you didn't see your dad last night. He denies he saw you. Funny how you don't talk to each other but you both sing the same tune."

Young Lauriat gave Donovan a glowering, very teenage, "I-hate-you-and-all-grownups" look.

"Take him downtown," Donovan said to the two other detectives—the men who had followed the teenager from the subway—who had walked up during the brief interrogation.

When they were gone, Donovan said, "Well, we have

the son. Now we have to round up the father. Any word on that, do you suppose?"

Mosko shook his head. "I would have gotten a call."

"This kid doesn't look like he would have a Natasha for a girlfriend," Donovan said.

"Come on, parents don't name their kids Dick and Jane anymore."

"I called mine Daniel."

"What did—does the rest of your generation—the sixties crowd—like for kids' names?"

"Vera, Chuck, and Dave," Donovan said.

"Yeah, well, you're very traditional for someone who considers himself an old socialist and who has three years in the sixties that he won't talk about. My generation calls kids stuff like Bret and Nicole and Tupak. This Natasha must be his high school sweetheart."

"Make sure someone talks to the mother," Donovan said.

"And the father. I have guys outside his apartment, below the tree house, at his office at Columbia," Mosko said. "So far no sight of him."

"Odd, because he's a creature of habit. He has only one interest in life—his research. Generally speaking, if he's not home he's at his faculty office or in the field."

"Maybe he's on the lam," Mosko speculated.

"I doubt that, but have guys call the airlines and find out. Maybe he's trying to beat it back to the rain forest, where you can live basically forever and all you have to worry about is being eaten by crocodiles, eaten by piranhas, or burned out by cattle ranchers who want to turn the jungle into pasture."

"Sounds like a hot deal to me," Mosko said. "Let's walk over to Broadway and get something to eat. I thought I saw a Twin Donuts back there."

"On Ninety-second," Donovan said, nodding.

"They have the best toasted coconut."

"I like butternut myself. Walk me home. I've had enough fun for one day. We'll pick up donuts on the way and I'll make coffee."

Mosko glanced at his watch and said, "It's pushing eleven."

"It'll take you under an hour to drive home at this time of night. Come in late tomorrow. I give you dispensation." Donovan gave his friend and associate the palms-up Papal blessing.

"What's this 'come in late?' " Mosko asked. "Between the cell phone and the cell modem, I'm never not working."

"Agreed, but you're never behind, either. And I sleep better knowing that things are being taken care of. Come on, I'll buy you a toasted coconut."

The two men started off in the direction of Broadway. After peering around the corner and watching them depart, the two drug dealers relaxed their guard and resumed their striding, with smiles, to a Mercedes full of white teenagers from New Jersey.

"I like going to your house, but I don't want to wake up Marcy or the baby," Mosko said.

Donovan shook his head. "The baby sleeps like a log and Marcy will be watching some tearjerker, made-for-TV movie."

"Marcy? You're kidding."

"It does something for her. Tell me why I spent one night last week watching *Waterworld* while steam cleaning the carpet. Even though I knew from minute one that the movie was nothing more than *The Road Warrior* with fish."

"It did something for you," Mosko said.

At Broadway, they turned left and headed south through a busy—even at that time of night—commercial zone of Spanish take-out restaurants and discount stores. The latter, painted in primary colors as storefronts are wont to be in

62

Caribbean neighborhoods, had names like Tip Top Bargains.

Donovan said, "Call in and get someone to go to Bronx Community and wake up Frank Lauriat's professors. Get the names of his friends. I want to know who Natasha is."

"You think she's someone he met at college?"

"That's where I met my woman," Donovan said.

"You never went to college," Mosko said.

"No, but I *taught* there. I was visiting professor of criminology at John Jay." Donovan was referring to the John Jay College of Criminal Justice, part of the City University of New York system.

Mosko asked, "How do you get to *teach* college, never having *gone to* college?"

"You get to be prominent in your field, son," Donovan said, offering his friend a smile and a pat on the arm. "And you get *there* by having great help."

Mosko smiled.

"I taught there two years, three nights a week," Donovan continued. "Marcy was working on her law degree at Columbia and the two schools had a joint criminal law program. After we started going out, she quit school to become a cop. The rest of the story you know."

Indeed he did. All of the men in Donovan's unit—numbering over a hundred, including technicians and assorted experts—knew the history of the tempestuous relationship between their boss and the beautiful, multiracial woman who once was an undercover policewoman and now was his wife. A few even realized how, while bringing light and love to his life, Marcy had unwittingly hurt his career. That happened because Deputy Chief Inspector Paul Pilcrow, the city's highest ranking black police officer but a racist, hated Marcy for being half Jewish as well as the daughter of New York State's most prominent black jurist, a respected and long-sitting member of the Supreme Court. Pilcrow also hated Donovan for his knack for getting into the headlines as well as for his friendship with the mayor.

Whenever Pilcrow thought of the Donovan family, the captain said often, his teeth itched.

"So you got her the badge," Mosko said.

"Yeah, and I got her shot at . . . and *shot*, once, while on an operation I was running. But the wound healed, and she even talked to her old law prof and got me a gig as a seminar associate at Columbia Law."

"I didn't know you taught at an Ivy League school."

"Another two years," Donovan said. "A workshop on law and community-based policing. But I quit eventually. I needed the time."

"What for?"

"For drinking and hanging out, in those days," Donovan said.

"You miss it sometimes. I can tell."

"I don't miss the pains in my stomach. I sometimes miss the time spent staring into space."

The two men continued down Broadway to Ninety-second Street, where Donovan bought a box of donuts before leading Moskowitz to an especially lovely stretch of Riverside Drive near Eighty-ninth Street, where his stately old apartment building stood across from the Soldiers and Sailors Monument.

After walking down the fifteenth-floor corridor, Donovan pulled his keys from his jacket pocket and turned the lock. As he pulled the door open, expecting only the sound of the TV playing to a wife who had fallen asleep on the couch, Donovan was surprised to hear conversation that included a man's voice. Mosko and he looked at one another. The voice belonged to Francois Lauriat.

The scientist was sitting on the couch sipping a cappuccino that was served in one of the fancy glasses that Marcy kept for company. He put down the glass and half stood, the deer-in-the-headlights look on his face again.

"Sit," Donovan said, taking off his jacket but not his shoulder holster, a bit of body language that spoke more eloquently than any collection of words. Lauriat sat back down and folded his hands in his lap like a good little schoolboy.

"Hi, honey," Marcy said, jumping up and planting a kiss on Donovan's lips. "Hello, Brian. What have you got, donuts? Oh, great! Did you get any chocolate?"

Donovan had.

"Are you okay?" Mosko asked.

"Sure. Why do you ask?"

"Miss Tofu eats chocolate donuts?"

"From time to time. Here, let me take them. I'll put up more cappuccino. Decaf, of course. Is that okay, Brian?"

"Yeah, great. Sitting here watching you eat a donut will be stimulation enough."

She headed for the kitchen, saying, "You guys will want to talk."

"If he gave you a statement already, there won't be any need," Donovan said.

Lauriat looked down at his folded hands, then up at Mosko, who had assumed the crossed-arms position that signaled incipient doom.

Donovan sat next to the scientist and said, "I met your son."

Lauriat looked up, startled, as if stung by a bee. "You saw Frank! Where is he! How is he?"

"Why so concerned?"

That made the man even more alarmed. He said, not quite stammering, "I . . . my son . . . How can you ask? . . . I was so afraid!"

"The two of you talk much the same," Donovan observed.

"How is Frank? Is he okay?"

"I ask again, why shouldn't he be? You tell a guy who's sitting on your couch, 'I met your son.' You expect he'll say something like 'great,' 'neat,' or, if he's young enough, 'cool.' What you don't expect is to hear this hysterical plea for information. So tell me, why are you so worried?"

Lauriat had come halfway out of his seat again, but now sank back into it, perhaps realizing he had given something away. Instead of speaking, he shook his head sadly.

"The kid's in jail," Mosko said.

"Jail! What do you mean, jail?"

"What do you think?" Donovan asked.

"When did you see him last?" Mosko asked.

"Last night! I didn't go down to take a walk like I told you! I went down to see my son! We were together the whole time that poor man was killed."

Donovan and Mosko exchanged glances.

"*Now* you say you were with your son. This morning you told me you saw no one. Which one was it?"

"I was with my son," Lauriat said, bobbing his head up and down.

"Why'd you lie to me this morning?" Donovan asked.

"It's bad policy to lie to the captain," Mosko said. "Do you read Steven Jay Gould?"

"Unh . . . what? Yes, of course I do. What's that got to do with . . . ?"

"You lie to the captain and you switch on his gene for pursuit."

"There isn't a . . . oh, *God*!" Lauriat released a big gulp of air that sounded, in part, like a wail. But no other sound was forthcoming, so Donovan repeated his question. "Why did you lie to me this morning?"

At last Lauriat took another breath, a quiet one, and said,

"I'm sorry about that. I was hoping you wouldn't find out he was there."

"He left his fingerprints on those beer bottles," Mosko said.

"So that's how you know about him," Lauriat said. "Can you tell me now if he's okay?"

"He's fine," Donovan said. "We took him downtown and are holding him. He asked for a lawyer."

"His mother is *dating* a lawyer."

"Oh, terrific move. Went from a man who lives in trees to a *lawyer*. Really climbing the mountain of accessibility, isn't she?" Donovan asked.

"She's not a bad woman," Lauriat said, without terrific conviction.

"Where did you talk to your son last night?" Donovan asked.

"What do you mean, 'where?' "

"You're a scientist. Be precise. Where, exactly?"

"By my car. *In* my car."

"While listening to the Chopin nocturne?"

"Yes."

"Are you sure you didn't talk to your son by the gazebo while listening to Pink Floyd?" Donovan asked.

"You're dating yourself, boss," Mosko said. "These days I think it's more like Nine Inch Nails."

"You didn't go to the gazebo?" Donovan asked Lauriat.

"God forbid, no. And neither did my son. Not for the whole hour between one and two."

The two detectives exchanged glances again.

"Did he?" Donovan asked Mosko.

"Not as of five o'clock."

"Check again."

"Check what?" Lauriat asked, watching Mosko take off

his coat, put his laptop on the coffee table, and begin pressing buttons.

"For moss on your boots," Donovan explained.

Lauriat looked back down into his clasped hands.

"Why didn't you go there?" Donovan asked.

"Because *she* was there," Lauriat said, looking up with tight lips.

"Who? The girlfriend? Vera?"

"What? Who's Vera? The name is Natasha. Where'd you get 'Vera?' "

"From an old song from my childhood. I hum it from time to time as I free-fall toward retirement age," Donovan said. "What's this Natasha's last name?"

"I don't know," Lauriat said.

"Come now."

"No, I really don't."

"Your son is accused of murdering someone in league with a girl and you don't know her *name*?"

"He calls her 'girl,' " Lauriat said.

"Girl?" Donovan asked.

Lauriat repeated the name, this time drawing out the sound, nearly growling, like "grrrl."

"If you're trying to provoke the dog, he's sleeping behind the couch at this time of night and won't come out for anything."

As they spoke, Marcy came into the room with glasses of cappuccino and a platter of donuts, summarily shoving Mosko's laptop to one side in order to make room atop the coffee table.

"Hey," he complained, but without taking his eyes off the monitor.

"Natasha Grrrl," Donovan said thoughtfully.

Marcy said, "Honey, you have that onto-something look on your face."

"The name rings a bell," he responded.

"She's *horrible*, a real little monster," Lauriat said. "If anyone killed that poor man, if was her."

"Don't beat around the bush, tell me what you *really* think," Donovan said.

"Mind you, I only was . . . *in her presence* . . . twice, but . . ."

"In her presence?" Mosko asked.

"Yes, she acts like she's a movie star, as if everyone should know who she is."

"Maybe she's a Calvin Klein model. Maybe she's a celebrity and you're not aware of who because you've spend the past twenty years up an elm."

"All I know is that Natasha is vicious and manipulative and has my son wrapped around her little finger. He'll do anything she wants."

"Including kill someone?" Mosko asked, though still absorbed in his monitor.

"No!"

"Did you see her last night?" Donovan asked.

"No. But I'm sure she was there."

"He said so?"

"They're *always* together. She's got her hooks into him."

"But let him out of her clutches for a whole hour in the middle of the night so she could sit alone in a desolate corner of Central Park?" Donovan asked.

"That must have been when she killed Cozzens," Lauriat said.

"And dragged his body into the pond by herself. Sounds like one strong girl."

"That's where the 'grrrrl' part comes in," Marcy said, handing out cappuccino and passing around the platter of donuts.

"What did you and your son talk about?" Donovan asked.

"I don't remember," Lauriat replied.

"I mean, he told me you never speak. Now you expect me to believe he let the girl he adores sit alone in the dark for an hour while chatting with you in the Range Rover and listening to Chopin?"

"That's what happened," Lauriat said, bristling defensively. "I can't help if you don't believe what I say."

"You'd be easier to believe if you hadn't lied to me this morning," Donovan said.

"He also lied to you about the moss, boss," Mosko announced.

Donovan put down his glass and leaned over to peer at the monitor.

"We found moss on the soles of your boots," Donovan said to the scientist. "It's the same moss that grows by the gazebo."

"*You're* strong enough to pull a body across the ground and chuck it in the pond," Mosko added, also addressing Lauriat. "And having worked in the Amazon, you'd know the terrain."

"You said just now you didn't go to the gazebo," Donovan added. "Another lie."

"You want me to see if Stephen Jay Gould has a Web page?" Mosko asked.

Donovan shook his head, then said, "You're in trouble, Francois."

Lauriat buried his face in his hands for a moment, then said, "I guess I need an attorney."

"I guess you do," Donovan told him.

"Like son, like father," Mosko added.

Donovan said, "Read him his rights and have a couple of guys pick him up and take him downtown. But don't let him *anywhere* near his son."

Marcy said, "Sorry, Francois."

He tossed his hands up. "A father has to protect his son," he said.

"Even when the kid says you walked out of his life when he was ten and haven't had anything to do with him since?" Mosko asked.

"Especially then."

As Mosko got on the phone to call headquarters, Donovan picked up the laptop and pulled it onto his lap, where it shared the knees with a butternut donut.

Lauriat fell into what seemed like the silence of clinical depression. Clearly uncomfortable about the arrest, in her living room, of the company she was entertaining, Marcy sipped her cappuccino in comparable silence.

Donovan dialed up the Internet and surfed around for what seemed to him to be forever but which appeared to the others to be no time at all. The muscles in his jaw relaxed into a smile. A split second later came that mischievous look his family and friends knew so well.

"What?" Marcy asked.

Donovan said, "The name—Natasha Grrrl—wasn't familiar, but I'd seen the schtick before. Look."

Marcy came over to the couch and sat next to him, pressing her thigh against his and dropping an arm around his neck.

She read out loud, " 'West Side Webgrrrl. What's that, William?"

"Exhibitionism, millennial style. When I was a kid, it was considered risque—or revolutionary, or de rigeur, depending on what neighborhood you lived in—for the girls to go braless in public. Now, they go braless at home—but invite the world in to watch them. There are thirty or forty girls like this one on the Web."

Donovan clicked the on button and was rewarded with a view—announced in bold-faced type as being "live"—of a teenager's bedroom. There were the usual: posters, in this case of movies of dubious distinction but hip pedigree—*Surf Nazis Must Die* and *Repo Man* among them. There were framed knickknacks and shelved gewgaws of the sort associated with craft fairs. There were a girl's clothes thrown everywhere. A prominently displayed TV, several phones, and a bed with a comforting array of stuffed animals. And, bustling around the room wearing white bikini panties and a tight white T-shirt that didn't nearly reach down to her navel, was a thin bottle blond who might have come from a Calvin Klein advertisement.

"What's this?" Marcy asked. "Who's this skinny mallink of a girl? Does she have a *camera* in her *bedroom* all the time? Hooked up to the Internet so thousands of people can watch her walk around in her underwear?"

Marcy was using the tone of voice she normally kept for women whom she despised deeply, commonly certain celebrities, Kathie Lee Gifford residing at the top of the list.

"Make that *millions* of people, and I'm sure that a lot of the time what she wears makes what you see appear over-dressed."

"People watch her *sleep*?"

Donovan nodded. "Sleep. Dress. Talk on the phone. And . . . see that door in the background? If that's a bathroom and she leaves the door open . . ."

"I don't *like* her," Marcy said. "Are you telling me that's Natasha?"

As if listening, the girl looked up—waltzed up, really, adding a little dance step as she traversed the blue-and-green braided rug—to the video camera that was hooked up to the computer and, quick as can be, lifted her shirt to expose, for half a second, the undersides of small breasts.

"Jesus," Marcy swore.

"And four hundred guys in Podunk just reached into their pants," Donovan said.

It was then he noticed that Lauriat had come out of his funk and had joined them in gaping at the monitor.

"That's her!" he said, almost gleefully. "That's Natasha! I told you there was something wrong with her."

"At least we know where she is," Marcy said.

Mosko had joined those gathered around the monitor. As his brain began to process the information traveling up his optic nerve, he said, "Is that *her*? What the hell's going on?"

"Art, son," Donovan said. "Performance art, if you want to be charitable. If you're not so inclined . . ."

"I'm not," Marcy said.

". . . Then what you see is art for the artless. Got no imagination but a pretty nice body? Turn yourself into a moving sculpture. Make your very existence relevant by waving it around and proclaiming it meaningful."

"What you just said sounds like the justifications of pornography I used to hear in the seventies. What's the difference between this and a strip show?" Marcy asked.

"There are no guys sticking twenty dollar bills under your waistband," Donovan said. "These sites began a few years ago with *real* performance artists. You know, the Yoko Ono sitting onstage in a paper bag crowd? Then Web sites popped up where some guy would let you watch his Halloween pumpkin rot over a period of months."

"Sounds like art to me," Mosko said.

"About two years ago these girlcam things started," Donovan said. "One girl set up a camera in her bedroom and pretty soon there were dozens. Recently the pros moved in."

"Hookers," Marcy said.

"Porno women. Punch in your MasterCard number and you can watch someone named Crystal leer at the camera while making it with her girlfriend. But a number of performance artists or, in this case, body poets, remain. Including, I see, Natasha Grrrl. She doesn't appear to be charging for the right to view her, so that lends a note of purity to the event."

Marcy frowned and made a stomach noise. "This is *very* provocative," she said. "I can't believe her parents let her do it."

"God knows what *they* do," Mosko said.

Donovan said, "I'll tell you this—it makes it kind of hard to go out in public, where you might be recognized."

"I told you she acts like a celebrity," Lauriat said.

". . . such as might be recognized by a middle-aged man with nothing in his life except computers," Donovan said.

"Harvey Cozzens," Mosko replied.

"The murdered man," Marcy said. "I *knew* you were wearing that onto-something look."

"Any chance the late Mr. Cozzens was into Web voyeurism?" Donovan asked.

"And somehow tracked down the girl and arranged to meet her in Central Park," Mosko added. "He wouldn't be the first middle-aged Internet pedophile to come to no good."

"He came on to her and was killed for it," Marcy said.

"Such as by *your* kid," Mosko said to Lauriat.

That sent Lauriat's face diving back into his hands, where he remained more or less silent—an occasional soft sob escaped his barricaded fingers—until Donovan's men came and took him away. While that happened, Donovan perused the Web site, making mental notes. Twenty minutes later and on his second donut and cappuccino, he said, "It looks like she set up her own Web site at a free home-page service, located in Denver, that's known for quirky stuff: astrologers, herbalists, purveyors of bizarre psychological theories, alien-abduction storytellers, fans of obscure TV actresses, and hippie conspiracy theorists who still believe that Paul McCartney died thirty years ago despite the fact he was knighted by the Queen a year or two ago."

"Does it list her real name?" Marcy asked.

Donovan shook his head. "I'll have to get it via the Denver cops in the morning. But I know the police commissioner there and he'll help me out." Donovan leaned forward and stared more intently at the screen. The girl had gone off camera, behind it, perhaps into the hall or an unseen room.

"She must have stepped out for a snack," Mosko said.

"It doesn't seem like she eats enough," Marcy observed.

Donovan said, "It may not list her name, but I swear there's something familiar about this girl."

"Have you seen her before?" Mosko asked.

"I don't think so, unless it was at the market, and I don't spend much time at the beer counter anymore. Anyway, I don't even know if we're *really* seeing her live. The whole thing could be a lie. What we see could be a recording made months ago. But this is a New York City apartment, I'm sure of it. Look at that room carefully."

He pointed out the high ceilings, paint and plaster that looked as if it were smoothed on with a trowel, grown ripply from decades of touching up, bare steam pipes rising in a corner, and a rectangular abutment that made another corner useless for furniture.

"If she's a few blocks from here, how come her Web service is in Colorado?" Marcy asked.

"It could be New Zealand as long as there's phone lines," Donovan replied. "And what makes me sure this room isn't far from here is the spiel."

He read out loud the explanatory statement, found on the opening page of the Web site, which declared Natasha Grrrl to be a "performance artist and body poet whose life force resonates with the growling, feral power that throbs beneath the smoking ruins of the twentieth-century American dream."

"I didn't notice any 'growling, feral power' " Marcy said.

"What I saw was a teenage slut in Victoria's Secret panties strutting her scrawny little body in front of the whole world."

Donovan smiled and patted his wife on the leg.

Mosko said, "Becoming a mom sure has brought out a conservative side I didn't know you had."

"All I can tell you is that my son, Daniel, will never go near girls like that."

"Weren't you a model at one point? Speaking of strutting your stuff."

"When I was sixteen, my mother got me a job as a show-room model in the garment district," Marcy said. "I tried on new lines of clothing for buyers. Then one of them felt me up and I was forced to break two of his fingers."

"Ouch," Mosko said.

"That was among the things he said."

"Did your boss make the sale?" Donovan asked idly.

"Yeah, but the guy had to sign the contract with his left hand. Anyway, I quit and went back to being a camp coun-selor, which is what girls should be doing at that age."

"You're especially cute when you get into this mommy mode," Donovan said. "You put a lot of growling, feral power into it. Which is a phrase I've heard before . . . some-where . . . years ago."

Mosko said, "We'll find out who she is, and . . ."

He cut short his declaration when a ruckus appeared on the computer screen. The three of them leaned forward to watch Natasha Grrrl run back into the room pursued by a milling crowd of parents and policemen. She stopped in mid-rug, looked into the camera for an instant and smiled—but this time did not expose anything beyond her youth—then flung herself onto the bed and cowered against the headboard, scooping up armfuls of stuffed animals. She pressed herself against the headboard looking fearful, while hugging Pooh Bear in one arm and a Teletubby in the other. As her parents argued violently, or at least seemed to in the silent video, a young uniformed policeman strode over to the bed and, ignoring the stuffed toys, slapped handcuffs on her.

Donovan winced as one of the cuffs also snagged Pooh Bear's arm, bonding him inextricably to the slender arm of the suddenly very small girl.

Mosko said, "Who are those cops? How did they get into our case? Wait . . . that fuck who cuffed her . . . that's . . ."

"Patrolman Lewis Rodriguez," Donovan said.

"Yeah! The kid with the mouth."

Marcy closed her eyes and shook her head sadly and silently, but said nothing.

Donovan said, "He works in the Central Park precinct. He knows the girl. Our old friend, Deputy Chief Inspector Paul Pilcrow . . ."

Donovan reached out and pressed a fingertip to the image of the deputy chief as it appeared on the monitor, strutting around, looking important.

". . . recently added oversight of that precinct to his portfolio."

"He's wanted to upstage you for years," Mosko said.

"Which he?" Marcy asked.

"Pilcrow, of course," Mosko said.

"And now he did it, with the help of Patrolman Rodriguez," Marcy said.

"Rodriguez called in 'sick' so we couldn't ask him what he knows about the girl," Mosko said. "All the time he was setting up this front-page bust so Pilcrow would look good. I'm gonna wring his scrawny rookie neck."

"There will be no need for that," Donovan said, staring intently at the image of the girl's mother and father. The woman was pretty and fortyish. The man was white-haired, sophisticated looking, and about seventy. "Know who that is?" Donovan asked.

"Her dad?" Mosko said.

"Yeah. But he's not just any dad. That's Gabriel Allen Cohen."

"The poet? The guy who bought the beer the other night? You got to be kidding me."

"The same. I'd recognize that face anywhere. And I remember where I heard the phrase, 'Growling, feral power' before. He used it in a poem in the late fifties. It was Cohen who bought the Steamboat Ferry Inn Ale and gave it to his daughter, the performance artist and body poet who's five years shy of legal age. Well, I guess that buying beer for his daughter is an improvement, considering the public heroin habit he sported for decades."

Marcy seemed unmoved by the argument. She sat in angry silence as Rodriguez and several other uniformed policemen carried the girl out of the room. Natasha had assumed the limp-framed posture of the antiwar protester that her father was during the Vietnam War, and the last view of her on camera was of a tender child being carried off by tough cops while Winnie the Pooh was shackled to her arm.

Donovan said, "Pilcrow has no idea of the nightmare this is going to be for him. Look at him in that room. He doesn't even know he's on camera! On the advice of a rookie cop, he just busted Winnie the Pooh while the whole world was watching. This will be a public relations disaster for Pilcrow . . . the mayor will have him for breakfast . . . and Pilcrow will take it out on the kid. You needn't bother wringing Patrolman Rodriguez's neck, Brian. He did it to himself."

"In the grand family tradition," Marcy said, getting up and going into the kitchen.

"What's she talking about?" Mosko asked.

Donovan shrugged. "It's late and she's tired. Let's all try to get some sleep. We need to rest up and stay sharp. That girl didn't kill anyone. If anything, she's managed—with some help from her dad, an old hand at manipulating the media—to turn her life and this case into a media event. Well, I guess that Cohen has gotten tired of being a recluse."

"I guess so."

"The girl will be out on bail by noon and on *Larry King Live* this time tomorrow. Her celebrity is assured. Her father is back in the news, once again battling the cops. And Frank Lauriat—or his father, the bird watcher, or both—will take the rap for killing Harvey Cozzens."

"You don't think that one of them did it?" Mosko asked. "The girl to protect her—oh, never mind."

"You were about to say?"

"Nothing," Mosko replied. "And the boy to protect his lady love from a middle-aged stalker who saw this skinny mallink of a girl, as your wife calls her, on the Internet and tracked her down. I'll subpoena Cozzens's computer tomorrow and also the records of his Web service provider. Let's see if he's been tuning her in."

"A visit to a Web site is called a 'hit,' " Donovan said.

"Yeah, but he's the one who got hit," Mosko said, getting up and switching off the computer preparatory to leaving for the drive back to Canarsie. "I'll see you in the morning."

Residents sometimes call New York City the center of the known universe. What it definitely is, no doubt, is the media capital. As Donovan predicted, on the following day the media went wild over the arrest of sixteen-year-old Natasha Cohen and her eighteen-year-old boyfriend for the brutal murder of Harvey Cozzens. All the media outlets pondered her arraignment and the subsequent press conference by Deputy Chief Inspector Paul Pilcrow. (The police commissioner and mayor, never known to miss the chance to take credit for high-profile arrests, were as wise as their best-known captain and stayed away; therefore, Pilcrow alone faced the cameras when an Eyewitness News reporter asked him, "How did it feel to arrest Winnie the Pooh while the whole world watched?")

Donovan also avoided the media and let his staff work with friends in the district attorney's office to run a lower-key arraignment of Frank Lauriat.

Both suspects were indeed out on bail, which was set relatively low due to their ages and the circumstantial nature of the evidence against them. The elder Lauriat was let go after a night of questioning, both of him and his ex-wife.

Lauriat and his former wife got together long enough to scrape up bail for their son, who was back on the street in time to see the right-wing *New York Post* screaming about the "murdering teenage slut and her punk boyfriend" being freed on bail.

And, more or less as Donovan had predicted, twenty-four hours after the arrest Natasha and her father were indeed on TV—not on *Larry King Live* but on *Geraldo Live*, which gratefully broadcast from her bedroom so she could resume her "body poet" career—this time with a much larger audience. With the Cohens was their lawyer, Boris Irwin, who first became famous for litigating censorship cases during the 1960s. With his help, Gabriel Allen Cohen was throwing the full weight of his prestige behind his daughter's innocence as well as her "right to express her growling, feral power in any media she chooses, including body poetry."

Donovan slept late that day, going into the office in the afternoon to review the transcript of the several interrogations to which all the suspects were subjected, as well as to read the reports from his small army of evidence collectors. As the day wound toward sundown, he found himself back by Fiddler's Pond—which uniformed cops were guarding from a horde of reporters—having gotten a report from Moskowitz that several items of interest, possibly including the murder weapon, had turned up. Several teams of investigators continued to drag the pond, using rowboats. Two divers in black wet suits, the backs of which were stamped with huge yellow letters reading NYPD, kept prowling the bottom of the pond using gloved hands to sort through the collection of rocks, mud, tin cans, and old sneakers along the bottom.

Mosko looked tired as he stood, hands in pockets, staring across the waters of Fiddler's Pond. The long shadows of late day made everything appear wrinkled and angry. The softness on display on a spring morning had turned to the sharp edges and cranky moods of day's end. Even Howard Bonaci, normally the most cheerful of Donovan's close associates, looked like he needed a nap.

"Are the fish biting?" Donovan asked, nodding at the men in boats.

"There's something swimming around in there and it ain't a fish and it ain't a cop," Bonaci said. "But I couldn't tell you what it is. The Loch Ness monster, maybe."

"Most likely a muskrat," Donovan said.

"Nah. Muskrats are fuzzy and brown and about the size of a football, not counting the tail. What I saw this afternoon was bluish black with fur like a seal and the size of a watermelon."

"With or without the tail?" Donovan asked idly.

"Without. Add a zucchini for the tail."

"Sounds like a mutant beaver," Donovan said. "Could be dangerous. Better shoot first the next time you see the thing."

"You ain't kidding," Bonaci replied, holding up a collection of evidence bags. One of them held a rusted old pistol.

"Are you gonna use *that*?" Mosko asked.

Donovan eyed the weapon suspiciously, then asked to hold the gun. Bonaci plopped the weapon, still inside its evidence bag, into the captain's hand. The weapon was red with rust and looked like one of the cast-iron antiques—

nineteenth-century railroad tools were an example—of the sort Donovan liked to seek out on weekend drives to Vermont. He stared at the thing for a moment, silently . . . silent long enough for Mosko to say, "Boss?"

Donovan shook off whatever had momentarily captured him, and said, "It's old. A Smith & Wesson like mine. A cop's gun from long ago. See if you can get the numbers off it and trace it."

"Will do," Bonaci said, taking the weapon back. In its place he gave Donovan a bag that held a knife, an old and decrepit and long one, with a blade that tapered so dramatically it more closely resembled a triangle.

"I think this is the murder weapon," Bonaci said. "It's about the right length—ten inches—and hasn't been in the water that long. There's no underwater growth on it. No algae. No snails or crawly things. And if you look closely you can see what looks like a mix of blood and dirt."

Donovan looked closely. What he saw was a reddish brown something stuck in a crevice where the blade met the hilt.

"I'll know more after the lab has had it for a few hours," Bonaci said. "But it looks like the killer tried to get the blood off the knife by thrusting it into the ground."

To illustrate, Bonaci used an imaginary knife to make a stabbing motion at the skunk cabbage that had been trampled by enough policemen's feet during the previous two days to have lost its odor.

He continued, "We found a mark like you'd get by doing that. It was in the ground at the old gazebo."

Donovan pondered that fact for a moment while he hefted the knife. "Where'd you find the knife?" he asked.

"In the water."

"No . . . *where* in the water?"

The man pointed to a spot in the middle of the pond,

halfway between the gazebo and the other shore.

"How far is that from the gazebo?" Donovan asked.

Bonaci shrugged.

"Measure it. I need to know if it's throwing distance."

"It is if you got a good arm," Bonaci said.

Mosko looked over at his boss, who looked back. Seeing the interchange, Bonaci said, "What'd I say? You got to have a good arm. Big deal. Those were both kids. Kids got good arms."

"One was a *girl*," Mosko said.

"What's that mean anymore?" Bonaci replied.

"This girl may be able to toss a sexy glance at her cybercam, but a large knife across a lagoon . . . I doubt it," Donovan said.

"Well, we'll measure the distance and find out. Hey, Cap, is it true this chick was parading around in the nude on the Internet?"

"She probably still is parading around," Donovan said, checking his watch. "It's going to be prime-time soon and her audience will have swollen. But nude I don't know about. Last night we were only treated to the Victoria's Secret duds. I haven't had the chance to get into the archival photos she has on her Web site."

"I got to get me a computer at home," Bonaci said.

"There are two years of archival photos in there," Donovan continued. "I'm sure that in at least one of them she forgot to wear clothes."

"She started this when she was *fourteen*," Mosko said, displaying the identical disdain heard in Marcy's voice the night before.

"Measure the distance from the murder scene to where we found the knife. I need to know if either of those kids was capable of throwing that knife that far. And another thing . . . check the rest of the shoreline of this pond to see if you can find any evidence that whoever dragged Cozzens's body into the water trampled down any skunk cabbage while exiting on the other side."

"We did that," Bonaci said. "Nothing."

Mosko said, "We checked for readable footprints, especially with mud on them. There *was* a mishmash of prints . . . none readable, *exactly* . . ."

"Meaning what?" Donovan asked.

"There's a partial of a sneaker print," Bonaci said.

"What kind of sneaker?"

"We don't know yet," Bonaci replied. "It's not a major brand. But in the mishmash there was what looked like pond mud yesterday. Today we got the analysis back."

"And?"

"And it is pond mud . . . from the edge of the pond. There were . . ." Bonaci consulted his notes. "Daphnia in it."

"What's that?" Mosko asked.

"A water flea," Donovan replied.

"Must infect dogfish, eh?" Mosko replied.

Donovan gave him a withering glance. "It's a common fresh-water microorganism."

"Glad to hear you hung onto your high school chemistry set."

"I read. I like to stay informed. It's a dirty job but someone's got to do it. You guys are telling me that whoever dragged Cozzens's body into the water got back out of the water the same way."

"That's the size of it," Mosko said. "He walked out of the pond, heading west, bloody and muddy."

"Which brings us to the next thing you wanted us to do," Bonaci said.

"Find out what happened to the clothes," Donovan said.

Mosko replied, "We interviewed the janitors and stuff at

the buildings where the two kids live. We talked to every Laundromat on the Upper West Side."

"No kids washed mud and blood out of their clothes in the past two days," Donovan said.

"Not one. And you know what? Cohen doesn't even have a washing machine in his apartment. Neither does the Lauriat kid."

"The janitors told you."

Mosko nodded. "In Cohen's case, the building's plumbing doesn't allow for individual apartments to have washing machines. You got to schlep down to the basement laundry room with the rest of the peasants. In the Lauriat kid's building, the plumbing is new and washing machines are okay but the kid and his mom don't have one."

"And since no teenagers were spotted walking home naked the night before last . . ." Donovan said.

"And an exhaustive search failed to turn up bloody clothes in trash cans, sewer drains, and Dumpsters on the streets between here and their homes," Mosko said. "So either these kids are as smart as O. J. . . ."

"Or they're innocent," Donovan said.

"The alternative is that their clothes were beamed onto a starship and warped away," Mosko said.

Donovan thought for a moment, then said, "They could have stripped down, killed Cozzens, then gotten dressed. No, too bizarre. And too much premeditation for these kids, who I see as sharing a whole flotilla of dysfunctional neurons."

"What's *that* mean?" Bonaci asked.

"They ain't too swift," Mosko translated.

"You don't have to be smart to be a body poet?" Bonaci asked.

"Nah, just have a sharp manager," Mosko replied.

"Did we look in every trash can in the park?" Donovan asked.

"Here's the problem—Pilcrow," Mosko said, a trace of hesitation in his voice.

Donovan rolled his eyes.

Mosko said, "Right. You got it. We can't do it without extra manpower, and Pilcrow now controls that as far as the park goes. I tried to slip it by him using a contact in the Central Park precinct, but the son of a bitch ratted me out to the deputy chief."

"Who did what?"

"Graciously allowed us to use his men in searching the park for the bloody clothes and the murder weapon . . . which, by the way, he doesn't know we found, assuming this is it in the bag here . . ." He pointed to the dagger that Bonaci held, once again, with the other bits of evidence.

"However," Mosko continued, "We got to fill him in on every step we take."

"And let him take credit if we find something," Bonaci added.

Donovan shook his head. "The man is bucking for police commissioner again. We're coming into another election year and Pilcrow is going to try to convince the mayor that he has the black vote in his pocket. As if the mayor can be fooled and the black population gives a rat's ass about the career of this pompous fool. So what do I have to do, let Pilcrow call the press conference?"

"I guess," Mosko said.

"Well, fine. I'm tired of being nice to reporters, even if such is a condition of my keeping the captain's badge. Let Pilcrow take credit if he can. I'm getting *really* interested in this case and need to spend all my time on it."

Mosko nodded, and said, "We're missing something, aren't we?"

"Bless you, my son," Donovan replied, patting his friend and aide on the arm. "You're starting to develop the sixth sense one needs to succeed in this business. We *are* missing something—and it's more than bloody clothes. Which, by the way, let's go all out to find, even if it means dealing with the devil. Get all the help you need. Look in every corner of this park. And while you're at it, canvas the Laundromats on the other residential sides of the park—east and north. In the meantime, I've got to talk to the girl."

"She ain't talkin', boss," Mosko said. "At least not to us. Her lawyer won't allow it."

"I think I know someone who can get me in the door," Donovan said, jamming his hands in his pockets and pondering the end of another day.

5. WINNIE THE POOH AND FORENSICS, TOO

You come highly recommended, Captain," Gabriel Allen Cohen said, opening the door and admitting Donovan to an apartment that immediately filled all his expectations—huge, old, honorable, book-filled, laden with treasures collected over a lifetime of world wandering.

"You, too," Donovan replied.

"I haven't seen Harry Spalding in—God, it must be twenty years now. I was bowled over when he called me this morning. He seems to be well."

"Harry is rich these days—but still cookin'." The old jazz musician had been a lifetime veteran of the dives and alleyways of Manhattan before being cleared of a murder rap a few years back by Donovan and, coincidentally, launched on a lucrative movie career.

"I can remember listening to Harry play piano at the West End forty years ago. We went way into the night together,

Harry and me, and I would write, scribbling notes on bar napkins, and he would play . . . wonderful stuff . . . Delta blues, Chicago funk, a little bebop when he got in the mood. Terrific times, those were. You would have been too young to go to saloons in those days."

"I would have been in my teens and able to go where I wanted," Donovan said. "Life wasn't all stickball. I snuck in with older friends some Saturday nights when the crowds were thick and I could pass for a Columbia kid."

The two men had walked a few paces down a hall that was narrowed to nearly shoulder width by jam-packed bookcases that faced one another and seemed almost ready to topple onto one another from the weight of accumulated volumes. Cohen stopped Donovan then, patting a hand on his chest and saying, sotto voce, "Harry says I can put my daughter's life in your hands."

Donovan replied, "If she's innocent."

"She says that she is and I believe her."

"But if she's guilty, I'll find out."

"Fair enough. I'm comfortable with that, and so is she. Ask her whatever you like. But my lawyer insisted on being here. He might not be so generous."

Cohen led Donovan into a large study that, if anything, had even more books than did the hall. The shelves ran from floor to ceiling, on all walls. A cutout in one of them admitted an old and honorable desk, oak with leather trim that was held in place by brass tacks. Magazines and manuscripts sat atop it, but in neat piles. An old turntable was hooked up to an ancient receiver that was jammed into one of the shelves, where it also served as a bookend for a series of foreign-language paperback translations of Cohen's books. In addition to a swiveling wooden desk chair, two pieces of furniture shared the room with the books—a raggedy loveseat that once was luxurious and an equally old armchair that had the appearance of a long-time acquaintance with a cat.

Natasha sat on the loveseat, her legs curled under her as young women do. Her old jeans were worn out at the knees, exposing white skin stretched taut by still-growing bones. A floppy pink sweatshirt let one shoulder slip out. By the standards of her Web site, she was overdressed. In the armchair sat a man of Cohen's age, thin and mostly bald, who wore an expensive wool suit, Saville Row and fashionably baggy, his slight frame within it giving the impression of a fierce asceticism that caused him to shrink out of the expensive clothes required in his profession. Donovan recognized him as Boris Irwin, who first gained fame in the 1950s and 1960s defending Freedom Riders and other civil rights workers in the South and only later added celebrity criminal law to his portfolio. Donovan recalled him as being the bane of the right wing, as one of those rare attorneys who occupied the stellar ranks but never lost his ethics. Donovan was impressed by the company, even by the girl, who maintained a demure silence as the introductions were made.

Saying, "There's something I want to get out of the way," Donovan pulled a slender volume from a manila envelope and handed it to Cohen. "I'd like you to inscribe this."

Cohen smiled as he opened the much-thumbed volume of poetry to the title page. "This is a first edition, nineteen fifty-seven," he said. "Wherever did you get it?"

"Do you remember the bookstore, Papyrus, on One hundred and twelfth and Broadway?"

"Of course I do. A classic West Side spot during the fifties and sixties. Only place you could get foreign and literary magazines without going downtown." Cohen wrote a line in the book and signed it with a flourish. "You bought my book there?"

"I was thirteen. I had read the Irish poets and my mother—she was a librarian and felt she could educate some sense into me, the poor woman—thought I should get into the Beats. She felt they would touch a chord with me."

"And did we?" Cohen asked.

"Far too well," Donovan said. "Before reaching the end of *On the Road* I was ready to thumb my way across the country."

"Did you?"

"I got around," Donovan replied, in a tone of voice that indicated this was as much information as he was willing to part with on the matter.

Cohen closed the book with a snap and handed it back. Donovan stole a look at the inscription, which read, "To a fellow truth seeker." Then he returned the book to the manila envelope.

"How does a bright thirteen-year-old go from poetry to becoming a *cop*?" Cohen asked, adding an emphasis to the word "cop" to let the captain know he generally disapproved of the profession.

"One thing led to another," Donovan replied, offhand.

The attorney spoke then, asking, "Did the road lead through Selma, by any chance? I *know* you, Captain, though it was many years ago and we were all much younger."

"May I sit down?" Donovan asked, and helped himself to the desk chair even as Cohen replied, "Please do."

Irwin continued, "Just after the attack on the bridge . . . not the Pettus Bridge, the other one on the road to Montgomery, by the sheriff, the Klan, and the dogs, there was this young man on our side . . ."

Donovan shrugged and swiveled the chair from side to side, making squeaks.

"Very tough, with a two-by-four. A little scary . . . took on this redneck who had a shotgun and put him in the hospital. Like I said, whoever this young man was, he was on our side. It was nineteen sixty-five."

Donovan drew a breath and said, "You're mistaking me for someone else. I have one of those faces that people are sure they've seen somewhere."

"So you weren't a civil rights marcher in Selma?"

"Like I said, I got around a lot in those days," Donovan said. "Don't remember being to Selma."

"I think you'd remember having been to Selma, Alabama, in nineteen sixty-five," the lawyer said, offering a terse smile.

"I only started taking gingko biloba recently," Donovan said, returning the smile.

Cohen's grin was broader than theirs and his eyes shifted in fascination from one man to the other, as if with the joy of having half-uncovered a secret.

"My father likes you," Natasha said then, her voice as fragile and chirpy as one would expect from a girl of her years.

"I still have an ounce or two of feral power left," Donovan said.

"An old turn of phrase that has become a cliché," Cohen explained. "Surprisingly, my daughter has adopted it. No doubt you know that."

"I checked out her site."

"How do you like it?" she asked.

He shrugged. "You're a performance artist. You are your performance. I'm not a drama critic."

"You don't disapprove?"

"I don't arrest people for their lifestyles," Donovan said sharply. "My sole interest is in murder, which flies in the face of my core belief—that good people should live forever. So— did you kill Harvey Cozzens?"

"No," the girl replied, after taking a quick look at her lawyer.

"Did Frank Lauriat?"

"No. Frank is a sweetheart. He couldn't harm a fly."

The lawyer cleared his throat and said, "I'm allowing my

client to be interviewed—despite grave reservations—because you come highly recommended, Captain. But I wanted to be here to make sure the entire conversation is witnessed."

"You want witnesses?" Donovan said, brightening. "Let's let the whole world watch."

The attorney offered a quizzical look.

"Let's go in her room," Donovan said.

"Okay!" Natasha said, gleefully uncoiling her legs and springing off the couch.

"As long as I can keep my clothes on, of course," Donovan said.

"I'm the only one who gets undressed on camera," she said.

"Not Frank?"

"Frank stays over, of course," she replied, unselfconsciously.

Cohen cleared his throat and said, "Since my daughter is going to have sex anyway, I'd prefer that it be where I know she's safe."

Donovan said that he understood.

"He even keeps extra clothes here," she added.

"I like to change my clothes a lot," Donovan added helpfully. "But tell me, what do you do in Central Park all night?" he asked.

"Laugh. Sing. Get fresh air. Practice Ishimani."

"Refresh my memory," Donovan said, getting to his feet and following her out of the study and down the book-lined hall. The others trailed.

"The religion of the Sionoyas tribe. They're stone-age Indians. Very wise."

Donovan said, "They live in the Amazon. Frank must have taught you about them."

"Yes! He's very smart."

She turned a corner and pushed open a door, her gait

getting visibly lighter as she entered her room. The space looked just like he saw it on the Internet, Donovan noticed. There were fewer clothes strewn around—maybe because the occupant had been away in jail and related court appearances for a day or more. But Winnie the Pooh was back on the bed, looking no worse for wear for his shackling, leaning against the wall in the very spot where the girl had cowered from Patrolman Rodriguez. Approaching warily, Donovan looked over Natasha's computer, a large Dell with custom components that took up the top of a gigantic antique dresser. One of the components was a video camera set on a tabletop tripod and wired to the computer. Seeing the camera, her performance personality switched on, something it seemed to do via autopilot, and she curtseyed mockingly and mouthed a silent "hi" into the lens.

Staying out of camera range, Donovan turned the camera away from the bed and aimed it at one wall, one that held a knickknack shelf.

"Hey," she protested.

"Art is not eternal," Donovan replied.

She pouted briefly, then sat on the end of the bed facing Donovan, who sat near the headboard and picked up Pooh, idly stroking the stuffed pet's arm where the handcuff had been. The other two men stood just inside the door, out of camera range.

Donovan asked, "When you go into the park to spend the night and perform Ishimani rituals, aren't you afraid of being mugged or worse?"

"No."

"Do you count on Frank to protect you?"

"No. He's spiritual and not physical. Frank is incapable of squashing a bug."

"Don't Ishimani rituals involve a mild trancelike state

brought on drinking tea made from the diluted venom of a poisonous tree frog?" Donovan asked.

Cohen chuckled.

"How'd you know that?" asked the lawyer.

"It was in *Scientific American* a few years back," Donovan said.

Natasha said, "We modify the ritual. You can't find poisonous tree frogs in Central Park."

"Are you sure?" Donovan said. "Nothing would surprise me. In fact, there's a serious proposal out there to introduce wolves to Central Park."

"Oh, I heard of that," the girl said excitedly. "I think that is *so* cool."

"You don't have to clean up the remains in the morning," Donovan said.

"No person should have to. The scavengers will do it. The crows . . ."

"The fish . . ."

She nodded. "It's the cycle of nature celebrated in the Ishimani rituals. Dust to dust."

"A guy goes from designing software to being eaten by crows in twenty-four hours. I suppose there are worse fates . . . torn apart by wolves *and* eaten by crows. All within a short walk of Zabar's, speaking of appetizers. So . . . if you didn't kill Harvey Cozzens, did you at least know him?"

Natasha gave her lawyer a look, and he shook his head. "I can't answer that," she told Donovan. "Sorry."

"Interesting," Donovan said, then raised himself off the bed and, still carrying Pooh, began to prowl the room, looking. "Did Frank know him?"

"I don't know," she said.

"They both were into computers. Not that it means much anymore. Did you see Cozzens last night?" Without getting on camera, Donovan stared at the knickknack shelf.

Again her lawyer wouldn't let her answer.

"Did you see *anyone* besides Frank in the vicinity of the gazebo that night?"

"Like who?" she asked.

"Anyone. Frank's father, for example."

"The Bird Man of Central Park? No, he wasn't there. The only one I saw when we were going to the gazebo was that cop."

"What cop?" Donovan asked.

"His name is Lewis," she replied.

"Lewis Rodriguez."

"That's him. He saw us go into the woods but didn't say anything."

"Were Frank and you together the whole time you were at the gazebo?" Donovan asked.

"The whole time," she replied.

"He never left you?"

"He never left me for a minute. I mean, he went into the bushes to pee, but that was only a few feet away and we never stopped talking. I could even hear him unzip his jeans, he was that close."

Donovan asked, "So you were at the gazebo and in Frank's company the whole time from when to when?"

"From twelve-fifteen to one-fifteen, about," she replied.

"Why did you leave then? I thought you usually stayed all night?"

"Oh, I didn't mean *all* night. We usually stayed until three or four. Frank wanted to. But that night I wanted to make love, so we came back here."

"What time did you get home?"

"One-thirty."

"Did anyone see you leave the park or go into your building?"

She shook her head. "Mom and Dad were asleep."

"Where *is* Mom tonight, by the way?" Donovan asked.

"At the theater with a friend," Natasha replied.

"What's she seeing?"

"Casablanca: The Musical."

Donovan frowned, then said, "The doorman didn't see you come in?"

"We didn't come in through the front door. We never do. We use the service entrance by the laundry room. The janitor says he keeps it locked, but he never does. Anyway, I know how to open it using a credit card."

The lawyer cleared his throat into his hand. She looked at him, turned a bit red, then said, "I'm not supposed to say anything that indicates criminal intent."

"Your attorney is as wise as the Sionoyas," Donovan said.

The crowd around Marcy's Home Cooking had thinned nearly to nothing by the time Donovan wandered in, Winnie the Pooh tucked under one arm, at eleven in the evening. A young couple sat in one of the two window tables staring into one another's eyes and lingering over herb tea. The piano player was noodling through a long improvisation on "Crepuscle with Nellie." And George Kohler had closed the kitchen and was quietly washing glasses behind the small bar. Daniel was asleep in his playpen, a handmade Vermont quilt covering his plump little body, while Marcy sat nearby at an empty table, her feet up on a chair, doing her homework. And Marcy had set up Donovan's laptop at the same table, which was cleared of tablecloth and place settings. When Donovan walked over she popped up and gave him a hug and a kiss.

"Hi honey, I'm home," he said.

"Hi, sweetie," she replied, tightening her arms around him and then letting him go so she could sit back down. "I made a sprout salad for you. It's in back."

"I'm not hungry," he said. "I brought a present for the baby."

He bent over the side of the playpen, touched his son's cheek, and pulled his blanket up closer to his neck. "Winnie the Pooh."

"That's the girl's bear. The one she was arrested with. I want this bear disinfected before it comes anywhere near my baby."

Marcy took the evidence bag and peered through the clear plastic. She said, "He's recovered from the wounds he suffered when he was shackled. I called Forensics. A courier is on his way."

She smiled and kissed her husband again.

"The sign of true love in a marriage is when your wife always finishes your thoughts for you," he said.

"As usual, Forensics is in absolute awe of the ease with which you circumvent the search and seizure laws," Marcy said.

Donovan took the bear back and put it on the table. Then he said, "Daniel can have Winnie the Pooh after Forensics is done taking samples of Natasha Cohen's hair, perfume, and whatever else . . ."

"Body lice, probably," Marcy said.

". . . off of him."

"I'm so proud of you. My man is so smart." Then Marcy waved him to a chair, saying, "Honey, sit down."

"What for?" he asked as she pulled the chair away from the table and patted the seat.

"There's something I want to talk about," she said.

"Uh oh," Donovan replied, looking around to see if he could spot the damage that was about to be reported. He couldn't. She showed no sign of betraying what the announcement might be.

He took off his jacket and sat. The monitor on his laptop

showed the most recent photo of Natasha's room. She had readjusted the camera. The shot now revealed a gap in the lineup of stuffed animals where Pooh used to be, but no girl.

"I've made a decision," Marcy said.

"Okay."

"I'm going to go back and finish my degree," she said proudly.

"I don't know if I could stand being married to a lawyer," Donovan said.

"Of course you can. You *like* lawyers. They're bright and concerned, like you."

"More than a handful of 'em are crooks."

"I won't be one of those. You know that. I want to go into public advocacy law."

"All because I conned Natasha Cohen into giving me Winnie the Pooh?" Donovan asked.

"No. I've been thinking about it for a long time."

"What about the restaurant?" he asked.

"I'll hire someone to run it," she replied.

"What about Daniel?"

"Mary can watch him when I'm in class. And I'll schedule my classes so I can spend the most time with him. I need to do more with my life. I've been off the police force for five years. I've started my own business and run it successfully. And I had a baby."

"Time to rest," Donovan said.

She shook her head. "Now I want to do something for people."

"Your mere presence on earth is enough."

"Thank you, sweetheart," Marcy replied, patting him on the knee. "Anyway, I talked to my old advisor. He's sending over some forms."

Donovan nodded, yielding to the inevitable. When Marcy got it in her head to do something, there was no stopping her. He liked that about her. Her decisions were always good. At least, they were good often enough for him to take the chance. "Doesn't Boris Irwin teach at Columbia Law?" he asked.

"Sure. A seminar in First Amendment issues. Why do you mention him?"

"He's Natasha Cohen's lawyer. I saw him tonight."

"Really," she said. "That's interesting. I guess he must have represented her father at some point."

"No doubt."

"Does he know anything about criminal law?" Marcy asked.

"Not enough," Donovan replied. "A sharper guy wouldn't have let me snag the bear."

"Did you know that he was a civil rights marcher with mom and dad?"

"Was he?" Donovan asked.

"I'm surprised that you didn't know that. You came of age in the sixties and love it when mom and dad talk about those days . . . it's a big part of that weird bond you have with my parents."

"I don't know if *love* is the right word to use in connection with the sixties, although it was tossed around a lot. I hated the injustice and get angry when I'm reminded of it. But I love knowing that we beat it . . . the good guys won . . . to an extent, at least. Look, I don't want the sixties to turn out to be my thirties."

"Explain," Marcy said.

"In the sixties my father talked about the thirties like it was the defining moment in his life. 'Times were tough . . . men were men and women were ladies . . . a guy was lucky to make ten bucks a week sweeping the streets.' And all that."

" 'I used to walk five miles in the snow to get to school,' " Marcy offered.

"We lived in the city," Donovan said. "The equivalent was walking twenty blocks to buy day-old bread for a nickel a loaf. Or so I'm told. Anyway, I don't want to be sitting here in today's world talking about the sixties in the same tone of voice. As much as it was an interesting time to grow up, the sixties are dead. Probably never been deader. I've forgotten those years and, to the extent it's possible, who did what to whom in Selma, Alabama . . ."

"That's where mom and dad were attacked on the bridge because they were an interracial couple," Marcy said. "If it weren't for some kid . . ."

"You want to know the defining moment in my life?" Donovan asked.

She nodded.

"When I married you," he replied.

She leaned over and kissed him. George Kohler, hovering nearby while cleaning off tables, applauded, then brought Donovan a bottle of Kaliber.

"Wotta performance," he growled.

Marcy smiled and said, "You're completely full of shit but I adore you."

"I adore you, too," he said, taking a sip of beer.

"Now that you've seen her in the flesh . . . what do you think of Natasha?"

"If you're asking 'guilty or innocent?' I just don't know. Her father is convinced enough of her innocence to let me talk to her tonight."

"But . . ."

"But they're being deliberately evasive and are giving me incomplete information, which only makes me suspicious."

Marcy said, "You turned the camera toward that tchotchke shelf. Did you see anything?"

He nodded. "The knickknack shelf is big enough to have held the knife Bonaci found. And something used to be there.

There's something occupying every other square inch. Get that archival photo back."

Marcy bent toward the laptop and used the mouse to navigate back through the archival photos Natasha Cohen kept on her Web site, past the bra-and-panties-only shots and the ones of her in bed with the covers pulled up, illuminated only by the light that came through the open bathroom door, past the shot of her wearing a cocktail dress as if on her way to a bar mitzvah. After perhaps a minute had passed, Marcy found a black-and-white photo that showed the knickknack shelf in a slightly enlarged view.

"On this page she had the camera go around and take closeups of every inch of her room, but she wasn't in it. If you want to see the plumbing and the cracks in the plaster, this is for you."

"Just the shelf," Donovan said, squinting at the screen.

"This is fun," Marcy said. "I can see why you got into the Web."

"It's all work, nothing but work," he replied.

The shelf had an image of a knife; from the way the blade widened precipitously as it joined the haft, the knife was the same one found in the pond. The picture was fuzzy, but to Donovan clearly it was the weapon that the crime lab was testing to see if it had been used to end the life of Harvey Cozzens.

"That's it. I'm sure it's the one." He took the mouse and used it to save a copy of the picture onto the hard drive of his computer. "In case they get onto me and delete the photo," he explained.

"What does Forensics say about that knife?" Marcy asked.

"They say 'tomorrow morning.'"

"What do you think?"

Donovan took another sip of beer, then opened the manila envelope he had carried back from the Cohen apartment.

He thumbed through it for a moment, then affected a scholarly tone and read the first few lines of a poem entitled, "Dirk, Bogarde, and Me."

George Kohler did not applaud. "I don't get it," Marcy said.

"Free verse," Donovan explained. "A dirk is a knife; a thin one, not at all like the knife we found in the pond, which is more like the kind of knife a knight in medieval Spain might carry as a sidepiece to his broadsword. Dirk Bogarde was an actor in old movies, the only one, as far as I know, named after a weapon. Anyway, there's a footnote to this poem that explains. In nineteen forty-eight Tommy Hertig . . . I don't have to explain who he was, do I?"

He had to, and did. "Hertig was a key Beat Generation poet, the heir to the fortune his grandfather made in the freight-shipping business before World War I. Hertig spent a lot of his money on heroin and travel, especially to North Africa, where he settled in Tangier and created a community of American exiles with literary aspirations. Hertig gave one of them, Gabriel Allen Cohen, then a young poet living in Tangier, a knife that he promptly nicknamed 'Bogarde.' This was to protect himself from the local inhabitants, not all of whom were friendly to literary heroin users from New York City who also happened to be Jewish. Nineteen forty-eight was the year Israel was born. Reaction around the rest of the Middle East wasn't universally enthusiastic."

"This is 'Bogarde?' " Marcy asked, touching the image of the knife on the screen.

"I would bet on it," Donovan said. "That isn't just any knife, although it looks to the untrained eye like an old fishing knife. It's an example of the Spanish daggers carried by El Cid's cavalry during the reconquest of Spain from the Moors. No doubt it was captured in battle by a Moorish soldier and brought home with him during the retreat."

Marcy said, "Tommy Hertig gave this knife to Cohen to protect himself in the wilds of Tangier in nineteen forty-eight."

Donovan added, "Cohen gave it to his daughter to protect herself in the wilds of Central Park."

"Protect herself from a middle-aged man who was stalking her after seeing her half naked on the Internet," Marcy said.

"To save herself from *someone*."

"Then she *is* the killer. Her or her boyfriend."

"We'll know tomorrow if that knife is the murder weapon," Donovan said. "After that, we'll worry about who stuck it in Cozzens's belly. In the meantime, did you save these archival photos on disk so we have evidence in case she trashes the site?"

Marcy nodded. "I also printed out every page. All the old photos have dates."

"One interesting thing about these cyber-exhibitionists is the compulsion to document everything. 'My socks drawer, November four, eleven-fifteen.' Not even the Nazis kept better records of their crimes."

"The tchotchke shelf was photographed March four," Marcy said.

"The knife was on it then. Now the knife is gone. She must have begun carrying it with her once the warmer weather began. All this is interesting supposition but nothing you could take to court. I need to know more. For one thing, was Cozzens *actually* a fan of Natasha's Web site?"

"Do you have his computer?" Marcy asked.

Donovan nodded. "We got the court order this afternoon and are picking up the computer tomorrow. Want to come?"

"You're not serious. I'm a mommy and have a full-time business. And I'm going back to school."

"Bring Daniel," Donovan said.

"What, you want your child as well as your wife with you on cases?"

"I want you with me every waking hour. Like it used to be when you were a cop and we worked together."

"Which got me shot at *and* shot," Marcy said. "I survived the experience of going to work with you, but I'm not taking a chance on Daniel."

"It was just a thought," Donovan said, a bit sadly.

Noticing that, she softened her tone and said, "Why does this bother you so?"

"I felt like having my family about me. This case is about to get a whole lot more complicated."

"You've done complicated before."

"This one is different," he said.

"How so? It seems clear enough to me. If that knife is the murder weapon and any of the hairs from her bleached-blond head are on the victim, the girl is guilty."

Donovan hesitated for a moment, then said, "Natasha says that the last person she saw before going to the gazebo with Frank Lauriat that night was Lewis."

Marcy gave her husband a look.

"She's convinced that he had the hots for her," Donovan continued.

Marcy was unusually silent. She stared at Donovan, then away at her sleeping baby son, then back at her husband. She said, finally and quietly, "Oh."

Donovan nodded. "Yeah. Here's one interpretation—Lewis saw her go into the woods. He was jealous because he was in love with her. He hung around and saw Cozzens stalking Natasha. To protect her, he killed Cozzens."

"Why not just arrest him?"

"Maybe Cozzens put up a fight."

"But then Lewis arrested *her* the following day."

"He woke up and realized what he had done and needed

someone to blame it on," Donovan said. "He was mad at the girl for taking up with someone else—Frank Lauriat—and then getting him into such a mess. So he turned her in. Then Pilcrow showed up and escalated what was, in essence, a nineteenth-century tragedy, as old as the gazebo, into a circus."

"Do you think that's what happened?" Marcy asked.

"No," Donovan replied. "I don't think Lewis Rodriguez is a murderer. I think he's a loose cannon, but no looser a cannon than I was at the same age. I guarantee you, though, that someone will dream up the scenario I just presented—Pilcrow, if Lewis does something to piss him off."

"Did I tell you he called before?" Marcy said.

"Lewis?"

"No, Pilcrow."

"For me?" Donovan asked.

"He didn't call for *me*. He wanted to talk to you."

"The man has my cell phone number. Why didn't he . . . oh, the hell with it. Life is too short for me to waste time figuring out Paul Pilcrow."

"He's afraid of you," Marcy said. "That's why he called me instead of you."

"Why would he do that?" Donovan asked. "You're the one who decked him. I only dreamed about it."

"Maybe, but *you* got him six weeks in the hospital."

"Did I ask him to jump in between me and a guy with a loaded crossbow?" Donovan asked. "I can't understand people who blame me for things that aren't my fault."

"You get the hottest cases. What Pilcrow doesn't get is the inherent danger of being burned. What will you do about Lewis?"

"I'll check his alibi for the time of the killing," Donovan said. "But I'll have to do it personally. Brian's contact at the Central Park precinct turned out to be a conduit straight to

Pilcrow. I know some people over there . . . lower level, street guys from the old days . . ."

"Are any of them sober?" Marcy asked.

"They're still alive," he said with a shrug. "I'll ask them informally."

Marcy said, "You don't want to let Pilcrow know that you're investigating his fair-haired boy."

"I don't want anyone to know. Pilcrow hates multiracial people. I think you're aware of that."

"It crossed into my consciousness," Marcy said.

"He'll turn on the kid in a second and go to the D.A. with the scenario I made up before. It's also *very* important that Lewis not know. He'll freak if he thinks I'm investigating him."

"Do what you can, darling," Marcy said, touching his leg lightly as she pushed her chair away from the table and stood up. "Are you hungry?"

"Starved," he said.

"I'll get your sprout salad."

"Did Pilcrow say what he wanted?" Donovan asked.

"Only that he may drop in tonight. Guess who he's having dinner with up in Harlem?"

"Well, I doubt it's your father."

"Daddy doesn't talk to racists, even black ones. Pilcrow is having dinner with Jefferson."

"What's this about? Never mind. I don't want to know. Can I get some French bread with butter with that salad?"

She shook her head. "Have the bread plain. It's good bread."

He grumbled, but relaxed and sipped his beer as she brought him a large wooden salad bowl filled with Boston and romaine lettuce, arugula, radicchio, the assorted wild greens sold as mezclun, alfalfa and mung bean sprouts, walnuts, apple slices, raisins, and dried cranberries. The French bread arrived with a small amount of butter—an "I love you" gesture from Marcy. He ate quietly while the other members of his extended family went about their business around him. After a while he took a second bottle of Kaliber and wandered out the front door onto the sidewalk, to watch the late evening traffic and other goings on. A *New York Times* truck clattered to a stop at the corner just long enough for a tightly bound bundle of early editions to be sent thudding to the pavement. Three or four people were shopping in the all-night fruit and vegetable stand on the opposite corner, and a trickle of couples were walking up Broadway, hand in hand, from the multiplex on 83rd. On a wooden bench in the mall that ran down the middle of Broadway during its long journey through the Upper West Side, three homeless men argued over a pint of wine amidst their fleet of shopping carts and overstuffed plastic bags. The only thing missing from the neighborhood's familiar, nestling-close-to-midnight scene, was the presence of detectives from the West Side Major Crimes Unit. Jefferson, once Donovan's assistant at the unit and now his successor as its chief, had moved the unit from its second-floor location above Marcy's to a modern, ground-floor compound that was part of the housing project on Amsterdam near 99th. Without what Donovan liked to call "the relentless thrum of hob-nailed boots" going up and down the stairs, buying breakfast at the Twin Donuts, and double- and triple-parking their unmarked cars, the neighborhood seemed both still and vulnerable, nearly fragile, with power at least subtly ceded to the hordes of halfway house people who lived on the Upper West Side. The large collection of residential treatment facilities for the mentally ill, recently incarcerated, and otherwise imperfectly connected to the mainstream of humanity, added to the neighborhood's reputation as welcoming artists, writers, actors, dancers, musicians, leftist politicians, perennial students of whatever, and garden-variety

107

eccentrics. An older man reciting Shakespeare's sonnets to the pigeons, consequently, would be given scant notice by other West Siders. That night no such literary impulse was in evidence; only three winos arguing over a bottle.

What *was* unusual, and duly noted by the trio, who shut up briefly to watch it, was the arrival of a black limousine that bore NYPD plates and a command emblem. It pulled up to the curb in front of Marcy's Home Cooking while Donovan kicked disconsolately at a wad of chewing gum that time had turned into a petrified pink rock permanently affixed to the foot-blackened concrete sidewalk.

When Pilcrow stepped out, it was with stiff bearing, either inbred or the result of long years aspiring to be more than nature intended and nurture allowed. When Pilcrow extended his hand to Donovan, consequently, it was with the fear that so doing would cause him discomfort if not actual, physical pain.

"Hello, Bill," Pilcrow said, surrendering his thin and carefully manicured fingers to Donovan's grip.

"Deputy Chief. Good to see you."

"Likewise."

"I heard you're on your way up to a late dinner in Harlem. Just stopping off to visit the poor folks along the way?"

Pilcrow smiled in a strained sort of way, his gaze fastening on the bottle in Donovan's hand. Continued sobriety was a condition of keeping the captain's badge, and Pilcrow was ever on the prowl for a terminal infraction. He kept his gaze on the dark, long-necked bottle until Donovan raised it and, resisting only with difficulty the urge to smash it over Pilcrow's sloping forehead, said, "Irish, but nonalcoholic."

"You understand, I wasn't checking."

"Of course not," Donovan replied.

"I'm glad that you know that. I would never go so far as to check up on an employee who's in recovery."

Donovan smiled, and said, "Besides, I'll do all my *real* drinking after you leave, with my friends over there."

He nodded in the direction of the winos, who had begun to fight openly over their bottle of fortified wine.

Pilcrow endured another smile.

"What can I do for you?" the captain asked.

"I heard you got in to see the Cohen girl this evening."

"You've been surfing the Web," Donovan said. "I could have sworn you weren't the type."

"One of my subordinates told me about it," Pilcrow replied.

"Another employee, eh? Yes, I *did* see her. Nice girl. Cute apartment. Lots of books. I got her dad to sign a book for me. Would you like to see it?"

Pilcrow had no interest in that.

Donovan continued, "Did you know that her attorney was a civil rights marcher in the South with Marcy's folks?"

"I didn't know that," Pilcrow said. "How did you get in to see Natasha Cohen?"

"A friend of mine is a friend of her dad's," Donovan replied.

"Who?"

"Harry Spalding."

"Harry Spalding. Harry Spalding. Oh, the piano player."

"And movie star, sort of, now that he's made the first of those shoot-'em-ups with Kurt Sharkey. He and Cohen knew one another from the jazz club scene many years ago."

Pilcrow nodded. "You *do* have contacts, I'll grant you that."

"I prefer to call them friends," Donovan said.

"Did you get anything on the girl?"

"What do you mean? Did she confess? Hardly. She denied responsibility for the murder or any knowledge of it."

"That's what she told us . . . before her lawyer got there and made her keep quiet."

"The girl was evasive, if that means anything," Donovan said.

"She should be," Pilcrow said. "She's guilty as sin."

Donovan nodded, but in a cursory sort of way.

"You don't agree?" Pilcrow asked. The man was accustomed to positive feedback from his cadre of yes men.

"It looks bad for her," Donovan replied. The captain was in the habit of denying Pilcrow straight answers to key questions. Pilcrow knew this, and also that he couldn't do anything about it. That made him angry, and when he got angry the veins throbbed beneath the skin of his temples.

"Is she your only suspect?" Pilcrow asked.

"Can you think of one as good?" Donovan asked.

"The boyfriend."

"Yes, the boyfriend. Admittedly . . . and I say that because his father is—was—a friend of mind, the kid is even a better suspect than the girl, but only if you subscribe to the old notion that men are inherently more dangerous than women. You know the saying, 'The most toxic chemical in the world isn't plutonium, it's testosterone.' The boy could have killed Cozzens to protect the girl. She's the type who's capable of engendering that . . . fostering it . . . in a man."

Donovan also was fond of changing his sentences to give Pilcrow definitions of words he thought the latter might not have in his vocabulary. That, too, got the deputy chief's goat.

"The two of them could have done it together," Pilcrow said.

"That too is a possibility," Donovan said. "And one I'd be more comfortable with if I could figure out what they did with the bloody clothes."

"Washed them, of course."

"It looks like they would have had to have done it at one

of the parents' houses, and that we can't find any evidence of that. No one saw them if they did. Of course, they could have done it by hand at Cohen's house, but only if you believe that her mom and dad would have known about it."

"He *was* a heroin addict," Pilcrow said.

"Gabriel Allen Cohen was a *literary* heroin addict, and during a time of the twentieth century when it was fashionable," Donovan said.

"My God, is there nothing that you and your liberal friends can't excuse?" Pilcrow said.

"When it does no harm to others, no," Donovan said.

Pilcrow worked hard at maintaining his stance as a black conservative. He was unwavering and brooked no opposition. His anger was capable of jamming him up emotionally, and did so at that moment. He was unable to respond to Donovan. Instead, Pilcrow looked away, composing himself.

Donovan continued, "I'll have a better idea how good a suspect Natasha Cohen is if the knife we found today turns out to be the murder weapon. I think it is."

Pilcrow turned back toward the captain, seemingly grateful for the return to the main topic. "I didn't know that you found the knife," he said.

"We found *a* knife," Donovan replied. "Like I said, I think it's the murder weapon. And I also think it belongs to the girl."

Pilcrow made a fist with his right hand and punched himself in the left palm. "I knew she was guilty," he said.

"Well, hold on now," Donovan said.

"No! *You* hold on. I know what you do. You never give me straight answers and you always leave yourself an out in case you're wrong."

Donovan shrugged. "It sounds like wisdom to me, Deputy Chief. Life is a very complicated thing, with many twists and turns. Sure, it looks bad for Natasha Cohen right now. But don't touch that dial."

Pilcrow returned to his angry silence, his hands, both fisted now, on his hips, and then he said, "You're always holding out on me, Captain! And this is another of those times, isn't it? I have a press conference tomorrow morning at which I'd like to make news."

"I told you what I know," Donovan said, choosing his words carefully.

Pilcrow looked him up and down, not bothering to hide the scrutiny. The scrutiny reminded Donovan of the extent to which his survival relied not just on continued sobriety, but on the support of the mayor and police commissioner, both of whom appreciated his brilliance and were amused by his unorthodox manner.

"I need to use the men's room," Pilcrow said, nodding in the direction of the restaurant. "Do you mind?"

"It's not my place," Donovan replied.

"It belongs to your wife."

"But *she* doesn't belong to *me*."

Sneering, Pilcrow pushed past the captain and walked into Marcy's Home Cooking. Donovan stayed by the curb, finishing his beer. Two or three minutes passed before Pilcrow returned, still angry.

"Did you find it?" Donovan asked.

"Yes." Pilcrow ducked into the back of his limo and Donovan thought that would be the end of him that night, but then the legs didn't follow the torso into the auto and it soon reappeared, arms clutching a black velvet box such as expensive scotch might come in.

"This is for you," Pilcrow said.

"You shouldn't have."

"There's something I need you to do. Test this." With that, Pilcrow opened the box to reveal a boxy automatic pistol, a Cyrcad Automatic, of a configuration the captain had never seen before. It looked brand new, especially in light of what accompanied it—a wristband that held a small electronic device that reminded Donovan of a Dick Tracy wrist radio, only smaller. Pilcrow took the gun by the barrel and handed it over.

"This is the latest thing," Pilcrow said. "This is, in fact, the *only* one the entire NYPD has."

"I'm no expert on firearms, Deputy Chief," Donovan said, nonetheless flipping the magazine out momentarily to make sure the weapon was unloaded. "But this wrist-band . . ."

"Is a radio transmitter, you're right."

". . . makes this most likely the new 'safe gun' that Cyrcad has been testing. You put on the wristband and that means that the weapon will only work for you. If a perp wrestles your gun away from you he can't shoot you with it."

"Precisely," Pilcrow said.

"Does it work?" Donovan asked.

"That's what I want you to find out."

Donovan tried to hand back the gun, but he was refused. Still he protested, saying, "You'd be better off getting yourself a beat cop who uses his weapon a lot or might be expected to. I hardly ever fire my weapon in anger anymore . . . about once a year these days. And I still use an old Smith & Wesson thirty-eight, not one of the new-issue Glock automatics."

Pilcrow was adamant. He said, "But you're the one most likely to figure it out. You are, after all, our most technological detective."

"Because I use a computer? Paul, have you been on the subway lately? Every third person is carrying a laptop. You know, when they told us we'd all be working on computers one day, they didn't tell us we'd also be lugging them around.

I'm not a computer expert. I just use one like everybody does."

"*Yours* has a satellite link," Pilcrow said.

"It's a cell modem, for God's sake. Works just like your average cell phone, and I see those at the *mall* these days. At the barbershop. Everywhere. And every patrol car in the Western world has a computer in it that does exactly the same thing."

"I don't care what you say, Captain Donovan," Pilcrow said, wearing his rank like a well-polished set of brass buttons. "You *will* test this weapon for us. It uses a nine millimeter load." Pilcrow reached back into the car again and this time produced a box of shells. He dropped it into the captain's palm.

"If you say so," Donovan said.

With but a cursory "goodnight," Pilcrow got back into his black limo and was driven off north up Broadway toward Harlem.

Donovan went back into the restaurant and looked around for the bear. It was gone. But Marcy was at the laptop, the screen in front of her showing a fashion layout from *Perfect*, her mother's magazine.

Donovan smiled. "Where's the bear?" he asked.

"In the ladies room," Marcy replied.

"I'm crazy about you," Donovan said, bending over and giving her a kiss.

"He was looking for it . . . he was looking for *something*."

"Whoever was monitoring Natasha Cohen's Web site for Pilcrow must have told him that I got my hands on evidence," Donovan said.

Marcy shut off the computer and closed its lid. "He didn't just ask you for it?"

"Not even Pilcrow is that stupid. Once evidence has entered the chain of custody, he can't simply walk off with it, especially if his sole intention is to display it at a press conference and say, 'I found this. We have the goods on the girl now.' I'll bet he thought I had Bogarde stashed in here. As things stand, he'll call a press conference for tomorrow morning and announce that 'his men'—" Donovan made question marks in the air with his fingers "—found the murder weapon."

He put the Cyrcad and its ancillary equipment onto the table. "I got a present. Christmas came early."

"What's that?" she asked.

"The new 'smart gun' that Cyrcad is testing. You put on the wristband, which has a radio transmitter, and—"

"Nobody can fire the gun except you. I read about it. So why do you have one?"

"Pilcrow wants me to test it," Donovan said. "He thinks it will malfunction and get me killed."

Marcy said, "Since your mandate these days is not to get shot at, that shouldn't be a problem."

"I use a computer, ergo, he thinks I'm into technology. The man has the imagination of a filing cabinet."

Marcy said, "Don't worry, darling. I'll figure out how it works and show you."

"I'm not giving up the Smith & Wesson. Remember the time I tried out a Magnum and it hurt my wrist?"

She remembered, and patted him on the hand.

Mary was bundling the baby, still sleeping, into his carriage. Marcy handed Donovan the laptop, took his beer bottle, and deposited it into the return rack behind the bar. George came out of the back, carrying the bear and a mop. He had a dish towel tied into a headband, making him look like a fat and sweaty samurai. He handed Donovan the plastic-wrapped Pooh and said, "The ladies room is now clean and Pooh-free. The customers have gone home. Now I would like to lock the doors, put on the wrestling match, and drink myself into a stupor. So get the fuck outta here and take the rest of your flock with you."

"Doesn't he work for you?" Donovan asked Marcy.

She shrugged. "I gave up trying to civilize him."

"Out," George said, pointing toward the door, which upon his words burst open, admitting the courier from Forensics.

"We're closed," George thundered.

The courier gave him a gesture that involved a flick of the fingers under his chin, in the direction of the victim, and a heartfelt *"va fungu."*

"Here it is," Donovan said, handing over the package and signing the chain-of-custody form.

"You're a trip, Captain," the man said as he turned and headed back toward the door. "Nobody gets stuff out of suspects like you do."

"She forced the bear into my hands," Donovan protested, but the man had gone.

"Here, take your son home," Marcy said, pushing the baby carriage up to Donovan and indicating for him to grab the handle bar.

Donovan looked down at the tiny thing, chubby-faced and pink and lying on his side, snoozing happily, now with a baby-blue blanket pulled up to his chin. Donovan's eyes filled with tears.

"My son," he said to himself, and pushed the carriage out into midnight on Broadway.

6. "Ain't Life Grand," Donovan Said

Long before crows entered his life, Donovan had a troubled relationship with birds. Pigeons, for example. Many years earlier, during his drinking days, he routinely greeted the dawn by bouncing beer cans off his bedroom window in an attempt, usually a failed one, to dislodge the noisily cooing pigeon who had adopted the window ledge as home and hearth. Later, with sobriety and the glimmerings of maturity, came a more tolerant attitude in the throes of which he allowed several generations of the birds to nest on his ledge. He even nurtured them, of a sort, leaving stale Wheat Thins and dried-up bits of cheddar cheese out there for his feathery companions.

Then came Marcy, as a permanent resident and then as a wife. The new, baked Wheat Thins were deemed too precious to share and the bean sprouts held no interest for the pigeons, by then in their seventh generation. Finally arrived the baby and his fragile health, and with him an obsessiveness about cleanliness in general and bird germs in particular. So once again, this time in the name of robust maturity, Donovan launched a campaign to drive the birds from his window ledges. He scrubbed, figuring Lysol and pigeons didn't mix. They ignored it. So did they 409, Tilex, and Murphy's Oil Soap. The birds didn't care for Clorox but weren't prepared to leave home in protest. And each rainfall washed it off. It took a commercial pigeon-chaser, a series of metal wires that resembled a wire brush turned turtle, to do the trick. Donovan considered the eight hundred dollars well spent, and wrote it off as just the latest example of how sobriety and maturity had wrecked his ability to associate freely with his old, slightly disreputable friends. The pigeons were gone.

But that was not how it seemed early the next morning as Donovan lay in half sleep, dreaming amidst a low-frequency, rhythmic chirping. Pigeons roosted again in this dream, cooing and strutting and making the soft buzzing sounds heard during the pigeon equivalent of rutting season. For a scary dreaming moment, the pigeons morphed into crows and then Nevermore, the one-eyed, man-eating bird that Donovan chased off the corpse of Harvey Cozzens, was rap-tap-tapping at Daniel's window.

Donovan sat upright, eyes wide, and heart pumping.

"What is it?" Marcy stammered, sitting up alongside him, the comforter tumbling to their waists. "Is the baby okay?"

"I had a bad dream," Donovan reported. "It's only the phone."

Donovan scowled at a new telephone that sat atop his end table. It didn't ring so much as purr. Donovan hated it.

"This goes out the window today. I thought the goddam birds were back."

"Oh, *honey*," she said, touching his arm.

He rolled over and picked up the phone, noticing at the same time, and in clear relief, that the window ledge was deserted. Donovan brought the phone to his lips and said, "What do you want?"

He listened for a moment, then hung up and said, "I have to go to the park."

"Check on the baby first. Who died?"

"Nobody. But Francois Lauriat was beaten up."

"What happened?"

"Apparently the poor, deluded fool went undercover in Central Park, looking for 'the real killer.' "

"Shades of the Simpson case," Marcy said.

"Except that Francois has a somewhat better chance of *finding* the real killers. I'd better get over there."

She looked at him with her big eyes, that reminder look,

and he said, "Yes, I know. Check on the baby first."

"You're a good father," Marcy said, and kissed him.

Right after he spotted the Emergency Medical Services van, with its boxy white Good Humor truck shape, flashing lights, and crackling radio, pulled up alongside Bethesda Fountain, Donovan saw the black bird. The old crow of his dream perched on the dead top branch of an oak, which was twisted like a Chinese puzzle and bare, the bark having been scraped off by years of claws. Donovan was certain the bird was Nevermore, perched alone and watching the proceedings below, which like those of the dawn a few days back also featured blood.

Lauriat was sitting up on a gurney, propped on pillows, while an EMS technician strapped a temporary cast on his left arm. Standing nearby was Patrolwoman Ebby, who was nearing the end of her shift and looked tired. Donovan walked up to the gurney and got Lauriat's eye. The scientist gave the captain a "poor me" sort of look.

Donovan said, "I'm sure this is going to be one hell of a story."

Ebby stepped in and said, "We found this guy right here by the fountain, Captain. He was half conscious and says he was beaten up by a gang."

"A gang of what?" Donovan asked. "Drag queens who got tired of cruising the Ramble and decided to mug an amateur sleuth."

"I was *not* playing amateur sleuth," Lauriat said. The act of moving his jaw brought him pain, and he said "ow" and touched the fingers of his free hand to a bruise, on his jaw line, that was the size of a lime.

"Yes, you were. You think your son is innocent and you came out here to prove it. Except you don't know what you're doing and pissed someone off enough to beat you up."

"I used to work in the Amazon jungle," Lauriat said. "I think I can handle Central Park."

"Think again," Donovan replied.

"They *attacked* me, and all I did was ask them if they saw anyone near the gazebo the night of the killing."

"Who attacked you, the inline skaters?" Donovan asked.

"How did you know it was them?" Lauriat asked.

Donovan pointed to a spot about twenty yards to the side of the fountain's edge, where a dozen, sixteen-ounce plastic beverage cups had been upended and laid out in a straight line, six feet apart, forming a slalom course. "This is how they practice," he said. "They use soda cups to make an obstacle course and they skate through it."

"The captain is right," Ebby said. "Most of the time they lay out their course on Park Drive West, but that's also where the *real* inline skating pros do their professional workouts. But the guys we're talking about can't play in that league and sometimes they come here."

"Did you see them tonight?" Donovan asked her.

She shook her head. "The first time I got round here was twenty minutes ago, when I found him."

"The skaters can't have been gone that long," Donovan said. "Given any more time and those cups would have been rearranged by something . . . passing bums, the crows . . ." Donovan looked up at the top of the tree, but Nevermore was gone again, off into the dawn mist yet again. "One of the wolf packs would have eaten them."

Ebby looked around with alarm and said, "That's only a rumor, isn't it . . . about the wolves?"

"Do you believe them when they say 'only a rumor?' " Donovan said.

"I ain't seen no wolves," Ebby replied, fingering her Glock automatic nonetheless.

"Stay sharp," the EMS technician said, as he finished

strapping Lauriat's forearm into the plastic cast.

"So the inline skaters beat you up," Donovan said.

"Yes," Lauriat said, bobbing his head up and down until that, too, caused him pain and he had to stop. "I mean, I *know* these young men. I see them around all the time, usually on Park Drive West. I park my car near the Crow's Nest. They know me and my car. It's unfathomable to me that they would attack me."

"Did they say anything?"

Lauriat shook his head. "Nothing substantive. The leader—I suppose he is the leader—mumbled something like 'we'll get you, you creep' and some other words that I couldn't understand. Why would he call me a 'creep?' I didn't do anything to him."

"How did you present yourself to them?" Donovan asked.

"I said, 'hello, we've never spoken, but I'm the man with the green Range Rover who studies birds by the pond. You may have heard about the man who was murdered . . .' And they *set on me*! It was unbelievable."

Donovan smiled. "Francois, this is New York City. The first thing you did wrong was tell them you have money—a Range Rover is an expensive vehicle. The second thing was reminding them that you can park in Central Park and they can't. The third thing was telling them you study birds for a living. Up to that point, if they thought of you at all, they probably assumed you were a game warden, Urban Park Ranger, or some other quasi-law enforcement person. No, you study *birds*. And here you are, asking them about a murder . . . implying that they're suspects. It's a wonder you're still alive."

"I don't know. I hear about ordinary people who look into crimes."

"In *books*, my friend," Donovan said. "And maybe . . . maybe, in this rights-conscious, litigious society . . . you can get away with amateur sleuthing in some little town in Maine, but in New York City you need power. There are only a few private investigators who are effective in this town, and they all have a kind of scary intensity that compensates for their lack of badges. I'm told I had it when I was a younger man. I think I can still call it up when I lose my temper. Moskowitz has it pretty much around the clock."

"I've noticed," Lauriat said.

"Brian walks into the zoo and the wild animals cower at the backs of their cages," Donovan said. "Sorry, Francois . . . you don't frighten anyone."

"I don't *want* to frighten anyone," the scientist said, moaning and pressing his bandaged head further into the pillows. "All I want to do is prove my son innocent. Bill . . . I know he's no murderer."

Donovan touched Lauriat's arm, taking pain to find a part that didn't hurt, and said, "You're a scientist. Look me in the eye and swear on all you've ever believed in the course of your life's work that you know for a fact, with absolute certainty, that he didn't do it."

Lauriat looked Donovan in the eye and started to speak, saying, "I swear . . ." Then he sighed, looked away, and sighed again.

"You weren't with him that night, were you?" Donovan asked.

Lauriat shook his head.

"You lied to protect your son."

"Wouldn't you do *anything* to protect your son?" Lauriat asked.

"It hasn't come up yet," Donovan replied. Then, looking away himself, he added, "I can see where it might. What *did* you do after you borrowed my sweater and went down the ladder?"

"Your sweater? Oh, you're right, I did. See . . . I'm so upset and hurting so much I can't recall borrowing your favorite sweater. I put it on and went down the ladder and stretched my legs. Stretched out in my car and listened to Chopin."

"And Frank and Natasha?"

"They were at the gazebo, where they always are at that hour of the night. I could hear their voices when the radio wasn't too loud."

"So could I," Donovan said.

Lauriat's eyes were misting over. "I like to hear his voice. I like to know he's there. It's true that we haven't spoken in years. He's still angry with me for leaving his mom."

"Why did you?"

Lauriat said, "I don't really know anymore. The differences between us seemed more important then. Anyway, it's done."

Donovan thought for a moment, then said, "I think this is sad. Marcy would say it's tender. Imagine this scene. Father and son haven't spoken for years. But there's enough love between them that they manage, through a fairly extraordinary combination of circumstances, to wind up fifty feet apart in the middle of the night—close enough to hear one another's voices."

Lauriat's eyes filled with tears. He sobbed for a while, then wiped his eyes with his bandaged hand. At last, he said, "It's not like we planned it."

"Didn't you?" Donovan asked.

"Well, I did make sure he knew that I would be conducting research in Central Park. I sent notices to his house. Just, you know, so he would be informed as to what his dad was doing."

Donovan smiled. "And he responded by bringing his girl to meet his dad—sort of. You know what Marcy would say? It's more than tender . . . it's *adorable*."

Lauriat broke down again.

Donovan continued, "There's the two of you, father and son, who came to this desolate place in the middle of the night to be with each other but can't make that final connection. There's fifty feet of trees between them."

Lauriat wiped his eyes again. Then he said, "I'll bet you've never seen anything like it."

"Maybe I have," Donovan replied.

"I realize now that I know nothing about this girl. Listen to me . . . calling her 'this girl.' I should call her 'Natasha.' Maybe she's not so bad after all."

"Perhaps not a 'murdering teenage slut,' " Donovan said.

"I honestly don't believe my son is capable of murder. Okay, and I'll say this too . . . that no one he falls in love with is capable of murder."

"It's possible that they're both innocent. Now, remember those slide shows you use to do of your time in the Amazon?"

Lauriat nodded.

"That was the last time the three of you were happy together, wasn't it?"

Again Lauriat nodded.

"And . . . let's see if I can remember the layout. Your Amazon research station was on a crane, right? And your base camp was . . ."

Lauriat said, "Down a path through the underbrush, about . . ." He paused for a second, his eyes like the lids of jam jars. Then he whispered, "Oh, my God!"

It was Donovan's turn to nod. "Ain't life grand?" he said.

"The two of us—my son and I—without thinking about it, reproduced the situation we lived in when we were happy as a family."

124

Donovan said, "There's a path that leads directly from the base of the Crow's Nest to the old gazebo, isn't there?"

"Yes."

"That's how you got the moss on your boots."

"I liked to know I could get there fast if there was an emergency," Lauriat said.

"Such as the kids being attacked by an older man."

"Such as that." Lauriat's mind seemed to wander a bit then, as if in the pondering of possibilities. Then he said, a bit absent-mindedly, "Sometimes I go over there and clean up after them. Pick up the beer bottles and put them in the trash can."

"But not that night," Donovan said.

"No. That night I went straight back up to the Crow's Nest. I had company. How did you know about the path? I thought it was my secret?"

"I saw a young police officer duck down it," Donovan said. "Listen, Francois . . . I like what I'm hearing from you, because it clears up some things. Including why the kids were into a watered-down Ishimani ritual."

Lauriat shook his head. That hurt, and he moaned softly, but then smiled and said, "Is that what they were up to?"

"Among other things."

"Another memory from the old days. I'm assuming there was no frog venom this time."

"Was there ever?"

"Not as the ritual was practiced—just for the fun of it—in the Lauriat family. We mostly like the meditative aspect."

"Like I said, I like what I'm hearing but have to warn you that, as you build a case for the innocence of your son and his girl, you're talking yourself into the role of number-one suspect."

Lauriat moaned again and closed his eyes.

Donovan asked, "Why'd you get divorced?"

"Is this important?" the scientist asked.

Donovan said that it was.

"Eleanor was bored with the Amazon and wanted to go home. She's a New York City native."

"And there's only so many piranha and crocodiles we New Yorkers can take," Donovan said.

Lauriat opened his eyes. He said, "And there was another woman."

"For Eleanor or for you? These days one has to ask."

"For me, of course."

"Who was she?"

"Laura, who I'm embarrassed to admit was the wife of a colleague. They broke up, too."

"She was down there?" Donovan asked.

"Indeed she was. Wonderful woman . . . quite a bit younger than me. I was flattered by the attention."

"And her husband?"

"Another researcher."

"Also studying birds?" Donovan asked.

"No. He was conducting canopy research into tarsiers," Lauriat said.

"That's a small carnivore, isn't it?" Donovan asked.

"Yes. Nasty little things, too. All fur and teeth."

"Kind of like a squirrel with an attitude problem."

"Yes, and immense ears and eyes," Lauriat said. "Creep up on other animals in the dark and eat them head first."

"I dated someone like that when I was a kid," Donovan said.

"As I was saying, the tarsier points up what you might call folklore in the research community—you are what you study. Oceanographers look like sailors. Dendroclimatologists—they study tree rings in order to deduce the history of climate—tend to resemble lumberjacks."

126

"You're about to tell me that you're a little flighty," Donovan said.

"I study crows. I have a black heart."

Donovan felt for the man, to an extent at least. He said, "Not that I've ever noticed."

But Lauriat was insistent. "I was thoughtless to Eleanor," he said.

"Tell me more about your cuckolded colleague. First of all, his name?"

"Rudolf Traks. He was a little man and could be nasty, like the tarsier. Not the kind of a man who could be pals with a woman. It was understandable that Laura turned to me. Traks almost *never* got away from his work, and when he did he was in a foul mood."

Donovan said, "Laura was caught between the piranha and a nasty husband."

"Precisely, and since she's an artist . . . was doing a series of watercolors of the rain forest for a company that was planning to market vegetable chips with jungle motifs . . . she was extraordinarily sensitive and readily hurt. I never could fathom what she saw in him."

"There must have been poetry in his soul," Donovan offered.

"He didn't *have* a soul," Lauriat said emphatically.

"What was the upshot?"

"Eleanor took Frank and moved back to the city. Laura moved in with me. Traks flew into a rage, insulted a grantor, and lost his funding. I hear he's back in the States, but doing what, I couldn't possibly say. We're not exactly friends, you see."

"I see. And Laura?"

"It lasted a year for us. But after we both came back to the States we drifted apart. She got herself an adjunct professorship in San Diego and now is teaching art there."

"Do you speak with her?"

"From time to time. The last phone conversation was a month ago."

"Does she know what happened to Traks?" Donovan asked.

"He had some rough times. She said he switched fields and recently has been trying to get some grant money again."

"But not to study tarsiers," I presume.

"There are none in America except in zoos. Why are you interested in Traks?"

"Wouldn't he be considered an enemy of yours?" Donovan said.

"Absolutely. Even today. He hates me."

Donovan said, "It's good to keep track of one's enemies. Mine often call press conferences, which facilitates surveillance. Do you have any other enemies?"

Lauriat shook his head.

"Not even Eleanor? I mean, I have some exes—one, anyway—who would like to see me dead."

"Eleanor and I have buried the hatchet," Lauriat said.

"That's good," Donovan replied. "So long as you didn't bury it in Harvey Cozzens's body."

Lauriat seemed to be shocked, and said, "My God, you don't suspect *Eleanor*, do you?"

Donovan nodded. "I'm an equal opportunity investigator," he said.

Lauriat forced a smile, then said, "I guess there was a time when I thought her capable of murder. But why would she want to kill that poor man?"

"If he was threatening Frank?"

Lauriat nodded soberly.

The EMS technicians had begun to shuffle around by way of showing that they had to leave, no matter the eminence of the detective who was interrogating their patient. Finally one said, "We patched the man up pretty good, Captain. But now we got to take him to the hospital."

"Where are you taking him?" Donovan asked.

"St. Luke's."

"My old E.R.," Donovan said. "Where I used to get patched up myself, after stickball accidents. There was this one time when I was trying to steal home and a guy threw open his car door suddenly and . . . well, let me say that I'm lucky to be able to have children." He patted Lauriat on the shoulder and said, "There's nothing to keep a man young like having sons, isn't there?"

"I'm glad you're getting to enjoy it," Lauriat said.

"Me, too. Look, when you get out of the hospital, I want you to go straight to your apartment and lock the door behind you. Send out for Chinese if you get hungry, but don't go out unless you check with me first." And to the EMS technicians, Donovan said, "Okay guys, take him away."

"My son is innocent, Bill," Lauriat said as they folded his gurney, with him on it, into the back of their vehicle.

"Aren't all sons so very innocent," Donovan said, more or less to himself, as the ambulance drove off, the wail of the siren driving a flock of chickadees out of a maple on the far side of the plaza.

"You were kidding about this wolf thing, weren't you?" Patrolwoman Ebby said when they were alone.

"I've lived in this town my whole life and seen a lot of weird stuff, but wolves in Central Park? I doubt it. A while ago this French company put a lot of effort into trying to get permission to *give* the city much-needed public toilets. Did you ever see one?"

She shook her head.

"The paperwork killed the project. Now imagine how many forms you have to fill out, how many hearings you have to hold, how many politicians you have to buy off, to get permission to release wolves in Central Park."

"I hear you."

"Still, if you could convince the mayor that the wolves would control the sidewalk vendors and stop jaywalking, he might go for it."

"What if they just did it in the middle of the night?" Ebby asked.

"The only way to get things done," Donovan said. "And if the guys behind the wolf project are aware of that, it's already a done deal. That howling you hear every full moon isn't junkies wailing from behind the cold stone walls of Belvedere Castle, it's a wolf pack on the prowl by the banks of Harlem Meer. If I were you, I wouldn't go on patrol alone anymore."

"You're freaking me out again, Captain."

"Where's your partner gone *now*, by the way?"

"Lewis? Oh . . ." She smiled faintly and shook her head. "He was put on three days' suspension."

"For what?" Donovan asked.

"The story is that the deputy chief was pissed at him over the teddy bear thing. You know what I'm saying?"

Donovan knew.

"I mean, it's not fair, Captain. The guy was nervous with all the brass and the TV news crews there. It was practically his first arrest, for God's sake, and it's a fuckin' circus. Pardon my mouth. So what if he slapped the cuffs on the girl and got the bear, too? Anyone can make a mistake. Don't you agree?"

"Oh, yeah. I've made a few."

"Do you have any pull with the deputy chief?"

"No," Donovan replied. "When does Lewis get off suspension?"

"Tomorrow," was the reply. "I mean, Lewis loses three

days' pay just because a reporter asked the deputy chief how it felt to arrest Pooh Bear?"

"The man has no sense of humor. So tell me, what's with these skaters?"

Apparently relieved to be off the topic of politics and back onto the familiar turf of law enforcement, Ebby said, "I can tell you who they are."

"Tell me."

"They call themselves the King Blades. Meaning roller blades, of course—not knives."

"Uh huh," Donovan said.

"There's about a dozen hard-core members. Most of 'em are Latinos who live in the twenty-third." By that she meant the 23rd precinct over on East 102nd Street, which included much of the neighborhood known worldwide as Spanish Harlem. "But a couple are black kids from the twenty-sixth," in West Harlem.

"My dad worked the twenty-sixth," Donovan said, looking northwest past Central Park Lake and Fiddler's Pond, now fully awake with another dawn, in the direction of West Harlem.

"Really? Your father is a cop? Still on the force?"

"He died in the line of duty. Shot during a bust. The killer got away with his service revolver and was never caught. It was a long time ago. I was just a young cop myself." Donovan caught himself delivering a monologue to the horizon, and his voice trailed off to a softly spoken ". . . Anyway."

"I'm sorry," Ebby said.

"So that's it for the King Blades. Latinos and blacks?"

"And one or two Irish kids from the twenty-fourth." That precinct was on the Upper West Side, Donovan's home turf.

He grinned. "My spiritual heirs," he said.

"Say what?"

"I always hung with a mixed crowd."

"Good for you, Captain."

"Are these King Blades bad guys?" he asked.

She shrugged. "They talk loud and don't like to share the road with anyone else."

"Like all inline skaters," Donovan said.

"But like I said, they ain't the NYRSA."

"The who?"

"The New York Rollerskating Association, the real pros. The bladers you read about in the papers. The King Blades . . . well, we got called on them a couple of times," Ebby said.

"What for?"

"For creating a disturbance, mainly. For playing the radio too loud and threatening those who complained about it. But they never actually *did* anything, so far as I know. But there was the purse-snatching thing."

"The purse-snatching thing," Donovan said.

"On three occasions, women accused them of stealing their purses," Ebby said.

"Did they?"

"I don't know. Somebody on roller blades . . . Latino, maybe . . . *was* stealing purses from women, like tourists, you know, and racing off at high speeds. And the finger got pointed at the King Blades."

"Because they skate and they're Latino," Donovan said.

She nodded. "And because every single night we saw them on the Park Drives some New Yorker lost her purse— your prime murder suspect among them."

"Natasha Cohen had her purse stolen by these guys?"

Ebby nodded.

"When?"

"Toward the end of last month. March something."

"What did she report was in it?" Donovan asked.

"She said 'personal items and money.' "

"How much?"

"Eighty dollars. We thought that the King Blades were behind it . . . not Severino, actually, because he seems to have the hots for her. Or maybe he did it to get even with her for rejecting him. Who knows with these people?"

"They're troublemakers, generally," Donovan said.

"You got it, Captain. They're loud and nobody likes them. Especially Lewis."

"Why him?"

"Aw, Captain, I don't know. Sometimes it seems like he's on a crusade to rid the streets—the Park, anyway—of Latinos who commit crimes or, for that matter, get out of line at all. He's Latino, you see."

"So I heard."

"He had words with them and was always on the lookout for something to pin on them. But he never found nothing. Nobody did. Captain, I don't know if the King Blades stole those women's purses or not. They could have. To the best of my knowledge, they're just a bunch of loud kids who hang out in the park, skate, and maybe smoke a little grass. But they definitely beat up on Professor Lauriat."

"Did he sign a complaint against them?" Donovan asked.

She shook her head. "He says he has to live alongside them. You know, watching his birds. Are the King Blades suspects in that murder you're investigating?"

Donovan nodded. "The more the merrier," he said.

"Well, that's *something*. I guess you'll be talking to them."

"Maybe not me personally," Donovan said. "At least not officially."

"You'll send someone?"

"Give me a name. Who did you say is the Genghis Khan of this little band of marauders?"

"The leader is Rico Severino. He's in his mid twenties.

Makes his living, if you can call it that, as a bicycle messenger."

"God, two of the most despised things in Manhattan—inline skaters and bicycle messengers. And the guy is loud and violent, too? No wonder your partner hates him."

"I think there's some kind of personal thing there, Captain," Ebby said. "But don't tell Lewis I told you."

"I can't say for sure that I'm ever going to run into him again," Donovan said. "But I'll keep your secret if I do."

"Lewis is a good kid," she said.

"I know."

"I want him to make out okay, you see? I want him to get through some of these things that set him off. Like Latinos who commit crimes. And like . . ."

"Me," Donovan said.

Her eyes widened. "You know about that? That Lewis has a problem with you, too?"

"I know about it." Donovan found himself staring at the horizon again. Far off, atop another half-dead tree a hundred yards or so in the direction of the pond, was another big black bird. Donovan couldn't be sure if it was Nevermore or not. Probably it was, he thought, watching him, like Lewis. Waiting for an opportunity.

"It's crazy. I got no idea where that comes from."

"I do," Donovan said, without taking his eyes off the faraway bird.

Ebby decided against pressing the matter.

Donovan sucked in a bushel basket's worth of early morning air, then expelled it. He turned back to the patrolwoman and said, "I'll be talking to your precinct commander in the next day or so. I'm going to spend some time in the park at night. I'll be undercover, if you want to call it that. Passing as a bum, something I'm well qualified to do."

Ebby gave a quizzical look to the captain. To younger

officers who didn't know him well, Donovan was something of a dignified man of middle years, not yet gray but with the look of experience, perhaps street experience, on him, who wore expensive, if frequently casual and usually well-worn clothes.

"Qualified, Captain?" she asked cautiously.

"Like the song says—it's a country song, and I hate country music—but I think it says, 'I've got friends in low places.' Well, not so much anymore. But my memory is pretty good."

"Okay," Ebby said. Humoring him, Donovan felt.

"There are some things going on in this investigation that can't be figured out from a distance. Someone has to be there. *I* have to be there. So I'll be notifying your precinct commander that I'll be conducting a surveillance . . ."

"Who of?"

"The name on the notification paper will be Rico Severino," Donovan said. "This will be an official matter, so anyone in the Central Park precinct who leaks it outside the family is going to be in deep trouble."

Ebby said, "Can I tell my partner?"

"Of course. He has to know. He's one of the two patrol cops in this sector of the park during the overnight shift. I'm sure he'll take this information and act appropriately."

"You just let me know if there's anything I can do for you," Ebby said. "Thanks," Donovan said. "I may come back to you. What you can do right now is write up the beating incident as being another case of a victim deciding not to press charges."

"Okay," she said, flipping through her book for her notes.

"That will give the King Blades the impression they really can get away with murder," Donovan said.

"And you'll be watching to see what happens," Ebby said.

Donovan smiled and nodded.

7. "THE LITTLE SQUIRT NEARLY GOT ME," DONOVAN SAID

Daniel lay on his back, flapping his arms and legs, trying to get a good slap at his father's face, which was just beyond reach and unsmiling. It wasn't an unhappy face—Donovan was, in fact, delighted to learn how to change a diaper—but something about the process of applying a patch of plastic-coated absorbent material to a wildly moving target left deep furrows in his brow. He struggled on, trying to immobilize the legs while positioning the Pamper.

"Why's he fighting me?" Donovan asked his wife.

"You tell me. He's a boy. It must be a testosterone thing."

"He doesn't fight *you* when you change him."

"I'm his mom and he adores me," Marcy said.

"What am I, chopped liver?" Donovan said, as a swinging foot just missed his chin. To celebrate the near hit, Daniel cackled in amusement.

"Sometimes it seems that way," she said.

"This kid is *not* holding still for me," Donovan said, the furrows on his brow coming to resemble the canyons of Mars.

"Try talking to him. Soothe him."

Donovan raised his voice into a higher octave and said, "Hi, Daniel . . . it's Daddy."

"You've been saying that same thing to him since he was in the womb."

"It worked. He came out with his hands up."

"Well, it's not working now."

"Hold still for Daddy," Donovan said, lowering his voice to a whisper and bringing his face close in while blocking a kick with his forearm. The kick stung, and Donovan said, "This kid is a tae kwon do prospect."

"I noticed that," Marcy said.

"Maybe if I . . . whoa!"

Donovan jerked his head back as a stream of urine shot into the late day nursery air. It missed his face by an inch, but fell on the top and sides of the changing table and splashed from there to the floor.

Marcy grabbed the Pamper away from her husband and held it over the baby. *"William!"* she said.

"The little squirt nearly got me," Donovan said.

"Go get the 409 and some paper towels."

"This wasn't my image of fatherhood. As somebody said, a baby is 'a big noise at end one and a complete lack of responsibility at the other.' "

"You'll get the hang of it eventually," Marcy said.

"Maybe if I get a hammerlock on him and pin the legs."

"That's *not* the idea. You have to talk to him."

"I thought I was. Oh well." He trudged off to the kitchen and returned a moment later with the cleaning implements.

"Where did you say Mary went?" he asked.

"For a walk in the park."

"Which one?"

"She didn't say."

"You just can't get good help anymore, even if they're related to you," Donovan said, bending to clean up the mess his progeny had left. As he did that, the baby cackled happily under his mother's care. Then Donovan trudged back to the kitchen and returned munching on an oatmeal-raisin cookie. "Look at him now. He's happy."

"He knows his mother is taking care of him," Marcy said.

Donovan leaned in and, blocking his son's arms so they couldn't strike out, kissed him on the cheek. The baby kept smiling, and this time cackled at his dad.

"See. We made up."

Marcy touched her husband's cheek and said, "You haven't shaved."

"I'm not going to for a while."

"You're really going through with this, aren't you?"

He nodded.

"Why?"

"I have to."

"You have to spend nights in Central Park passing for a homeless man?"

"Not a homeless man. An artist who needs the solitude of the night to ease the pain."

"A drunk with nowhere to go."

"A lost soul," Donovan said.

"Isn't this something you can get Brian to do? He's from Brooklyn."

"Brian will be with me much of the time. And if it makes you feel less alone, his wife isn't happy about it, either."

"Brian Moskowitz is twenty years younger than you and in better shape," Marcy said.

"I'm in pretty good shape," Donovan objected.

She kissed him on the cheek, then made a face at the stubble of beard. "Of course you are, honey. You work out every day. Your tummy is flat." She poked it with a finger, then said, "Sort of. But your back hurts when it's cold. And what about your shoulders where you took those shotgun pellets years ago?"

"I'll take ibuprofen with me," Donovan said.

Marcy put the baby into his blue, terry cloth sleeper and zipped it up. Then, with her husband following, she carried him into the living room, sat on the couch, and unbuttoned her blouse.

Donovan sat next to her. "I'll be careful," he said.

"You'll be *armed*, won't you?"

"Of course. But honey, you *know* that Central Park is a lot safer than it was during the days Johnny Carson used to make fun of it."

"It didn't have *wolves* in it then," she said.

Donovan said, "There are no wolves in Central Park. That's only a proposal. And you know it will never get approved."

"Keep your gun where you can get at it," she said.

"I always do that, even going to the market."

"And come home at a reasonable hour. When will you be home tonight?"

"One or two," he replied, picking up the remote and switching on CNN but setting the volume low.

"That's too late," she objected.

"I'll be out all night at other times."

"We'll see about that," Marcy replied, snatching the remote from him and switching to Lifetime, the channel for women.

"Maybe you can come with me one of those nights?" he asked.

"What, go undercover with you in Central Park?" she laughed.

"We're a good team, you and me. It would be just like the old days."

"The old days when working undercover with you got me shot," she said.

"That was years ago. And I wound up in the same hospital with shotgun pellets throughout my shoulders. Remember? Jefferson took them—all one hundred and two that the doctors were able to get out—and had them mounted and hung on the wall behind his desk."

"Yeah, and you left the hospital with that Rodriguez woman on your arm," she said.

"I was young," Donovan sighed.

Marcy touched his hand with her free one, then said, "I'm a mommy now. I'm retired as far as crime fighting goes. And you're a daddy. No more getting shot at. How many times do I have to say that?"

"I'm not going to get shot at," he insisted.

"Every time you say that . . ."

"Okay, okay," he replied, leaning over and kissing her on the cheek.

"Let Brian get shot at. He's from Brooklyn."

"Fine," Donovan said.

They were quiet for a time, watching Daniel take his bedtime breast. On television, a made-for-TV movie showed the plight of a teenager fighting back against the local high school football star who had raped her. Donovan never could figure out why his wife liked to have those movies on every night, especially since she nearly always fell asleep before the first commercial. Maybe that was the idea, he thought.

Finally, she said, "So what are you going to do in Central Park? Hang around and get people to talk to you?"

"That. And watch."

"Who are your suspects now?"

"The two teenage lovers, Natasha and Frank. Francois. Rudy Traks. Rico Severino and the rest of the King Blades."

"And Lewis," she said.

"And Lewis."

"Did I tell you that I logged onto Natasha's Web site this afternoon?" Marcy asked.

She hadn't told him.

"Guess what she did?" Marcy asked.

"If this is something obscene, I'm not in the mood," Donovan said.

"It is."

"Then don't tell me," he said.

"Her site is no longer entirely free," Marcy said. "To get

to the photo archive, you have to plug in your MasterCard number. She's charging five ninety-five a month—three months' minimum."

Donovan rubbed his eyes. The glare from the televised saga of the misunderstood teenage girl was giving him a headache.

"I guess you would say, 'so much for art,' " Marcy said.

He nodded.

A few hours later, Donovan was inspecting himself in the hall mirror. The hall leading to the bedrooms had a gigantic mirror that someone early in the building's one-hundred-year history had built into the wall. It was trimmed with mahogany that was covered with at least twenty coats of paint, a fact that Donovan once, during one of the many idle moments back when he was drinking, had determined by chopping off a piece and inspecting it using his boyhood microscope.

The mirror was nearly full-length, running from ankle to shoulder, and probably covered the full frame of the average nineteenth-century male. But because the hall was under six feet wide, it was impossible for Donovan to back far enough away to get a good view, and pressing against the opposite wall meant disrupting the framed family photos that were tacked up the entire length of the hall.

Donovan tried, and in so doing knocked a framed eight-by-ten off its nail. It crashed to the floor but the glass did not break. Donovan picked the picture up and put it back on the wall. The photo showed a much younger Donovan and Marcy, looking young and tough and bulletproof, standing in front of a rowboat that figured in a long-ago case. She cradled not a baby then, but a shotgun.

He straightened the frame and returned to examining his wardrobe. Donovan wore his painting pants—the ones with the holes at the knees, the tears at the corners of the pockets, and the belt loops two of which were hanging loose like tiny pennants. There was a thick but very worn belt with a buckle, the fake gold plate mostly worn off, from the Pro Football Hall of Fame in Canton, Ohio, and a Marlboro T-shirt, also quite worn, that showed a cowboy with a butt hanging from his lower lip. The working class saloons of the outer boroughs, Donovan knew, were thick with unshaven men wearing cigarette-company T-shirts.

Over the shirt was a canvas vest of the sort worn, at one time at least, by professional photographers. It had dozens of pockets, loops, and other holders for whatever gear a man might need in the field, whether film canister or battery or corkscrew or ammunition. Over everything was a cheap and ancient cloth greatcoat, a raggedy light gray tweed that Donovan bought a decade earlier at Canal Jeans in SoHo for fifteen dollars. It covered him from shoulder to calf and had immense pockets each capable of holding a hero sandwich—double, with everything—a liter of liquor or wine, or a snub sawed-off shotgun. The pockets had, in fact, been used to carry each of those things at one time or another.

Donovan adjusted his attire, as much of it as he could see in the mirror, and trudged off to the door.

Marcy stood there, holding a paper shopping bag and some other stuff.

"I'm going," he said.

She fixed his collar in the partial light, and then looped a scarf—a ten-foot, broadly striped woolen one—around his neck.

"I want you to wear your Doctor Who scarf," she said.

"It's springtime," he objected.

"It gets cold after dark. The Weather Channel says it's going down to fifty tonight."

"That's not cold enough for a scarf."

"It is if you're sitting on the cold, damp ground. Listen

to your wife. Did you bring your ibuprofen in case your back acts up?"

He nodded, thrust a hand into a pocket of the greatcoat, and shook the bottle.

She said, "Here's the rest of your stuff."

"You're Jewish-mothering me," he said.

"I am what I am," Marcy said, using her brooking-no-argument tone of voice. "Here's your cell phone. I set it on buzz. You won't hear it when it rings, but you can feel the vibrations."

"I know what 'buzz' means in this context," Donovan said, sticking the phone in an inside pocket.

"Here's the Cyrcad. Are you using the shoulder holster?"

He said that he was. "I have it on."

Donovan took the gun from her, withdrew the magazine, and inspected the load, then pushed it back in and put the gun in the holster.

"Do you have the wristband on?" she asked.

He held it in the air and shook it proudly.

"You look like a punk rocker. I checked it out and it works just fine. To be safe, try not to get the wristband wet."

"I promise to come in out of the rain," Donovan said.

"Do you still have the Smith & Wesson?" she asked.

He hiked up his right pants leg and showed her the holster.

She said, "Here are two speed loaders. I gave you the loads with good stopping power. You'll have a total of eighteen rounds. In case the Cyrcad punks out on you, that should be more than enough bullets for a night in Central Park. How many wolves are there in the average pack?"

"Ten to thirteen," he replied.

"So you'll be okay. Shoot the alpha male and the rest will panic."

"Got it."

"Just don't get shot at."

" 'Don't get shot at' is my mantra these days," Donovan said.

"Mandate."

"Both."

"Good. Here's your beer." She handed him the shopping bag, which actually was three ordinary Food Emporium bags stuck inside one another. "There's a six-pack of Kaliber for you and a six-pack of Beck's for you to give out. No drinking the real stuff."

"I don't drink," Donovan sniffed.

"Watch out for Pilcrow, William," Marcy said. "He'll be looking to catch you with a real beer in your hands. If he does, that's the end of the captain's badge."

"Pilcrow will never go into the park at night. Too many crazy white people."

"But there will be spies."

"Yes, there will," Donovan agreed.

"You'll have to stop at a deli and buy your own cigarettes," she said. "But no smoking."

"I wouldn't think of it."

"Remember that you're wearing a tweed coat, and tweed soaks up smoke like a sponge. I don't want a coat that smells of smoking hanging in my hall closet."

"*Our* hall closet," he said.

"Our hall closet."

"A man needs props, that's what the beer and cigarettes are."

"When is Brian meeting you and where?"

"Eleven, at the bandshell."

"What's playing?"

"Shanghai Love Motel, but the show will be over by then. Noise regs."

"Who is . . . ? Oh, never mind."

Donovan said, "I've been hearing about this band for three years but have never actually *heard* them. But Brian likes rock and roll, and he'll fill me in. I'm mainly going there because the bandshell tends to be a flash point for the various social conflagrations that occur in the park. People go to a concert and then fan out to Bethesda Fountain or the Seventy-second Street Transverse or to Strawberry Fields to hang out."

"You be careful," Marcy said.

"I'm always careful," Donovan replied, then put his arms around her. They hugged for a long time, then kissed for longer than that. She pulled back and said, "Kiss the baby before you go."

Donovan set down the shopping bag and walked along the hall to his son's room and pushed open the door, slowly and gently so the old and massive but squeaky hinges would behave themselves and stay still. A triangle of light from the ceiling fixture in the hall fell over his son's chubby face, which otherwise was lit only by the soft glow from a teddy bear night light and the small bulb in the nursery monitor. The boy was angelic with soft eyes gently shut, Donald Duck binky beginning to slip from moist lips, and breath coming in little puffs, the beating of butterfly wings. Donovan slowly lowered the side of the crib and bent to press his lips against the baby's cheek.

Daniel stirred slightly, perhaps feeling the day and a half's growth of beard. "Sorry, kid," Donovan said.

Marcy wrapped her hands around Donovan's forearm and squeezed it. "That's what you say? 'Sorry, kid?'"

"I love you, son," Donovan said.

"That's better," she replied, then watched as her husband raised the side of the crib. Then she walked him to the door.

• • •

As Marcy predicted, it was cold once the sun set and, left Central Park in darkness broken mainly by the modest and oft-times flickering light from ancient streetlamps. But even at ten in the evening, a stream of pedestrians, bike riders, and bladers entered the park through various portals leading from Central Park West, many of them apparently intending to ignore warning signs that proclaimed the park closed at midnight.

Donovan walked into the park through the 93rd Street entrance, a break in the thick granite wall that few chose. The bulk of nighttime visitors from that part of Manhattan traversed the busy 86th Street entrance, which had the advantage of being wide and brightly lit by virtue of also being a crosstown transverse. The 93rd Street entrance, by way of comparison, was dark and at night chosen mainly, it seemed, by those who were slinking into the park under cover of obscurity carrying contraband, assortments of substances. Donovan had walked the five blocks, three of them long avenue blocks, from Riverside Drive to Central Park West, stopping at a deli, as planned, to buy a pack of cigarettes. By the time he got to the park entrance he was slightly disheveled and a bit sweaty, despite the rapidly falling evening temperature. His disguise was working. As he trudged by a young couple who were enjoying an evening flirtation under a Central Park West streetlamp, Donovan saw that they eyeballed him carefully, in their eyes that vague fear and loathing that well-bred folks can seldom hide when they see a bum, a potential mugger, or an acutely lost soul. Maybe they just recoiled from the inevitable and sorry consequence of aging in the city.

Donovan found himself humming "There But for Fortune" as he ducked inside the portal.

A streetlamp—a walkway lamp, actually, an old one, bent like a shepherd's crook and only half the height of the streetlamps familiar alongside American roads—illuminated a patch of concrete path that ran past the base of the trunk of a horse chestnut. The temperature seemed even lower in the park than on the street and Donovan felt the beginning of an ache in his lower back. He set the shopping bag down on the concrete and stretched, and when that didn't help very much he made a fist with his right hand and used his left to pull it against his lower back. That helped take away the ache. For insurance, he scooped up a horse chestnut that had tumbled from the tree and ripped away the husk. Then he took the shiny brown nut inside and rubbed it for a moment, as rural men did for centuries to ward off rheumatism, before plunking it into a pocket alongside his cell phone. Then Donovan picked up his bag of beer and started with it down the path in the direction of the bandshell.

The bandshell resembled a clamshell—no fancy scallop or overwrought oyster shell here—that had been magnified to gigantic proportions and embedded in the soil near the end of a promenade that brought daytime strollers or nighttime mischief makers from more southern parts of the park to Bethesda Fountain. This white concrete shell backed into a grove of trees and underbrush and held in its lap a motley array of chairs that, while permanent, seemed always in disarray. This was because events, scheduled or otherwise, occurred almost daily. When a Latin or rock band or jazz or rap group wasn't officially scheduled, someone who aspired or pretended to musical ability would clamber onto the plain stage with guitar or boom box and hold his own. The audience could be overflowing or meager but seldom nonexistent. There was usually someone drunk enough or bored enough or with time to kill before embarking upon some form of mayhem to stretch out on one or more of the chairs and pay at least some attention to the performance.

As Donovan walked up, by that time pulling at a bottle of Kaliber and affecting the devil-may-care look of a man for whom the possibility of walking into a tree was something of little consequence, the rock and roll quartet that had graced the stage, in a scheduled appointment promoted by a local radio station, was abandoning it. A dozen or so followers and friends of the band loitered about and watched while the musicians loaded their instruments into black boxes and carted them into the back of a rented Ford van. Out at the fringe areas of the audience, an assortment of random drunks and late-night wanderers lay about, some looking about ready to move on, others apparently waiting for the party to begin. Among them Donovan recognized Moskowitz, his body builder's torso bulging out a garish yellow T-shirt that bore a cartoon showing a man in the final stages of passing out as well as a legend that read:

ONE TEQUILA

TWO TEQUILA

THREE TEQUILA

FLOOR!

The narrator was a yellow worm gaudily dressed in a bandolier and sombrero, the brim of which was decorated with lemon wedges and salt shakers.

Moskowitz also wore battered gray sweatpants and a gray, zipper-front hooded sweatshirt that was unzipped all the way to the bottom. He sipped from a small bottle that he kept hidden in a Dunkin' Donuts bag. "Evenin', boss," he said, wagging the bag and bottle as if it were a semaphore flag.

"What are you drinking?" Donovan asked.

"Who wants to know?" Mosko replied.

"Without the Brooklyn attitude, *por favor.*"

"Jeez, you're like Pilcrow," Mosko said, opening the bag and producing a small, clear, bottle.

"I'm responsible for your well being," Donovan said. He took the bottle and held it up to catch the light from one of the bandshell lights, one of the few not yet doused following the end of the concert. "Dr. Brown's Cel-Ray Soda? You got to be kidding me. You brought Dr. Brown's Cel-Ray Soda? It takes a strong man to bring celery soda to a stakeout."

"It's a Jewish thing. I wouldn't expect you to understand. Besides, this ain't no stakeout that I can see. More like a hangout."

Donovan handed the bottle back. "The answers are here, son. I can feel them."

"I can feel it getting cold," Mosko said, looking off at the band, which was nearly done with loading its equipment onto the truck.

"You should have worn warmer clothes," Donovan said.

Mosko plucked at his T-shirt until he got a pinch of it, a bit of skin-tight cotton, to stretch out from one of his pectoral muscles. "This is first-grade cotton," he said.

"Charming."

"Do you like my worm?"

"It's not a worm. It's . . ."

"Okay, so it's a caterpillar, right?"

Donovan shook his head. "Butterfly larva. A gusano, if you want to know, and it mainly comes in bottles of mezcal, not exactly tequila."

"You got this bit of information off the Internet, right?" Mosko said.

"Off a liquor bottle, many years ago. It stuck. How was the band?"

Mosko nodded in the direction of the van, which was about to drive off down the promenade toward 72nd Street. "They're good. I like these guys. They're the ones you sent me to see when they were opening at the Bitter End for Jeff Buckley. Too bad the son of a bitch drowned. I may buy their CD. You ought to listen to rock and roll from time to time."

"Never," Donovan said.

"I heard this rumor you used to be a big rock and roller when you were a kid," Mosko said.

"Hey, I gave up when I grew up. You haven't seen me with a stickball bat recently, have you? Or bubble gum?"

"Not recently, now that you mention it."

"Same thing with rock and roll. I grew up. I gave my famous record collection away. I told you that."

"To who?"

"A kid," Donovan said, his voice carrying that end-of-the-page finality.

The van had gone and so had that part of the audience that wasn't drunk. Donovan drifted off, too, Mosko walking by his left shoulder, and they headed north to the 72nd Street transverse and over it. A broad stone balcony overlooked Bethesda Fountain and the plaza surrounding it, on which Francois Lauriat lay and bled not too long before. A sprinkling of couples stood at the stone rail, looking down at the party scene below. Donovan and Mosko joined them in watching the disco bladers whirling around overturned plastic beverage cups, a circus company in tight pants and tank tops all done in basic, luminous colors. A boom box blasted disco hits from the 1970s.

"Kind of a retro crowd, isn't it?" Donovan said.

"These are disco classics, boss. Donna Summer and Sade."

"Is this what you listened to when you were a kid?"

"Me? Not a chance. I was pure punk."

"You? A punk rocker? You got to be kidding me."

"It's the real deal," Mosko insisted. "The Sex Pistols and the Ramones. PIL."

"What pill?" Donovan asked.

"Public Image Limited. The band that Johnny Rotten formed after the Sex Pistols broke up."

Donovan looked amused. He stood back and held his

partner and friend by the shoulders, at arm's length, trying to imagine him as a teenager. "I'm calling up this picture of you with orange hair," Donovan said.

"It was purple with a mauve streak down the middle," Mosko said.

Donovan smiled, and shook his head. "The picture isn't coming up. You and purple hair—with or without the mauve streak—is rough on the imagination."

"Right now I'd pay real money to have it back," Mosko said, patting the round patch of white scalp at the top and back of his head. Circled all around with curly black hair, it made him look like an Irish Jewish monk.

"Were there tattoos to go with the hair?" Donovan asked.

"Come on, you know that there were."

"I don't know that. It was a guess."

"You've seen me with my shirt off," Mosko said.

"When was this?"

The sergeant thought for a moment, then said, "Maybe not. Okay, take a gander at this." He handed Donovan his bottle of soda while using two hands to hike up the T-shirt. There, proudly displayed—if a bit fading—over his heart was a small but noticeable marking: thin crossed bars of equal length separating the letters NYHC.

"Very nice," Donovan said. "I always knew that one day you would make your mama proud."

Smiling, Mosko said, "I know you think that stands for 'New York Health Club,' but—"

"New York Hard Core," Donovan said.

Mosko expelled a puff of air that made his cheeks bulge out. "I hate you sometimes. You know that."

"I know."

"You didn't get that off the Internet."

"I'm getting bored of the Internet. No, I learned that one talking to a kid."

"What kid?"

"The same one I gave my rock and roll records to," Donovan said. "So look, did you hang out in Alphabet City with punks in mohawks and go slam dancing at CBGB's?"

"Nah, the punks in mohawks were dirty fuckers. I hung out in the punk body building division. We celebrated the body. You won't find any piercings in this body. Beyond the hole in the head my wife says I have for deciding to spend nights in Central Park with you."

"I thought you told me your wife went along with everything you want," Donovan said.

"I never said quietly," Mosko replied.

Donovan took a longish and quiet look at the bladers below, who had begun slaloming around the fountain to the tune of "Night on Disco Mountain." Donovan said, "These aren't the kids we want."

Mosko shook his head. "This bunch is harmless, say the Central Park precinct cops. The guys we want—the King Blades—are usually over on Park Drive West this time of night. Want to go over there?"

Donovan did, and the two men headed off in that direction.

8. IT DIDN'T DO SQUAT FOR THE FROG

It was a cloudless night, unlike the night of the murder, and a crisp and clear feeling was in the air. A hansom cab trotted across the 72nd Street traverse, its top-hatted driver sitting back and letting the horse follow the well-traveled tourist route that began at Grand Army Plaza and the Plaza Hotel and wound through the populated and safer sections of the park. In the open-to-the-air back of the cab, a thirtyish couple held hands and nuzzled while a five-year-old, his eyes wide from the thrill of staying up late and taking a horse-and-buggy ride in the big city, pointed out every tree and lamppost.

As they walked along the pedestrian footpath heading west, they were passed by every manner of getting-about person—among them joggers, both men and women and of all ages, in spandex decorated with assorted sports manufacturer logos; bladers, similarly dressed, some with crash helmets and elbow and knee pads, some carrying bottles of water or *something*; bicyclists, many sharing with the bladers that king-of-the-road attitude that had turned them, according to the perception of the general public, from environmentally aware pioneers to road nazis, in a short period of time. Among them were a few walkers and, among *them*, the occasional stumbler, bumbler, or lost-looking soul who seemed disconnected from the balance of humanity.

It was the latter march that Donovan and Moskowitz joined, parting from the more mobile group when the 72nd Street traverse crossed Park Drive West. Most of the bladers, skaters, cyclists, and joggers turned south and headed down Park Drive West toward the safer parts of the park that adjoined Midtown. But the parade route of the lost souls was north, up alongside Park Drive West, toward the danker portions of the Upper West Side and, if they kept walking, Harlem.

Half a mile north of the traverse the two detectives came upon a stretch of Park Drive West that was unusually well lit because of the confluence of new mercury vapor streetlights and old scrawny trees that did little to block the light. There was no vehicular traffic at that time of night, the park drives (other than the transverses) being closed to cars, and the numbers of joggers, cyclists, and Rollerbladers who were unaffiliated with gangs were reduced by geography. The park drives ringed the park like a belt; traffic on them, even unmotorized traffic, flowed counterclockwise. To get to Park Drive West in the usual manner it was incumbent upon one to go first through Harlem. That was a chance that the faint-hearted were unwilling to take, at least after dark. So the King Blades had their stretch of Park Drive West essentially to themselves, to use for their nightly competitions.

There were about twenty skaters on the road that night—ranging in age from mid-teens to nearly thirty, and seeming to represent Latins, blacks, and whites, as Patrolman Ebby thought they would. And while they dressed in all manner of duds, including hip-hop baggies, skin-tight spandex, and neo-preppy khaki, all wore at least one item of clothing that was either orange or black.

"These guys look like a swarm of bumblebees," Mosko said, as the captain and he walked up, by that time accustomed to the roles they were playing and lurching slightly from side to side, on the cusp of intoxication.

"Bumblebees don't swarm," Donovan said.

"Maybe they flock. Look at the black and orange motif. These must be gang colors. The report I got on the King Blades doesn't mention gang colors."

"Did you ever take a look at venomous animals?"

"Not since I graduated high school, no."

"Orange and black are common colors in many species—bees, birds, lizards, amphibians. I don't suppose you've ever seen an Amazon arrow poison frog?"

Mosko said, "Actually, yes, I did. Two days ago on the D train."

"The natives of the rain forest dip their blowgun darts in the poison and use it to paralyze their prey," Donovan said.

"The Amazon again. Are you trying to tell me that there's a connection between these guys and Lauriat other than that they beat him up the other night?"

Donovan shook his head. "I'm only pointing out that, for

154

an animal, when you're venomous it pays to advertise. I mean, what good does the poison do for the tree frog if the hawk bites his head off anyway because he's a plain, green frog? So the orange and black warns the hawk to stay away."

"It didn't do squat for the frog when the Indians came around," Mosko said.

"Maybe they're color-blind," Donovan said dully.

"I get it, I get it," Mosko said.

"Anyway, as a result of orange and black being the universal signal of danger, many sports teams have chosen those as their colors."

Mosko said, "I'm impressed with you, you know that?"

"But the King Blades aren't a real gang, no matter what they wear," Donovan said.

"More like a bunch of guys who get together in the park to show off how good they skate. And to pick up girls."

"And assault the occasional bird watcher," Donovan said, leading the way—*stumbling* the way—along the footpath. This path had narrowed to a dirt trail, the concrete giving way to a well-trod dirt track that was mottled with dandelions and roots and wide enough for one. Mosko walked behind, one hand under Donovan's arm as if to steady him. To announce their arrival, Mosko switched on his boom box, which hung from a strap slung over one shoulder, and played WBGO, the Newark jazz station that long had been the captain's favorite. The melodious piano bebop playing at that moment was an American Beauty rose amidst the weeds of hip-hop that clattered from the King Blades' gigantic blaster. Several members of the group twisted their heads disapprovingly in the direction of the newcomers.

The detectives walked past the skaters and crossed a small plot of grass to plop themselves down against the gnarled trunk of a century-old gingko biloba tree. A spray of sea-green, cleft leaves, each the shape of a shovel blade, hung over their heads like an immense Chinese fan. The gingko biloba grow in quantity in Central Park, where older Chinese men and women gather each fall to harvest the olive-shaped nuts, which then are boiled, seasoned, and skewered on pine needles to be part of the first meal of the new year.

"You couldn't sit under a spreading chestnut tree like a normal person, could you?" Mosko asked, eyeing the oddly shaped leaves with deep suspicion.

"This is a gingko biloba," Donovan said, proud of the discovery he had made that afternoon in a Central Park guidebook.

"Those are the pills you take."

"As I recall, yes, they are."

"To help you remember those three years in the sixties that you won't talk about," Mosko said.

"What three years? So, which of these mobile hooligans is Rico Severino?"

"The tall one," Mosko said, pointing his beer bottle in the direction of a six-foot-something man of perhaps twenty-five who was dressed in black spandex from shoulder to mid thigh; parallel orange stripes ran up the left and right sides of his outfit. Severino had several gold piercings—two in the left ear, one in the left nostril—and a yellow bandanna that was tied around his neck. He was one of the skaters who had taken note of the newcomers—no one else dared be in that corner of the park as midnight beckoned—and was watching them suspiciously as they sat against the gingko biloba with their beer and their jazz.

Donovan stared back, lighting a cigarette and puffing a blob of smoke into the night air in front of him. The light from the streetlamps threw the shadows of the gingko leaves onto it.

The King Blades had been engaged in a competition that involved doing figure eights with their feet, crossing them from one side to the other, while snaking along a row of forty-ounce fortified malt liquor bottles—recently, the drink of choice of ghetto youth—that they had placed along the line that separated the cycle and jogger lanes. After a brief interruption caused when Donovan and Moskowitz arrived and sat under the tree, the competition resumed. Much of the point, Donovan surmised, was to impress three Latin-appearing girls in sausage-skin–tight miniskirts and sort-of leotard tops, orange or black, of course, worn over Wonder Bras. The girls sat on a bench across the street from the tree and engaged in what appeared to be an amused speculation about the newcomers.

"They're wondering if we're gay," Donovan said.

"What? You and me?"

"Gay men cruise the Ramble at night . . . even now, after a series of assaults by wandering punks from the outer boroughs. So two men sitting together at night not far from the Ramble could be thought of in that way."

"Especially when one of 'em is young and cute," Mosko said, nudging his boss in the ribs with an elbow.

"What does that make me? Old and . . . no, don't tell me."

"Patrician," Mosko said.

"I'll accept that," Donovan said.

"That is, when you're not dressed up like a bum who's spending the night in the park. Look, while we're sitting here . . ." Mosko looked at the skaters for a moment, then back at the captain, and said, ". . . and being ignored, why don't I give you an update. There's news."

"Okay," Donovan replied, opening a second bottle of Kaliber.

Mosko took out a steno pad, a thin one of the type used by reporters. He used to carry one of those in his pants pockets in the days before Donovan computerized the department.

Mosko flipped through several pages of scribbled notes.

"Where's your laptop?" Donovan asked.

"In the trunk of my car. Tonight it occurred to me that carrying a five thousand dollar laptop might slow me down in case I had to fight."

"What's the news?"

"The news is that we got the forensics report back on the knife," Mosko said.

"And?" Donovan asked.

"It's the murder weapon," Mosko announced.

"I had a feeling. What did they find on it?"

"Traces of type AB blood, which is the same blood group as the victim."

"And relatively rare," Donovan said.

"The blood was caught in the crack between the blade and the handle, which as it turns out is three-point-five millimeters wide."

"About one-eighth of an inch."

"Practically the Grand Canyon," Mosko said. "And repository to all sorts of interesting shit."

"Including?"

"In addition to the blood, there was dirt and traces of moss . . . such as from the ground at the gazebo," Mosko said.

"Where the killer thrust the knife into the ground in an attempt to get rid of the blood," Donovan said.

Mosko continued, "There was also . . ." He stared at a word that he had stretched out, in block letters, from one side of the paper to the other. He said, "Octyl methoxylcinnamate. Proud of me?"

"Very," Donovan said. He looked at the word and, after a second, said, "This is a familiar chemical name but I can't remember where I've seen it before."

Mosko reached up and plucked a leaf off the branch that hung over their heads and handed it to his boss. "Chew on this and maybe it will come back to you," he said.

Donovan shook his head. "I'm a modern American who takes his meds in pill form. I don't know where I saw the name of this chemical before."

Proudly, Mosko said, "Forensics says it's an ingredient of facial moisturizers."

"*That's* where I saw the word," Donovan said.

"You use moisturizers on your face?"

"The labels of Marcy's cosmetics bottles are my john reading when I can't find my copy of *New York Review of Books*," Donovan said. "And I see how the moisturizer got on the knife."

Mosko nodded. "You squeeze it out of the bottle onto your hands. You put a good schmear on your face. You pick up the knife and it gets on there. And, you know what?"

"What?"

"You pick up Winnie the Pooh," Mosko said.

"We got the results back from the tests on the bear?" Donovan asked excitedly. "And we found . . . what is that chemical name? Boxy-cinnamon?"

"Boxy-cinnamon it is. You were expecting an argument from *me*?"

"On the bear? This stuff was on the bear too?"

Mosko bobbed his head up and down, smiling. "Along with a number of strands of bleached blond hair and a smidge of Chanel 'Rouge Noir' lip pencil. That ties Natasha to the murder weapon. And if we need any more, Forensics ID'd the knife as being what you said it was—a Spanish dagger of the type that Tommy Hertig gave to Gabriel Allen Cohen in nineteen forty-eight."

"I'll be damned," Donovan said. "A grand slam. All evidence points to the girl. They must be celebrating in the DA's office."

"I heard that the assistant DAs assigned to the case all went out for a night on the town," Mosko said. "Just like us."

Donovan took a swig of Kaliber, and Mosko joined him in a beery salute to the gods of forensic science.

"They consider that it now is an open-and-smut case," Mosko said after a moment.

"And Natasha has wrecked whatever sympathy factor she may have had by charging admission to see her half-naked on the Web," Donovan said.

"I heard about that. So tell me, boss . . . if this is a lock for the prosecution . . . lock her up and throw away the key . . . the girl is absolutely guilty . . . what are we doing in Central Park at . . ." He consulted his watch. "At midnight?"

"I don't believe in absolutes," Donovan said.

Mosko nodded in mute recognition of the hard-learned fact that things were seldom neat, clean, and absolute when the captain was involved. Donovan simply didn't gravitate toward the open-and-shut cases.

"Well, since you don't believe in absolutes and, in fact, are absolutely turned on by things that come up and complicate matters, chew on this: There were two other things found on the murder weapon."

Donovan whipped his head in the direction of his associate. "What?" he asked.

"A kind of oil," Mosko said. "Forensics isn't familiar with it and is trying to run down the chemical formula. But it's probably something Gabriel Allen Cohen used to lube the knife."

"He doesn't strike me as being the type to maintain his weapons," Donovan said.

"Me either. He probably did with the knife what you used to do with your medals. Stuck it in a shoe box until one day he needed it to give to the girl to use in protecting herself."

"You yourself thought it was an old fishing knife. What was the other thing found on the knife?"

"Some fibers from that jacket," Mosko said.

"Which jacket? The murder victim's?"

"Yeah, the blue-green jacket that you've been obsessing on."

"Who says I've been obsessing?" Donovan asked.

Mosko hooked a thumb toward his chest. "Yours truly," he said.

Donovan said, "I don't *obsess* anymore. When I was planning to give up drinking . . . in the months and years . . ."

"Eons, the way I heard it," Mosko said.

"That I was planning to give up drinking, my greatest fear is that I would obsess on alcohol and not be able to think of anything else. But when I finally *did* it, my mind was clear. I never wanted another drink, and if I thought of anything a lot it was 'what in the world was I afraid of?' "

"You obsessed on it. You're doing it now."

"I am not," Donovan said. "I'm just talking."

"Unh huh."

"You brought the matter up. If I *obsess* on anything, it's only on my family."

"Whatever you say," Mosko said.

"And sometimes on your performance evaluation,"

"Oops," Mosko said.

"As for the *jacket*, let me explain," Donovan said.

Mosko nodded, took out a ballpoint pen, and prepared to take notes.

Donovan said, "The jacket issue may help you understand why we're cooling our butts on the grass in Central Park on this increasingly cold evening," Donovan said, pulling his coat more tightly about him.

"You're not convinced by the evidence against Natasha and her boyfriend," Mosko said.

"Let's leave that aside for a while."

"Okay—tell me about the jacket."

"Francois has this famous blue jacket," Donovan said. "You know how I'm attached to my L. L. Bean tote bag?"

"It's been everywhere with you," Mosko said.

"Francois is similarly attached to his L. L. Bean jacket . . . waist length, zipper front . . . the color is teal."

"Teal," Mosko replied.

"Bluish green. Or greenish blue. Whichever way you wish," Donovan said. "He took it with him to the Amazon. It's rainproof and has a big collar you can turn up. He wore it every time I saw him walking his dog in Riverside Park . . . when the weather was cool, of course."

"And?"

"And the night of the murder, when he went for his walk at one in the morning—we now know it was really to be near his son, if not to actually *talk* to him—Francois borrowed my sweater. The jacket was in the cleaners, he said."

"Was it?" Mosko asked.

"That's one thing you can obsess about tomorrow," Donovan said. "He uses the cleaners at Ninetieth and Broadway."

"You got it."

"I don't see why he would lie to me at that point," Donovan said, "having brought up the matter of clothing in the first place."

"So Lauriat put on your sweater. Which one?"

"The old black one."

"And went down the ladder," Mosko said.

"But, that night, he didn't go near the gazebo, which he did on other occasions, to be near his son or—and this is important—to clean up after him. My presence nearby made Francois self-conscious about it. I had made a remark about the kids before he left. Francois hung out in his Range Rover and listened to the Chopin nocturne. Which, by the way, the station really did play that night between one and two. I checked. There's a complete listing on its Web site."

Mosko said, "All this is fine and dandy, but why is it important what jacket Lauriat was wearing?"

Donovan said, "It's important because Francois, who usually wore a teal jacket, didn't go to the gazebo and wasn't murdered. But Harvey Cozzens, who wore a blue-green jacket that night, did and was."

Mosko's eyes widened. In the midnight light of the street-lamps, he looked like an owl. He thought for a moment, clearly tossing around possibilities, then said, "Lauriat's jacket is teal. Cozzens's is blue-green."

"Can you tell the difference?" Donovan asked.

"Unh . . . I don't know."

"Can you tell the difference in the middle of the night by the blue light from a can of Sterno and do it while you're creeping up on someone from behind?"

"No," Mosko said emphatically.

Donovan said, "In my opinion, there is a good chance that, had Francois gone to the gazebo that night wearing his teal jacket, to clean up the kids' beer bottles, he would have been stabbed to death. According to the coroner, the first blow was struck from the back, before the killer could see his victim."

"You're saying that Lauriat was the intended victim," Mosko said.

"It's a possibility."

"Who would want to kill a guy who spends his life up in trees studying birds?"

"The name is Rudolf Traks," Donovan said.

Mosko reopened his note pad and wrote down the name.

"He's the ex-husband of the woman that Francois had an affair with in the Amazon. This is the affair that broke up

Francois's marriage and started him on the path that brought him to where he is today."

Mosko said, "You told me he had an affair but skipped the details. Can I have them now?"

Donovan filled his associate in, concluding by saying, "Traks is an expert on tarsiers."

"I had a Dodge Tarsier once. Great mileage but lousy suspension. It fell apart on me one morning crossing the Brooklyn Bridge."

Scowling, Donovan said, "A tarsier is a nasty little thing with fur that creeps up on its prey in the middle of the night and eats it head first."

"What a thought. I'll sleep well tonight." Mosko looked around, the rustling of a couple of leaves having become sufficient to set him off on a flight of imagination.

"Are you looking for tarsiers or wolves?" Donovan asked, picking up a rock and tossing it off to one side, into underbrush that grew up to and partly obscured a gaggle of small boulders.

"There are no wolves," Mosko said. "You told me."

"Do you believe everything I say?" Donovan asked.

"Don't bust my hump, boss. I don't like things that creep up on me."

"And I do?"

"I'd rather deal with something I can stare down and stomp," Mosko said.

"I'd rather deal with something that you can stare down and stomp, too," Donovan said.

"Do you know where this Traks guy is now?" Mosko asked.

Donovan said, "I have a lead." He fumbled around in one of his inner coat pockets for a while before coming up with a single sheet of paper that had been folded into quarters. He unfolded the paper and handed it to his sergeant.

"What's this?" Mosko asked.

"A printout of National Science Foundation grants awarded this year for research in the natural sciences in the New York City area."

"Traks is in the city?"

"Could be. If you look down the page, you'll see that the NSF awarded one hundred and forty-three-point-six thousand to an R. Traks for a project entitled 'Habitat destruction and aggression in *Rattus Norvegicus* in an urban park.' "

"Is 'R. Traks' Rudolf Traks?"

"Probably. Scientists generally identify themselves by last name and initials, at least on scientific papers. And Traks, five or six years ago, wrote several papers on habitat destruction and aggression in the tarsier in the Amazon rain forest canopy."

"Sounds like our man. But what's the 'rattus' whatever that he's studying now?" Mosko asked.

"The brown rat," Donovan said.

Mosko's eyes went back to owl-like dimensions. "Wait a minute. Are you telling me that one of our murder suspects is getting paid a hundred and forty-three grand to study *rats*?"

"That's what I'm telling you."

"How can I get a piece of this?"

"Eat your Wheaties and do your homework, kid," Donovan said. "Twenty years of schooling and you, too, can watch rats for a living."

"Come to think of it, I'm a cop. I do that now. So what's this about habitat destruction and aggression?" Mosko asked.

Donovan smiled. "I found and read the proposal. Here's the story. The mayor has a campaign to rid the city of rats."

"What a shocker," Mosko said.

"Yeah, stop the presses. Now that he's dispensed with jaywalking, made the cab drivers take polite lessons, banned pornography and the First Amendment, and, generally, turned the city into Minneapolis, but larger, he's turned his attention to rats. This is designed to make him into a viable candidate for President at some point."

"You better vote for him. He likes you and has saved your ass from Pilcrow a number of times."

"The man knows I think he's a nice guy despite the fact he would have us all walking down the street, single file, nobody talking out of turn, like the well-behaved little kids he remembers from going to Saint Dominic's Catholic School in the fifties."

"Weren't you an altar boy at Saint Dominic's?" Mosko asked.

"Don't start in on religion," Donovan growled. "So anyway, the mayor orders the parks department to get the rats out of the park by plugging up the holes between boulders where they nest. Leave it to the mayor to ban holes between boulders. So the rats feel the pressure of their habitats being destroyed and respond by getting nasty with one another."

"I think we can sell this scoop to *Hard Copy*, boss," Mosko said.

"I'm with you," Donovan replied. "Anyway, the rats are gnawing on one another and this is an excellent opportunity for a scientist to study what happens to a mammalian community when habitat destruction causes an outburst of hostility."

Mosko said, "God, this really *is* the land of opportunity. Even the parks are paved with gold."

"Your job tomorrow will be to find out if Traks is working in Central Park, where exactly, and for how long. Don't let him know we've discovered his presence. Just find out his situation . . . where he's been and all . . . and get back to me. Tomorrow night."

"Same time?" Mosko asked. "Same tree?" He parked his

beer bottle at the base of the gingko biloba and opened another.

"No. Another spot. I'll call and tell you where."

Mosko finished his note-taking and stowed his pad in his shoulder bag. He said, "You think that Traks was using his research job to case this part of the park and figure out Lauriat's movements?"

"Could be," Donovan said.

"Traks is presumably an expert on hunting at night."

"To study nocturnal hunters he would have to know something about the topic," Donovan said.

"And figured out when Lauriat was likely to go to the gazebo to clean up after the kids and what he would be wearing," Mosko said.

"You're a smart guy, you know that? You have to get out of Brooklyn."

Mosko said, with a dismissive wave of the hand, "Man, I'm smart *because* I live in Brooklyn. I got a lovely house, a reasonable mortgage . . ."

"An above-ground pool," Donovan added.

"And I'm half an hour from the city."

"From 'the city.' Boy, you *are* a Brooklynite. Calling Manhattan 'the city.' "

"That's how we say it."

"Brooklyn is part of the city," Donovan said.

"No it ain't," Mosko insisted.

"And you're maybe half an hour from *the city* driving at four in the morning."

"Hey, there's a lot of times that's exactly when I'm driving home," Mosko replied, looking up at the starry sky. "I'll check on the whereabouts of Traks when I get up, first thing in the afternoon."

Donovan said, "Do us all a favor and, before you go to

bed, leave a voice mail message for someone to get going on it."

"That's an absolute thing," Mosko said.

"When *are* you going home tonight?" Donovan asked.

"In about an hour. If I can get home by one or two I'll . . ."

The two men stopped talking when Rico Severino, who had been staring for some time and conferring with others in the group, came over, a pair of sneakers dangling from his waist beside a black fanny pack. Now, inline skaters look like giants when rolling, for the skate adds several inches of height. But when forced to hobble across grass they resemble the clown on stilts at the circus. Severino was a tall if slender man, with ample muscles displayed beneath the yards of spandex. So his approach, uninvited and during the felonious hours of the night, was threatening.

He said, "How you guys doin'?" The voice, slightly Latin accented but mainly hard-edged and annoyed, seemed to reach down from the blackened treetops, the man was that tall atop his blades.

"We're cool," Mosko replied, closing his notepad.

Donovan said nothing, but watched the incipient encounter with the jaded eye of a veteran meteorologist—or a Key West bartender—who had seen too many hurricanes blow ashore and well knew what the early breezes were like.

"We haven't seen you here before," Severino continued.

Mosko said, "Then we got something in common. We haven't seen you here either."

Donovan could hear his friend's voice forming into the hard ball of humor and threat—Groucho Marx with a nuclear weapon—that so unnerved those stupid enough to challenge him.

Undeterred, or stupid, Severino asked, "What are you doing?" He pointed at the notepad.

Mosko looked over at Donovan, who replied, "We're performance artists."

Picking up the thread, Mosko looked back at Severino and said, "We appear off-Broadway."

"What we're doing tonight is working on our act," Donovan added.

"Your act," Severino said.

"You got a problem with that?" Mosko said.

Donovan loved that phrase. Classic Brooklyn street corner:

"What are you doing just sitting there?"

"I'm eating some fuckin' Jujubes. You got a problem with that?"

Severino must not have been a fast learner, and body language might have been ancient Aramaic to him. He folded his arms, threatening, and when he did so, two fellow skaters peeled off from the crowd and came up to join him. They also endured a period of hobbling across the grass before they could join their leader in cross-armed stance. Severino said, "We like to have this area to ourselves. So why don't you two get lost?"

Slowly, silently, Mosko uncoiled his legs and got to his feet, and as he rose the biceps rippled on either side of the fifty-inch chest and his nostrils flared and jaw tightened into that look that frightened animals. Severino stood his ground, but looked a lot less sure of himself. And his henchmen took a step backward each, one of them nearly falling in the attempt to put his blades in reverse. Then Severino also took a step backward.

Mosko said, "I didn't hear what you just said. You want to repeat it?"

There was an awkward silence in which Donovan sensed that Severino was looking for a way out, any way out. The captain wasn't sure, but he thought the man's Adam's apple was quivering. Severino reached into a pocket and, as the two detectives' fingers touched their sidearms, pulled out a well-worn Zippo lighter and began flicking the top open and shut nervously.

One of Severino's pals reached forward, tentatively, as if in fear of burning his fingers, and touched the leader of the King Blades on the upper arm. "Rico . . . maybe we should . . ."

Severino shook off the fingers.

Then Donovan broke into a grin, reached into his Bean bag, and produced a bottle of Beck's. "Come on, fellas, have a beer." And he tossed the bottle to Severino, who was startled and forced to unfold his arms to catch it.

Severino's friends grinned back, all the more so when Donovan tossed bottles to them.

"Live and let live," Donovan said. "We're minding our own business. Have a beer and go about yours."

The moment before, Severino was standing, tensed up, with his arms folded. Now he was holding a beer, his anger abruptly out of synch with the relief around him.

Donovan gave Mosko a bottle, and the sergeant twisted off the cap and took a mighty swig.

Finally, fumbling with the words, Severino said, "I thought you were spying on us."

"Why would we do that?" Mosko asked.

"I don't know. Why are you here? There are better places to sit."

"This is a gingko biloba tree," Donovan said. "Sitting under it helps us remember our lines."

Severino nodded, as if that was the most logical explanation.

If Severino could have scuffed his feet on the ground while wearing skates, he would have. He said, "Hey . . . I'm sorry."

"No harm done," Mosko replied, sticking out a beefy paw to be shaken.

"What's a performance artist?" one of his friends asked.

Donovan said, "It's kind of like poetry that you act out. Have you guys heard on the news about the girl who's been arrested for killing a guy?"

Severino's friend, the one who spoke earlier, smiled and said, "Yeah, yeah. We heard about her, didn't we, Rico?" Having been emboldened by the beer, the man moved closer and nudged Severino with the back of his beer hand. "We heard about her, didn't we?"

Severino said nothing. But the muscles in his brow tightened and this time his Adam's apple definitely quivered. He used the back of his right blade to stab at a small root that stuck out of a sandy patch that separated clumps of grass and dandelions. His friend looked at Donovan and shrugged.

Donovan told Severino, "She's a performance artist. I'll tell you what—you write down your address and I'll send you an invitation to our next performance. At the Shining Path Poets Café in the East Village. You be our guests."

"I can't sit still long enough to watch a show," Severino said. "Look, I'm sorry I gave you a hard time. You guys take it easy."

"Like I said, no harm done," Mosko said.

"See you around," Donovan added as the three young men half walked, half hobbled back to the pavement, there to soar once again and rejoin their group.

When they were out of earshot, Mosko said, "I noticed that he was a little uptight when the subject of Natasha Cohen came up."

Donovan nodded, and said, "But if he had killed Cozzens and his friends knew, they wouldn't be poking him in the ribs like that one guy did."

"Are you sure?" Mosko asked. "Gang members have been known to brag about killings."

Donovan said, "The King Blades aren't the Bloods or the Crips. These are vaguely wacked-out athletic types—inline skater stoned chic—who perform their little figure eights in the park to impress girls."

"I think you're right."

"That notwithstanding, have someone check out the laundry room where Severino lives and all the Laundromats in his neighborhood."

"We're doing that," Mosko said.

"And, tomorrow night, I want a team of detectives down here asking all the members of the King Blades their whereabouts the night of the killing."

"That should shake them up," Mosko said, glancing over at the gang. Unnerved by the encounter with Donovan and Moskowitz, despite the peace offering of beer, the King Blades had shut off the boom box and were beginning to decamp, perhaps moving on to another spot in which to whirl and dance.

Donovan said, "They're moving north, in the direction of Harlem."

"We scared them."

"*You* scared them," Donovan said.

"We're a good team, you and me," Mosko replied. "Maybe we *should* work up an act."

Donovan checked his watch and kept an eye on the group as it headed up Park Drive West. Then the two men chatted for a while longer, about blading and whether they would ever try it, about whether blading competitions constituted performance art, and finally, about the hour.

It had drawn close to one in the morning and the moon was tilting toward the West Side. Ten minutes' worth of explanation occurred about hearth, home, and the drive to Canarsie at a time when the Brooklyn-Queens Expressway was going through an especially bad bout of spring potholes. Donovan walked Mosko halfway to his car, then said good night and turned north himself.

He chose that direction not to follow the bladers, but to reach the edge of the Great Lawn, where a full moon, even one that had slipped a few days past fullness, was sure to attract celebrants. Donovan found several, praying, ruminating . . . he wasn't sure what, perhaps marking the rotation of the cosmos with nothing more than silent awe. They sat, cross-legged, in a semicircle on a dollop of lawn that separated Belvedere Castle from its service road.

A whimsical combination of fantasy and military—the Magic Castle meets the dreariest fortress ever cobbled together from the stones of medieval Spain—Belvedere Castle was built in 1869 on Vista Rock, the highest point of land in Central Park, as a lookout. What it was designed to look out for was never entirely certain. It had been a century or two since the last hostile Indian rampaged through Manhattan Island. Over time, Belvedere Castle became a weather station and, finally, the venue for Central Park nature exhibits. It also was listed on tourist guides and drew a fair number of camera-clicking foreigners. But not at one in the morning, when Donovan trudged by it on the course of his uphill, northward trek.

The worshippers, or whatever they were, occupied ragged grass wedged between the service road and a granite outcropping. They sat, Donovan noted, at precisely the spot where the shadow, cast by the moon, of Belvedere Castle's spire, touched ground. The four men and two women, wearing identical dark gray robes, kept silent and ignored the captain despite his watching them from a distance of no more than twenty feet in the middle of the night. After half a minute, he moved on, skirting the western edge of the Great

Lawn, which was roped off and surrounded by assorted equipment—supply vans, carpentry stuff, piles of lumber, the makings of a grandstand, light towers, lights, show biz sorts of things. A large wooden sign read, EARTH DAY MEGACELEBRATION, COMING SOON. Donovan noted it and moved on.

He had Park Drive West to himself. The King Blades were gone, and he didn't know where. Most likely they turned east and went crosstown at 96th Street. As Donovan approached the northern end of the park, he entered a wild and rocky zone, not landscaped or done so long ago one couldn't tell, but resembling scenery found off the beaten path in Vermont.

It wasn't that the city neglected the northern park. The Lasker Pool and Rink and the Dana Discovery Center, on opposite sides of Harlem Meer in Central Park's northeast corner, were popular places and tended as well as any frequently visited facilities might be. But the edge of the park along Central Park North, from Harlem Meer on the east to the blockhouse on the west, was a bit of frontier dominated by miniature ridges, granite faces, and forgotten trails on which, anywhere but New York City, one wouldn't be startled to see mountain goats. A decade earlier, well before Donovan and Marcy became husband and wife, her friend was murdered nearby. That was the case that caused the falling out between Donovan and his old sergeant, Jefferson, and also the arrival of Brian Moskowitz.

Somewhere in the middle of the ridge, apart from the roads and trails and not easily accessible, a path appeared in the scrub and led up toward the crest of the rocks. As for those rocks, they might not have seemed big by the standards of mountain America, just granite outcroppings thirty or forty feet high, the cracks between which were stuffed with whatever types of trash trees might grow. And, Donovan supposed, thousands of holes in which rats lived and perhaps fought with one another for the benefit of a scientist. But by New York City standards these rocks at the northern end of Central Park were the continental divide on which rock climbers practiced rising three or four stories and scaring off all but serious adventurers, no more so than in the middle of the night.

It had been years since Donovan scrambled up that rock face. Tired and seeing only by the light of the moon, he nonetheless found the path he remembered and, walking awkwardly upward, ten feet and then twenty, thirty and then forty, at last he stood at the height of the tops of the trees that lined the walk that paralleled Central Park North—110th Street.

The top of the rock face at that point was flat, marked only by occasional bursts of wild blueberry bushes. Wind and rain swept the rock often enough to push the cigarette butts, crack vials, and the shattered yellow glass from malt liquor bottles into crevices, leaving bare rock that served as a midnight playground, in years past, for West Side boys with beer cans and courage, and served eternally for Milton of Central Park.

Donovan found the man sitting not on the rock but on a cheap aluminum, nylon-web folding chair carried up from someone's garbage. He was seventy at the very least, and perhaps a decade older than that, a slump-shouldered legend among park regulars although he would speak to just a few, with skin that was wrinkled the way skin gets when its owner spends a lifetime—including the nights—out of doors. He had a white beard that was chest length in parts but elsewhere was cut back to barely an inch in length, and a quarter-sized patch of recently cut stubble occupied, for no apparent reason, a spot low on one cheek. The man wore gray corduroy bell-bottom pants and a white shirt—the kind, made of synthetic material, with straight-across hems and pockets sewn low on them—favored by the older Latino men Donovan still saw playing dominos on card tables along the side streets of the West Side and El Barrio.

Milton's eyes were closed, but flew open when Donovan crunched a crack vial beneath one foot. The wrinkles deepened on his face and the yellow age spots that were splayed across his brow like balloons at a child's party stood out in the moonlight. Before he saw who the visitor was, his fingers tightened around a ten-inch length of lead pipe, capped on both ends, that rested across his lap.

"Easy, old man," Donovan said.

"Oh," the man replied, or maybe the sound was "eh." Then he said, "It's you . . . Willy Boy." And he put down the pipe.

"I brought you beer," Donovan said, setting down the shopping bag and taking from it the three remaining bottles of Beck's.

"My brand?" the man asked, leaning over and squinting at the bottles, which Donovan then set on the rock.

"Of course. What did you think I'd bring you, Old Milwaukee?"

"Why not six?"

"I gave the other three to a group of wandering minstrels I encountered during the trek up this magic mountain. So where are you sleeping these days?"

The man jerked his head several times to the west. "Down there, where the rocks meet the wall. I got a spot where the cops can't find me." He looked back at Donovan and scowled, "Most of 'em, anyway."

"Are you safe there?" the captain asked.

"Which of us is truly safe anywhere? Not me here. Not you in your fancy apartment on Riverside Drive."

"How much is that bit of wisdom going to cost me?" Donovan asked.

"Truisms are free. I only charge for poems."

"I want to buy a poem."

The old man shook his head. "Not tonight. Milton has shut down for the day. Come back tomorrow."

Donovan said, "I want to buy a poem about . . ."

"Bring food," the man said.

"Schaller & Weber roast beef, center cut, medium rare. On French bread. With butter . . . unsalted."

"And more beer. Make sure it's cold. You were saying about a poem?"

"I want one about a man who studies rats," Donovan said.

"A man who kills rats?"

"No. Studies them. Where they live. How they behave."

"Rats behave like rats. It's their destiny."

"That's not the poem I'm paying for," Donovan said.

"Like I told you, truisms are free. This man is a scientist?"

"Among other things. He works at night."

"I can write this poem for you," the old man replied.

"I thought you might," Donovan said.

The old man reached out with a thin hand, the slender fingers of which were delicate, but dirty, with nails that were chewed down nearly to the knuckles. He waggled the fingers at the beer bottles on the rock below. Donovan picked one up and twisted off the cap. The man snatched it and took a sip.

"You haven't come to see me in years," he said then.

"I've been busy."

"Doing what?"

"Marcy and I got married. We have a son."

The old man looked over, and a glimmer of a smile appeared on his face. Then it disappeared, and he said, "Don't fuck it up like you did the other one."

Donovan sighed, stretched up tall, and joined his hands behind him and tugged at his lower back, which was hurting again. He fetched himself two ibuprofen and washed them down with a sip from his third bottle of Kaliber. Then he took the horse chestnut out of a different pocket and rubbed it. Eyeballing this procedure, the old man said, "My back hurts too, when the night turns cold."

"Try this," Donovan said, dropping the nut into his palm. "I'm going home to my family."

9. ONE TIME A SANITATION WORKER REALLY *DID* FIND AN ALLIGATOR

His second night in the park was a colder one. Preceded by a day's worth of threatening clouds, a mass of cold air had swept down from the Great Lakes, driving nighttime temperatures down to April levels. As midnight approached, the mercury was headed for the forties. A cold breeze blew from the northeast, softly rustling the newly minted leaves on the trees that ringed the pool.

In light of the change in the weather, Donovan exchanged the photographer's vest he had worn under his coat the night before for his old, floppy black sweater, the one with the turtleneck that had become stretched out in the course of years of putting on and taking off and which now hung loosely in front. He also abandoned the massed grocery bags as carriers for beer. This time he filled his sturdy L. L. Bean tote bag with beer—now that he needed bribes for both Milton *and* passersby. And he brought other stuff: sandwiches for Milton and himself, and his laptop computer (disguised in a brown paper bag) in case he felt like working.

As things turned out, that's exactly how he felt. So he found himself a spot to sit—on a patch of moss at the foot of an ivy-covered boulder with a view of the waterfall just off

Central Park West up on the northwest edge of the park. He chose a spot where no one could come up behind him. Neither could anyone see the light from the monitor, so long as he kept the instrument angled away from the stone footpath that circled the pond, coming within ten feet of his hiding spot. Assorted berry bushes and an ill-tended blackberry bramble kept all but the nosiest prying eyes from spotting him. Before too long the crickets that had been silent since his arrival resumed making a ruckus.

Donovan pulled the bag off the laptop and switched it on. He turned down the light on the screen, after finding that it reflected too brightly off the rock at his back. Then he settled in for an hour's worth of reading e-mail, answering queries, checking status reports, and, finally, browsing about the Web. In the course of the latter, Donovan read the history of Central Park, read a review of a biography of Calvert Vaux, the designer of Bethesda Fountain and Belvedere Castle, among other park structures, digested an opinion about how the activity of American and European scientists fit into the politics of the Amazon rain forest, and plunked down his credit card number to buy three months' worth of time on Natasha Cohen's Web site.

Donovan was not surprised—and a little relieved—to find that no pornography, nor even severely titillating pictures, lurked at the end of his browsing. Instead he found several poems, including two of her father's oldies as well as a new composition, fully pastoral by Cohen's old standards, something about a turtle climbing out of the water and onto a forked log as being symbolic of struggle and difficult moral choices. As for the girl, her writing was what he expected from a teenage girl, irrespective of her dad's literary skills or her own claim to be a "body poet:" musings on love and freedom that, he judged, were two beats to the hip side of Hallmark cards. Its merit as art notwithstanding, the poetry gave Donovan the thought that Natasha had at least one or two normal teenage attributes. The ordinariness of her sentiments diluted the seminudity found amongst the photos. (A shirt-lifting photo was there, as well as a blurry photo of her naked butt as she walked into the bathroom, and an arty close-up of a nipple, lit from one side by a desk lamp that she had twisted sideways for the purpose.)

There were several other additions to the site. A counter listed Donovan's visit as being the ninety thousand four hundred and thirty-eighth of the past month. People had been surfing into her site, she claimed, at the rate of nearly ten thousand a day "since the bust." In keeping with that phrase, she had begun a Natasha Cohen Legal Defense Fund that included a diatribe, written by her father, against prosecutors in general and what he called "the prudery of millennial America" in particular. An order blank encouraged visitors to further call upon their credit lines to buy copies of his books.

Suddenly, Donovan was aware that the crickets had stopped chirping. He shut off the laptop and returned it to its paper bag and the safety of the tote bag. The air had fallen silent as a graveyard at midnight. Only the constant tinkling of the waterfall remained. Even the traffic sounds—normally an eternal presence in Manhattan at any hour of day or night—seemed to be gone. But the small hairs at the back of Donovan's neck were tingling and his spine straightened, back pain or none. He retrieved his automatic from its shoulder holster and held it in front of him, muzzle pointed up, while pressing his back against the stone.

There was no way anyone could see him from the footpath. Unless, of course, he or she was specifically trying and had some experience with finding men hiding in the woods after dark. And who, what casual stroller, would be looking for a man hiding against the rocks behind a bramble that was en route to nothing, in an obscure part of the park at night?

Maybe it's an animal, he thought. *A dog . . . not a wolf, of course, let's not be ridiculous, but you can't know for sure, one time a sanitation worker really did find an alligator in the New York City Sewer System . . . actually, it was a caiman, and only two feet long, still big enough to take off a hand.*

Then Donovan heard feet, a man's shoes walking slowly, deliberately, roughly, looking for something. Stopping every few paces to ponder. Donovan thought, maybe *he's* thinking of wolves, too.

Donovan held his breath as the man stopped just the other side of the bramble. The man was looking and listening, the captain was sure. Through a softball-sized break in the bushes, Donovan, his eyes accustomed to the dark, could see the polished-black brogans and freshly pressed blue pants of a uniformed police officer. That man stood by for twenty, thirty seconds before starting off again down the path. At first he used the same deliberate, searching pace; but abruptly he began walking faster and soon was gone.

Donovan started breathing again and returned his weapon to its holster. He got his cell phone and punched in seven digits.

"Where are you?" he asked.

"Ninety-sixth and Riverside," Mosko replied. "I just dropped the bagels off with your doorman."

"Hurry up. I want to get on with it."

"What's the matter? Are you okay?"

"Nothing's wrong," Donovan said. "Of course I'm okay. But I had a visitor."

"Who?"

"I'm not sure. Just get over here. You know where I am."

"How will I find you when I get there?" Mosko asked.

"Walk down the path whistling 'Dixie' and I'll yell."

Mosko said, "I'm from Brooklyn. I don't whistle 'Dixie.'"

"Then make it 'The Battle Hymn of the Republic'," Donovan replied.

"You got to be kidding me," Mosko said as his boss hung up the phone.

Ten or fifteen minutes later and still alone, Donovan heard someone whistling "Frere Jacques" and called out, "Over here."

"Over where?" Mosko asked, stopping in the same spot as did the uniformed officer.

Shining his Mag Lite on the route through the brambles, Donovan said, "Here . . . Shelly Berman . . . over here."

"You expect me to go over there?" Mosko replied.

Donovan did, and Mosko complied, and accompanied by a modicum of cussing, he arrived at the site and sat down. He was dressed more warmly than the night before, this time sporting a Kingsborough Community College sweatshirt over new jeans.

"No tree?" he asked.

Donovan shook his head. "Tonight is boulder night." He shut off the flashlight and, before too long, Mosko reported that his eyes were getting used to the night. At that hour in that location, the walkway lamps were infrequently spaced. And the moon was largely hidden behind slowly moving gray clouds.

"So who dropped in on you?" Mosko asked.

"Did you tell the Central Park precinct cops where I would be staking out tonight?"

"Like you said."

"Then they knew I would be here," Donovan replied.

"Who did Pilcrow send to spy on you?"

"I didn't see his face, but my gut and ears tell me it was Patrolman Rodriguez."

"That guy again? So he's off suspension."

"Apparently."

"How do you know it was him?" Mosko asked.

"I recognized his walk," Donovan said.

"His walk? You remember the sound of his *walk*?"

"He clomps around in his brogans. He's a kid and not used to them yet. Besides, sending Rodriguez makes perfect sense from Pilcrow's point of view. The kid has a problem with me *and* he needs to do something to redeem himself following the Winnie the Pooh episode. Getting the goods on me would solve both dilemmas going on in the kid's head."

Mosko gave Donovan a strange, vaguely disbelieving look. But he kept quiet on the matter, wisely. Donovan was his boss as well as the most intuitive man he had ever met.

"He came down the path walking like he was looking for something," Donovan continued. "He stopped every few paces to listen and look around. And when he didn't find me, he sped off. Trust me on this—it was him."

A bit unsure of himself, as he often was when unable to discern what Donovan was thinking, Mosko said, "I don't understand why you don't just grab the little bastard by the throat and tell him to leave you the fuck alone."

"When the time is right, 'the little bastard' and I will have a talk," Donovan said, offering to the evening stillness a faint smile.

The crickets had fallen silent upon Moskowitz's arrival. They started up again. In addition, sirens erupted on both the west and north sides of the park . . . ambulances heading to St. Luke's emergency room along Broadway and 110th Street. Donovan and Moskowitz listened to them grow closer and closer together until the sounds converged outside the E.R., located at 113th and Amsterdam.

After the sirens stopped and Donovan could imagine EMS personnel squabbling, as New Yorkers do in all situations, over who would push their gurney through the double doors first, Mosko said, "So where's the old man you told me about?"

"He's not *here*," Donovan said. "He lives about half a mile to the north, in the rocks along One hundred and tenth Street."

"Maybe that was him in the ambulance," Mosko said.

"You better hope not. He knows everything that happens north of the Great Lawn."

"Who is this guy? The way I heard it, he's some kind of guru."

Donovan shrugged. "He's an old man with a gift for platitudes. When you're a kid and open to all manner of possibilities, when all the world seems wondrous and new, it's easy to be impressed with an older man who says things like 'Rats behave like rats. It's their destiny.' That sort of stuff sounds profound, when you're a kid."

"It sounds like horseshit to me," Mosko said, shaking his head. "I mean, 'a rat must be true to its destiny' or whatever, what the fuck else is a rat gonna *do*?"

Donovan said, "His name is Epstein, but everyone calls him Milton because he writes poetry."

"This Epstein is homeless?"

"No. Central Park is his home."

Mosko said, "Now, to me that sounds like 'a rat must be true to his destiny.' And he's lived here how long?"

"Thirty-five or forty years that I can attest to," Donovan said. "But for a while there was an SRO on Columbus Avenue."

SROs, or single-room-occupancy hotels, were largely a phenomenon that predated the astronomical rent rises and apartment-construction boom of the 1980s and 1990s, during which so many livable spaces in Manhattan were converted to upper-middle-class housing.

"Epstein sells poetry?" Mosko asked.

"Call him Milton. He gave up his real name years ago, claiming to prefer something that illustrated what he did."

"In that case, why didn't he call himself 'Hobo Epstein'?"

Donovan said, "Hobo is what he is, not what he does. Believe me, you don't want to have this conversation with him. He'd only turn it into a poem . . . write it on a three-by-five card . . . and sell it to you for five bucks."

"That's what literature costs these days? Five bucks?"

"Five-ninety-five a month, three months minimum, if you don't like collecting three-by-five cards and want to read your literature on Natasha Cohen's Web site. Which I checked out just before, by the way."

"You paid to see the good parts?" Mosko asked, giving his boss a wink and an elbow to the side.

"There was nothing to print out and tack up on the squad room wall—not that so doing wouldn't earn you a sexual harassment suit these days," Donovan said.

"A shame."

"Mostly, there were appeals for money and pitches for her dad's old books. I found the whole thing kind of sad. I loved that man once. It's hard now to watch him demean himself by using his kid's Web site to make a buck."

Mosko said, "Gabriel Allen Cohen sells it on the Web. Your friend sells it in the park. What's the difference?"

"None, I guess. At least Milton's poems could give us a lead. I asked him to write a poem about a man who studies rats."

"Rudolf Traks?"

"He said he would."

Mosko reached into his shoulder bag for his computer, hesitated, then said, "Can I use this here?"

"As long as you don't attract wolves," Donovan replied.

When Mosko had finished booting up his laptop and finding the file he wanted, he said, reading from the screen,

"Rudolph Traks. Awarded a contract from the National Science Foundation just the way you thought. Got a permit from the city . . ."

"Only one?"

Mosko shook his head, then said, "Ummm . . . four. Filed a notification with the Central Park precinct . . ."

"So the beat cops would know where he is, if they figured out that he even exists," Donovan said.

"Yeah."

"Go on."

"Traks also got permission from the Central Park Conservancy," Mosko reported.

"Which administers the park."

"And had to file paper of various kinds with the People for the Humane Treatment of Animals, the ASPCA, the New York Metropolitan Animal League, the Parks Department, and the West Side Coalition of Environmental Organizations."

Donovan said, "If Traks wasn't a raving maniac before coming to New York, having to do all this paperwork sure would have made him one."

"I'm with you," Mosko said. "During all of this time he listed himself as living at the Stuyvesant Gardens Residential Hotel on Broadway and Ninety-five. Your neighborhood."

"I wonder if he comes into my wife's restaurant," Donovan said.

"If so, I'm sure she can handle him."

"I'm more concerned about Daniel than about her."

"Boss, I know your wife. Any guy comes within ten feet of the kid without being invited will wake up in St. Luke's emergency room. Don't worry about *your* family. Better you should concern yourself with the happy Lauriat clan."

"Why?" Donovan asked. It was *his* turn to develop eyes that resembled an owl's.

"Because Traks listed his institutional affiliation—you know, where he works these days—as being Bronx Community College."

"Where Eleanor Lauriat teaches," Donovan said.

"Traks is adjunct visiting professor of biological sciences as of January. He has a one-year appointment."

"So he may not be staying," Donovan said. "He takes a job for a year and leaves town. In the meantime, he studies rats and kills his old enemy . . . only he fucks it up and kills the wrong man."

Mosko said, "Of course, he could have taken this temp job 'cause it was the only one he could get. When your entire resumé has to do with studying tarsiers in the Amazon rain forest, the headhunters aren't exactly breaking down your door."

"Not the human resources headhunters anyway," Donovan said.

"Traks takes a job . . ."

"At Eleanor's college. Too much of a coincidence. She had to have helped him get it. Saw the posting on a bulletin board and gave him a call. Introduced him to the dean. I wonder if she's sleeping with him."

"Wasn't she dating a lawyer?" Mosko asked.

Donovan nodded.

"I wonder if Lauriat knows about this," Mosko added.

"I doubt it. My sense is he would have told me. He has no problem shooting his mouth off about his enemies. It's only his son he clams up about. Did you check on Lauriat like I asked?"

"Yeah. He's out of the hospital and recuperating in his apartment in your building. I assumed you would know."

"It's a big building, and I don't know what goes on in every corner of it," Donovan said.

"I hear he's on the phone trying to raise the money for

his son's bail. There's a bail hearing in the morning."

Donovan said, "The fact that the DA is even considering the possibility of bail means that the case is weak. Interesting. I wonder if Francois can come up with the money. I suppose he can."

"Want to hear about Traks?" Mosko asked.

"Sure."

Mosko scanned down the page, then tapped a finger at the screen. He said, "I tried to pin down exactly where in the park Traks is pondering rats, but couldn't find it."

"Milton will tell us that," Donovan said.

"Who *is* this guy to you, your old swami?"

"When you're a kid and impressionable, he can seem profound," Donovan said. "He likes to have kids around him— the juvenile James Deans, you know what I mean? The nineteen-fifties teenagers who wore black, smoked cigarettes, drank Chianti out of those bottles with baskets around them, had circles pressed into their wallets from carrying condoms, and listened to black music."

"You and your pals," Mosko said.

"Guilty as charged," Donovan said.

"You fed him."

Donovan nodded. "He only eats Schaller & Weber roast beef. Medium rare. Bought from this one East Side deli where he used to shop back before whatever crashed in on his life did so. Look, he's a good man. Had a nervous breakdown, I guess you'd call it. Sometimes—if you try to get too close to him—he'll push you away by spouting gibberish about circuits shutting down."

"You love these people," Mosko said.

"The world must take care of its artists and eccentrics," Donovan said.

"He sounds like a garden-variety schizophrenic."

"The line between art and madness is a fine one best trod with care," Donovan said.

Mosko fished a five-dollar bill out of his wallet and, holding it by one end, waved it in front of his boss. "Write that on a three-by-five card and I'll buy it," Mosko said. "When do we meet Milton?"

"Soon."

Mosko scrolled further down into his file. He said, "In that case I got some loose ends I want to clean up. Remember that white powder we found in Cozzens's wallet?"

Donovan remembered.

"I thought it was cocaine. Bonaci thought it was angel dust."

"What is it?"

"Certs."

"A breath mint?" Donovan asked.

"A peppermint one. He must have sat on it for a month to get it ground up that fine."

"That's the one thing computer guys do. Sit."

"What kind of guy carries a breath mint in his wallet?"

"An insecure one," Donovan said.

Mosko said, "I guess so. I'll tell you one thing. Bonaci's got to find some way of speeding up the testing procedures. It shouldn't take two or three days to find out that a white powder is Certs."

Donovan said, "I find myself wishing we could have let Pilcrow have the white powder for his press conference. So he could hold up a pinch of it in an official plastic envelope and declare that his 'employees' had uncovered a fiendish drug aspect to the tale of the murdering teenage slut and her punk boyfriend."

"I hear you. Okay . . . let's talk about Cozzens's computer. Or, I should say, computers. With an *s*."

"You got the hard drive," Donovan said.

"You bet. The one at his home *and* the one at his office. I got the report this afternoon."

"Let me guess—the deceased tuned in Natasha Cohen's Web site."

"*Tuned* in! More like *crashed* in. We have records of multiple visits to her site as well as—get this—two hundred and sixteen e-mails sent to her. You can get both her e-mail address and her dad's off the site."

Donovan knew. He said, "I fired off a few myself a little while ago."

"You e-mailed Natasha Cohen and her dad? I thought the lawyer told you to buzz off . . . no more questions."

"He never said I couldn't chat them up about life, liberty, and the pursuit of happiness."

"What's the point?"

"The point is to see how hard it is to get their attention. Her attention in particular."

Mosko brightened, and said, "Maybe to see how hard it is to get her to come and meet you in the park."

Donovan said, "You're a bright kid, you know that? You'll go far."

"This is how Cozzens got to her."

"So they *did* know each other."

"Absolutely . . . at least in cyberspace. The only proof I got that they met in real life is the blood on the knife, but that doesn't seem to impress you."

"I'm impressed," Donovan said. "Just not convinced."

"I can tell you one thing, though. The deceased sure *tried* to meet her. He began by chatting with her about, I don't know, poetry or something." Mosko's face displayed a fleeting mischievous look, and he said, "Kind of like you're doing. But then he began hocking her to meet him in the park. By the fountain."

"Which is not far from Fiddler's Pond and the gazebo," Donovan said. "Did she go?"

"Not so far as I can tell. She kept replying, 'yeah, yeah, not today.' Just like a woman. Want to know how Cozzens described himself?"

"Sure," Donovan said.

"First of all, he said his name was Craig."

"Craig?" Donovan laughed.

"Yeah. Craig Towers."

"A Tom Clancy name. Like Jack Ryan. Good, rock-solid Americana. I love it. You can see him standing six-foot-four, former Yale quarterback, square jaw, perfect hair."

It was Mosko's turn to laugh. "That's him! Thirty-two, single, financially secure, just like they tell you in the singles ads. I guess it's hard to pick up teenage girls when you're a chubby middle-aged nerd with no future."

"Except that spent staring, glassy-eyed, at a monitor. What did *her* e-mails to *him* say?"

Mosko said, "She treated him to some of her poetry."

"Lucky man."

"Mostly she wrote about wanting to be appreciated, wanting to be loved."

"She wasn't in love with Frank, Junior?" Donovan asked.

Mosko said, "The records we got off the kid's hard drive contain *thousands* of e-mails back and forth and lots of talk of love."

"She told him she loved him?"

"Over and over. But a lot of the time, the two of them exchanged nothing more than agreeing when to meet in the park."

"*Really?* So that's how Cozzens was able to find her. He hacked his way into her e-mail."

"Not all computer types are hackers, boss," Mosko said. "For one thing, it ain't all that easy."

"I know that, but . . ."

"While Natasha might have never told Cozzens anything to lead him on, she dropped enough hints as to where she hung out."

"What sorts of hints?" Donovan asked.

Mosko said, "She wrote a couple of poems about Fiddler's Pond. She carried on about the old gazebo as a symbol of decay. She described it in the moonlight. She talked about dancing half naked in the moonlight, under the canopy of the weeping willow. She might as well have drawn a map and e-mailed it to him."

"Do you get the impression she did this deliberately?" Donovan asked.

"I don't think so. My feeling is she was being a kid . . . you know, all enthusiasm and no sense. Was in love with what she was doing and, while shooting her mouth off about it, gave away too much. And she talked too openly about taking off her clothes. You know, taking off her clothes on the Web."

"What kind of things did she say?" Donovan asked.

"Well, she talked about nudity as a freedom issue, but . . ."

"A horny and unhappy middle-aged computer nerd might have been driven wild," Donovan said.

"You got it," Mosko said.

"Let's assume that Cozzens couldn't talk her into meeting him so he stalked her. She has a thing about the full moon . . . mentioned it in a couple of her poems I read on her Web site."

"And a couple she e-mailed to Cozzens," Mosko added. "He got the idea to lurk near the old gazebo on Fiddler's Pond during the full moon and wait for her to show up. She did, but with her boyfriend. Cozzens flew into a rage and attacked them. She stabbed him . . . or the boy did . . . using her knife."

"In that case, why not just *tell* us?" Donovan asked. "She could have made a clear case for self-defense. Probably gotten an award from the people who chase down cyberstalkers."

"Maybe she was afraid of having the world know she hung out in the park with her boyfriend," Mosko said.

"The girl didn't appear to be afraid of publicity," Donovan said.

"In any event, Cozzens stalked her and got killed for his trouble."

"What else did you find at Cozzens's home? Anything I would be interested in?"

"No. Nada. Zilch. Just clothes and junk. But it's all still under lock and key if you want to look for yourself."

"Any porno? Child pornography?" Donovan asked.

"Nope. A lot of computer mags. Now, on his hard drive we have evidence that Natasha wasn't the only cybergirl he chased after. He corresponded with two others . . . one in Christchurch, New Zealand, and another in Seattle."

"But no stalking?"

"Not in person. Kinda hard if you don't have one fuck of a lot of frequent-flier miles."

"And he didn't."

"There's no indication he ever set foot out of New York."

"Okay. Now it would be nice to know what's on *her* hard drive, but they're fighting the subpoena," Donovan said. " 'She needs the hard drive for her business,' the lawyer says. And she'd had plenty of time to destroy all suspicious files. What else do you want to tell me about? You said there were a number of loose ends."

Mosko made a monotonal sort of humming noise. Donovan was reminded of the thrumming of his grandmother's ancient Singer sewing machine, one of the black enamel ones with structural elements that were curved like Coke bottles, while it was on idle. Then he popped the screen with a fingertip and said, "You remember you asked me to measure the distance from the murder scene to where we found the knife?"

Donovan remembered.

"Let me say this about that—we bought a knife in about the same shape and weight as the murder weapon."

"Where'd you get it?"

"A barbecue supply shop in North Carolina. Did you ever have North Carolina barbecue?"

"Nope."

"Very weird. You get a glop of rice, a piece of cornbread, and a glob of shredded pork that you pour your own barbecue sauce on. Some folks like to shred up that pork real good so this one place sells these fat, sharp knives that bear some resemblance to the ancient Spanish one that Cohen brought home from Morocco. It's a bit like a bowie knife, too."

"I'm not into weapons," Donovan said, a bit impatiently. "Save the details for Bonaci, who would collect tanks if his backyard were big enough."

Mosko continued, "We shaved down the haft and added some bulk to the blade. Then we got Bonaci's kids to see how far they could chuck it."

"And?" Donovan asked.

"And Howard's girl—she's fifteen and skinny like the Cohen kid—could throw it at best forty feet. But her brother—seventeen—could toss the knife twice as far."

"This kid isn't a high school baseball pitcher or anything, is he?" Donovan asked.

"Nah. He's a wuss, like the Lauriat brat. And also into computers. It's like a goddam epidemic in that generation.

But holding the knife by the tip and throwing it overhand, he could toss it eighty feet."

"How far was it between the murder scene and where we found the knife?" Donovan asked.

"Seventy-five. And if you're thinking that the murderer dropped the knife while wading across the pond away from the gazebo, forget that too."

"Why?"

"Can't do it. The pond is six feet deep in places."

"Six feet?" Donovan asked. "That little splash of water is *six feet deep*? I don't believe it."

"I swear on my mother's grave," Mosko said.

"Your mom still ain't dead."

"Nonetheless. We measured the depth."

"The killer could have swum," Donovan said.

"And make his clothes bloody *and* soaked through and through?" Mosko asked. "I don't think so. Bloody and damp is enough to have to get rid of, which is something I want to talk about in a minute. The killer didn't wade *or* swim across the pond, 'cause he left no evidence of having come out on the other side. And to walk ashore there you got to beat down a lot of bushes."

"What do you think happened that night?" Donovan asked.

Mosko picked up a twig and, using it as a pointer to jab at the air, said, "The killer . . ."

"And who is that?"

"Frank Lauriat. To protect his girl from a stalker."

"Okay, let's fly with that premise for a while," Donovan said.

"Cozzens shows up at the gazebo and surprises them . . ."

"Just shows up? With Frank Junior there?"

"Maybe the kid went into the bushes to have a squirt. The older guy lunges at the girl . . ."

"I would sooner buy the notion of him showing up and drinking with them or something and then getting out of control," Donovan said.

"There was no alcohol in him. No drugs."

"Okay. So we finally got the autopsy results back. About time. Was there anything else of interest in it?"

"Stomach contents," Mosko said.

"Which were?" Donovan asked.

"Two Big Macs and a large order of fries. And a package of Jujubes."

"Dessert. Anyway, it's low fat."

"And he came in his pants," Mosko said.

"Excuse me?" Donovan asked.

"The guy came in his pants, and not too long before he died, either," Mosko said.

"We're sure of this?"

"Absolutely."

Donovan said, "Cozzens stalks Natasha to the gazebo. Hides in the bushes and watches. Jerks off."

"He made a noise and gave himself away," Mosko said.

"It could have happened that way," Donovan said.

"So the kid grabs the knife and stabs Cozzens," Mosko continued. "Or both Natasha and Frank stab Cozzens. Then they drag him into the water . . ."

"Why?"

"To get rid of the evidence."

"It didn't work," Donovan said. "When the crows found Cozzens in the morning, his corpse was floating."

"The perps are kids," Mosko said. "They panicked. They wanted the body away from a place they were associated with. Maybe they thought it would sink or drift away."

Donovan nodded.

Mosko continued, "The Lauriat kid throws the knife away . . ."

"From where?"

Mosko looked puzzled. He said, "From where? From the murder scene, of course. From the gazebo."

"Why not from where the body was when they pushed it into the water?" Donovan asked.

"Oh . . . you mean it would be a shorter throw."

"Exactly. How far a throw?"

"Thirty or forty feet. So the girl *could* have done it."

"What happens then?"

Mosko said, "They go back to shore. They clean up the beer bottles."

"Which they didn't always do. Remember that Francois used to clean up after them. What then?"

"They went home," Mosko said. "Back to her apartment."

"What about the bloody clothes?" Donovan asked. "The bloody *and* wet clothes?"

"I was building up to that. Remember I was gonna get help from Pilcrow's men to search every trash basket in the park?"

Donovan remembered.

"We searched them. Every can. Every basket."

"And found nothing, right?" Donovan said.

"Not a goddam thing. We also checked all the sewer drains. All the catch basins. The Dumpsters behind Belvedere Castle, Lasker Pool, the Zoo, the Metropolitan Museum, Tavern on the Green, and the other tourist spots."

"No bloody *or* wet clothes."

"Not so much as a hankie with a nosebleed on it. Boss . . . we looked in every hole except the ones between boulders where the rats live . . . don't want to piss them off more than they are already."

"Absolutely not," Donovan said. "I guess the killer took the clothes with him."

"Or carried a shovel to use in burying them, but that seems unlikely and we haven't spent much time on it. However . . ."

Mosko's voice had that about-to-unwrap-the-birthday-present tone, and Donovan looked at him. "However?" he asked.

"I wasn't satisfied on the trash can front, so I checked Fire Department records. It seems that at about three in the morning the night of the killing . . ."

"Right after we think it took place," Donovan said.

"There was a fire in a trash can located along Park Drive West near the Ninety-third Street entrance," Mosko said.

"Where I entered the park last night," Donovan said.

"Yeah. Four fire trucks responded. Must have made enough racket to wake up Mia Farrow . . ."

"With all those kids I don't think she sleeps very well anyway," Donovan said.

"And Carly Simon and Alec Baldwin and Kim Basinger and the rest of the hippie celebs who live on Central Park West."

"What about the fire?"

"Someone doused the contents of a trash can with lighter fluid and touched it off," Mosko said.

"Interesting," Donovan said.

"Now, no record was kept of the contents of the can. I mean, the Fire Department wrote it down as a kid prank or something a drunk might do. Homeless guys used to torch garbage cans to stay warm in the dead of winter, but it's not that cold . . ."

"And being homeless is a crime these days."

"A garbage truck hauled off the contents, which by now, sad to say, reside in the Fresh Kills Landfill on Staten Island along with fourteen million seagulls. Nobody thought to save the burned contents 'cause nobody thought they might be valuable until this afternoon when it occurred to me."

Donovan patted Moskowitz on the arm. "Don't blame yourself. I didn't think of checking Fire Department records *at all*."

Mosko said, "Funny the incident never made Police Department records. You'd think that there's four fire trucks responding to the park and a cop or two would take note. The cops that night were Ebby and Rodriguez. But then, cops don't write up every incident they happen to see."

"If the perp burned the clothes . . ."

Mosko interrupted, saying, "That fire *had* to be the perp burning the clothes. It's too much of a coincidence otherwise. The problem I got with the scenario is, what'd he wear home?"

Donovan said, "You've noticed that the Ninety-third Street entrance to the Park is en route between Fiddler's Pond and the Cohen apartment?"

Mosko said he had noticed.

"It could have happened this way: The girl stabs Cozzens while the boy is taking a leak or whatever," Donovan said. "They pull the body into the water. The girl takes off the bloody clothes and puts on the boy's sweatshirt. She walks home in that."

"In just a sweatshirt?" Mosko asked.

"You told me that one of the things that makes America great is that girls strut down the block in their panty hose. Haven't you seen girls wearing just a sweatshirt that comes down nearly to their knees?"

"And nothing else?"

"This prudish side of you is fascinating," Donovan said. "Okay . . . sneakers, too."

"That sneaker print we found at the murder site? It was a man's size nine."

"Any particular brand?"

"Yeah, the one sold at Sole Warehouse, the discount chain, for twelve bucks."

Donovan said, "It would be my luck there's no hundred-and-sixty-buck pair of designer sneakers in this case. Well, if we can ever get past Natasha Cohen's lawyer we'll subpoena her closet and get to the bottom of this wardrobe problem. Damn Pilcrow; he was so eager to bring her in he didn't go armed with a search warrant for the contents of her room."

"I can't get past the fact she might not have worn any . . . I mean . . ." Mosko waggled his fingertips at his midsection and said, "No undies?"

"If they got bloodstained too, no undies," Donovan said. "But that probably didn't happen. What *could* have happened is that the sweatshirt hung down to her knees—Frank Junior is a lanky brat—and she walked home looking like every other . . ."

"Murdering teenage slut," Mosko snarled.

"You're an American original, my friend," Donovan said. "I was going to say, 'like every other adolescent moppet.' We don't know that Natasha killed Cozzens. We don't know that Natasha and Frank killed Cozzens."

"Come *on*."

"In fact, we don't know much at all. Mankind doesn't know much of anything, 'cept for what we can extrapolate from the inexorable cycling of the cosmos."

Mosko gave the captain a funny look, then said, "You been readin' them poems again, haven't ya?"

"When is Earth Day Megacelebration?" Donovan asked.

"When is who what?"

"A special edition of Earth Day," Donovan said. "There's going to be a massive celebration on the Great Lawn. I noticed the preparations for it last night. And the radio this morning said that a million people are expected there and in Sheep Meadow."

"Who's appearing? Michael Jackson?"

"No."

"Paul Simon again? Barbra Streisand?"

"I don't think so. But I assure you that the mayor and the cardinal will address the crowd."

"I would think that they'd know enough to stay away from you by now," Mosko said.

"I'm not going to be anywhere near. The Pope will address the crowd also, I hear, via satellite. So will the Archbishop of Canterbury and the Orthodox Primate of St. Petersburg."

"Oh . . . it's a Jesus thing," Mosko said.

"Kind of. But there will also be the President by satellite, a lot of new age mumbo jumbo, a fair amount of tree hugging, and several dozen rock bands."

"Michael Jackson *will* be there."

"Not if I'm nearby and carrying a gun," Donovan said. "The bands will be the usual suspects who sing at Farm Aid, Fisherman Aid, Rain Forest Aid, and Rock Stars with Alzheimer's Aid. I think the event is this weekend."

"Sunday," Mosko said. "I heard some talk about some big thing on Sunday."

"Let's try to be home with wives and children by then," Donovan said.

"If you're predicting that we'll wrap up the case by then, hooray! I'm on your side."

Donovan wasn't. "I'm suggesting that there are too many loose ends. Some of which you were going to tell me about. Any more?"

Reluctantly, maybe growing tired as the night pressed on, Mosko scrolled down the screen until he found the entry he wanted. Then he reported, "You asked me to check on the blue-green jacket . . . sorry, the *teal* jacket . . . that Lauriat said he sent to the cleaners at Ninetieth and Broadway."

Donovan nodded. "Did you?"

"Yeah, he brought it in three days before the killing, pretty much like he said. It had a stain on it."

"What flavor?"

"Oil. The cleaner couldn't get it all out. So we took the jacket for evidence and are having the stain analyzed. To see if it's the same weird oil we found on the knife."

"Good man," Donovan said.

"That's my report for tonight," Mosko concluded. "That's all there is, except for the fact we're still canvassing laundromats and have yet to find anything."

"Keep trying."

"But I'm pretty sure the perp burned the bloody clothes," Mosko said.

"So am I. Keep canvassing anyway. It's something that Pilcrow would think of and if we don't do it, he'll show up and demand I tell him why not."

Donovan yawned and pressed the back of his head against the ivy that coated the stone behind him. The leaves crinkled softly, a gentle sound that was very much like the muted clicking of Mosko's fingers on the keyboard. Donovan closed his eyes and listened as his friend finished what he was doing and closed the file, an action that made a contrasting series of chirps.

"You changed the beep," Donovan said.

"This afternoon."

"What *is* that sound? It's familiar."

"*Star Trek* communicator," Mosko said.

"I don't watch much TV anymore."

"Not even The Learning Channel? Your favorite?"

"It's not as good as it used to be. And I get bored with

abbreviated knowledge. I'm trying to find the time to read more books."

"Want to play some poker before I shut the computer off?" Mosko asked.

"I want to go see Milton," Donovan replied.

10. "I Come in Peace for All Mankind," Donovan Said

....

The temperature dropped and a wind came out of the broad avenues and narrow cross streets of Harlem and blew across the tops of the antediluvian boulders that formed the backbone of the north park. Despite the breeze the leaves were still, as if the early morning air was too thin and pale in its youth to bother them. The climb up the rocks seemed steeper this time . . . if only because two men making the trek expended exponentially more energy than one.

Arriving at the summit, with both of them huffing a little from the effort, Donovan and Moskowitz found the white-haired old man seated in his folding chair, angled directly at the waning moon. Within a second after Mosko's foot crunched a sun-blanched twig, the poet reached for his lead pipe.

"I come in peace for all mankind," Donovan said, and the man let go of the weapon. It fell onto the rock face with a deep metallic ring.

"Willie Boy. Who's that with you?"

"My friend, Brian."

Still the old man didn't turn around. "Is he one of the good ones?" he asked.

"He's one of the best," Donovan replied.

"If he is a good man and true friend, let him step forward. If not . . ."

"I'm not paying for that," Donovan snapped. "Send it to Hallmark."

The poet sighed, and said, "Some nights you can't even give it away."

"I've had those," Mosko said.

"I brought food and drink," Donovan said. "Would you like to eat now, or talk?"

"Both."

Trailed by Mosko, Donovan walked up to Milton and laid a bag of offerings at his feet. As Donovan stooped to pluck from it a bottle of beer and remove the top, the old man scrutinized the captain's companion.

"You're a big one, aren't you? Where did you get those muscles?"

"Ralph Avenue," Mosko replied.

"Your gym?"

"Nah, nothing like that. I was driving one day on my way to Roll 'n' Roaster and I saw them laying in the road."

Milton accepted the bottle and, drinking from it, told Donovan, "I like this friend of yours."

"I'm getting real fond of him myself," Donovan replied, unwrapping the sandwich and balancing it on the man's bony knees, which he drew together to form a platform.

"Your taste in friends remains excellent," Milton continued. "They all are interesting. Your woman . . . the one whose father is a judge . . . do people still mistake her for that actress? What's her name? Something religious . . . Hare Krishna? Hallelujah?"

"Halle Berry," Donovan said. "From time to time. Mostly they see her as a mommy these days. So . . . you were going to write a poem for me."

"And so I did." With that, the old man reached underneath his coat and into a shirt pocket and pulled out a patch of brown paper, roughly four by six inches, torn from a grocery bag, crumbled and refolded. Near a corner was a bar code and a mark made in purple crayon. On the paper the man had written, using a laundry marker, these words:

The rat man
sleeps
eyes quivering
peaceful
teeth gleaming in starlight
alone

Donovan read the words out loud while gesturing, with one hand, and at an angle where Milton couldn't see it, to Mosko to keep his opinions of the poem to himself. To the old man, Donovan said, "I like it."

"It's not bad, if I say so myself," the man offered. "It gets to the point . . . is part haiku and part couplet . . . it is what it is."

"Ten dollars," Donovan said.

"Twenty."

Donovan gestured for Mosko to get out his wallet. "Pay the man," he said.

Mosko did as he was told, fishing a twenty out of a wallet that was thick with small bills and family photos. Milton took the twenty, kissed it, and put it in the same pocket from which had come the poem.

"Thank you," he said.

"The thanks are on me," Donovan said. "Now . . . the details about the sonofabitch, please."

Taking a swig of beer, the old man said, "He's a nasty fucker. Works mainly over by that culvert . . . storm drain . . .

call it what you will . . . at the northwest corner of the reservoir."

"Not that far from Fiddler's Pond," Mosko said.

"He's got a small camp set up in the rocks. I thought he was like me at first, a man who prefers to live within nature, but no! This one has a *permit* on his sleeping bag, and a *permit* on his camera tripod, which he uses to photograph his rodents, and a *permit* for his gun."

"Gun?" Donovan asked.

"He told me about it—his way of warning me off, the man being a nasty little varmint himself. A wise man once said . . ."

Donovan raised a finger—to admonish against clichés as well as to warn that he wouldn't pay for them—but Milton said, "This one is free. A wise man said that a man . . . sorry, a *person* . . . I almost forgot you consider yourself a feminist."

"I consider myself amenable to fair positions."

". . . that a person is what he works at. I *am* a man of nature. Mike Tyson *is* a man of violence. You *are* . . ."

"Impatient," Donovan said.

"That, too. Well, the rat man is a rodent, a nasty one with teeth. Stay away from him. Or shoot him on sight."

"What kind of gun does he have?" Mosko asked.

"I didn't see it. Only heard about it."

Mosko looked concerned, and when he caught Donovan's attention cast a disparaging glance down and to the left into his leather shoulder bag. "I don't know why that gun permit didn't come up in the computer searches we did," he said.

"It might not have been keyed in yet," Donovan offered.

"I'll see tomorrow."

Milton said, "Rudy—that's what name the rat man goes by—told me he needed the gun for self-protection here just like he did when he worked in the jungle."

"He told you he worked in the jungle?" Mosko said. "As opposed to the rain forest?"

" 'The jungle' is what we called 'the rain forest' before it got a PR man," Donovan said.

"He did say it was the Amazon jungle," Milton added.

"That's our man," Donovan said.

"I don't like him. I think he's dangerous."

"So am I."

"More so when you were a young man," Milton replied.

"Don't give me a hard time. I've handled worse guys than him every day of my life. Besides, if things get too rough, I'll have Brian rip his head off."

Mosko nodded faithfully.

"You always were sure of yourself," the old man said.

"The culvert on the northwest corner of the reservoir, you said?"

"Rudy works at night and sleeps by day. Sometimes in the sleeping bag that I told you about. Sometimes he goes out of the park entirely."

"To the residence hotel he lives at on Broadway," Mosko said.

"He has a fence next to the culvert—like the one the bird man has around his tree, except more expensive—and sleeps in there between the bushes and the rocks where it's nearly impossible to see him from the path." The old man sucked in his breath and some beer and continued. "That's not a bad spot he's found, by the way. When he leaves I may take it myself . . . if the mayor would hurry up and get rid of the damn rats, of course."

The two detectives lingered with Milton for another half an hour, exchanging opinions on what the poet called "living within nature"—being homeless—and the vicissitudes of New York City life that had grown to make that way of life difficult over the years. But soon the hour got seriously late and the moon ducked behind a large and dreary cloud, and the old man showed signs of tiring. Donovan and Moskowitz got up—they had taken up acolytic positions on the rock near his feet—and offered a few parting pleasantries. Then Mosko folded another twenty into the man's hand and said, "The captain here tells me it's my duty to help support the arts."

"Willie is wise," Milton said.

"Tomorrow I'm going down to the south end of the park to lay some bucks on the other guy."

"What other guy do you mean?" Milton asked.

"The other poet who lives in Central Park. You *know* there are two."

"Oh, him."

"The guy who will only accept food gifts from Zabar's," Mosko said.

"He used to be a West Sider before he got the call," Milton explained.

"The call?" Mosko asked.

"To live within nature, of course."

"The call of the wild," Mosko said.

"The call of the streets," Milton replied, with finality.

"Anyway, I'll give the other poet money, too."

"There are *three* of us now," Milton said; his voice was flat this time, as if in deliberate understatement of the importance of his words.

"Donovan's eyebrows arched like boomerangs. "Three?" he asked.

The old man nodded slowly, his expression changing again, to a slight smile.

"Sure. You don't know that the *eminence grise* has joined us? Part-time; at least."

"The who who?" Mosko asked. "The what grease?"

"*Eminence grise,*" Donovan explained. "It means 'gray eminence' in French."

"Oh, pardonez moi! You must have forgotten that I don't *parlez vous*."

Scowling, Donovan said, "Milton is referring to a distinguished older gentleman."

"Like you in ten years if you keep your nose clean."

"Twenty," Donovan snapped. "Milton is telling us, considering that the number of *eminence grise* poets living in New York City these days is limited, that Gabriel Allen Cohen has been seen living in Central Park."

Mosko's jaw actually dropped. Donovan had never seen that actually happen in a human being except for when they were faking it for effect. Such as in the movies.

Without a word, Mosko reached into his pocket and got another twenty dollar bill and stuffed it in Milton's shirt. The old man reached two thinning fingertips into the pocket and caressed the sixty dollars he had just earned. Enough to live on for a month, living within nature, that is, even doing so within the City of New York.

Donovan fingered the point of his chin and said, "Let me guess . . . lamppost T one three five seven B."

Milton's eyes widened and he looked up at the man, once a boy, he had known for decades. "That's the broken one?"

"With a four-inch or so chunk of metal broken off the base at the edge of the hatch that electricians use to get at the wires," Donovan said.

Silent for a moment—his jaw had returned to its normal position—Mosko looked at his boss and said, "You're havin' one of those moments, aren't you?"

"What moments?"

"The ones that piss Pilcrow off so much because he will never have one. Okay, I'll play straight man for you again— what in hell are you talking about?"

"I told you I've been reading the poems they posted on

the Web . . . his and hers, father and daughter," Donovan said.

"I read some of them," Mosko said. "And her e-mails. So did the deceased. That's how he must have figured out where the gazebo is."

Donovan said, "That's how I decoded the meaning of 'T one three five seven B.' It's mentioned in one of Gabriel Allen Cohen's poems, but obliquely, and it's hard to figure out just what it means. It refers to a lamppost. The city keeps track of them by numbers, and there are guidebooks written for bird watchers, tree lovers, and other nature fiends, that use the numbers so people can find something. Such as the spreading chestnut where the yellow-breasted hairsplitter nests, for example."

"You keep insulting Pilcrow and I'm gonna have to turn you in," Mosko said.

"The designation 'T one three five seven B' refers to a lamppost, on the edge of the Ramble, which made it into the horticulture guidebook. You know . . . horticulture?"

Mosko slipped into his Groucho Marx voice again . . . the wrong Marx brother, but it was in the middle of the night. He said, "Sure I do, you can lead a whore to culture but you can't make her think."

Donovan smiled. "As I was saying, that lamppost earned a place in the guidebook by virtue of standing next to an especially fine example of a Sumatran willow."

"Leave it to you to know what one looks like," Mosko said.

"Cohen's poem also mentions that kind of tree. And he writes of a special place of solitude, and a casual reader will think it's in Sumatra but of course it isn't, it's in Central Park on the edge of the Ramble. The impression I get is of another quiet hiding spot, like the old gazebo, where young lovers . . ."

"Or old eminences . . ."

"Can quietly and without interruption exercise their particular passions," Donovan said.

"Such as write poems, make love, or kill someone," Mosko said.

"I suspect that Cohen has been hanging out there at the same time his daughter and her boyfriend were lighting Sterno cans, practicing Ishimani rituals, and . . ."

"Carving up uninvited guests."

"By the bank of Fiddler's Pond. Which is right nearby, by the way. Fathers look after their children."

"Cohen *was* there," Milton reported.

Both detectives turned their attention back to him. Donovan asked, "Two nights ago, the night there was a murder in Fiddler's Pond, you saw Cohen at the Ramble?"

"I did indeed."

"Where we just talked about?"

"Exactly. He stopped by the bench there for a minute, then went into the woods by the pond."

"You were there?" Mosko said.

Milton nodded. "Most of the night."

"Why there?"

"Why not? For one thing, I like the shadows the moon casts on the cobblestones. When you live within nature, such pleasures are among your most enjoyable."

"When did Cohen arrive and when did he leave?" Mosko asked.

"His eminence arrived around midnight and left around three," Milton said.

"You're sure?"

"Beyond sure."

"You looked at your watch?" Mosko asked.

The old man bristled. "Watch? A watch is a convenience

for the wrist that exacts a toll from the soul. I tell time by the moon."

"By the moon?"

"Exactly."

"How do you know when it's lunch?" Mosko asked.

"I sleep during the day," Milton said.

"You can't tell time by the moon," Mosko replied.

"Sure he can," Donovan said.

"And this is accurate?"

"I've seen him do it. From the position of the moon along the plane of the ecliptic he can tell the time within ten or fifteen minutes."

"What's the plane of the eclectic? Oh, fuck it. I don't want to know. Get this over with—tell me what time it is."

Milton considered the heavens for five seconds, perhaps seven seconds, before saying, "It's quarter to three."

Mosko glanced at his watch, holding it up to the moonlight to read the dial.

"Well?" Donovan asked.

"I'm going home," Mosko said. "Back to Canarsie where things make sense."

"First we visit the rat man," Donovan said.

"I'm getting this picture of myself on the witness stand, and there's my fellow Brooklynite Alan Dershowitz, looking at me and saying, 'Tell me again, Detective Moskowitz, just how you knew exactly what time it was,' and there I am explaining about how the moon travels down the plane of the eclectic and it's better than a fucking Rolex. I'm going home."

"First we find Traks."

The nest that Rudolph Traks had built for himself at the northeast corner of the Central Park Reservoir looked new, bounded by that mint-green, plastic-coated, chain-link that the security-minded use when they want their fencing to appear environmentally aware. The reservoir itself was girded by more traditional fence, as well as a jogging track around which New Yorkers both ordinary and famous—Madonna and her bodyguard, for example, or Geraldo Rivera—were known to sweat. In most spots the fence that ran around the reservoir was the old-fashioned kind of chain-link that rusted. Its purpose seemed mainly to prevent joggers from becoming swimmers or suicides, and to that end clung to the shoreline, allowing entrance mainly to the Canadian geese that stopped over en route to their day jobs—despoiling suburban golf courses. The jogging part was, for the most part, very close to the water. But here and there the track bent away from the water and skirted other things: rock outcroppings, random bursts of trees, and, at the designated spot, a storm overflow pipe that cut under the path and emerged on the other side as a culvert that disappeared into another pipe that cut below yet another rock outcropping and sloped underground, probably, Donovan thought, to merge with the New York City sewer system.

The green fencing surrounded a puff of trees—young maples, the regular kind, not silver maples—that grew in the cleft where the second storm drain disappeared under the rocks. Donovan could see why Milton thought the spot a good one to sleep in (apart from the rats, of course). It was isolated by reason of its ordinariness. On the way to nowhere and not attractive itself, the maple grove was dark and apart enough to provide a safe sleep while occupying an open area that the occasional roving band of muggers and rapists would be unlikely to notice.

The green fence was a sore thumb, hardly a convincing environmental gesture. Marked every few yards with signs reading RODENT CONTROL AREA, it also encouraged passersby to pass along. Approaching it, Mosko said, "What does 'rodent control' mean? Doesn't it mean, like, they're killing rats?"

"More like the city is boring them to death with red tape. Remember all those permits Traks got? They went into establishing the rodent control area," Donovan said.

He led the way up to a smallish chain link door that was closed with a stainless steel chain, the links of which were forged from quarter-inch steel. It shone in the moonlight and stood against the mint green of the fence and the black of the night within the maple grove. The chain was locked on the inside by a huge, double-steel padlock.

Donovan fingered the chain. So doing made a prominent clink. He said, "Never lock yourself inside a cage. It's bad psychology. Displays poor self esteem as well as bad planning. Makes you look afraid of something. Not only that, rats don't respect fences."

"At least we know he's in there," Mosko said.

Donovan nodded. "Call him out."

Mosko kicked at the bottom of the door, making a clatter that echoed off rocks near and far. If any rats were nearby and in a jittery mood, the racket surely sent them scurrying into their cubbies—aggressive neighbors notwithstanding. He yelled, "Rudolf Traks! Police officers! Come outta there!" When there was no response, Mosko called the man's name a second time.

Donovan pulled his Mag Lite out of a pocket and shone it into the darkness, which filled an area, behind the fence, wide enough and deep enough to comfortably fit a Poconos vacation cottage. He could see nothing.

"Rudolf Traks!" Mosko yelled again, augmenting the command by kicking the bottom of the door a second time.

That got results. Out of the darkness came a figure, dark clad, slight, eyes wide and apparently luminescent in the beam of Donovan's Mag Lite. Traks moved slowly, his smallish feet eerily making no sound. Donovan noted that he wore all black: wool pants, sweater, parka, and pea cap. His buzz-cut hair was black but showed glimmerings of gray.

Traks stopped a few paces back from the fence and his left hand twitched toward a pants pocket. Within a second, both detectives had their weapons in their hands. To Donovan, the automatic seemed boxy and awkward and the electronic wrist band was a fancy watch, as Milton would say if he knew of it, far beyond an insult to the soul.

Mosko snarled, "That hand better not come out of your pocket with anything harder than your dick in it."

Traks's hand snapped back up where it was before.

"Are you Rudolf Traks?" Donovan asked, putting away the gun and gesturing for Moskowitz to imitate him.

"Yes . . . who . . . what *is this*? I've done nothing wrong." The man's voice was angry but controlled, and fearful, very fearful, suspicious and unnerved. He said again, "I haven't done anything."

"That's what we're here to establish, Mr. Traks. I'm Captain Donovan of the New York Police Department. This is my colleague, Sergeant Moskowitz."

"*You're* a police officer?" Traks said, looking with undisguised loathing at Donovan's hobo getup.

"Yeah, well, they've relaxed the entrance requirements in recent years," Donovan said.

"Captain Donovan is Chief of Special Investigations," Mosko said. That was to no avail, for Traks continued to gape at Donovan as if he were a plague carrier.

Traks said, "You've interrupted a valuable experiment. I could have lost data."

"No, you didn't," Donovan said. "We're a random occurrence, Traks. You can filter us out when you do the statistics. How are you conducting this study, videotaping them?"

"Yes . . . basically."

"And review the tapes later on to spot aggressive patterns?"

"Yes. So you know something about my work?"

"I don't know a damned thing about your work. But how else would you do it?"

"There are ways, but you're right. Tape is the best for the conditions. And I'm sorry for getting upset a minute ago. You didn't disrupt my study in any serious way."

Donovan said, "I take it you don't really need to be here all night."

Mosko looked at his boss.

"Correct," Traks replied. "I stay here generally but not absolutely. To change tapes when I need to. To prevent my subjects from chewing the power cables. To guard the equipment from being stolen."

"Ergo the King Kong chain and the big padlock," Mosko said.

"And the firearm," Donovan said.

"The . . . what? Oh, my gun. How do you know about that?"

"Don't you have a license?" Donovan said.

"Yes . . . of course I do."

"We'd like to see both the gun and the license," Donovan said.

Traks replied, saying, "It's in my camp."

"What's in your pocket?" Mosko asked.

"A flashlight," Traks replied, taking it out . . . slowly, as he might have seen it done in the movies . . . and showing it to them. It was identical to Donovan's.

"Where were you two nights ago?" Donovan asked.

"Two nights ago?"

"April seventeen," Mosko said.

Traks had eased off most of his initial suspicion and some

of his fear while they were talking about science. But his mood suddenly switched. Donovan was reminded of pictures he had seen on the Discovery Channel of a chameleon changing from light to dark green while stepping onto a new leaf.

"That was the night that man was murdered," Traks said.

"Where were you?" Donovan asked.

"Do you suspect me? Are you accusing me of *murder*?"

Donovan shook his head. "If we were accusing you we'd be hauling you off. Where were you?"

"Lauriat put you up to this."

"*I* put me up to this and we found you. Where were you two nights ago?"

"I was here," Traks replied.

"All night?" Mosko asked.

"Yes."

"From when to when?" Donovan asked.

"I arrived an hour before dusk. I worked until about five in the morning. At that time I went to sleep."

"Here?" Mosko asked.

Traks nodded. "In my sleeping bag," he said.

"You go to sleep on the ground a few feet away from a rat's nest?" Mosko asked.

"They know me. And I spray myself."

"With what?" Donovan asked.

"Rat poison," Traks said.

"You *spray yourself* with rat poison?" Donovan asked.

"I suppose it's wrong to call it 'poison.' It's a kind of repellent. It works beautifully."

"You could make a fortune selling this in the inner city," Donovan said.

"The product is not that well known," Traks said. "A small company in Belgium manufactures it, but their market is exclusively garbagemen and other municipal workers in the old cities of Europe. But a few rodent researchers know about it. It really works on rats."

"I wonder if it works on reporters," Donovan said.

Traks offered the most fleeting of smiles. "Try a can," he said.

"I think I will. I've been spending nights in the park . . ."

"I was wondering," Traks said, taking another long and appalled look at the captain's ratty attire and stubble of a beard.

". . . and you can never be too careful. Where can I get a can?"

"I have a spare. You can pay me what I paid for it. But I don't spray it on myself, exactly. I spray the sleeping bag and an area around it. The spray is oil-based and sticks like crazy. It smells bad, too."

"I'd like to see your operation," Donovan said. "I'm sorry if that disturbs your subjects. I promise we won't stay long."

Donovan expected a fight. Instead, Traks gave a resigned sort of shrug and said, "As you said, I can fix the statistics later. You must have a scientific background."

"Nope," Donovan said. "Just a familiarity with crime statistics. You can cook them, too."

"The mayor does, every election year," Mosko added. "That's how he got the rep for being this big crime fighter."

Traks pulled back the sleeve of his right arm to better get at an elastic band that held a key. Donovan recalled the round elastic that secured gym locker keys to wrists back at St. Dominic's Roman Catholic High School. Traks had something very like them, and used his left hand to stretch out the smallish stainless steel key that opened the padlock. There was the rattle of chain and Traks pulled the door open to admit the detectives. Then the chain went back on the door and was relocked. "You can't be too careful," Traks said.

"There's a killer on the loose," Donovan added.

The key snapped back against the small man's wrist.

He got his flashlight back out of his pocket and used it to guide the two detectives along a newly cut path that snaked through the middle of the grove to arrive at a clearing, ten by fifteen or so, that itself was ten feet from a collection of boulders that was mossy-faced, laced with cracks, and peppered with holes.

"Good thing the mayor doesn't know about this," Mosko said.

Donovan said he agreed. He surveyed the camp and found a site he might have made himself. A sleeping bag, an old-fashioned one, colored forest green to fool Indians, elves, and grizzly bears, was laid out carefully and neatly just off center. To its left was a canasta table, also old, perhaps a hand-me-down, on which sat a battery-operated Watchman. A stack of tapes was nearby, as was a smaller pile of manila folders and a spiral notebook. On the far end of the clearing was a heavy duty photographer's tripod atop which sat a professional Ikegami video camera. The business end of the camera sported an attachment that Donovan took to be related to night vision.

"That's an expensive camera," Donovan said. "What are you using? Infrared?"

"Yes and yes," Traks replied, walking to the vicinity of the table and switching on a battery-operated fluorescent lamp that hung from a tree limb. The camp was bathed in the slightly bluish, entirely antiseptic-looking light. Donovan heard a scampering sound, leaves rustling and claws on rocks.

"Bye, bye, rats," Mosko said.

Traks shrugged. "They'll be back. This is their home."

Donovan looked at the rock face and the ground at the base of it. The rodents were nowhere to be seen or, after a very short time, heard. "Fast on their feet, aren't they," he said.

Traks nodded. "They're feeling a lot of pressure on their habitat. When you pack creatures into tiny spots where they're on top of one another, among the results is violence. Tonight wasn't too bad. They all just fled. They didn't take it out on one another. They're more afraid of you two than they are of each other."

"It's him they're afraid of," Donovan said, patting Mosko on a bulging bicep. "He has that effect."

"I can imagine," Traks replied, adding a nervous smile, his second of the encounter.

"The lesson here is that overcrowding breeds aggression."

"As social planners learned after they built all those low-income housing projects that now have to be torn down and replaced with something livable," Donovan said, "You can't stack poor people who drink."

Traks said, "I see you *do* understand basic science. I should pay you to write my grant proposals. Yes, my work does have ramifications for people."

"I'd like to make copies of your tapes. May I?" Donovan asked. "Those for the past week."

The scientist thought for a second, then said, "Sure. Why not?"

"Can you bring them to my forensics office tomorrow to be copied. My guys have a high-speed dubbing deck."

Traks agreed. He said, "Afternoon would be best. That will let me get a little sleep."

"You'll be sleeping here?"

"Right here," Traks replied, pointing at his sleeping bag.

"Sleeping comfortably, knowing you're protected by a stout fence, rat repellent, and a weapon," Donovan said.

"Can we see the gun?" Mosko said. "And the license?"

Traks agreed, and showed the detectives a small, cedar-wood case that was laid out on the ground near the head of the sleeping bag, where it imitated a miniature and misplaced foot locker. "It's in there," he said, pointing with a toe.

"Get it, please," Mosko said.

Traks went to and stooped alongside the case, and touched it with his fingers. There was a brass catch held in place not with a padlock, but with a twig, a fast-release mechanism of the sort Donovan would devise were he to live in the wild. "I'll take it out slowly," Traks said.

Donovan smiled and watched as the man produced, gingerly enough to be showing them a Faberge egg, a small Ruger revolver, narrow in barrel and somewhat dainty overall. He handed it to Mosko, grip first, appropriately, and followed it with a laminated piece of official paper.

"This is a Ruger Bearcat, Captain," Mosko said. "Shoots twenty-two caliber long-rifle slugs. It's a plinker."

"What that's mean?" Traks said.

"A 'plinker' is the weapon of choice when Mr. Rabbit's been eating your rutabagas and you want to send him to that big garden plot in the sky," Mosko said.

"Or if you might need to shoot a rabid rat," Donovan said.

"Which is exactly why I got the gun," Traks said.

Mosko returned the gun and gave the license a once-over. Then he said, "It's legit."

"I told you," Traks said, before returning the gun and license to the case and reinserting the twig in the catch.

"We're sorry for bothering you about the gun," Donovan said. "I can see that you're not planning to hold up any banks using that thing. Now, let's get down to the main thing I want to talk about. A while ago I mentioned a murder and asked you about it and you said, 'Lauriat put you up to this.' Why did you say that?"

Traks changed appearance, again chameleonlike, from a scientist who was enjoying talking about his work back into a small and suspicious man. Unsure of himself, he said, "I . . .

assumed . . . that Lauriat was the one who gave you my name."

"I didn't mention Lauriat. You were already thinking of him. Why?"

"Why . . . his son is accused of murder. He's looking to put the blame elsewhere."

"Why would he think of *you*?" Mosko asked.

"I don't understand."

"Me, someone accuses my son of killing someone, I think of blaming . . . I don't know, a mugger. A robber. A thief."

"A roving band of inline skaters," Donovan added.

"Or a homeless man who camps out nearby and stays up all night," Mosko said. "Not a guy I used to know in the Amazon jungle."

"Why'd he come up with your name?" Donovan asked.

"Lauriat knows I don't like him," Traks said.

"Guys don't like other guys all the time without a corpse being involved," Donovan said. "I don't like my boss and he doesn't like me but we seem doomed to spend a lifetime together. What happened between the two of you that you would assume he named you as a murder suspect?"

"He didn't tell you?" Traks said.

"Maybe he did and maybe he didn't. He didn't tell us about what?"

Traks stammered, the words coming out of him in staccato chunks. "He . . . stole . . . my . . . wife!" As he spoke, the man's face turned red, not a pleasant sight in the fluorescent light.

Donovan was struck by the response, which seemed old-fashioned enough to have occurred in a black-and-white movie in which all the men wore hats and all the women were coquettes.

"Tell me about it," Donovan said.

Traks looked around, then stepped backward and sat on

the gray metal folding chair that was shoved up against the canasta table. Donovan could see Mosko thinking, *he has to sit to talk about it?*

"We were all working in the Amazon, he on his project and me on mine. We didn't even know each other well, mainly through the Internet café in the nearest settlement."

"Which was?"

Traks said, "A general store and, I guess, you would call it an inn or cantina, that had a PC hooked up to the Internet. They charged people the equivalent of two dollars to spend an hour on the Internet and send e-mails to all their relatives in the States."

"I've heard of that kind of joint," Donovan said. "It's the cheapest way for many people in South and Central America to keep in touch. Much cheaper than regular mail, and more reliable too. So that's where you met Lauriat?"

"It was where *we* met him," Traks said. "Laura and I were there one Tuesday afternoon, buying provisions and sending e-mails . . ."

"To whom?" Donovan interrupted.

"To my grantor. My university. I was working for the University of California at San Diego then. To my wife's sister and her husband in Salt Lake."

"Okay . . . sorry for interrupting."

"No matter," Traks said. "Laura and I were in the cafe when they came in—Eleanor and Francois—and we didn't even know they were nearby. I mean, the natives said something about a bird man, but for some reason I thought that, whoever he was, he was Brazilian, not American. We aren't the only ones sending scientists into the rain forest. Brazil has quite an impressive program itself."

"Why were the Lauriats there in the cafe?" Donovan asked.

"To do the same thing we were—buy food and send e-mail. To the same kinds of places, as I remember. Eleanor had to communicate with her department chair . . . something about her sabbatical. She was on a two-year leave so she could accompany her husband to the Amazon."

"Not too shabby a life," Mosko said.

Traks replied, "Well, she also was supposed to finish her book."

"Which was on what?" Donovan asked.

The scientist smiled faintly, a pencil-fine grin, as "hard" scientists sometimes do when getting a whiff of a fuzzy project sprouting in the humanities. He said, "It had something to do with, in her phrase, 'elucidating the Marxist subtext of the predator-prey dynamic in the Third World rain forest.' "

"What's the 'predator-prey dynamic'?" Mosko asked.

"The big fish eat the little fish," Donovan said.

"And the little fish see it coming and reproduce like crazy to compensate," Traks added.

Mosko shook his head and smiled, but not a pencil smile, a big and full one. "People get paid for this," he said.

"Studying aggression in rats is starting to look better to you, isn't it?" Donovan said.

"You bet."

The captain returned his attention to Traks. "What happened to her book?" Donovan asked.

"She never finished it."

"Why? She couldn't figure out what was Marxist about big fish eating little fish?"

"No, I think she understood that well enough," Traks said. "Eleanor didn't finish the book because she fled the rain forest after her husband began sleeping with my wife."

"Let's talk about that a little, do you mind?" Donovan asked.

Traks said that he didn't. Donovan didn't believe him but

pressed the topic anyway, gesturing with his hand in a way that told the scientist to continue.

"The four of us began to exchange visits," Traks explained. "After all, we were the only Americans in the province. Practically the only ones who spoke English. So it was natural we would get together, despite the obvious competition between our programs."

Mosko asked what he meant.

Donovan answered, saying, "His subjects ate Lauriat's subjects."

"Essentially true," Traks replied. "The four of us played cards . . . canasta." He tapped a nervous finger on the table beside him. "And we shared dinners and conversation. Not that there was all that much for Lauriat and me to talk about. You see, we really didn't like each other."

"Even before he stole your wife?" Mosko asked.

Traks nodded. "From the first moment."

"Hate at first sight," Donovan said.

Again the scientist bobbed his head up and down. "I guess you would call me a lone wolf. I don't like people very much, and I admit it. I'm happiest working, and happier alone and working. I suppose that's why I chose the field I did."

"Sitting alone in a clearing in the woods all night watching animals run around is your idea of a hot time," Donovan said.

"Exactly. And you think it's funny, don't you?"

"Not at all. I know lots of people who are good at one thing and interested in it alone. It doesn't make them weird . . . only dedicated. If you were a workaholic Wall Street type whose idea of a hot time was to sit up all night waiting for the morning report from Tokyo on . . . I don't know, widget futures . . . the *Wall Street Journal* would put you on page one."

"I see you understand," Traks said.

"I know a guy whose sole interest is the competition among mammals at Aqueduct," Mosko said.

"What's Aqueduct?" Traks asked.

"A race track," Donovan replied.

"My work is all that ever mattered to me," Traks said.

"I get the impression that your wife mattered to you," Donovan said. "You got so upset about talking about Lauriat having stolen her that you had to sit down to talk about it."

Traks nodded, and Donovan thought he was embarrassed at the admission. The scientist said, "Let me rephrase my reply to your statement: My work is the only thing that *has* mattered to me since that man stole Laura from me."

"You were furious at first."

"Livid. I was beside myself."

"You could have killed him," Mosko said.

Traks shook his head. "No. I was an angry man, but I was never a killer. I am not physically strong." To illustrate, he flexed a muscle, but because of his clothing Donovan could get no idea of the man's strength or lack of it. "I have endurance—you have to in order to work in the rain forest—but strength, no, not really."

"You don't need much if you have a sharp knife and an opportunity," Donovan said.

"And the anger to stab someone thirty or forty times," Mosko added.

"Is that how often that poor man they found in the pond was stabbed? No one deserves that. Do I hate Francois? Well, I *did*. And I suppose I still do. But want to kill him, no, of course not. And anyway, who said anything about killing Francois? How did you arrive at that?"

"The victim was dressed like Lauriat," Mosko said. "In a blue . . . I mean, *teal*-colored jacket."

Traks laughed, and out loud, too, the anger vanishing as quickly as it arrived. "Ah, the famous Bean jacket."

"You know it?" Donovan asked.

"I remember when he got it . . . ordered it over the Internet, and had it delivered to the café. It was ridiculous, really, a jacket designed for Maine winters in the Amazon rain forest. But, you see, it was part of the Laura thing."

"Explain."

"Laura thought that she looked like one of the women in the L. L. Bean catalog. One of the models."

"Did she?" Donovan asked.

"In a way," Traks said. "And she loved Bean clothes . . . had a supply of their khaki walking shorts as well as a cable-knit sweater in exactly that teal. I suppose that Francois bought the jacket to impress her. That's what I thought, anyway. He always was much more image-conscious than me." Traks snorted, saying, "Canopy researchers. Heads in the clouds. Big shots. Who else would fail to be satisfied with stealing a man's wife, but would have to *humiliate* him by taking her a hundred feet up a tree to have sex."

"As if the sex itself wasn't enough," Donovan said.

"Precisely," Traks replied. "Francois had to flaunt it. Had to make fun of me. Having sex with my wife on top of a tree while I was working."

"How'd he get away with it?" Mosko asked.

"Eleanor had gone to Amazonia for a few days to shop. I was working nights. My subjects *are* nocturnal, after all. Francois's subjects were active mainly during the day. So while I was working he was with my wife. Hey, Captain . . . I thought of something."

"What?"

"If you want to discuss strength, talk about a man who will climb to the top of a tree and still have the strength . . ."

"Not to mention presence of mind . . ."

"To have sex."

"I'd be afraid of falling," Mosko said. "Even if there was

227

a solid floor beneath me. I mean, I never even liked the top bunk in a bunk bed."

"Were they in love, Lauriat and your wife?" Donovan asked. "What did they say?"

"Love was never a part of it," Traks replied. "I'm sure of that. It was pure sex, and some adventure, of course. Laura was bored with the jungle after a while. And I was forced to stay to finish my project, not only because I was committed to do it but also because I needed the money. I was never a wealthy man, like Francois."

"Lauriat has money?" Mosko asked.

"Family money," Donovan said. "He's not filthy rich or anything."

"Maybe a little dusty rich," Mosko said.

"Like that. And he probably has less money, now that he's divorced and Eleanor has half of it. Mr. Traks, are you sleeping with Eleanor Lauriat?"

Traks tensed up and what color was left in his face went away. After a few seconds, he said, "No. Ridiculous."

"How did you end up at Bronx Community College?" Donovan asked.

"She took pity on me," Traks replied. "She knew that I came back from the Amazon broke and beaten. I lost my grant because I could no longer focus on my work after Laura cheated on me and left me. Once you have failed on a grant, not because the science was bad or you had no luck, but because you couldn't complete the work due to personal problems, it is hard to get another. Eleanor saw a research opening posted on a bulletin board and called me. But sleeping with her? No, of course not."

"I had to ask," Donovan said.

"Besides, I think she has a relationship," Traks continued. "I am not sure who with."

"So that's how you came to be in Central Park studying rats," Donovan said.

"That's it," Traks replied.

"Have you run into Lauriat?" Mosko asked.

"Yes," Traks replied.

Donovan was surprised, and said so. "I didn't expect that," he admitted.

"Oh, sure. We ran into each other one day. Early in the afternoon."

"When was this?" Donovan asked.

"In early March," Traks replied.

"Where?"

"Oh, in the . . . I think you call it the Ramble. He was on his way to his research area. I was stretching my legs after having slept to noon on the ground. I was stiff and needed to walk it out."

"Did you know he was working in the park, too?"

"Of course. Eleanor wouldn't have left out a fact like that. She warned me I might run into him. She warned *him* he might run into me. The two of us apparently spent a good deal of time worrying what might happen if we ever *did* run into each other."

"And what happened when you did?" Mosko asked.

"Nothing. It was highly anticlimactic. We spoke briefly of our research, never brought up our ex-wives, and that was it. The whole thing was over in two minutes. We shook hands and walked off."

"Very gentlemanly, eh?" Mosko said.

"That is how scientists are," Traks replied.

"And you never saw him again?" Donovan asked.

Traks shook his head. "Not since then. I was relieved that the hatred was over. After meeting him, I felt that the entire matter had been concluded. I had closure."

"That's nice," Donovan said.

"I don't suppose that you believe me."

"Why not? The two of you settled the matter sensibly and without violence or even the threat of it."

Traks said, "I know it sounds like an unbelievable coincidence, the two of us winding up working a mile apart in Central Park."

"Not to a New Yorker it doesn't," Donovan said. "Sooner or later, everyone and everything comes to New York City. All the time I run into someone I haven't seen in years."

"Then . . . am I in the clear?"

Donovan smiled. He liked a man who got right to the point. He replied, asking, "When was the last time you killed anything?"

"I shot an anaconda in the Amazon. Nothing since."

"Not man or beast?"

"Neither," Traks replied.

"And you stayed here all night. Didn't go out from dusk to dawn?"

"As I told you."

"Didn't see or hear anything?" Donovan asked.

"I heard fire sirens around three, maybe a little after. But other than that, nothing."

"Then you're in the clear," Donovan replied, edging toward the trail leading away from the camp.

Traks rose to escort his guests back to and through the gate.

"Thank you for your cooperation, Mr. Traks," Mosko said, encasing the man's hand in his own and shaking it. "I hope we haven't disrupted your work too badly."

"Don't worry about it," the scientist replied.

"I'll send someone around to pick you and the tapes up tomorrow afternoon. Around two okay?"

"That will be fine," Traks replied.

11. THE FAMOUS CAPTAIN DONOVAN, PASSED OUT IN THE PARK

When they walked far enough away from Traks's little corner of Central Park to be out of earshot, Mosko said, "What do you think?"

"I believed him," Donovan said.

"But as you've told me before, a guy can be believable *and* guilty as hell."

"True, but this one sounded honest. He hated Lauriat, and for good reason. Then he got over it, as a grown man will."

Mosko asked, "Does it bother you that Milton thought he was an evil man with a dangerous streak and you and I found him okay?"

"Milton is usually a pretty good judge of character," Donovan said. "On the other hand, he did tell us he wants Traks's spot to sleep in."

"Milton has a stake in our hating him," Mosko said.

"That's right," Donovan replied.

"What do you want Traks's tapes for?"

"I mainly wanted to get him out of his fenced-in enclosure so Bonaci can get a cast of his footprints. Did you check out those sneakers he was wearing?"

"Small. He has a foot like a kid."

"A man's size nine, I bet," Donovan said.

"We'll find out."

"And I *am* really interested in seeing his tapes."

"What could be interesting about videos of a bunch of rats running around?"

"Get the tapes and I'll show you," Donovan replied.

"And what are you planning to do with *this*?" Mosko asked, tossing the sixteen-ounce can of rat repellent up into the air and catching it.

"Have it analyzed," Donovan replied.

"Looking for what?"

"A peculiar brand of oil that so far has eluded elucidation by our esteemed forensics team," Donovan said. "Remember the oil found on the murder weapon?"

"You think . . . ?"

"The oil on the knife could have come from the rat repellent? Yeah, that's what I'm thinking. Traks said it sticks like crazy."

"Crazy enough to last through a plunge through a body, a thrust into the ground, and a night under water?" Mosko asked.

"Let's see," Donovan replied.

The two detectives walked to Central Park West and found Mosko's car at just that time of night when the city that never sleeps dozed momentarily. It was after the bars had closed and the drunks had gone home but before the garbage trucks starting making their daily racket. Looking south down Central Park West, Donovan saw but a lonely yellow cab lazing along, not even trying to make the lights, down around 72nd Street, looking in vain for a fare.

Mosko opened the door to his car and got behind the wheel. "Drop you off?" he asked.

"No, thanks. I'm going back into the park."

"You're spending the rest of the night?"

"Yeah. I want to check something out."

"Well, be careful," Mosko said, starting the engine.

"I'm always careful these days," Donovan said, and waited until his friend was a few blocks away and headed for the next transverse before turning back into Central Park.

Donovan trudged along, at last feeling the burden of

sleeplessness, feeling it more with each step, until he reached the periphery of Fiddler's Pond. He avoided the area of the gazebo and the yellow crime-scene tape that surrounded it still, a brightly colored Flintstones Band-Aid that sought to bind an ugly wound.

Turning to his left, Donovan followed a cobblestone path that curved gently east and then southeast before twisting back northward, leaving behind a loop, on the edge of the Ramble, that left the captain pondering a dense and unlit wild of boulders and waist-high brush that adjoined a strip of skunk cabbage and meadow grass directly across the water from the old gazebo. Donovan found an indentation in the scrub just beyond lamppost T1357B . . . less than a path, more like a deer trail, and that's what he would have suspected it of being were he anywhere but in Central Park. He pushed his way down it, the brush scraping his legs, at the knee level, on both sides, until reaching the Sumatran willow, planted years before and forgotten by all but the occasional wandering naturalist or peripatetic *eminence grise*. Its canopy protected a clear patch large enough for one person to lay down in comfortably or for two or three to sit in for a moment of secluded, if uncomfortable, conversation.

Donovan lowered his bag to the ground at the foot of the tree and sat beside it. He was close enough to the cobblestone path to hear footsteps should they occur, but far enough away to go unseen. The scrub made for a good cover and even the moon conspired in Donovan's privacy; it was close enough to the western horizon to cast long shadows that were easy to hide in.

He closed his eyes, opened them, then closed them again and tried to drift off while sitting, like a New Jersey Transit commuter on the 7:11 from Spring Valley, and feeling more secure than lying down. Sleep eluded him and when he opened his eyes, better adjusted to the darkness, he could see the water of Fiddler's Pond between the broad leaves of the skunk cabbage, which drooped in the moonlight like elephants' ears.

Still hoping to sleep, Donovan lay down on his right side, curling into a fetal position and loosening his coat to make it more comfortable. He rested his head on his gloves, which he had put together and folded over to approximate a pillow. He closed his eyes again, and after a moment became more acutely aware of the sounds of the park at night—a cricket making a racket a few yards away, something scraping around in the leaves off to the east, one of Traks's rats, maybe, and finally a splashing in the pond; a water rat was not out of the question, maybe even the mutant beaver that Bonaci thought he spotted. No wolves, Donovan was pretty sure. Still, he took the Cyrcad out of the shoulder holster and held it in his right hand, his finger off the trigger but close by, the gun under the coat, the muzzle pointing up, just in case he was wrong about the wolf thing. Donovan thought of Marcy's advice: Shoot the alpha male and the rest of the pack will lose heart. Thus nestled into his hiding place, Captain Bill Donovan of the NYPD fell asleep.

An hour later, about five in the morning and still dark, with no hint of pending daybreak, Donovan woke up to the sound of feet. A man was walking down the footpath, walking deliberately, his feet still unaccustomed to the heavy brogans that clumped distinctly along the cobblestones.

Donovan kept his eyes shut; he could hear perfectly. The intruder walked to the end of the path, looking around, searching for something as before. Then he stopped. Donovan opened his eyes to see a flashlight, a standard police issue one, scanning the scrub. He shut his eyes again and listened as the intruder came right to him, pushing aside the bushes, shining the flashlight as if it were a searchlight scanning the wall around a prison in search of an escapee.

When the light landed on Donovan's face, he could see the glow through his eyelids. Then came the voice, familiar and scornful.

"So this is the famous Captain Donovan, passed out in the park next to a bag of beer."

"Hello, Lewis," Donovan said, without opening his eyes.

"Is this what you've come to . . . sleeping in the park with your beer?"

"It's Kaliber. Nonalcoholic. I haven't had a real drink in ten years. Superbowl of nineteen eighty-nine was the last. Check it out."

If the young officer was taken aback, he didn't show it. He said, "What happened, did Marcy throw you out?"

Donovan opened his eyes. "Only one woman has done that," he said. "How *is* your mom these days?"

"Mom is fine. So let's say that you're not drunk. What are you doing?"

"Working," Donovan replied.

"Working?" Rodriguez laughed. It was a bitter laugh, bitter and nervous.

"Investigating a murder. I notified your precinct, per regulations. That's how you knew to look for me. And you found, me, too, on only your second try of the night."

"Where were you before?"

"Uptown by the waterfall. I heard you walk by. Then I met my partner and went to see an informant. After that we spoke to a suspect. Now, are you ready to ditch the anger, come down off your high horse, and stop being so hard on your old man?"

"You're lying there unprotected," Rodriguez shot back. "I could have killed you."

"You think so? Reach down and pull back my coat."

"What?" the young man asked, startled.

"Do it."

Rodriguez stooped and, the flashlight in one hand, peeled open Donovan's coat with the other to find himself staring at the muzzle of the Cyrcad.

The young man's dark complexion went white in waning moonlight and he rocked back onto his heels as his father put the weapon away.

"You walked up to an unknown man in the dark protected by nothing but a flashlight. Who could have killed whom?" Donovan asked.

Wordlessly, but breathing fast and shallow, Rodriguez sat back against the tree and dropped the flashlight on the turf beside him. The beam disappeared off into the bushes. Donovan got up and sat beside him. Their shoulders touched.

After a long time, Rodriguez said, "I can't compete with you. You always win."

"Very few guys your age can compete with their dads in their own profession, unless we're talking about sports or something," Donovan said. "And detective work isn't an athletic event—it's a game of mind. Don't worry. You'll get it. You've already got the drive."

"God, I hated you for so many years."

"But you couldn't stay away. You kept *turning up*, usually with a sneer on your lips but, at least, there you were and I was always glad to see you."

"I hated you for leaving Mom."

"Like I said . . ."

"And I hated you for being drunk all the time."

"*We* were drunk, and not all the time, we *did* function."

"Yeah, well, she says it was just you."

"It was bad, but it was mutual. She denied it then, she's denying it now. Look, Rosie was the one who wanted me to quit the force and come work with her in the bar. And I wouldn't do it. That was the start of the end, not so much the drinking. And anyway, what do you remember of us

236

drinking? You weren't even born when we broke up. In fact, I didn't know she was pregnant and it took me two years to figure out I had a son. All she told me—other than to stay away, that is—was that she was going to live with her grandmother in Union City."

"I know, but . . ."

"So everything you've learned about me comes from her. And from your pal Pilcrow, who by now you've learned you can't trust, I presume."

"Tell me about it," Rodriguez said.

"Did he tell you to spy on me?" Donovan asked.

"He made it clear that I could get back in his good graces if I got the goods on you. You know about the Pooh thing, right?"

"Yeah, I saw that happen."

"Jeez, I feel like such an idiot. I don't know what's the matter with me."

"We've all had those moments. Your mom can fill you in on some of mine."

"She has," Rodriguez said, this time with a laugh.

Donovan smiled, and said, "Is she really okay or are you just saying that?"

"She's really okay."

"And things are still good between her and her husband?"

"Yeah. The miscarriage shook them up, but she's okay."

"Is she going to try again?" Donovan asked.

"I don't think so."

"Where are you living these days?"

"Still on a hundred and ninth."

"Do you still have my old record collection?"

"Of course."

"I thought you would have given them away," Donovan said.

"They were *yours*," Rodriguez replied.

Donovan was pleased with that answer, and after a moment of feeling pleased, asked, "Can you handle a piece of advice?"

"Do I have a choice?"

"No."

"What is it?" Rodriguez asked.

"Don't let Pilcrow know you're multiracial," Donovan said. "The man is a racist and will turn your life into a living hell."

"He thinks I'm Puertoriqueño."

"That's typical. Thinks everyone with a Hispanic last name is Puerto Rican."

Rodriguez said, "Frankly, I live in greater fear of him finding out I'm your son."

"That would do it," Donovan agreed.

"Why does he hate you so much?"

"For some of the same reasons you do," Donovan said. "I'm a pain in the ass. A loose cannon."

"Still?"

"Well, not so much anymore. But Pilcrow has a long memory."

"I don't hate you anymore," Rodriguez said.

Donovan touched his son on the arm, briefly.

"He also hates me because of Marcy."

"Being multiracial."

"Being multiracial when part of it is Jewish. That's an old problem in some parts of the black community. At least Tom Jefferson, my old sergeant, only hated her because she was light-skinned, and he wasn't all that serious about it. It was more of a game. But Pilcrow means it. And, I guess, he hates her 'cause her folks are rich and famous. And 'cause she looks like Halle Berry and he looks like Clarence Thomas."

Rodriguez smiled. "The deputy chief also hates you because of your smart mouth," he said.

"Oh, *that*," Donovan replied.

"I think you're funny . . . sometimes."

"How did you hook up with Pilcrow anyway?" Donovan asked. "I mean, the deputy chief and a rookie cop?"

"He asked my precinct commander what cops were on duty the night Cozzens was murdered," Rodriguez said. "It really ate away at him that you found the body. As if you weren't already good, here was a body *delivered* to you. He was looking for someone who might know something that would make you look bad."

"And did you know anything that fit the bill?" Donovan asked.

Rodriguez shrugged. "All I knew is that Natasha frequented the spot where the murder took place."

"How well did you know *Natasha*?"

"Not as well as I would have liked to. She's gorgeous, you know."

"Do you really think she killed that man?" Donovan asked. "Or that she and Frank Lauriat did it?"

"I arrested her, didn't I?" Rodriguez said.

"Guys arrest people for all sorts of reasons. Because they're black. Because they're Jewish. Because they're gorgeous and ignoring you."

Lewis gave his father a sharp look, then looked away and smiled slightly.

"My mouth again?" Donovan said.

"Your mouth again. I know what you're thinking . . . did he arrest her to get even with her for having a boyfriend?"

"Did you?"

"No. I did it because I thought she was guilty. I still do. And what do you think?"

"What does the great Captain Donovan think?" Donovan asked.

This time it was Lewis who touched his father on the arm. "I didn't say that . . . you did."

"Well, the Great One doesn't know. I have a few ideas, but nothing resembling a conclusion. So help me out here. What *did* you see that night?"

"I saw Natasha and Frank go into the woods on their way to the gazebo," Lewis said.

"What time was this?" Donovan asked.

"About midnight. A little after. Twelve-ten or fifteen."

"Was anyone with them?"

"No."

"Was anyone else around?"

"Nope."

"What did you do after you saw them go into the woods?"

"Headed north, where I heard noise. The inline skating guys were up there causing a disturbance."

"The King Blades," Donovan said.

"Yeah. You know about them?" Lewis's face hardened up at the mention of this group.

"I met them last night. Their chief bandito was getting out of line . . ."

"That happens a lot with Severino," Lewis said.

"So I hear. Mosko had to threaten him. He settled down."

"Who is Mosko? Oh, Sergeant Moskowitz, Mister Personality."

"That's the man. So what were the King Blades doing the night of April seventeen?"

"The usual," Lewis said. "Harassing passersby. Acting like they own the park. Looking for someone to rip off."

"I heard that you were trying to nail Severino for those purse snatchings," Donovan said.

"I'm sure he's the one . . . they're the ones. He has two guys who are his henchmen, also skaters."

"I met them."

"What happens is they create a disturbance . . . such as by running into a woman carrying a pocketbook. Or they stage a fight during which they bump into her."

"And Severino skates off with her purse," Donovan said.

"Yeah, that's it," Lewis said. "It's penny-ante stuff, but it keeps him in beer and marijuana."

"All cops start with penny-ante arrests," Donovan said. "My first was a guy stealing car radios."

"Really?"

"And that was before stealing car radios became a city-wide problem. Right out of the starting blocks, I was ahead of my time."

"I thought I had him a few days ago," Lewis said.

"How so?"

"A woman got her purse snatched behind the Metropolitan Museum," the young officer explained. "She was a wealthy lady and had about eight hundred bucks in cash in it plus credit cards. She said that a bunch of skaters stole it in the middle of a disturbance."

"Severino's M.O.," Donovan said.

"Yeah, but she couldn't positively I.D. him or any of his friends. *But* I found the purse . . . minus the money and credit cards, of course."

"Where?"

"In a culvert by the northwest corner of the Reservoir. I think that's where Severino has been throwing out the purses he snatches after he empties them."

"What did you do with the purse?" Donovan asked.

"Well, I turned it in for evidence. But you know how it goes—when you're a uniformed cop, a rookie, at that—no one on the detective level will pay attention to you."

"Not *no one*," Donovan said.

"As far as I know the purse sits there waiting for someone to get around to running prints and comparing them with the ones we have on file for Severino dating back to a time I busted him on suspicion but had to let him go."

"Do you still have the evidence number?" Donovan asked.

"Umh . . . yeah . . . hold on a minute."

As his father waited, the young man poked around in his pockets until he was able to produce a slip of paper with a number written on it in ballpoint pen. He handed it to his father.

"Let me look into this," Donovan said.

"This is *way* below your league," Lewis said, almost apologetically.

"One thing I *can* do is move evidence along. My man Bonaci is this city's crime-scene genious."

"The guy with the forensic science van? I hear he's awesome."

"The price sticker on that van was awesome," Donovan said.

Lewis's smile returned. "Okay, so busting Rico Severino for being a serial purse snatcher is more my speed than catching killers. If you can help me, I'd really appreciate it. Here's how I got into the thing of arresting Natasha. Like I told you, Pilcrow was looking for the cop on the beat that night, hoping he had some information you didn't. As it turned out, the cop on the beat was me and I did happen to know the name of the girl at the pond. So I told him. Actually, I told my sergeant and the word went up the ranks in, like—"

"Twenty seconds," Donovan said.

"About that. So Pilcrow called me in and said I could make a big name for myself by bringing her in. It would look good, a rookie cop under his command making this humongous bust. He would feature me at the press conference and all that. And maybe . . . I'm sorry . . . maybe I thought I could show you up. Maybe I wanted to make you proud of me."

"I was proud of you before," Donovan said. "I'm even more proud of you now."

"Why?"

"You're my son," Donovan said. "And you've come a long way on your own. Going into your dad's field given the ambivalent feelings you've had about me was a gutsy move. I'm impressed."

Donovan smiled at Lewis, then reached over and gave his hand a quick squeeze.

"The end of the story is that I arrested Natasha, who I really liked. I guess I had a crush on her. And I guess I *was* mad at her for being with that other guy. Do you think she did it? Please tell me."

"It's possible she didn't," Donovan said.

"Really?"

"There are better suspects."

"Who?"

"Rico Severino," Donovan said.

Lewis appeared to be surprised by the suggestion. He thought for a second, then said, "No. He couldn't have."

"Why not? He had the hots for Natasha."

"So did every guy who met her or saw her on the Web. You'd have to suspect half the male population of New York."

"Maybe I do," Donovan replied.

"Besides, he couldn't have killed that man," Lewis said. "He left the area. I *chased him* out of the area."

"What time was this?"

"Twelve-thirty," Lewis replied. "Twenty to one."

"Did you see him—them—leave?" Donovan asked.

"Oh, yeah. They headed back uptown. They cleared out

and I watched them leave. They were gone by quarter to one."

"And what did you do then?" Donovan asked.

"I followed them for a few blocks, then headed across the Great Lawn and back to the precinct."

"When did you get there?"

"One-thirty," Lewis replied.

"What did you do then?"

"Took a dump and went on break. I caught a cup of coffee at the luncheonette over on Madison and Seventy-fourth. You know the place?"

"With the four-dollar bagels. Sure, I know it. When did you get back on patrol and where?"

"Two-fifteen at the Fountain. Then I walked south past the bandshell."

"So the King Blades could have doubled back and gone to the gazebo and you wouldn't have known it," Donovan said.

"They didn't," Lewis replied.

"How do you know that?"

"I ran into them by the bandshell. They were dug in . . . all set up like they had been there for a while and were planning on staying all night. Besides, why would they have gone to the gazebo? They didn't see Natasha going in there . . . they couldn't have."

"You're positive of that?" Donovan asked.

Lewis nodded, and added, "I saw the two of them cross Park Drive West and go into the woods toward the gazebo. There was no one else there."

"Unless someone was hiding in the bushes," Donovan said.

"I wasn't looking for anyone hiding in the bushes . . . that night, anyway," Lewis replied.

The gray light of predawn had begun to diffuse across the

sky, replacing the moon, which had at last dipped behind the Manhattan skyline. There was enough light to see by, and Lewis picked up his flashlight and clicked it off (the batteries were largely drained anyway). Donovan pointed over the tops of the bramble, over the glassy surface of Fiddler's Pond and the skunk cabbage and the overhanging willow that obscured a stretch of shoreline. The bare bones of the old gazebo and, around it, a wisp of crime-scene tape, were coming clear to the eyes.

"That's the murder scene," Lewis said, his voice containing a hint of surprise, enough to tell Donovan that the young man didn't really know where he had been sitting.

"And so it is," Donovan replied.

"Is that why you camped out here? To see the murder scene at dawn?"

"I'm not the only one." Donovan pointed up to the top of a tree, where sat a black bird, a crow, Nevermore, perched aware and watchful, glaring with its one eye at the two men below.

"Friend of yours?" Lewis asked.

"I'm not sure. Maybe. Yeah, that's why I'm camped out here. To watch the murder scene and gather impressions. It's what I do."

"Gather impressions? That's how you investigate murders? By gathering *impressions*?"

"It's one of the ways. I figure if you sit alongside a problem long enough . . . not staring at it all the time, just being adjacent and glancing over from time to time, you can solve it."

"I don't know," Lewis said, smiling as if undecided whether to believe his dad, but finding some interest in the idea anyway. "Impressions," he said idly, looking up at the bird and then back down at the water.

"I'm searching for a ripple in the force," Donovan said.

"Have you found one?"

"I think so."

"Want to share it?" Lewis asked.

Donovan said, "Stand up."

"What?"

"Go ahead, stand up."

"Okay," the young man said, pushing himself to his feet and brushing some leaves from his pants legs. But before they hit the ground, there came a piercing cry from the old bird atop the tree followed by a cacophony as the entire *murder* of crows awoke and gave vent to the primal cries of alarm designed to warn of predators and, maybe, scare off the easily intimidated.

"Jesus," Lewis said, and sat back down. Safely returned to his dad's side, he joined in watching as the crows debarked, a rackety mob flapping and screaming off into the approaching day. Half a minute later, the two policemen were alone again.

"That was the ripple in the force you were looking for?" Lewis said. "It was more like a tidal wave."

Smiling proudly, Donovan bobbed his head up and down.

Lewis looked at him and then back at the ruins of the old gazebo. "The birds are frightened by people?" he said.

"By strangers. You scare them. So do I. But the Lauriats . . . father and son . . . don't. Neither does Natasha."

"How do you know that?" Lewis asked.

"I was up there in that tree house . . ." Donovan pointed at the Crow's Nest, vaguely visible in the canopy on the far side of the pond. ". . . the whole night, from about midnight until dawn, when I spotted the body. The murdered man's body, laying in the pond."

"And the crows were quiet the whole time," Lewis said.

"Right. They complained a bit when I climbed the ladder, but not much because Lauriat was there, and he assured me that they were used to him. But they raised holy hell when Nevermore . . . that's the name of that bird I showed you before . . ."

"You know their names?"

"Not 'their.' Just his. They screamed like crazy when dawn broke and Nevermore found the body and started breaking the fast. But between midnight and then . . . nothing."

Lewis said, "And you take this to mean that the birds knew the killer?"

"Or that the killer was already at the gazebo when the murdered man got there," Donovan said.

"Laying in wait," Lewis said.

"Laying in wait," Donovan replied.

Lewis sighed deeply, then asked, "Does that rule out Severino?"

"It might."

"Does it rule out anyone else?"

"You," Donovan said flatly, without emotion, to deny the words the impact they would normally have.

"Me!" The young man appeared to be flabbergasted, and he pulled back from his father for a second before thinking about it, then leaning back in.

"If I didn't think of it, someone else would," Donovan said.

"Okay," Lewis sighed. "You said that detection is a mind game. I get it. I had the hots for her and was furious that she went into the woods with another guy. I was the last one—other than him, I guess—to see her before she went to the crime scene. Why did I kill Harvey Cozzens?"

"He was lying in wait for her and attacked. You killed him to protect her. But you were still pissed off, so you let her take the rap for the murder, after you got home and had the chance to think of a way out of the mess."

"Why didn't she finger me?" Lewis asked.

"Who says she hasn't?" Donovan asked.

"She hasn't talked to you, word has it."

"Well, she *did* talk to me, but not about that. Anyway, you're in the clear."

"I don't know. That sounds like a flimsy scenario to use in hanging a murder rap on someone."

"Guys have been sent up the river on flimsier ones," Donovan said. "Especially guys of color."

The young man looked at his father, this time fondly, and said, "That's why you were waiting for me, isn't it? So you could see if the crows would react to my presence."

Donovan grinned.

"How'd you know I would come?" Lewis asked.

"Like I said, you say you hate me . . . hated me . . . but you *always turn up.* I knew you would. Like that time at the tree house when you stepped out of the woods and into that clearing at the base of the tree. You remember that?"

Lewis remembered.

"There's a path leading directly from the tree-house tree to the old gazebo, isn't there?"

"How'd you know that?" Lewis asked.

"You stepped out of it."

"What's it mean?"

"Maybe nothing," Donovan said. "But it could mean that Lauriat was able to get from the tree to the gazebo without walking all the way around."

"Sure he could," Lewis said. "If he knew the way. Does that help your case?"

"Every little bit of information helps. What are you going to tell Pilcrow about finding me tonight?"

"I don't know. What would you suggest?"

"The truth."

"I found you, but you were clean and actively engaged in honest police work."

"That will piss him off, but it's the truth."

Lewis said, "Ah well, who cares? Everything pisses him off. So what if he kicks me out of his command."

"No matter what you've heard, I'm not without influence in this town," Donovan said. "I'll make sure you land on your feet. Just don't ever, *ever* let Pilcrow know you're my son."

"Thanks for the advice," Lewis said. He hesitated for a second before adding, "So look, does what you told me about the crows suggest anyone in particular who might have killed Cozzens?"

"Natasha and Frank Lauriat still could have done it," Donovan said. "So could Lauriat senior. So could persons unknown who could have lain in wait."

"Like who?" Lewis asked.

"I don't know," Donovan said, getting to his feet and, while Lewis dutifully looked away, going around to the far side of the tree to relieve himself. When he was done, he returned to find the young man on his feet, brushing himself off and looking very much the professional police officer who was, at that moment, also eyeballing the contents of Donovan's bag.

Lewis plucked a bottle of Kaliber and held it up to the growing dawn light.

"Is this stuff any good?" he asked.

"Yeah. Tastes just like a good, dark beer, but without the alcohol. Try one."

"I'm on duty."

"So am I," Donovan said.

"I don't drink anyway," Lewis added.

"Still? You still don't? Good for you."

"Not so much as a drop."

"You shouldn't. I'm duty-bound as a dad to point out that you have alcoholics on both sides of your family."

"Awright. Don't preach."

"*Now* you sound like a son," Donovan said.

Lewis put the bottle back, then turned to his father, opened his coat, and peered suspiciously at the Cyrcad.

"What's that thing?" he asked. "What happened to your Smith & Wesson thirty-eight?"

"Pilcrow ordered me to try this out."

"Is that the radio-controlled Cyrcad?"

"Yep."

"It's gonna get you killed," Lewis said. "Lose it."

"I hardly ever draw my gun anymore," Donovan said.

"Lose it," Lewis repeated, more emphatically that time. "If you got to have an automatic, get the nine-millimeter Glock like I use."

"You're preaching," Donovan said, reclosing his coat against the early morning cold and leading his eldest and newly rediscovered son out of the woods and back to the cobblestone path. When they got there, Lewis grasped his father's hand, shook it, then pressed it between both of his. He said, "I have to go back on patrol. I have to make a swing through the Great Lawn. Pilcrow is afraid that there's going to be a lot of trouble in connection with the big Earth Day celebration on Sunday. And I'm on duty Sunday, backstage."

"I'm afraid that Pilcrow could be right this time," Donovan said.

"Me, I'm convinced that Severino and his pals will be primed to rip off tourists during the party," Lewis said. Then he added, "I'm going to get him for *something*, if only purse snatching."

"Go get 'im," Donovan said.

"Where are you off to? Home?"

"Coffee first," Donovan said.

250

Half an hour later he pulled into a booth in the luncheonette, on Madison near 74th, where he once paid four dollars for a bagel with cream cheese; he had been talking about it since. Across from him sat a man of sixty-five some-odd years, half bald and with a beer belly that loomed, shelflike, over a lower body that somehow had been stuffed into newly bought jeans. A black vinyl zip-up jacket bore, over the left breast, the insignia of the Sheepshead Bay Boat Club. The man looked over Donovan's getup, then smiled and pinched him on the cheek, grasping a quarter-sized bit of bearded skin and squeezing it.

"Working late or drinking early?" the man said.

"Working late and on my way home," Donovan said. "Good to see you."

The waitress came over, and Donovan ordered a cup of coffee, half decaf and half regular, and an English muffin with butter and marmalade. When she left, he grumbled "seven bucks" and left a ten-dollar bill on the table.

"German tourists," Shea replied. "They're everywhere on Madison Avenue these days, every block, couples mainly, paying exorbitant prices for everything. Who would have thought that Madison in the seventies would turn into a popular shopping thoroughfare? The average American can't even afford to take a deep breath in this neighborhood."

"So I heard."

"And the way they *smoke*, these Germans. Like smokestacks, one cigarette after the other."

"And we thought they grew out of that tendency to march, lemminglike, into the flames. I heard you quit."

"Two years now," Shea said.

"Good for you."

"You still dry?"

"Ten years now."

"Well, congratulations. Who woulda thunk it? Me, well, a guy's got to have *one* vice."

"You still fish, don't you? Isn't that what you guys do at the Sheepshead Bay Boat Club?"

"We talk about it. Mostly, we drink. All winter we sit in the bar drinking and talking about fishing. All summer we sit on the porch drinking and talking about fishing. Twice a year, spring and fall, we put our boats in the water and pull them out and then sit down in them or next to them and drink and talk about fishing."

"Sounds like the old days," Donovan said.

"You miss it sometimes?" Shea asked.

"Like I've told you before, sometimes I miss the point-lessness."

"Pointlessness," Shea said.

"Yeah, the opportunity to give your neurons a few hours' rest. A time to do nothing but watch the neighboring neurons die off. Look, I need to know about Lewis Rodriguez."

"You're still following that kid. Why?"

"He's an interest of mine."

"Like thinking too much, right?" Shea said.

"Yeah, my substitute for liquor. Like that," Donovan agreed.

"You want to know what he was doing the night that guy Cozzens was killed in the park."

"That's what I want to know. What he was doing in the wee hours. Specifically, when did he take his break? You were working the desk then, right?"

"All night, every night, wearing out my butt the same way I do on the porch of the boat club. Yeah, the kid took his break per usual, all right. He came in at one-thirty, picked up a copy of *The News* and went in to inspect the plumbing, then walked over here to get a donut and be insulted by the prices. I know he was here because he brought me back a bagel. Four bucks. He's a good kid."

"I know."

"So are you gonna tell me why you're so interested in him?"

"No," Donovan said emphatically.

"Well, that's okay with me, if you don't want to tell me what it is with this kid and you, that's your business. I owe you a couple of times over. And there's old times sake."

"I appreciate it. You're a pal."

"Well, like I always say, us old-timers got to stick together. Say . . . I heard you became a dad."

Shea reached across the table and over the coffee cups and silverware and shook the captain's hand.

"Yeah," Donovan said proudly.

"How's it feel?"

"Good. It feels good."

"You have a son, right?"

"You got it," Donovan said.

"How old?"

"A couple of months."

"Jesus, my kids are out of college and one has a kid of his own on the way," Shea said. "I can't imagine what it would be like to have a baby boy in the house."

"It feels good to have a son at any age," Donovan said, then added, "Are you among the cops who have to work Sunday?"

"Yeah, and that was one of my fishing days, too," Shea said. "I got to run the command post backstage. You gonna be around?"

"It's a possibility," Donovan said.

"Stop by for coffee."

"I may do that," Donovan replied. "I may bring friends."

And then the two men fell into a long conversation about parenthood that took them well into the morning rush hour and made it that much harder for Donovan to get home, which he did in time to kiss his wife good morning and pile into bed and pull the covers over his head.

12. A Power Spot, Where the Elemental Forces of the Cosmos Converge

He awoke late in the day to find himself alone in his big apartment, which seemed all the more cavernous with no one else there except the aging Yorkie, who as ever was wandering in and out of rooms, investigating the assorted creaks and squeaks that came with the century-old West Side apartment. Donovan showered and dressed while watching the sun fall below the horizon on the far side of the Hudson where the wooded cliffs of the Palisades were flecked with high-rise apartments, yet below an abandoned waterfront restaurant, once a grand Hudson River cruise ship, lay foundered and rotting on its side. While his hair dried, Donovan sat at the computer in his den and read his e-mails and sent out a few more, finally smiling to find that a lure he cast the night before had landed a fish. After logging off the computer he packed more beer, both regular and nonalcoholic types, into his Bean bag and headed off for his third night in Central Park.

Donovan made only one stop en route: at Marcy's Home Cooking to pick up a sun-dried tomato and smoked mozzarella sandwich, and kiss his wife and child. Then he walked across 86th and entered the park about an hour past sundown, when the night had begun to take over. On his way along Park Drive West he noticed that the King Blades were not at their usual spot. Judging by the easy and unhassled manner of the others enjoying that part of the park that night, and by the absence of boom box music, the skaters were nowhere near.

Donovan walked briskly, skirting that edge of Fiddler's Pond where the old gazebo stood, now ringed by crime-scene tape no longer, until he entered the Ramble and found lamppost T1357B. He walked down the looping cobblestone path and, soon thereafter, stood at the edge of the clearing in the midst of which grew the Sumatran willow, beneath which he had buried the hatchet with his eldest son. Another familial scene was in progress—Gabriel Allen Cohen, his daughter, and her boyfriend—the latter having made bail only that morning—sat beneath the tree, on a blue woolen blanket that glowed from the small blue flames that flickered from two Sterno cans. The three of them huddled like Mojave around a campfire on a chill prairie evening, sipping what appeared to be tea from identical metal cups. Three sets of eyes met Donovan's.

"Ishimani ritual herbal tea?" Donovan asked.

"There's no such thing," Cohen replied.

Wide-eyed and nervous, Frank Lauriat said, "Tasha and I made most of that up."

"This is Red Zinger," Cohen added. "Want some?"

"No, thanks," Donovan replied. "Anyone for a beer?"

He set his Bean bag down on the ground and from within it took a six-pack of Steamboat Ferry Inn Ale. He set it on the blanket next to one of the Sterno cans. The girl eyed it, reached for a bottle, then looked at her dad nervously and asked, "Is it okay if I have a beer?"

Donovan laughed. "This is wonderful," he said. "You dance naked in the moonlight in Central Park. You take off your clothes for all the world to see on the Internet. You bring your lover home to have sex in your bedroom next to

Winnie the Pooh. Well, maybe not any longer, since you gave the bear to me for my baby. But you still need your dad's permission to have a *beer*?"

"Alcohol can kill you," the girl replied.

"But dancing naked in the moonlight in Central Park can only get middle-aged voyeurs killed," Donovan replied.

"I'm sorry about that man," she said. "I really am."

"Come, Captain, sit down," Cohen said, as his daughter got herself a beer and twisted the cap off.

Donovan lowered himself to the blanket and wriggled into a reasonably comfortable position on the edge of it, facing the three suspects.

"I'm glad you could come here tonight," Donovan said. "I'm surprised that your lawyer let you."

"He spoke with your father-in-law," Cohen replied.

"Oh, so you're getting the whole *mishpocheh* in on it, are you?"

Natasha turned to her boyfriend and said, "that means 'extended family' in Jewish."

"His honor refreshed Boris's memory," Cohen continued. "We're convinced now that you're a man of honor."

"Thank you," Donovan replied.

"I was put off by the cop thing."

"Well, on the day that everyone on earth begins behaving according to just laws, there will be no need for cops and I will retire," Donovan said. "Until then, I'm a reality and I need to know who killed Harvey Cozzens."

"Why?" Frank asked. "He was a creep."

"It's *okay* to be a creep," Donovan said. "Being a creep doesn't hurt anyone, at least not seriously enough to warrant execution."

Cohen added, "The next step after killing creeps is killing everyone we don't like."

"And *that* puts us back in Nazi Germany," Donovan said. "So did you kill him?"

"No," the three of them said at once.

"Who did?" Donovan asked.

"We don't know," Natasha replied. "We didn't see him that night. Everything we told you about what happened was true. Frank and I went to the gazebo to hang out. We didn't see anyone except that cop . . ."

"Lewis Rodriguez," Donovan said.

She nodded. "And then we went home to make love. And that's *it*."

"What did you do while at the gazebo?"

"Talked," she replied.

"Listened to the radio," Frank said.

"I heard you talking and playing the radio," Donovan said.

"And we made out a little," she said. "Warmed up, I guess you would say. Did I dance naked in the moonlight? No. Not that night."

"Have you ever met Cozzens?" Donovan asked. "Did you ever even talk to him on the phone?"

"Never," she replied, and the other two shook their heads.

"How'd you know he was a creep?" Donovan asked the boy.

"Tasha forwarded some of his e-mails to me."

"I've seen them too," Donovan said. "They make him seem like the ideal American male."

"Yeah, and I was jealous of all the attention Tasha was paying to him on the Internet," Frank said.

"You're too naïve to have killed anyone," Donovan said.

"What do you mean?" the boy asked.

"You just gave the investigating officer in a homicide a motive for murder," Cohen said.

"I'm afraid so," Donovan replied.

"But I didn't kill anyone," the boy protested. "I was with Tasha the whole time. We didn't see this guy Cozzens at all. I just wanted to be honest with you. She spent too much time e-mailing him, leading him on . . ."

"I did not," the girl protested.

"Not intentionally, of course," Frank said quickly. "Tasha is just like that . . . innocent, kind of."

"Asking permission to have a beer," Donovan said.

"She didn't know that the guy was this middle-aged creep who would *stalk* her. We didn't know that until we saw pictures of him in the paper after he was killed. I mean, I guess he was stalking Tasha. What do you think?"

"He was," Donovan said. "But my suspicion is that he only wanted to catch a glimpse of her in the flesh, dancing in the moonlight. I think he was watching the two of you from the bushes, and never would have gotten the nerve to have stepped into the Sterno light."

"We didn't see anyone," Natasha said again.

"How closely were you paying attention to the bushes?" Donovan asked.

"Oh. Not very closely, I guess," she said.

The boy added, "There was no one but us on the path in from the road. There couldn't have been anyone in the water, could there?"

"I doubt it," Donovan said.

"That leaves the bushes on either side," Frank said.

"Which ones did you go into when you had to take a leak?"

"The ones to the left. As you face the water."

"To the north," Donovan said.

"Well, I went into there once that night . . . just a foot or two, you know, to keep it away from where we were sitting. You don't want to pee too close to where your girl is sitting."

"I get a kick out of you two," Donovan said.

"I didn't see anyone," the boy concluded.

"There's a path leading off to the south," Donovan said. "Did you know that?"

Both teenagers shook their heads. The boy added, "I'm blind as anything in the dark."

"He *is*," Natasha agreed. "One night I walked away from him and then came back and he got real scared and thought I was a ghost."

"The path is a narrow one, hard to spot even during the day," Donovan said. "I think that Cozzens was hiding in there, watching you the whole time you were at the gazebo."

"Creep," Frank said.

Donovan gave Cohen a quizzical look, and said, "What about you, do you know where that path is?"

And the poet shook his head, saying, "I've never been to the gazebo."

"Not ever?"

"Never," the man said again.

Donovan said, "It's an interesting place."

Frank said, "Tasha believes that it's a power spot, where the elemental forces of the universe converge."

"Could be. Look, Mr. Cohen . . ."

"Please call me Gabe."

"Next opportunity I get," Donovan said. "So you've never been to the gazebo, but you've been here, under this tree, many times before."

"Oh, sure. Many times," the poet said.

"How did you know that?" Natasha asked.

"It's in one of my poems. Yes, I've been here."

"Including the night of the murder," Donovan said.

Cohen looked at the captain, unsure of himself, and his daughter looked at him; she appeared to have been caught off guard by the news.

"You were here?" she asked.

Reluctantly, Donovan thought, Cohen nodded his head. The captain added, "From midnight to about three, correct?"

"Correct," Cohen said, sighing.

"Daddy . . . were you *spying* on me?" she asked, in a hurt-teenage-girl sort of voice.

"So much for asking permission to have a beer," Donovan said.

"I wasn't spying on you," Cohen told his daughter. "But I wanted to be nearby in case you got in trouble. So I stayed here, beneath the Sumatran willow . . ." He twisted around and rapped the trunk of the tree with his knuckles, perhaps knocking on wood for luck in getting out of trouble with his daughter. "Where I would be close enough to come help if you needed me."

"Close enough to hear someone scream," Donovan said.

"Yes," Cohen said, looking down at the blanket, then saying, "But I fell asleep and didn't hear a thing. I'm afraid I'm not as good at staying up all night as I used to be."

"Lately I've proved to be a lot better at it than I would have imagined," Donovan said.

"I can't believe you spied on me," Natasha said.

"I was trying to be there for you," Cohen said. "In case you needed me."

Donovan said, "Let's face it, you put yourself at risk when you took your clothes off on the Web and then began writing about dancing naked in the park."

"I didn't say *where* I did it," the girl protested.

"Yes, you did. You dropped enough clues for a blind man to find you on a cloudy night," Donovan said.

"I *told* you," Frank said.

"Cozzens figured out how to find you from your poetry, the same way I figured out that the alphanumeric phrase T one three five seven B referred to that lamppost over there."

Donovan nodded in the direction of the lamp, the light from which was just visible through the trees and leaves.

Looking down the tall amber neck of her beer bottle, Natasha said, "I was writing poetry. But I got my inspiration from real life." Then she turned to her father and said, "I was trying to write like *you*."

Cohen reached over and stroked her hair for a few seconds.

"There are all sorts of complications that arise when you try to compete with your father in his own field," Donovan said.

"Boris told me that your father was a policeman," Cohen said.

"And so he was," Donovan replied.

"Mine was a tailor," Cohen said.

Donovan said, "Tell me, if you were sitting here that night and heard your daughter scream, what would you have done?"

"Why, protect her, of course."

"How? Do you have a gun? A knife?"

"I have a cell phone," Cohen replied. "I would call nine one one, and then I would run over there and, I don't know, flap my arms or something. I'm not a violent man. As I think you know, my whole life has been in opposition to violence."

"Mine has been picking up the pieces afterwards," Donovan said. "You say that you don't have a gun or a knife, but you *had* a knife, didn't you?"

Cohen seemed a little surprised, but recovered quickly. He said, "You mean the Moorish dagger that I got as a gift from Hertig? The one aggressive object I ever permitted in my house? I gave it to Natasha to use in protecting herself during those nights in the park. But she lost it."

"It was stolen," Natasha said.

"During the robbery," Donovan said.

She bobbed her head up and down. "I left my goddam purse on a bench while I went into the woods to take a leak. I thought that Frank would keep an eye on it, but *he* had to go, too."

Donovan smiled, and upon seeing it, she said, "We *were* drinking beer."

"I understand."

"And one of the skaters stole it."

"How do you know it was a skater?" Donovan asked.

"We were sitting watching them, and one of them—the big shot, if you know what I mean—has the hots for me."

"He's a creep," Frank said.

"That would be Rico Severino," Donovan said.

She said, "Yeah, that's him. I told him to get lost and stop bothering me. I told him just that night. And he stole my purse to get even, I'm sure of it."

"There was no one else around?"

"There were people, I guess. But we were watching the skaters and I'm sure that one of them took my purse and they all skated off. Probably it was Rico. To get even with me. They do that, you know—steal purses."

"Why were you watching them?" Donovan asked.

"No reason," Frank replied.

"Yes, there *was* a reason," Natasha replied. "I was trying to show you how dangerous inline skating is by forcing you to watch those jerks."

"She's always mothering me," Frank said sheepishly.

"So you skate, too," Donovan said to the boy.

"He used to," Natasha said.

"I also used to skateboard," Frank said.

"That's even worse," she said.

"But at least skateboarders don't steal purses," Frank said.

Natasha returned her attention to the captain, and said, "That cop we saw that night . . . Lewis? He says he is going to get Rico for stealing purses, but I don't know."

"Somebody is going to get Severino for something," Donovan said. "Why didn't you list the knife as having been stolen when you filled out a police report?"

"Because it wouldn't look good for me to have a knife," she said. "I mean, how would it look for me to be in the park drinking beer and carrying a knife?"

"Not too good," Frank said.

"So you reported that you lost eighty dollars and 'personal items,' " Donovan said.

She nodded.

"Why are you so interested in the Moorish knife?" Cohen asked.

"Why do you think?" Donovan replied.

"It's the murder weapon, isn't it," the poet said.

Donovan nodded.

"Oh, my God," Natasha said, pressing the tips of three fingers to her lips.

"That doesn't look good for us, does it?" Cohen said.

"It would look better if she had reported the knife stolen," Donovan said.

"This is what I get for breaking my rule and allowing an aggressive weapon into the house," Cohen said. "Where did you find it? The papers didn't say anything about my knife."

"We found it not far from the body," Donovan said. "The papers don't know about it yet."

"And it's definitely my Moorish knife that killed Harvey Cozzens?"

"Beyond a doubt. Did you clean your knife regularly while you owned it? Such as oiling it?"

"No," Cohen said, not quite laughing.

"I don't think he ever looked at it," Frank said. "Tasha kept it up on a shelf."

"Did *you* clean it?" Donovan asked the girl.

"No. I just stuck it in my purse—in a special compartment built into the side for you to hide secret stuff you might need."

"Like knives . . ."

She smiled, a wicked sort of smile, and said, "Like Mace, vibrator, K-Y, Viagra, all sorts of things a girl needs these days."

Cohen looked away, apparently having reached the outer edge of his ability to applaud his offspring's sexual freedom.

"Was this a safe compartment?" Donovan asked.

"Oh, sure. Very safe. You wouldn't know anything was in there unless you were *really* looking. Only Frank and I knew how to get in there."

"Did you keep oil in there?" Donovan asked.

"Why? We had the K-Y."

"Not that kind of lubricant. Oil, as in the type you use to keep a knife clean."

"Of course not," she replied. "Why do you ask?"

"Do you guys use any odd or unusual oil around the house? Stuff that the knife might have come into contact with?"

"Just Three-In-One Oil," Cohen said. "The little can you get from the hardware store. For squeaky hinges. There are a lot in my apartment."

"And you never kept oil in your purse," Donovan asked the girl.

"You mean like mineral oil?"

"Anything."

"Keri Oil," she replied.

"My wife uses that," Donovan said. "I've read the label while . . . never mind. Keri Oil isn't what I had in mind. I don't suppose you own any rat repellent."

"I don't *think* so," she replied, a bit haughtily.

"Can I search your apartment?" Donovan asked. "And yours," indicating the boy's.

"My lawyer won't allow that," Cohen said.

"Neither will mine," Frank added.

"Can we talk to your moms?" Donovan asked.

Again the reply was negative.

"Why are you asking questions about oil?" Cohen asked.

"Oh, I'm just trying to keep up with my scientific guys. Do you believe in science? As I recall, you didn't for quite a while."

"I also didn't believe in making money for quite a while," Cohen said.

"You've changed," Donovan said.

"You noticed that we've begun charging for access to much of the site."

Donovan said he had noticed.

"I suppose that makes me a child pornographer, charging admission to see pictures of my daughter half naked. Is that what you think it makes me?"

"I ain't the lifestyle police," Donovan said. "Catching murderers is my one and only career goal. You'll have to get your disapproval from Ken Starr or the mayor."

"I wasn't fishing for disapproval," Cohen said.

"It was *my* decision, daddy," Natasha chimed in.

"We need the money for her legal defense fund," Cohen said.

"So it doesn't hurt to toss off a couple of new poems after . . . how many years?"

"Since I published a new work?" Cohen asked. "Thirty some-odd years."

"Was it hard for you?" Donovan asked.

"You do what you have to do for your daughter. Did you like what I wrote? Speaking as an old reader."

"I liked the one about the turtle crawling out onto the

forked log as being a symbol of struggle," Donovan said.

Beaming, Cohen said, "I'm especially fond of that one, too. It has a kind of Wordsworth quality, wouldn't you say?"

"I'm not a poetry reader, generally speaking," Donovan said. "I couldn't tell you Wordsworth from Woolworth. Was he the one who wrote 'The Charge of the Light Brigade?' "

"That was Tennyson," Cohen said.

"I just like the turtle," Donovan said, pointing out in the direction of the pond. "It's great what you can see here at daybreak."

Cohen followed the captain's finger, thought for a moment, then, seemingly distracted, replied, "Yes . . . it is."

"Dad's poem is also about tough moral decisions," Natasha added. "That's the symbolism of the forked log."

"I got that," Donovan said.

The peaceful buzz of the city's background noise was briefly overridden by the hissing sound of a far-off jet plane, heading down the middle of Manhattan, on the roundabout approach to LaGuardia Airport. Natasha and her boyfriend glanced up at it.

"Why would my daughter have killed a man with her own knife unless maybe in self-defense?" Cohen asked. "She's too smart for that."

"Is that what happened?" Donovan asked.

"No," the girl insisted. "I told you exactly what went on."

"You went to the gazebo. Tell me again, at what time did you get there?"

"About twelve-fifteen."

"How do you know what time it was?" Donovan asked. "Did you look at your watch?"

She shook her head. "We watched *The X-Files* and it's over at midnight. We went to the park."

"And tell me again what time you headed home?"

"About one-fifteen," she replied.

"Why'd you only stay an hour?" Donovan asked.

"We had a movie coming on cable at one-thirty," she said.

"Which one?"

"*Surf Nazis Must Die,*" Frank replied.

"One of my favorites," Donovan replied. "So you were home by one-thirty and you put on the movie."

"No. We skipped the movie, made love, and fell right asleep," she said.

"It's a dumb movie anyway," Frank said.

Donovan turned to Cohen and said, "When you got home from the park . . . around three or three fifteen, I guess . . ."

"About that," Cohen agreed.

"Did you see the kids in her room?"

"Of course not. They always have the door closed, and it would be prying for me to open it up when I know they're in there."

"When did you wake up?" Donovan asked the girl.

"Five," Natasha said. "I sleep like a rock and I remember Frank woke me up, with his sweats on and everything, ready to go. I walked him to the door and sent him home. He's too embarrassed to stay for breakfast."

"You find these patches of old-fashioned morality in the damnedest places," Donovan said.

"To me, it's silly," Cohen said. "Frank is always welcome for breakfast, or any other meal, and I make a hell of a stack of pancakes."

"So that's it, eh?" Donovan said. "The two of you got to the gazebo at twelve-thirty, left at one-fifteen, and didn't see anyone but Patrolman Rodriguez."

"That's it," Natasha replied.

"And *you,*" Donovan continued, addressing Cohen, "You got here at midnight . . . ahead of them."

"I knew they were coming. I left while they were still in the living room watching TV. I didn't want Natasha to know I would be there, looking after her."

The girl gave her father an I-forgive-you look, one followed by a swig of beer.

"And you fell asleep at about when?" Donovan asked.

"I guess right around one," Cohen replied. "I was really tired."

"And you didn't hear anyone scream, you didn't hear anyone anything, and you woke up at three. What woke you?"

"Something in the bushes," Cohen said.

"Something like what?" Donovan asked, looking around.

"A big dog, I think. It was kind of like a German shepherd, but you know I couldn't see it very well, and I hit it on the nose with my cell phone and it ran off. Amazing how people let their dogs run wild in the park."

"Amazing," Donovan said.

"So I went home. But no, I didn't hear a scream. I didn't hear anything. I walked home and went to bed."

"When we talked at your apartment, why did you refuse to tell me whether or not you knew Cozzens?" Donovan asked.

"I was afraid you'd think I had a relationship with him, since we were exchanging e-mails," she replied.

"That sounds sensible enough of a fear to have," Donovan said. He was getting cramped sitting in the one spot, so he adjusted his position and, while so doing, got himself a bottle of Kaliber and opened it. "Anyone else?" he said.

"Go ahead, Frank," Natasha said to her boyfriend.

"Can I?" the boy asked Donovan.

"You're old enough to fight for your country, you're old enough to drink," Donovan said. And he gave the boy a bottle of the ale. And after the boy twisted off the cap and tossed his head back, taking a drink, Donovan picked up one of his feet and looked at the sneaker adorning it.

"Hey," Frank protested.

"Nice sneakers," Donovan said.

"I bought them for him," Natasha said. "They're very expensive."

"I wear cheap sneakers," Donovan said. "I get them at Sole Warehouse."

"He used to wear the cheapest sneakers," Natasha said.

"K-Mart," the boy said.

"But I finally got him into something good."

"What are those, size tens?" Donovan asked the boy.

"Ten."

"I'm an eleven," Donovan replied, letting go of the foot.

"Is that all, Captain?" Cohen asked. "Because if it is, we have to go. We're tired. Well, *I'm* tired. I can't speak for these two . . ."

"You do quite well," Donovan interrupted.

"But only because I know what they're thinking. Natasha has something to do on her Web site, and I believe that Frank has to get home to see his mother."

"It's a condition of my parole," the boy said.

"Explain," Donovan said.

"I have to be home by ten P.M. and my mom has to certify it by calling a number."

"When can you leave in the morning?" Donovan asked.

"Eight."

"And can you go anywhere you want?"

"Yes. Except out of the country."

"Where are you going tomorrow?" Donovan asked.

The boy thought for a moment before saying, "I don't know."

"You're not going to see your father?"

Frank looked surprised. He made an odd sort of face, then

said, "Why should . . . ?" But then Natasha poked him in the side, and after saying, "Ow," he added, "Of course . . . I'll go see my father."

"He *did* hock everything he owns to post your bail," Donovan said, feeling a little foolish for scolding.

"That was so *great* of him," Natasha said, chirping merrily and doing it so well that Donovan couldn't tell if it was forced. But he felt that it was. She continued, nudging her boyfriend again, gentler this time, "Frank owes him so much."

"Especially given that they hadn't spoken in years," Cohen added.

"Well?" Donovan asked the young man. Who thought for a prolonged moment, then breathed deeply and said, "I love my father. I forgive him for leaving my mom."

"You managed to camp out a stone's throw away from his research base," Donovan said.

The boy nodded, adding, "I wanted to go over and say hello. But I couldn't."

"Then his father came to his rescue with the bail money," Natasha said.

"And I'm ready now to bury the hatchet," Frank added, punctuating the thought with a sip of beer.

Donovan stared at him a bit, then looked over at the other two. Then he smiled and told the boy, "That's wonderful. So you'll go see him when?"

"First thing in the morning," Frank said.

"Unfortunately, he's not in town," Donovan said.

The three of them hadn't expected that development, Donovan felt. They exchanged quick and surprised glances, and then Cohen said, "I thought he was home, recovering from his wounds, from the other night when he was beaten up. I read it in the paper. He was investigating the murder, they said, and was beaten up by thugs."

"They're everywhere," Donovan said. "On the streets, in

the bushes, everywhere. Frank, your father had to go to Washington to see his grantor. He's getting an advance on his next research project. To help pay your bail."

"When will he be back?" the boy asked.

"Sunday. I asked him to join me at the Earth Day Mega-celebration."

"Why there?" Cohen asked.

"To finish some business we started out doing," Donovan said. "He was telling me about crows, especially how they react to the presence of strangers. I'm interested in seeing what the arrival of one million or more strangers will do."

"I guess I can't see him tomorrow," Frank said, and in a tone of voice that gave Donovan the impression he meant it.

"You'll join us Sunday," Donovan said. "All of you will."

"How will we find you if there are going to be a million people there?" Cohen asked.

Donovan fished a business card out of his shirt pocket and handed it to the *eminence grise*. Then the captain said, "There will be a police command post in the backstage area. I'll be there, having a cup of coffee. Ask for me about two."

13. "I Love Turtles," Donovan Said Out Loud

When Cohen and the two young lovers were gone, Donovan took out his cell phone and called the elder Lauriat. The captain gave some instructions to his friend, and endured a lot of quizzing and backtalk before finally being assured that the scientist would do as he asked.

Then Donovan called his wife to tell her he loved her, and then put the instrument back in his pocket and got to his feet and picked up his bag. He left the campsite at the foot of the Sumatran willow and trudged around the rim of Fiddler's Pond, ducking in and out of the mid-evening foot and cycle traffic on Park Drive West until he came to the path that the teens took to get to the gazebo. His arrival upon it brought forth from the treetops not exactly a screeching protest, but a loud and angry murmuring that reminded the captain he remained a stranger to the crows.

Not only was the crime-scene tape gone, the site of the murder had been cleaned up to discourage souvenir hunters. That appeared to have been an unnecessary precaution, for when the captain reached the gazebo he found himself alone. Only the marks left by the rakes used to straighten up the scene of the crime reminded him that people had recently been there.

He put away his Mag Lite after lighting a Sterno can brought along from Marcy's Home Cooking, where its normal function was to keep a chafing dish warm. He set this light in the middle of the space, between the two benches, where he imagined the teens would have placed it.

Then he laid out a blanket on the ground, again between the benches, in fact right where his men had examined Cozzens's body. He placed his Bean bag near one end, close to the water. Then he got his sandwich—that night it was smoked turkey with sun-dried tomatoes on seven-grain bread—and a bottle of Kaliber and, using his Mag Lite again, found the spot where Bonaci had showed him the dead man's shoeprint.

Donovan stepped into it and poked around a bit and, by bending a sassafras branch that twisted, gnarled and bent, at waist level, found that he was, indeed, on a path. It was a very narrow one, really just a way of pushing the bushes aside, but it did lead, and very quickly, to the base of the Crow's Nest. Smiling, he returned to his starting point and sat down, approximately cross-legged, at precisely the spot where Cozzens had gratified himself while watching Natasha and Frank.

Donovan sat for half an hour in the spot occupied by Cozzens just before his death. After his eyes became accustomed to the dark, Donovan could see every detail of goings-on at the gazebo clearly in the light of the Sterno can. The flickering blue had a surreal quality, like a graduate school art film or an old and washed-out color monitor. The question was, could someone in the gazebo see *him*?

The murmur of protest from the crows was repeated, but louder. Then footsteps on the main path were accompanied by the whistled tune "Goodbye, Yellow Brick Road." Mosko stepped into the blue light wearing a black jacket over new jeans and carrying his shoulder bag and a paper bag from Burger Demon. "Yo, Cap?" he called out.

Donovan said nothing as Mosko looked around.

"Whaddya doin', watering the ivy? I'll hang out."

Still Donovan didn't respond, and unable to find him with simple glances, Mosko cruised the perimeter of the clearing looking more closely. "Cap? You okay? You passing a stone or something?"

"I'm all right," Donovan snarled.

"Where the hell are you?" Mosko asked.

"Over here. In the direction of the Crow's Nest."

Mosko looked at the pond, then around again, and said, "Okay, let's see if I can remember. This ain't a New York City kid thing. You face the pond, which is east. That means your right hand is facing south."

To illustrate, he pointed off to his right.

"And since the tree house is south . . ."

"You're a fucking genius, you know that?" Donovan said, standing and pushing his way out into the clearing.

Mosko turned to face him. "Is that where Cozzens hid out? Where Bonaci found the shoe print? Yeah, I guess it is. Could you see me okay?"

"Perfectly."

"So that's it, then. Cozzens stalked the girl to this spot and got off watching her and the boy. Did you find out what they were doing here?"

Donovan sat down on the blanket near his Bean bag and took out another beer. He said, "They were making out. When time came to finish the act, they went back to her place."

"Oh, they wanted privacy so they decided to do it on the Web," Mosko said.

"She turns the camera away from the bed when her boyfriend is over," Donovan said.

Mosko sat next to his boss, reaching into his shoulder bag and taking out his laptop and a bottle of Cel-Ray soda. Then he pulled a Demon Burger with cheese from the paper bag and set it down on the blanket alongside a large order of fries.

"I got one for you or I can eat both of them if you're not hungry," Mosko said.

"I ate already," Donovan said. "You have them both. You need to feed those muscles."

"You got that right," Mosko said, taking a bite out of a burger and chewing it in the soft blue light.

Donovan stared at the pond, looking across it in the direction of the Sumatran willow. He was trying to spot the light from lamppost T1357B, but couldn't. It wasn't so much the distance, which was not great. The problem was the branches from the willow . . . not the exotic imported one, but the regular American willow that grew alongside the gazebo and had branches that dipped down into the water . . . they hid the view in that direction.

After enough burger settled in his stomach to settle the growls, Mosko said, "Tell me again how you got the Cohen bunch to come and meet you in the park tonight."

"I e-mailed them," Donovan said.

"I *know* that. You told me last night that you were doing it. What you didn't say is how you convinced them to trust you some more."

"I let them think they have something on me," Donovan said.

"I guess that would appeal to their lawyer," Mosko replied. "What is it?"

"What, *you* want something on me too?"

"You bet your life, Cap," Mosko said.

"Dig up your own dirt. Anyway, they came."

"And? And?"

"Frank Lauriat gave us a motive for murdering Cozzens," Donovan said.

"What is it?" Mosko asked.

"He admitted he was jealous of the amount of attention that 'Tasha' . . .'"

"Who?"

"His pet name for her," Donovan said.

"Cute. Tell me more."

"Frank was jealous of all the e-mail traffic she was directing to Cozzens," Donovan said. "And he was aware that she left lots of clues to where she hung out in Central Park."

"I told you," Mosko said. "Maybe it was deliberate."

"I still think it was innocence," Donovan said, adding, "As for Frank, he thinks that Cozzens was a creep and doesn't seem to be too sorry he's dead."

"The kid agrees with me."

"Frank also isn't too keen on his dad, despite the fact that Francois has been going through seven hells ever since this whole thing started and this morning bailed his son out of jail," Donovan said.

"What happened?"

"Well, you'd think that when your dad hocks everything

he owns to get you out of jail, the least you could do is plan to go over and thank him," Donovan said.

"In most families the thanks would involve donating a pound of flesh," Mosko said.

"But Frank wasn't planning on doing that. It took coaxing from Tasha to get him to agree."

"This kid sounds like a creep himself. I wonder what she sees in him."

Donovan gave his friend a beats-me sort of glance.

"Give me the bottom line here," Mosko said. "Did these people tell you anything that changes your mind about what happened that night?"

"Not too much. Cohen admitted he was across the water there, beneath the Sumatran willow, all through the event, but says he slept through the murder and didn't see or hear anything. That may be true because I don't see how he could have gotten to the gazebo to kill anyone without Milton or the crows spotting him. And Milton said he left at three."

"Quarter to three," Mosko corrected.

"Close enough. Now, Cohen did tell me he had never been to the gazebo at all, and I'm pretty sure he was lying. I'll know for sure in the morning."

"Why would he lie about that?" Mosko asked. "What's wrong with saying, 'sure, I was there a year ago?' "

"Don't know. As for the kids, they pretty much repeated the tale she told me back at her apartment. They went to the gazebo, fooled around for an hour, and went home."

"Okay," Mosko said.

"Once there, they made love and fell asleep. The boy got up at five and went home, despite the fact that Cohen makes a mean stack of pancakes."

"I love you limousine liberals," Mosko said.

"I don't have a limousine," Donovan replied.

"Cohen lets the kid's lover spend the night and then offers to make breakfast."

"Better that than they do it in the park," Donovan said. "Where did *you* do it when you were a kid?"

"Not in the *park*, that's for sure," Mosko said.

"Where?"

"Canarsie Pier."

"Oh, pardon me," Donovan said.

"It's safer and privater," Mosko said.

"Sex in the back of a Chevy was never safe and seldom private," Donovan said.

"How would you know? You grew up in Manhattan and didn't have a car until you grew up."

"I heard rumors," Donovan said.

"Where did *you* do it?" Mosko asked again.

"I'm your boss and don't have to say."

Without letting go of a french fry, Mosko elevated his middle finger in the direction of his boss. Then he said, "Basically, what you're telling me is that you coaxed three of our suspects to the park this evening and didn't get anything really new out of them."

"Not true," Donovan said. "I learned that Cohen is hiding something and that Frank had a motive for killing Cozzens. I also found out he hates his dad still. Oh, and that the Cohens never maintained that knife and only kept Three-In-One Oil in the house. I forgot to tell you that."

"Do you believe them?" Mosko asked.

Donovan said that he did. "To lie effectively on that question they'd have to know what answer would be best for them, and they couldn't have. One person would have a fifty-fifty chance of being right. So when three people answer the same way you tend to believe them."

"Did you learn anything about how the knife got to where it is today?" Mosko asked.

Donovan nodded. "Cohen gave it to his daughter to use in protecting herself during those nights in the park. Frank and her were watching the King Blades one night. She had the knife in her purse, which she left on a bench so she could go pee. Frank was supposed to be watching it, but *he* had to pee, too. When they got back, the purse *and* the King Blades were gone."

"And you believed them?" Mosko asked.

"It's not out of the question," Donovan replied. "At least it was something sort of new."

"If they didn't have anything new to tell you," Mosko said, "why'd they talk their lawyer into letting them meet you in the park?"

"Yeah, interesting question, isn't it?" Donovan said.

"What do you think?"

"I think they wanted to tell me something."

"What?" Mosko asked.

"There was some information they wanted to impart. But what is it?"

"To convince you of their innocence," Mosko said.

"That's one possibility."

"Did they succeed?"

"Nope," Donovan said.

"Will they let us search their apartments?"

"Nope."

"I didn't think so."

"They're not being *that* cooperative," Donovan said.

"They just want you to *think* they're being cooperative," Mosko replied. "But we can't search their places and we can't talk to the wives."

"Only to the dads," Donovan said. "Tell me about Rico Severino."

Mosko crumpled up his burger wrapper and deposited it in the bag. Then he opened his laptop and switched the machine on. "I thought you'd never ask," Mosko said. As he found the file he wanted and scrolled down it, Donovan saw in his associate a growing excitement that must have been seen in those unwrapping the Dead Sea Scrolls.

Mosko found the page he wanted and said, proudly, "The boys really rang Severino's chimes last night."

"Tell me about it," Donovan said.

"Frazier and Rosenblatt and half a dozen others caught up with the King Blades near the pool, which seems to be the pad from which they put on their skates and launch their nightly raids on the law-abiding users of Central Park," Mosko said.

"Without the commentary," Donovan said.

"Hey! What would life be like without a little Tabasco? So anyway, we separated them and took down their individual accounts and compared them. Generally speaking, they agree with what Patrolman Rodriguez told you this morning."

"Including the timeline?" Donovan asked.

"Yeah, including that. They got chased away from this here frog pond by Rodriguez around quarter after twelve. They were pissed about that but, hey, not pissed off enough to take on a cop. And they seemed afraid of Rodriguez anyway."

"That's good."

"I guess it can't hurt," Mosko said. "A couple of them said something about him being 'scary.'"

"Remind you of anyone?" Donovan asked.

Mosko shook his head. "Anyway, they went over to the fountain and then to the bandshell, where they stayed until three in the morning. Then they drifted south to the skating rink, where they disbanded about five in the morning and went home."

"Which fits what Rodriguez said." Donovan replied.

"But," Mosko added, "they can't account for their activities after two-fifteen or two-thirty. We're relying on their word that they didn't double back to the region of the gazebo. However . . ."

"They all had the same story," Donovan said.

"Yeah. Which makes it unlikely that they're lying. Unless they rehearsed it."

"Did you ever get that many people to rehearse anything?" Donovan said. "I mean, we're not talking about the chorus line at Radio City Music Hall here. These are street kids."

"Who say that Severino was with them the whole time and they never went back to the pond," Mosko said. "Which makes it look like he can't have killed Cozzens. However . . ."

"What's *this* however about?" Donovan asked.

"Maybe we *are* dealing with the chorus line at Radio City Music Hall." Proudly, Mosko added, "When we executed the search warrant on Severino's apartment today, guess what we found?"

Donovan shrugged.

"A pair of sneakers from Sole Warehouse," Mosko said.

"It's a big chain," Donovan argued.

"Yeah, with a store two blocks from Severino's apartment."

"Really?"

"You bet. And get this . . . you couldn't tell it when he's wearing those inline skates, but Severino has small feet for such a tall guy. He's a size nine."

"Severino? What is he, six-one?"

"He only looks that tall in the skates. Without them, he's five-eleven. And he's got little girl's feet. Well, comparatively."

"Were the sneakers you found in his apartment a match

for the print at the murder scene?" Donovan asked.

"No, but they were the same model," Mosko said. "Same model and same size."

Donovan frowned. "I don't know about this," he said. "I also buy shoes at a chain—Payless. These chains have every style of shoe and they have two types of every style—two loafers, one penny and one with the little tassels, and so on—and sell gazillions of them. I'll bet that store in Severino's neighborhood sells a hundred pair a week of those sneakers."

"A hundred twenty-five," Mosko said. "We asked."

Donovan said, "I appreciate all you're doing in trying to nail this kid, and I'll repeat what I told Patrolman Rodriguez this morning—eventually some cop will get him for something. But I just don't know why Severino, or any of the King Blades, would want to kill Harvey Cozzens."

"To get even with her for rejecting him," Mosko said. "The guy is an asshole, and a proud one with a temper, and I can tell you from experience . . . *bitter* experience, you would say . . ."

"A lifetime spent in Brooklyn," Donovan added.

"That there's nothing as dangerous as an asshole with a temper," Mosko concluded.

"Nonetheless, you forced him to back down the other night, and he gave up without a fight."

"So he's got a few braincells. Look, here's what happened the night of the murder. Rodriguez ran Severino and his gang off. That pissed him off and reminded him of the slight he got from Natasha Cohen. He wanted to strike out at someone. Rodriguez is a cop. He didn't know that we're cops too, but wrote us off as being too scary."

"*You* were scary," Donovan said. "All I did was sit there and hand out beer."

"Whatever," Mosko said. "Severino couldn't get even

with Rodriguez, so he got even with the girl. He killed a man using the knife he stole last month along with her purse."

"And got a dozen street kids to swear they were with him all night?" Donovan asked.

"Yeah, just like that. They're afraid of him."

"I don't know," Donovan said.

"Stop fighting me on this," Mosko said.

"Come up with something we can take to the DA," Donovan said, sipping his bottle of Kaliber and then picking up a pebble and tossing it into the water. "Like, did Frazer and Rosenblatt ask Severino about the knife?"

"Sure. He denied it. What did you think he would say?"

"I was wondering," Donovan said.

"How could he admit having the knife without at least admitting that he stole the girl's purse?" Mosko asked.

Donovan said, "I just want you to get something solid on the guy."

"I got it right here," Mosko said, plunging a hand into his leather bag and removing an evidence bag. Inside it was a small tube that bore the image of an inline skate. He handed the bag to the captain.

Donovan peered at it in the slight blue light, then shone his Mag Lite on the object so as to better read the label. "What's this supposed to be?" he asked.

"It's called 'Sensory Loob,'" Mosko said. "It's high-performance racing oil formulated specifically for inline skates. Something about the ball bearings."

"Where'd you find this?" Donovan asked.

"On Severino. He kept it on him, in his fanny pack. Which must be the same place he kept the knife after he stole it from Natasha."

"Why do you say that?"

"Because," Mosko said, drawing the words out for as

much dramatic effect as he could, "this oil matches the oil Bonaci found on the murder weapon."

Donovan looked at Mosko. "A match? An exact match. You're sure?"

"Absolutely positive. It's the same stuff. A highly unusual oil designed for high-performance applications. Like inline skates."

"And sold nowhere else?" Donovan asked.

"Not that we can find," Mosko said.

"What about the oil used in Traks's rat repellent?" Donovan asked. "Did you get that tested today like I asked?"

"I did and it doesn't."

"Does it match the oil on the murder weapon?"

"Nope. In fact, the oil in the rat repellent is more like the oil used in that Keri Oil that Natasha uses, but not exactly. *Not* the stuff on the murder weapon."

"So Traks is off the hook. Well, partly off the hook. I'll be damned."

"And you liked him as a suspect," Mosko said.

"I liked them all," Donovan replied.

"But him in particular, because he has the reputation for being mean, and he plays with rats."

"Did you get his tapes dubbed?" Donovan asked.

"Yep. I had the copies brought to your apartment. Marcy wasn't in, so I had them left with the doorman. You want to tell me what you're looking for?"

"I want to talk to the rats," Donovan said.

"Come again?"

"I think the rats are going to tell me something."

"You talk to the crows. You talk to the rats. You're a regular fucking Dr. Doolittle, aren't you."

"That's me," Donovan said.

"Wasn't there something in your past about pigeons? And a big, nasty turtle?"

Donovan shrugged. "I like turtles," he said.

"Severino is the killer," Mosko said.

"*Someone* who skates could be," Donovan said.

"You mean one of the other members of the King Blades," Mosko said.

"No, I meant that Frank Lauriat could have done it," Donovan said.

"He skates?"

"Skated. I just found out tonight. When her purse was stolen with the knife in it, she was trying to convince him how dangerous inline skating can be."

"Marcy skates," Mosko said.

"Marcy can do anything," Donovan said.

"The Lauriat kid can't have killed Cozzens," Mosko said. "The girl took him home with her before the killing and then kept him there afterward."

"And so she did," Donovan said. "And *that*, I think, is what the Cohen clan came here tonight to tell me."

"They came here to give him an alibi," Mosko said.

"And if you believe what any of them say, it's a good one."

"I think they're *all* lying, the three of them," Mosko said.

"The girl might not be," Donovan replied.

"I think she's the biggest liar."

"Did you know that the history of Ishimani rituals includes human sacrifice?" Donovan asked, grabbing a french fry from his colleague and biting it in half.

Mosko gave him one of those looks, then silently shook his head.

"To complete the ritual, you needed a tribal elder . . ."

"An *eminence grise*," Mosko said.

Donovan nodded. "And you needed at least two young people . . ."

"But not necessarily virgins, I guess."

"The Web site I got this off of wasn't that specific," Donovan replied. "And you needed a ceremonial dagger."

"What was the purpose of this ritual?" Mosko asked. "To restore the tribe's growling, feral power?"

"How did you know?" Donovan asked.

"Your friend, Milton, alibis Cohen up until three in the morning."

"I love Milton, and have known him since I was a kid, going back to the time when homeless people were not homeless but hoboes who Bob Dylan wrote songs about, but the man ain't infallible."

"He can tell time by the moon," Mosko said.

"Sometimes he nods off," Donovan said.

As dawn was threatening to break, it was clear that the day before the big Earth Day celebration was to bring one of those glorious El Niño climate surprises that New Yorkers, like many other residents of the continental forty-eight, had come to be acquainted with. For a front had come through shortly after Mosko left and Donovan fell asleep, and following it the cool evening prepared for warm day. All the woods seemed to come alive, even before the crows normally awoke. There was something in the air, an electric something, and the crackling of small twigs being crinkled beneath padded feet that crept stealthily along, purposefully, making as little noise as possible.

Donovan was a light sleeper and very attuned to shifts in the environment. At home, he customarily awoke five minutes before the baby did for his bottle. And while he set the clock radio every night, he always awoke before it clicked on with *Morning Edition*. And thus when he felt the atmosphere around him tighten up and heard the crinkling of the twigs he opened his eyes just as a big, black, and wet nose brushed his cheek.

285

A puff of foul breath, and Donovan jerked his head away and grasped the Cyrcad beneath his coat and in that instant came the high, piercing cries of a crow and then the cries of a hundred crows. Leaves and twigs flew, kicked into the captain's face as the animal turned tail and fled. He caught a fleeting glimpse of gray fur mixed with white disappearing into the spring foliage amidst the horrible racket from above. The beating of many, many wings, and once again silence fell on the bank of Fiddler's Pond.

Pointing his Cyrcad into the bushes and finding nothing but leaves, Donovan sat up. Far above him the old crow looked down from a dead top branch. "You weren't much help," he said as the bird gave a final, nearly rejoicing caw and flapped off, its wings beating the air laboriously as crows do when taking flight.

Donovan stood and looked around. Whatever it was that woke him was gone. He put the gun back in its holster and went into the bushes to urinate. Then he returned to his makeshift camp and sat back down. He gazed out at Fiddler's Pond, trying again to see the Sumatran willow that grew just the other side of the glassy surface. Again, the view of it was hidden by the drooping branches of the American willow. And, rising from the water a handful of yards from shore, hidden from the view of anyone but those at the gazebo, was the forked log he had read about in Cohen's poem. Atop it, all but its rear feet out of the water, was an eastern painted turtle.

"I love turtles," Donovan said out loud.

He lay back down and closed his eyes and half an hour passed. The sun came up and traffic noises, although far-off ones, arrived to replace the sounds of dawn. Then there was another noise, wheels on forest trail, and he heard a familiar and loving voice saying, "Honey? Honey?"

"Over here," he replied, sitting up and adjusting his clothes so that he looked less homeless.

Donovan had intended to stay on the ground, but when Marcy and the baby carriage she was pushing burst into the clearing, he scrambled to his feet and ran over and wrapped her in his arms.

"Hi, honey," she said.

"Good morning," he said, hugging and kissing his wife before picking up the baby and planting a kiss on his cheek. "Hi, Daniel," he added.

She took the baby from him and put him back in the carriage, saying, "Your disguise works. You look like a bum. You can hold the baby after you clean up."

"I've been sleeping," Donovan replied.

"It's time to come home to your wife and child. Enough of this already."

"My work here is done," he said grandly.

"Good," she replied. "Did you see any wolves?"

"Only one, about an hour ago."

"You didn't see a wolf."

"It was gray and white. It might have been a German shepherd. Do they come in gray and white?"

"Do I look like an expert on German shepherds?" she asked. "Do I look like an expert on German *anything*?"

"It came up and pressed its nose against my cheek while I was sleeping," Donovan continued.

"I think that wolves are more aggressive," Marcy said.

"I didn't have to shoot it. It ran off."

Marcy kissed her husband on the cheek and said, "My man sleeps in a murder scene and fights off a wolf single-handedly in the middle of the night."

"I'm ready to sleep in my own bed," Donovan said.

"About time. It's Saturday. The weekend. You don't have to work today."

"Tomorrow is Earth Day," he said. "I have to work then. We discussed this. You're coming with me."

"I don't want to be apart from you," she replied, kissing him on the cheek and hugging him for a while.

"Lewis will be there," Donovan said.

"I like Lewis."

"And the Cohen clan."

"Are they the guilty ones? So tell me, did you figure out who killed Harvey Cozzens?"

"Not yet. I have some ideas and I got a few insights last night."

"Such as?"

"See that turtle?" he asked, pointing at the creature.

"Charming," she replied. "You're not bringing it home with you."

"Who says I want to?"

"I'm not going through another turtle episode. I remember the one in the bathtub ten years ago."

"It was fifteen years," Donovan said.

"It feels like yesterday," she replied. "No more turtles. What was your insight?"

"To wonder why a man would swear he never set foot in a spot and then go on the Internet with a poem that describes a scene you can only see from that spot," Donovan said.

Marcy looked at the turtle again, and at the tree branches that shielded view of it from the rest of the park. "Cohen," she said. "That poem you read to me off the girl's Web site. About the turtle and the forked log. That log?"

"That log," Donovan replied.

"Cohen told you he never came here and he lied."

Donovan nodded.

"Why?" she asked.

"Don't know."

"Okay, what was the other insight you got last night?" Marcy asked.

"That Nevermore and his flock . . . sorry, his *murder*, of crows aren't infallible sentries."

"Explain."

"That wolf crept up on me and the goddam birds overhead didn't utter a squawk until I startled the beast," Donovan said.

"That wasn't a wolf you saw last night," Marcy said. "It was a German shepherd."

"The point is that it's possible to creep up on someone in this spot even with the birds overhead," Donovan said.

The baby stirred in his carriage, and Donovan bent over and tucked the covers in around him.

"Who killed Harvey Cozzens?" Marcy asked again.

Donovan shrugged. "Probably not Lewis," he said.

"Good. What about Natasha and her boyfriend?"

"It's possible. They're good suspects. I have to agree with Pilcrow on that."

"I never thought I'd hear you utter those words," Marcy said.

"You'll never hear them again," Donovan said.

"What about Cohen?"

"He's a possible. He could have snuck over here after the kids left and done it. To protect his daughter."

"Severino?"

"Maybe. Twelve alibi witnesses notwithstanding."

"Traks?"

"A definite possibility," Donovan said. "After I talk to the rats I'll tell you."

Marcy said, "Rats, turtles, wolves. I think you've had enough nature for a guy who grew up in the city. Let's go home."

He bobbed his head up and down, then began to scoop

up his possessions and tuck them into his Bean bag. The motion startled the turtle, who tumbled back into the water of Fiddler's Pond. The ripples spread concentrically outward and soon disappeared far from shore.

"I'm hungry," he announced.

"I'll make breakfast," she said, turning the baby carriage around and pushing it toward the trail that led away from the gazebo.

"A man sleeps in the wood all night and he wants a man's breakfast," Donovan said.

"Pancakes. A whole stack of pancakes."

"Good."

"With butter and real maple syrup," she replied.

"And bacon."

Marcy grabbed his hand and squeezed it. "Today you get whatever you want."

"Let's go home," Donovan said with a yawn.

14. SUNDAY IN THE PARK WITH DONOVAN

The crowds came in from all over the New York area, to partake of the Earth Day celebration in the City of New York. Having left their cars, trains, and buses, celebrants came on foot to Central Park, across Fifth Avenue and Central Park West and South, past the bandshell and the fountain, through Strawberry Fields and around the lake and Fiddler's Pond and around all the other places famous and forgotten, to gather on the Great Lawn that spring Sunday. Because only a few hundred thousand could squeeze onto the Great Lawn at once, the crowd spilled over into Sheep Meadow and the other open areas of Central Park, where huge TV projection screens were set up to allow the entire million to share in the day's festivities. Whatever happened on the three stages set up at the east side of the Great Lawn would be shown on those immense screens as well as beamed by satellite around the world. As for the stages, one was going at all times; on the other two, stagehands were either setting up or taking down equipment belonging to the various bands, theater companies, dance troupes, and performance artists.

Said Donovan upon spotting the latter, "I'm sure that Natasha Cohen would be up there, wiggling around in her T-shirt and panties, were she not under indictment for murder."

He got no argument from Marcy, who hadn't mellowed from her original position that there was "something wrong" with the young woman.

The two of them, Donovan and Marcy, entered the park through Strawberry Fields shortly after noon, he in jeans and a polo shirt, she in a matching polo shirt but cutoff jeans and her inline skates, which made her appear several inches taller than him. They drifted along with the crowd, heading north up Park Drive West, which for the occasion was fully given over to the crowd. No jogger or skater could go in the opposite direction; that would be like swimming upstream in the Rockies.

When they got to the Great Lawn, Donovan and Marcy found themselves on a wide corridor that bisected the crowd and led straight up to the central stage. Along it were booths, tables, and like spaces at which various persons sold wares. Taking an hour or more to stroll along it, the couple passed astrologers, soothsayers, gurus, Christians early and reborn, mystics, Earth-asteroid–collision doomsayers, druids, witches and warlocks, Jews for Jesus, Hare Krishnas, death cultists, crystal and pyramid merchants, organic food growers, survivalists, Greenpeace, those dedicated to saving dolphins and baby seals, and recording companies hawking CDs that captured the sound of waves lapping against the shore of New Patagonia.

"I thought today would mean more," Donovan said.

"You mean, more than another excuse to sell T-shirts," Marcy said as a full-bearded man walked by carrying an armful of them. "I guess I've grown jaded." She smiled, and added, "I'm getting old."

"You're getting better," Donovan said, kissing her on the cheek (and having to rock forward onto his tiptoes to do it).

Then a familiar voice said, "I can't take any more of this."

They looked over to see Moskowitz, muscles bulging beneath a T-shirt that read BROOKLYN—CENTER OF THE FUCKIN' UNIVERSE. He had come out from behind the blue police sawhorse barricade that surrounded the backstage area.

"If it isn't Benny the Bodybuilder," Marcy said.

"I heard that you guys used to fight all the time," he said.

"Some of the time," Donovan corrected.

"Could I see one of those times?" Mosko asked. "This lovey-dovey shit is wearing me down."

"Sorry, no can do," Donovan said.

"Couldn't she throw a plate at you or something? I used to hear about flying plates."

"A figure of speech," Marcy said.

"Oh well, I guess it's best if we all have good feelings about today," Mosko said.

"There's a lot of it in the air," Donovan said, regarding the balmy skies and puffy white clouds that drifted languidly over the skyline.

"There's a lot of pot in the air today," Mosko said, sniffing it. "Too bad Timothy Leary is missing this."

"Who says he *is*?" Donovan replied.

Marcy scuffed one skate against the ground and leaned on her husband's shoulder, taking advantage of the artificial height to play with the hair on the top of his head.

"Do you *enjoy* being on those things?" Mosko asked her, pointing at her skates.

"I like being able to look down on your bald spot," she replied.

He made a harrumphing noise. "Where's the kid?" he asked.

"The *baby* is home with his nanny," Marcy said. "I'm not subjecting him to this circus."

"Why are *you* here?"

"To be with my husband, of course. To spend a beautiful Sunday in the park."

"To chase down Rico Severino if need be," Donovan said.

"You're retired," Mosko told her.

"But not yet dead," she replied.

Donovan nodded over in the direction of the NYPD command van, a huge blue and white motor home that was parked behind and to the right of the southernmost of the three stages. While a klezmer band disassembled and stored its equipment on the boards above, a parade of uniformed policemen, augmented by casually dressed men who were unmistakably detectives, moved in and out, drinking coffee behind the barricades and slipping around and under it to disappear into the crowd.

The three of them moved out of the corridor and around the front of that third stage and then slipped through the barricades and into an enclosed area between the stage supports and the mobile police HQ in which everyone they encountered was, in one way or another, in law enforcement. Further back from the stage, the blue sawhorses curved along the edge of a paved access walkway turned, that day, into a roadway for police and other official vehicles as well as a conduit for celebrants. Several handheld radios suddenly came alive with crackled orders and three patrol cars suddenly disappeared from their parking spots along the edge of that road, and Donovan could see that they had only been there as placekeepers for the limousines that moved, grandly and with much self-importance, out of the wooded area to the east and up to the cusp of the celebration.

"Here comes the brass," Mosko said.

Donovan checked his watch. "The mayor's speech is half an hour from now. He's early."

"He must have come early to score some grass," Marcy said.

"*That* is something I would pay good money to see," Donovan replied.

"Your friend, the mayor of the City of New York, soon to be a candidate for the Republican nomination for President, sitting cross-legged on a blanket at Strawberry Fields blowing a little weed," Mosko added. "We could charge admission."

"Unfortunately, he's only here to give a speech and get the publicity," Donovan said.

There were two limos, moving slowly, with the crowds, as if they were manatees swimming among schools of herring. The first one pulled way up and stopped and out popped Deputy Chief Inspector Pilcrow, looking starched, as usual, and eager as a beaver in a lumberyard. He scurried to the back of his limo to wave the mayor's vehicle into place, then rushed to open the back door as other officers pulled back the barricades to make way.

Donovan started forward, but Marcy's hand on his arm restrained him—for a moment.

"Give the poor man a break," she said.

"Give who a break? Pilcrow or the mayor?"

"All of them," she replied, as the mayor stepped into the

sunlight followed closely by the red-robed Roman Catholic Cardinal of the Archdiocese of New York.

"I know my calling," Donovan said, slipping away from her grasp and striding up to the officials. Seeing him coming, Pilcrow took the mayor by the arm and tried to hurry him and his companion in another direction, more toward the stage but really just *anywhere* but near Donovan. If the mayor hadn't discerned the fact, Pilcrow had become painfully aware that standing too close to the city's most famous detective could be hazardous.

But the city's chief executive spotted Donovan despite Pilcrow's best efforts and took two steps in the direction of the captain, saying, "Bill . . . I was hoping you'd be here. With your wife?"

Unable to avoid it, Marcy skated over and smiled prettily, trying to slouch down so as not to seem a full foot taller than the diminutive mayor. They shook hands, and he said, "Great to see you again. How are you. How's the baby?"

"Good, the baby is good."

"And your folks?"

"The same."

"Tell your father I read his opinion in *State of New York v. Philip Morris* and thought it was absolutely brilliant. A first-rate piece of work."

"Thank you. I'll tell him."

Smiling benevolently, the cardinal said, simply, "Mr. and Mrs. Donovan."

"How are you, Your Eminence?" Donovan asked.

"Very well, thank you," the cardinal replied.

The mayor smiled and patted Donovan on the arm and said, "I hear that you had a body delivered to you the other day. Never let it be said that we don't try to make things easier for our detectives."

Donovan smiled. "Thanks," he replied.

"How is that case going? Does the case against the Cohen girl and her boyfriend look solid?"

"Of course it does, your honor," Pilcrow said then. "I'm sure that Captain Donovan agrees with me."

"Yes indeed," Donovan replied, making eye contact with the mayor and exchanging impish smiles.

"Well, we must be going," the mayor said, allowing Pilcrow to pull him back in the direction of the stage. "His Eminence and I have to deliver our remarks."

"See you around," Donovan replied, giving a little wave as the trio walked off, Pilcrow delivering an evil-eye glance over one shoulder.

When they were gone, Mosko walked up and said, "I hate to keep sounding like the William Bendix character in old war movies, but *man*, I can't stand brass."

"The time will come when you will have to," Donovan replied.

"I hope I never get promoted that high," said Mosko.

"Keep wearing that T-shirt to meetings with brass and your wish will come true," Marcy said.

15. WWW.MURDERINGTEENAGESLUT.COM

Have there been any sightings of the Cohens?" Donovan asked, cupping a hand over his eyes and scanning the backstage area and the pedestrian-clogged road running by it, looking like the ancient mariner sweeping the horizon.

"Not yet, boss," Mosko replied, glancing at his watch. "But it's early, twenty to two. And I don't think they're clock-watchers."

"Except when it comes to timing their alibis," Donovan said.

"Yeah, suddenly seconds count. Well, they ain't here, but your pal Lauriat is."

"Where is he?"

"In the van. He's afraid to come out in the open."

"The poor guy," Marcy said. "You scared the wits out of him."

"I did? *I* did? The man's work was interrupted by a body and a group of outlaw skaters jumped him. Where are the King Blades, since we're on the topic?"

"The last I heard, they were set up on Park Drive East near the Metropolitan Museum doing skating displays and collecting coins from the tourists," Mosko said.

"Is Patrolman Rodriguez keeping an eye on them?"

"Yeah, just like you asked. And to make sure he doesn't fuck up, I assigned Frazier and Rosenblatt to keep an eye on the whole bunch of 'em."

"I want to make sure he's okay," Donovan said.

"So you dispatched him to deliver the message to Severino that Natasha Cohen wants to see him about something. This afternoon. Here." Mosko kicked the ground to accent his point.

"That's what I did. What about Traks?"

"He's coming. He didn't want to, but since a million people tramping around have thrown his rats off their feed, so to speak, he didn't see what he had to lose. And he says he wants to make up with Lauriat."

"I'll bet he does," Donovan said. "Wants to make up a letter bomb."

"Your pal Shea says he's gonna set up the table the way you want it," Mosko said.

"I knew I could count on him."

"He said he'd rather be fishing, but . . ."

"The man fishes for pop-tops," Donovan said. "He can catch just as many here."

Mosko led the way around to the far side of the mobile van, through a fenced-off region where several patrol cars were parked, to an area where the barricades included a triangle of small trees and an oak picnic table near a public drinking fountain. The fountain was on the other side of the barricades, so passersby stopped there every minute or so to slake their thirst on their way to the celebration. A patrolman stood guard by the barricades, watching an entry point that fell between the drinking fountain and the parked cars. Next to the picnic table, a hundred-gallon blue and white Igloo cooler stood up against the base of a Weber charcoal grill.

"I love New York," Donovan said, planting himself at one end of the picnic table bench and holding his wife's hand while she sat next to him and rested her skate-clad feet atop the cooler. "Only here could you have a barbecue in this rustic setting . . ."

"Surrounded by a million wackos," Mosko said.

"And get free beer, too. What kind did you get?"

"Shea got O'Doul's Amber. Your other brand. No real stuff behind police lines . . . at least not with Pilcrow around."

"Does he know about this?" Donovan asked, looking warily at the back of the stages, a few hundred feet away, and the bustle of activity thereby.

"Nah. He's too busy keeping the mayor away from you."

"I'm hungry," Marcy said.

Donovan beamed. "In honor of Earth Day, I thought we'd eat healthy today."

"I'm proud of you, honey."

"So I had Frank stock up on franks and burgers . . . Ball Park, not turkey or Hebrew National franks, and chopped chuck with enough fat in it so I can hear it crackle when it sits on the grill."

Marcy frowned, but said, "I love you anyway."

"Hey, you got your restaurant and I got mine," Donovan

continued. "You got Marcy's Home Cooking and I got Donovan's American Picnic here, a little celebration of salt and saturated fat."

"What else did you get?" Mosko asked.

"Potato salad. Corn on the cob."

"I don't suppose that salad crept its way in there," Marcy said.

Donovan stared at her until she said, "No, of course not. No salad. Stupid of me."

"Apple pie with vanilla ice cream and coffee with caffeine in it and cream and sugar," Donovan said.

"I feel like I'm sitting in a field in Iowa," Marcy said.

"*Exactly* the intention of the designers of Central Park," Donovan said.

"Let's enjoy ourselves, babe," Mosko said, squatting beside the cooler and lifting her feet up and off the top of it. "Have a beer."

"Here we go," a voice said then, the voice belonging to Shea, who came from between two police cars bearing a platter of food. The platter bounced against Shea's mammoth belly, which was covered by a ragged old and lovingly food-stained apron lettered CHEF DADDY. He put the platter on the picnic table, removed a plate from it, and advanced on the grill.

"You're a good man," Donovan said.

"As for your other guests, the latest word is that the Cohens are on their way and should be here in a few minutes."

"We're following them, of course," Donovan said.

"You bet. And the rat guy is on the concourse . . . that's the main corridor with all the goodies for sale, the one you came up. He's checking out a display of compact disks."

"The waves in New Patagonia?" Donovan asked.

"Don't know," Shea replied. "Brian, you want to take

over running this surveillance so I can do what God put me on the planet to do . . . cook and eat?"

"You got it," Mosko said, taking the cell phone the man produced from the pocket of his apron and walking a little away from the picnic.

"What about Lauriat?" Donovan asked.

"He refuses to come out until you get here," Shea replied, flipping a burger patty onto the grill. It made a satisfying crackling sound as the fat burned off.

Donovan said, "I'm here."

Shea called out, "Brian, get the doc." And Mosko spoke into the cell phone and a minute later Lauriat's face appeared at the door of the police van, looking around like a prairie dog pondering a stroll away from the burrow.

Donovan smiled and waved at him; it was the sort of smile and wave one gives to a frightened child. "Francois, come out and play," Donovan yelled.

"Is it all right?" the man called back, looking from side to side, from the back of the stage to the tree line.

"Yeah, I doubt that any of our suspects can shoot worth a damn and you're out of knife range," Donovan said.

Gulping visibly, Lauriat went down the three wooden steps that led from the van to the ground and walked gingerly toward the picnic table. Marcy called out, "You're surrounded by cops. The only one who has to worry is the guy carrying the donuts."

When he arrived, he looked around again and said. "Maybe, but you're sitting away from the rest of them."

Donovan took off his jacket to reveal his holstered Cyrcad. The radio-controlled automatic weapon was much bigger than the captain's old Smith & Wesson revolver, and made him feel like he was carrying an artillery division. Maybe, he thought, the sight of the thing would be a billboard advocating good behavior.

"I guess I'm safe," Lauriat said, relieved.

"Sit down," Donovan said, handing the man a beer.

Lauriat did so, after shaking Donovan's hand and giving Marcy a kiss on the cheek.

The scientist said, "This whole thing has been so upsetting for me."

"I know," Donovan said.

"First that man was killed. Then my son and that girl were arrested. Then I was beaten up. Then you tell me not to see my son, after he finally agrees to talk to me."

"Sons are funny that way," Donovan said.

"Can you explain?"

"Later."

"Did anyone ever catch those men who beat me up?"

"We're working on it," Mosko said, strolling closer with the phone pressed against his ear. "Hi, doc."

"Hello," Lauriat said, in a way that suggested uncertainty as to whether Moskowitz was friend or foe.

"Your colleague is coming round the bend," Mosko said.

"Who?" Lauriat asked, doing the prairie dog thing again until Donovan feared he would twist his head off; the captain rested a comforting hand on Lauriat's shoulder. "Who's coming? Traks? Is *he* coming today, too?"

"I invited the whole kit and caboodle," Donovan said.

"And Frank, my boy? He'll definitely be here?"

"At this very moment, he's at Strawberry Fields saying a mantra for the restless soul of John Lennon. Or maybe just getting a drink at the water fountain. At any rate, he's on his way."

"Yo, Cap. The Cohens have got your pal, their lawyer, with them," Mosko said.

"I had a feeling that would happen. Well, everybody's got a lawyer these days, and considering what the Republicans have been up to in Washington, we all need one."

"You didn't invite the *gang members*, did you?" Lauriat asked, horrified at the thought.

Donovan bobbed his head up and down.

"Oh my God."

"Don't worry, I only invited one of them, Severino."

"He's the one who did it," Lauriat said.

"If he gets out of line I'll shoot him or my colleague here will twist his head off. So while we're waiting, have a dog and settle down," Donovan said. "Frank, one dog for my friend here."

Shea gave the man a hot dog on a paper plate and pointed to a display of condiments on the far end of the table. "Eat," he said.

"Is this low fat?" Lauriat asked.

Marcy laughed.

"Tell me," Donovan said, "How did you raise the money to bail out your son? Did you get an advance on a grant or something?"

"There's no such thing," Lauriat replied, taking a tentative nip out of the end of his frankfurter and then nibbling more. "In fact, I'm behind on the crow research. I may never get to document their use of tools."

"Don't seem to see the buggers around today," Donovan said, cupping a hand over his eyes as he did before and scanning the treetops.

"They don't like it when too many people are around," Lauriat said. "That's why Fiddler's Pond is so attractive to them."

"I noticed how they react to strangers," Donovan said.

"Oh yes, that's true. The night I brought you they were uneasy about your presence. But I calmed them. As I indicated, they're very bright. They trust me. And they learned quickly that you were safe."

"I guess you could get away with just about anything without upsetting them," Donovan said.

"Well, I don't know," Lauriat said.

"You could, for example, creep up on them in the night."

"I don't have to. They know me, and you're aware of that. But to be honest, they won't react to someone who is very good about navigating in the dark. If they're far enough up in the treetops, and you're very quiet, you can slink along without arousing them. But you have to be good at it, very good. A woodsman, you know."

"Natty Bumppo," Donovan said.

"Who?" Mosko asked.

"Hawkeye. *The Last of the Mohicans.* Classic Comics? No, not you."

"I saw the movie," Mosko said.

Donovan asked Lauriat, "Could an expert on nocturnal animals . . ."

"Tarsiers, you're thinking," Lauriat said.

Donovan nodded. "Could such a man creep up to the gazebo without waking the crows?"

"Traks could," Lauriat said. "He's very quiet in the forest, and very cunning." Again the scientist looked around nervously. "Where did you say he was?"

"Buying a compact disk of the waves lapping against the shore in New Patagonia," Mosko replied.

"Oh," Lauriat replied. "Maybe he's put in for a project there."

"Maybe," Donovan replied.

"New Patagonia is pretty far away."

Donovan thought that Lauriat had lapsed into daydreaming of such a possibility. If so, the reverie didn't last long. For Traks came walking up the path, against the flow of foot traffic, slipping readily, catlike, between the flow of humanity and the blue sawhorses. Once again he wore all black, a

303

woolen turtleneck and cheap cotton and polyester slacks. On his feet were sneakers—cheap ones, Donovan could see, but not the brand offered at Sole Emporium. He had a canvas bag, also black, slung over one shoulder.

Traks identified himself to the uniformed policeman guarding the gap, between the sawhorses, that led to the picnic area. That officer glanced over at Shea, who nodded. Traks walked quickly to the picnic table, breaking into a big grin and saying, "Lauriat!"

"Hello, Traks," Lauriat said, raising himself up slightly and sticking out his hand.

"Good to see you. You're looking better. That was terrible that those kids set on you."

"I guess I put myself in harm's way," Lauriat replied.

"But we did nothing like that living in the jungle, eh?" Traks said.

"No," Lauriat replied, with a little huff of a laugh. "We did nothing like that."

"We were rich Americans . . . by local standards . . . living among stone-age Indians and river pirates, sitting in the trees conducting our studies. I guess the locals got a good laugh out of us."

"I imagine that plenty of American dollars trickled down from those tree houses," Donovan said.

"We spent enough at the local supply merchants," Traks agreed. "Like we're spending now, at the delis along Broadway. Lauriat, I found this marvelous place near Ninety-second Street that sells the barley-and-mushroom salad you like so much."

"I know the place," Lauriat replied.

So did Donovan.

Traks continued. "But of course you would. You are a local here, having kept an apartment in the city for many years."

"Have a hot dog," Donovan said.

"Traks is a vegetarian," Lauriat said. "A famous one. Has sworn never to eat meat."

"For nearly two decades now," the man bragged.

"A vegetarian who studies carnivores," Donovan said.

"Nothing will make a veggie out of you faster than seeing one animal rip the head off another," Traks said.

"Listen to the man," Marcy said.

"Have potato salad," Donovan suggested.

Traks agreed to that, and within half a minute Shea produced a paper plate bearing a mound of it. Traks took a plastic forkful, chewed and then swallowed it, and said, "Why are we here? Certainly not to reminisce about our days in the jungle."

"I'm more interested in your nights in Central Park," Donovan said.

"Especially that one earlier this week," Mosko added. "Cap . . . the Cohens will be here in a minute or two."

"We *discussed* the night of the murder," Traks said. "And I still can't help you. I was in my study enclosure the entire time in question. Just me and my rats. I didn't see anything. I don't know anything."

"How are the rats today?" Donovan asked.

"Hiding," the man replied tersely.

"So, apparently, are the crows," Donovan said.

Looking around again, Lauriat said, "They don't like people, generally speaking. But they know that people leave behind a lot of garbage. The crows are someplace nearby, watching. When everyone goes home, they will move in."

Donovan looked at Traks and said, "Your rats have an interesting relationship to people."

"What are you saying?" Traks asked.

"I'm saying that I looked over the raw tapes you were

generous enough to let us copy. Smart of you to time-code them."

"We do that routinely to allow us to go back and see exactly when a particular event happened," Lauriat said.

"Such as when your friend here left his enclosure."

"I didn't leave the enclosure that night, I told you," Traks said.

"Oh no?" Donovan replied. "Well, I can tell you that when you were in your camp the rats kept to their normal routines, scurried in and out of their holes, followed their normal trails, had their usual fights, the things you're getting paid to—what's the two-dollar word for 'explain' that scientists love to use—to *elucidate*. But every morning when you left the enclosure the rats were all over your living area . . . rat repellent or no. And when you came to the gate to let us in, they ran all over your cute little campsite."

"And," Mosko said.

"And on the night of the murder, at one-thirty in the morning on the night of the murder, the rats overran your camp again," Donovan said. "Funny with that camera. You can see them rushing right at it the second you leave. On the night of the murder they kept at it for over two hours . . . abruptly scurrying away at about twenty-five to four."

"That means you lied to us, pal," Mosko said.

"You left your enclosure and were away for two hours at exactly the time that Harvey Cozzens was killed," Donovan said.

Lauriat moved away from Traks on the bench, perhaps unconsciously, Donovan felt, but noticeably. If the other man saw the movement, however, he gave no indication. Instead his previously jovial mood disappeared and he hardened, glaring at the captain with eyes that might have fit on a rat . . . or a tarsier.

Mosko said, "Not only that, Traks, you were away from

your camp every night for the week before at the same time. On all the tapes you gave us, you were away between one-thirty and three-thirty, more or less. And I know what you were doing—casing Fiddler's Pond and getting ready to kill; learning your victim's habits."

"Why would I want to kill a man I didn't know?" Traks said.

"You didn't want to kill Cozzens," Mosko said. "You wanted to kill *him*." With that, he pointed at Lauriat.

"Francois? Me, kill Francois. Why?"

"Revenge for having stolen your wife and fucked up your career," Mosko said.

"Why did you lie to us about that night?" Donovan asked.

Traks looked down at his potato salad, which he had barely touched, and thought for a moment. Then he replied, "I *did* leave the enclosure that night."

"I know," Donovan said.

"And you went to Fiddler's Pond, looking for the man who stole your wife and wrecked your career," Mosko said.

Traks shook his head. "No. I didn't do that. Anyway, I read in the paper that you found the murder weapon. How was I supposed to have gotten *that*?"

"You were the one who stole Natasha Cohen's purse with the knife in it," Mosko continued.

"Why would I do that?"

"To have someone to blame the crime on," Mosko said.

Traks shook his head and said, after a minute, "I did go out that night, like you said. But not to kill anyone."

"Where'd you go?" Donovan asked.

Traks looked around, smiled faintly, and said, "I walked up to Broadway to buy a Demon Burger."

Marcy looked away so her husband couldn't see the smile, but he did anyway.

"You went to Burger Demon," Donovan said flatly.

The man nodded.

"That's a checkable fact," Donovan said.

"Please, check it."

"We will," Mosko said.

"And the reason you went out every night at one thirty," Donovan said, with an involuntary sigh, "is that Burger Demon closes at two."

"How do you know that?" Marcy said, whipping her head around.

"I get paid to know things," Donovan replied.

"Have you been sneaking out to Burger Demon in the middle of the night?" Marcy asked.

"If I had, I would have known where this guy was going on his nightly forays," Donovan said.

"Why would a guy be so ashamed of going out for a fucking burger that he wouldn't tell the cops about it?" Mosko said.

"I never thought you'd catch me," Traks said.

"Your rats ratted you out," Donovan said.

"I've been proud of my reputation for being a vegetarian," Traks said. "Sometimes I think it's all I have left. And, as you know now, it's a sham. But the real reason I didn't tell you about it is because you would then suspect me of murder."

"We would have anyway," Donovan said.

"I have no alibi, as I think you call it, for the time of the murder."

"You don't pay much attention to anything beyond science, do you?" Mosko said.

"What do you mean?" Traks asked.

"The sergeant is saying that the people at Burger Demon are your alibi," Donovan said.

"But surely they won't remember one face," Traks said.

"That came in every night between one-thirty and two in the morning?" Donovan said. "Just before closing."

"Wearing black," Mosko added.

Donovan said, "You always remember the pain in the ass who comes running in just before closing time. Get someone to take this man's picture and show it to the night shift at Burger Demon."

"Will do," Mosko said

Traks looked pleased, Donovan thought. The little man stared down at the lump of potato salad before him and was still staring a minute later when Shea slapped a burger in front of him. "Live it up, guy," Shea said, returning to his grill.

"You're off the hook for the time being," Mosko said. "And you'll be off the hook for good the second that someone from Burger Demon IDs your picture. In the meantime, enjoy the afternoon."

"Here comes the Cohen tribe," Donovan said.

They entered the picnic area the same way as did Traks, between the blue barricades, and were a splendid-looking bunch, too. The Cohens, father and daughter, wore white, he a white business shirt, but tucked into white painter's pants that were closed with a belt made of twisted hemp. His feet were clad in Indian water-buffalo-hide sandals and he carried a PBS tote bag. His daughter's white outfit consisted of tights and a long and oversized tee shirt that carried a single word—YES—on the front. On the back, however, was lettered her Internet address, a new one, Donovan could see:

www.murderingteenageslut.com

On her feet she wore clunky, pure white sneakers.

Frank Lauriat and Boris Irwin were dressed more familiarly, the boy in jeans with a heavy-looking fanny pack and a somewhat garish, vertically striped polo shirt, the lawyer in a blue blazer over an Oxford shirt and gray slacks. As for mood, unlike the ebullient-looking Cohens, the boy and the attorney looked uncomfortable. Young Lauriat consistently shifted his head from side to side, causing Donovan to wonder if there wasn't something genetic about the prairie-dog behavior.

Possibly more nervous than his son, Lauriat fairly leaped to his feet, in so doing knocking both his legs against the side of the picnic table. "Ow," he said, rubbing one knee as he turned and twisted off the bench and rose to embrace his son.

Donovan rose alongside his friend but somewhat more smoothly, and moved with Lauriat, close enough to feel the boy's spine stiffen as his father's arms enclosed him. Donovan noticed that the boy kept his hands folded across his chest, as if to protect his heart from his dad's love. The captain looked at the hands and also at the fanny pack, which had a lump in it that bulged down over one of his back pockets.

Suddenly weeping, Lauriat said, "I'm so glad to see you . . . It's been so long . . . I'm so sorry."

The boy said nothing, but his hands lowered slightly so that they were no longer crossed.

Lauriat continued: "I know you didn't kill that man. You couldn't have. You've always been gentle . . . and poetic, and . . ."

"Thanks for bailing me out," the boy said finally.

Donovan thought, *He spoke! And that's enough for Lauriat.* And indeed it was, for the man stopped weeping and relaxed his grip on the boy and took a half-step backward.

"It was . . . I know it's not much, after the way I hurt you and your mom, but . . ."

"Do you have anything left?" the boy asked.

"Anything? Anything what?"

"Any money left."

Lauriat looked perplexed, grasped for words, and said,

"No . . . not much. But the rent's covered and you'll always have a place to stay if you want it. Is . . . is there something wrong with staying with mom?"

"Mom's dating now," the boy said.

"I heard . . . a lawyer."

"Yeah," the boy replied, the word coming out like a tiny laugh.

"Sure . . . you can come and live with me," Lauriat said, brightening and, Donovan was sure, looking warm inside as a relationship with his son appeared to be coming back. They embraced again, and this time the boy's arms were at his sides, not across his chest, and his hands even flicked up to touch his father's arms as they went around him.

Donovan suddenly leaned forward, said, "Hey, this is great with you two," and clapped both of them on their backs several times, one of the claps landing on the boy's fanny pack.

Said the younger Lauriat, "I don't know if I'll have to come live with you. But I might like to some day."

"A room will always be there for you," Lauriat said.

Then the boy said, "This is my girl." And he drew Natasha into the conversation; she smiled ear to ear and said, "Hi!" in that bright way only teenage girls seem able to do.

Donovan backed away from the knot of people just as Cohen got into it, pumping Lauriat's hand and looking for all the world like a small-town mayor campaigning for re-election. As Donovan returned to the picnic table, Mosko sidled up him and stage-whispered, "Was it a gun?"

"It felt like a rock," Donovan said, shaking his head in reply.

"You can kill someone with a rock," Mosko said.

"Not while you and I are carrying guns," Donovan said, adding, "Where's Severino?"

Tapping the cell phone, Mosko said, "at Eighty-sixth and closing."

"And Lewis is with him?"

"Who do you think I'm talking to?" Mosko replied.

"The two of you are friends now?" Donovan asked.

"The kid is growing on me. He loosened up after talking to you and doesn't seem so angry anymore."

"That's good. Did Lewis say anything about Severino?"

"Just that he ain't coming alone," Mosko reported. "He's got the rest of his merry band of petty thieves with him."

16. "HI, I'M THE MURDERING TEENAGE SLUT"

I'm trying to picture this . . . Lewis is on foot, in uniform, keeping up with a dozen skaters?"

"That's it. But you got to figure, these guys are doing their little pirouettes along the way, figure eights, and they got the three skate molls with them, the Puerto Rican babes in the tight skirts and push-up bras."

"Sounds like a damn gypsy caravan," Donovan said.

"Yeah, and having a uniformed cop walking along behind only adds to the festive nature of the procession," Mosko said. "I'll tell you one thing that Rodriguez related to me . . . his impression that these guys are still solid."

"Meaning?"

"Meaning that they're sticking to their story," Mosko said. "They weren't anywhere near Fiddler's Pond when Cozzens was killed. They speak as one voice, and that voice says that Severino couldn't have done it."

"Hmmm," Donovan replied.

Mosko tilted his head in the direction of Lauriat and the Cohens, who were chatting happily and giving off the impression that nothing had ever gone wrong. Said the sergeant,

"Wasn't your friend calling Natasha a murdering slut the other day?"

"Or words to that effect," Donovan said.

"He got over it," Mosko replied.

"Yeah. He's so glad to be reunited with his son that he's prepared to put up with anything. Dads will do that."

"Put up with being murdered?" Mosko asked.

"Let's try not to let that happen," Donovan said.

"It's going to be rough to burst this guy's bubble."

Donovan nodded, and added, "Let's get this over with before Severino gets here."

Smiling, Mosko went over to the knot of celebrants and, stretching his arms out fully, said, "Come on, folks, let's sit down and enjoy the afternoon. We've got some basic food here, and the captain wants to have a few words with you."

Hearing that, Traks rose and, smiling in a way that Donovan had not imagined, beckoned the others to him, saying, "Sit down and eat. The policeman here wants to accuse you of murder. And when he's done with that, you can have a burger."

Natasha looked at the black-clad man, then smiled, and said, "Cool."

"Hello, Mr. Traks," Frank Junior said, shaking the man's hand.

"Hi, Frank. I haven't seen you since you and your mom left the camp. How are you?"

"Fine."

"So this is your girl."

"Hi, I'm the murdering teenage slut," Natasha said sweetly.

"Natasha," Boris Irwin said sharply, but with the trace of a smile.

"Oh, come on, Uncle Boris. Captain Donovan isn't here

to ensnare me. He's a wise man who understands that Frank and I are innocent."

"Watch your wallet," Traks said, sitting back down.

Donovan ignored this, and Lauriat introduced Traks to Cohen as "the man I worked with in the Amazon."

Cohen perked up. He said, "So you know the Ishimani rituals too?"

"God, no," Traks snorted. "I was there to work, not engage in Stone Age rituals. And work I did . . . until that no longer was possible." As he said that, he looked away from Lauriat and then down at the ground.

Donovan distributed beer to those that would have it and led the small talk that went on until everyone had a plate in front of them and settled down. Then he stood at one end of the picnic table and said, "Mr. Traks here was right . . . to a point. I have a couple of questions."

"My client knows what I feel about that," Irwin said.

"But showed up nonetheless," Donovan replied.

"Against my advice. And I understand they met you the night before last. Also despite my wishes."

"Controlling poets is like herding cats," Donovan said.

"Fortunately, only one of them is *that*," Irwin replied.

"Natasha is an *artist*," Frank retorted, a remark that caused Marcy to look at the girl and then look away so that the scowl went unseen by all but her husband. In that instant, both Marcy and Traks were looking away, but in opposite directions.

"We have decided that we will cast our lot with the captain," Cohen said then. "He may ask us what he wishes. We reserve the right to select what we answer."

"And I hope you'll listen to *something* I say," Irwin added.

Donovan said that was fair. Then he cleared his throat and said, to Cohen, "You lied to me."

The poet looked at him.

"I don't like it when people lie to me," Donovan added. "It switches on my gene for pursuit."

Cohen sighed and said, "This would be about the turtle, wouldn't it?"

"Yep," Donovan replied.

"Turtle?" Lauriat asked.

"Fiddler's Pond has a resident turtle," Donovan explained. "I mean, it could have a couple, for all I know, but I refer to this one that greets the dawn by climbing up onto a forked log that sticks out of the water right near the old gazebo."

"I know the log," Lauriat said. "I have a tape of Nevermore sitting on it, playing with a twig."

"Who's Nevermore?" Traks asked.

"A crow," Donovan said.

"Not just any crow," Lauriat said.

"The boss bird. Likes to keep an eye—*the* eye, since he only has one—on what I'm doing here in the park." Donovan looked around but, apart from a few pigeons swirling around far above the crowd, saw no birds. "I had hoped he would visit us today, but he seems to have better things to do. Anyway, this eastern painted turtle climbs onto the log, making for a pretty picture. That *he* wrote a poem about."

Donovan indicated Cohen.

"Only one problem," Mosko added.

"You can only see this picture if you're standing—sitting, laying down, or crouching in the bushes, for that matter—at the old gazebo. The down-hanging branches from a willow hide the scene from outside eyes."

Cohen jumped in, saying, "The captain asked me if I'd ever been to the old gazebo. I told him no."

"Gotcha," Donovan said.

"He caught me in a lie."

"Why?"

"To prevent you from thinking I was a murderer," Cohen said.

"The thought would have crossed my mind anyway," Donovan said.

"I told you to watch your wallets," Traks chimed in.

"The forked log in the poem symbolizes difficult moral choices," Mosko added.

Donovan thanked him.

"In my case, I had to choose between my natural tendency to protect my daughter and my firm belief that she was entitled to be free of the surveillance that *we have had quite enough of* in today's America," Cohen added, looking around at the many policemen coming and going in the backstage area.

Donovan caught himself tapping his foot impatiently. "When did you go to the old gazebo?" he asked.

"Oh, many times over the years."

"It was daddy's hideout before it was mine," Natasha said.

"So you know all the trails and everything around there," Donovan said.

"If you're asking, could I find it in the dark? No, probably not. My eyes aren't what they used to be, and anyway, I have never been to the gazebo at night. I left that to my daughter and her boyfriend. It's all I can do at night to find the Sumatran willow on the other side of the pond, and I only can find that because the way is paved and well-lit."

"What use would you have been in an emergency, then?" Donovan asked.

"Like I said, if Natasha screamed I would use my cell phone to call the police." Cohen scanned the blue-clad figures wandering around and said, "They *do* have their uses."

"But she didn't scream that night," Donovan said.

"No. And I fell asleep."

"But even asleep you would have heard your daughter scream," Donovan said.

"Oh yes, I assure you that I would have. You're a father. You can hear your baby cry, can't you?"

"From a mile away," Marcy added.

"I'm a light sleeper," Donovan said.

"He's very protective of his son," she concluded. And husband and wife exchanged smiles.

Then Donovan said to Cohen, "You fell asleep at one and woke up at three."

Cohen nodded.

"The wolf woke you up," Donovan said.

"Wolf? It was a dog."

"Gray and white?"

Cohen bobbed his head up and down.

"It was a wolf," Donovan said. "Woke *me* up the other morning."

"Whatever," Cohen replied. "At least we survived the encounter."

"And you went straight home and to bed and didn't see anything except your daughter's closed door. Which you presumed she was behind with her lover."

"I know she was," Cohen said.

"Do you? You didn't see them," Donovan said.

"Well, she told me."

"I was in there and I was with Frank," Natasha said.

"The whole time? From about one-thirty until five?"

She nodded.

"Are you sure?" Donovan asked. "You told me you sleep like a rock."

She said, "I do. But . . . I mean, I fell asleep with Frank next to me, I guess it was somewhere between one-thirty and two, and we woke up together at five."

Donovan said, "If you sleep anything like my wife, Frank could have run out to Burger Demon, eaten a Demon Burger with fries, and gone back to you and slipped back under the covers without you knowing."

Marcy swiveled around and said, "You have been to Burger Demon, haven't you?"

"I swear on his mother's grave," Donovan said, nodding at Moskowitz.

"My mom ain't dead," Mosko replied.

Frank Lauriat shifted warily on the bench.

Traks said, "Do you still have your wallet?"

"While we're on the subject of clothes," Donovan said to the boy, "when we talked under the Sumatran willow, Natasha told me that when you went to the park with Natasha the night of the murder you were wearing jeans."

"She said that?" the boy asked.

"Actually, what she said was that when you went into the bushes to take a leak, she could hear you unzip your jeans."

"Who cares what I was wearing?" the boy said.

"She told me that when she woke up at five in the morning and you were ready to go home, you were wearing sweatpants," Donovan said.

"So what?" he said.

"What happened to the jeans?"

"I took them off," Frank replied.

"When?" Donovan asked.

"When we wanted to make love," the boy said, in a tone of voice that suggested the captain was a fool for asking. Which was, in fact, how he was coming to feel.

"What did you do with them?" Donovan asked.

"Threw them on the floor and then kicked them under the bed."

"Why did you switch to sweatpants?"

"The jeans were kinda dirty," the boy admitted.

"Is that them?" Donovan asked, pointing at the pants the boy was wearing at that moment.

"Those are new jeans I just bought him," Natasha said. "When he couldn't go visit his father yesterday, I took him to Canal Jeans. I said to him, 'you have got to get rid of those filthy things you left at my place.' "

"Where are they?" Donovan asked, increasingly frustrated.

"Which?" she replied.

"The ones he wore to the park the night of the murder," the captain said.

"Oh, those," she said. "I hated those jeans. You know the kind a guy wears until they're falling off?"

"He knows," Marcy said over her shoulder.

"I told him to burn then," Natasha said.

Donovan gave her a look. Not a piercing look, exactly; more of an I-can't-believe-you-said-that look. "Did he?" he asked.

"I threw them *out*," she laughed. "You should have heard him wail."

"When did you throw the jeans out?" Mosko asked.

"Yesterday afternoon," Natasha replied.

"You just put them in the household garbage?"

"Yeah."

"There's no weekend garbage pickup in her neighborhood," Donovan said.

"I'll get some guys over there," Mosko said, walking away and talking into the cell phone.

"Are you going to get my jeans back?" Frank asked.

"Almost certainly," Donovan replied.

"Can I have them back when you're done?"

"I think so. Speaking man-to-man here, a guy works hard for his filthy jeans and is entitled to them."

Marcy made a face at him.

"There are two circumstances under which you can't have them back," Donovan continued. "One is that they now reside, in the form of ashes, in the Fresh Kills Landfill. The other circumstance is if your girlfriend really did chuck them in the garbage and, when we find them, they're covered with Harvey Cozzens's blood."

"I didn't kill that man," Frank protested.

"You're gonna have to convince me," Donovan replied. "And so far, the large serving of insouciance I've been getting from the bunch of you . . ."

At that point, Cohen interrupted with a translation, saying "lighthearted unconcern" to his daughter and her boyfriend, who nodded appreciatively.

". . . only goes so far toward convincing me of your innocence," Donovan concluded.

"I could have told you he wasn't buying it," Irwin said to Cohen.

"Frank can't have gone out of my room after I fell asleep," she continued. "He would have been on camera."

"I thought of that and went back over the records from your Web site for that night," Donovan said. "And remind you that the camera doesn't take in the whole room. He could have slipped out of the room a couple of times in thirty seconds," Donovan said.

"Or gotten down on his knees and crawled along the carpet," Marcy added, turning back to the group at last.

Mosko said, "I think that your boyfriend here could have gotten out of bed, avoided the camera, put on his jeans, stuck his sweats under his arm, returned to the gazebo, killed Cozzens, dragged the body into the pond and thrown the knife there, cleaned himself up . . ."

"A fringe benefit of wading into the pond is being able to wash yourself off," Marcy added.

". . . Burned the bloody clothes, put on the sweats, and went back home to you," Mosko concluded.

"But I didn't know the creep was at the gazebo," the boy protested.

"Maybe you did," Mosko suggested. "Maybe you saw him in the bushes after all and went back to get him."

"Maybe you *both* went back and killed him," Marcy said.

"Why would we want to do that?" the girl asked.

Donovan tossed his hands up. "Pick a reason: because Cozzens was stalking you and you wanted him to stop. Because it was spring and there was nothing better to do. Because you listened to an Ozzie Osbourne record and he told you subliminally to take a life. Because first-degree murder is the ultimate performance art."

"If my daughter wanted to kill someone for art's sake she would do it on the Web," Cohen said.

"That's not really funny," Mosko said, "Because it's only a matter of time before someone really *does* kill someone on the Web."

Donovan continued, asking, "Why do teenagers kill these days? There doesn't have to be a good reason."

"I didn't kill that man," Frank said again.

Bristling somewhat, Mosko said, "Who says you wanted to kill *Harvey Cozzens*? Maybe . . ."

Donovan cut him off with a sharp "no," taking his friend by the arm and leading him away from the group, over by the police barricades, where the suspects couldn't hear them talk.

"Why'd you shut me up?" Mosko asked.

"This isn't the time," Donovan replied.

"The kid's guilty. He got the knife from her purse that time she went into the bushes to pee. He made repeated visits to the gazebo to case the joint and get the old man's schedule down. You know, the nightly walks your pal took, followed by cleaning up the beer bottles? On the night of the murder, the brat left the girl's room the way I said and went back to the gazebo to kill his father. But when he got back to the gazebo that night, expecting to find his father cleaning up the beer bottles, the kid found Harvey Cozzens sitting there . . . wearing a jacket that was hard to tell from the one his dad always wore. He hasn't seen his dad in years, and the girl told us he can't see for shit in the dark. He stabbed the man and then, when he found out he got the wrong guy, flew into a rage and carved him up. Then he dragged the body into the pond, washed up, burned the bloody clothes, and went home to his clueless, poetry-scribbling chicky. Case closed. Prosecution wins. Here comes the camera crew for a post-verdict sound bite: 'Detective Moskowitz, now that you've convicted Frank Lauriat of murder, what are you going to do?' 'Go to fuckin' Disney World, what else?' "

"This isn't the *time*," Donovan said.

"Oh, *man*, when will it be the time?"

"Soon."

Donovan placed a hand on his friend's shoulder blade and urged him back to the picnic table, where he found a bunch of people watching his every move, with silent dread, he was sure.

His voice deep and rich, Shea said, "You must have let the batteries run out on the boom box, Captain, 'cause it suddenly got very quiet around here."

"Can I have a burger?" Donovan asked.

Marcy said, "Darling, you can have anything you want."

Shea handed Donovan a platter, and the captain took it back to the place at the head of the table where he stood the moment before. Of the assembled, only the attorney had the courage to break the silence. He said, clearing his throat, "My understanding is that Mr. Cozzens was killed with a knife that once belonged to my client and her father."

"That's correct," Donovan said.

"And that said knife was stolen from her along with her purse."

"So goes the story."

"How is Frank Lauriat supposed to have acquired that knife?" Irwin asked.

"He was the one who stole it," Mosko said.

"And when was this?"

"When the girl went into the bushes to pee, her boyfriend *did* leave her purse on the park bench to be stolen by the inline skaters. But only after taking the knife out of it and hiding it in his fanny pack," Mosko said.

"And I suppose you'll say that he did this because he planned to kill Mr. Cozzens."

"He planned to kill *somebody*," Mosko replied, earning himself a look of warning from his boss.

Frank seemed confused by the drift the proceedings had taken, and returned to familiar ground. He said, "I wish I had those jeans back. They were the ones I wore to see the Wallflowers last year at Wetlands."

"Isn't that Bob Dylan's kid's band?" Donovan asked.

"Yeah," the boy replied. "Jakob Dylan is awesome. Do you like the Wallflowers?"

"I don't like rock and roll generally," Donovan said. "I mean, I *did*, up until disco came in, and then I gave up. Lately I've been softening, after discovering that my baby boy smiles and bounces around whenever you put on a Beatles record."

"And once again the apartment is full of speakers," Marcy added.

"I have a feeling you're getting the jeans back," Donovan said to Frank Lauriat, after looking over toward the gap in the barricades and spotting Rico Severino being ushered through the barrier by Lewis Rodriguez. The other members of the King Blades looked angry at being excluded, but Severino waved for them to settle down and they did so, setting up an obstacle course made of sixteen-ounce drink cups turned upside down and beginning to do skating tricks in exchange for money from the steady stream of passersby.

Hobbling across the grass as he did when approaching Donovan and Mosko as they sat beneath the gingko biloba, Severino's look of anger turned swiftly to astonishment and *then* anger, fury almost, upon spotting the two detectives.

"You two . . . you're *cops*? I don't fucking believe it!"

"Believe it, pal," Mosko said.

"You . . . with the muscles . . . you threatened me that night."

"Do you have a lot of brain cells?" Mosko asked the man.

"Yeah," he said defiantly.

"Well, you take good care of them corpsuckles, because you're gonna need them before the day is through."

It wasn't clear to Donovan that Severino was still listening, for the man had noticed Natasha Cohen and Francois Lauriat and appeared to be straining his corpsuckles in an attempt to figure out what was going on.

"Hi, Rico," the girl said, but not in a friendly way.

"Hey," he replied. "I heard you want to see me."

"Who's your friend?" she asked, looking beyond the skater to Lewis Rodriguez, who never looked better, having polished shoes *and* buttons, and even seemed a bit taller that day; a new pair of shoes perhaps. Rodriguez stepped around Severino, who was not in custody, after all, but rather had been conned into attending.

"Hello, Lewis," she said, her voice softer and calmer, in another register entirely, the poetic one, and the coquettishness in her voice earned her a dirty look from her boyfriend.

"Hi, Natasha," Lewis replied.

"I forgive you for arresting me," she said.

"I didn't want to do it. Really. It's a long story, but I'm sorry."

Cohen grinned just as Irwin frowned. A roar of applause from the crowd on the other side of the stages told the picnickers that the mayor and the cardinal had begun their speeches.

"It's okay, really. I don't mind. I'm sure that Captain Donovan will get me off . . . Captain Donovan and Uncle Boris, of course."

"Thank you for including me," Irwin grumbled.

"What did you want to see me about?" Severino asked the girl.

"I didn't ask to see you," she replied. "Who told you that?"

"This cop," Severino snorted, hooking his head defiantly in the direction of Rodriguez. Who, ignoring the insult, had gone over to where Marcy had gotten to her feet and stood with her arms in the hug-me position. He hugged her.

"Hi, Lewis," she said.

"Hi, Marcy. How are you?"

"Just great."

"And Daniel? How is he?"

"Sensational."

At that point Mosko walked over to the two of them and stared, first at one and then the other. After a moment of this inquisition, he said, "You two can't know each other."

"We nearly didn't," Marcy said.

"What the hell is going on here?" Mosko asked.

"A good question," Traks added.

"What's happening here, Professor Traks, is that this young inline skater is going to help us discover just which one of the people here killed Harvey Cozzens and why," Donovan said.

"I told you, I was nowhere near the murder scene," Severino said rapidly.

"Doesn't matter," Mosko told him.

Donovan turned to Lauriat and said, "Francois . . . is this the man who assaulted you?"

Swallowing a gulp of air or saliva or *something*, Lauriat said, "Yes, it is. This is the man."

"You old fool," Severino snapped. "I'm gonna get you good now."

"You don't talk that way to my father," Frank Lauriat blurted, getting to his feet for an instant before his father pulled him back down to the bench.

"I'm no longer afraid of you," Lauriat said.

"So that's one count of assault we got you on," Donovan said. "Patrolman Rodriguez will read you your rights in a minute. But if you think that you can race off on those fancy skates and get away, I'd like you to meet my wife, Sergeant Marcia Donovan, retired. Who is a great skater and, not incidentally, a ninth-degree black belt in kung fu. You want to flee? Have a ball."

Severino looked around and seemed to be thinking of it, but then realized he was trapped in a sea of cops and gave up. "Okay," he said.

"And there's more," Donovan continued. "Sergeant Shea?"

Shea reached behind the grill and got a large plastic evidence bag that he tossed to the captain. Donovan held it up so that Severino and the rest of them could see it. The bag contained an expensive-looking purse.

"See this bag?" Donovan asked. "Brushed suede Gucci, seven hundred and fifteen dollars at Bloomingdale's. Guess where Officer Rodriguez found it?"

Severino looked away and appeared to be listening to the cardinal's invocation.

"He found it in the culvert near the northeast corner of the Central Park Reservoir—where you threw it—where you throw all the purses you steal from women in the park."

"I didn't steal nothing," Severino said.

"Funny, 'cause your prints are all over it. And that makes you a bona fide purse snatcher. Congratulations, schmuck. You just got busted twice in five minutes by a rookie cop. And one of those charges, keep in mind, is very serious—felony assault. I wonder if they have an inline skating team at Sing Sing. Officer Rodriguez, read the man his rights."

Lewis did so, finalizing the recitation by slapping on a pair of handcuffs.

"And you know what?" Donovan continued. "The last one to wear those cuffs was Winnie the Pooh, so consider yourself a lucky man. You're sharing iron with a legend."

"I want to see a lawyer," Severino said.

"This one's available," Donovan said, nodding at Irwin.

But that man shook his head. "I already have a client. It would be a conflict."

"After you talk to your lawyer, whoever he is," Donovan continued, "tell him that I can get you off the hook . . . just like I'm getting Natasha Cohen off the hook."

"I told you," Cohen said to Irwin. "I told you we could trust this man."

"And I can do this right now, very easily," Donovan said.

"How can you get me off the hook?" Severino asked.

"Tell me about the night you stole Natasha's purse," Donovan said.

"You mean it? You can get me off the hook?"

"Francois?"

"I agree to drop charges if you cooperate with the captain to his satisfaction and mine," Lauriat replied.

"What happened that night?" Donovan said.

"All right . . . I'll tell you . . . I stole the purse, Natasha's purse, about a month ago. Are you happy now?"

"Almost. What did you get out of the purse?"

"Eighty bucks," Severino snorted.

"That's it?"

"And a bank card that had expired. Yeah, that's it, eighty bucks."

"You didn't find anything else?"

"Like what?" Severino asked.

"Like a knife?" Donovan said.

The man laughed. "You mean the old knife?"

"Yeah. The old knife."

"It wasn't worth shit. It was an old fishing knife . . . like old men carry to the waterfront to cut bait. I couldn't figure out what she was doing with it . . . probably found it someplace and carried it for protection. I *have* a knife, since you're asking . . . a good Swiss Army knife that cost me two hundred bucks. A genuine item."

"What did you do with 'the old knife?' "

Severino snorted, "I carried it around in my fanny pack while my boys and me made a lap of the park and then I tossed it out with the purse."

"That's the same fanny pack you keep your Sensory Loob in, isn't it?"

"My skate oil? How'd you know about that?"

"I guessed," Donovan said. "Where did you dump the purse?"

"In that culvert, just like you said."

Donovan smiled and Mosko smiled with him.

"Why that culvert?"

"It's isolated and people don't go there."

"Why?"

"The fucking place is full of rats," Severino said, his voice showing disgust.

"And so it is," Donovan replied.

It had been a while since Traks had made a smart remark; quite the contrary, he now stared nervously at the captain. Donovan saw this but chose to ignore it. Instead, he glanced at the back of the stage, where a commotion as well as the resumption of live music—a performance by the Brian Setzer Orchestra playing an old Louis Prima tune called "Jump, Jive, and Wail"—meant that the mayor and the cardinal were returning to their limo and walking in the general direction of the picnic.

Donovan turned to Natasha and Frank and asked, "What time did you two say you heard fire sirens the night of the murder?"

Frank and Natasha looked at one another, then both shrugged. "I didn't hear fire sirens." she said.

"What about you?" Donovan asked the boy.

He shook his head. "No . . . nothing."

"Did you ask us that before?" she asked the captain.

"No. That was a trick question."

"*I* heard fire sirens," Cohen said.

"I was hoping you would say that," Donovan replied.

"It was right after three," the poet continued. "Remember I told you I fell asleep beneath the Sumatran willow and didn't wake up until three?"

Donovan remembered.

"Well, I was walking home and there were fire trucks on Park Drive West. I couldn't see where the fire was, though."

"It was in a garbage can," Mosko said.

"The killer of Harvey Cozzens was burning the bloody clothes," Donovan said. "Three fire trucks responded."

"I heard the sirens too," Traks said, a bit tentatively, Donovan thought.

"I know," Donovan replied.

"You told him," Mosko said.

"You told me you heard the sirens as you were working

in your enclosure," Donovan said. "But that was a lie . . . the fire in the trash can happened a mile and a half away and your enclosure, as well as the culvert nearby, are in a low-lying area shielded by trees. You couldn't hear the sirens from there."

"I admitted I lied to you about being there at that time," Traks said, his voice now quite tentative.

"I know," Donovan said.

"I went out to Burger Demon and got a Demon Burger."

"I don't think so," Marcy said.

Traks looked at her. "What?" he asked.

"The night of the murder there was an electrical short in a Con Edison junction box," Donovan said. "Knocked out lights along a stretch of Broadway that included Burger Demon as well as my wife's restaurant."

"The freezers went off and I lost a hundred dollars' worth of zabaglione," Marcy said.

"All the restaurants along Broadway in that neighborhood were closed," Donovan said. "Including Burger Demon. So there was no trip to buy a Demon Burger. So when you heard the sirens you weren't in your camp and you weren't out for a burger. That's two lies. Want to go for three?"

"I don't know what you're saying," Traks said, his voice breaking.

"Remember you told me you were never at the old gazebo?" Donovan asked.

Traks nodded, his head bobbing up and down jerkily; Donovan had the impression he took a moment to make up his mind whether to reconsider what he said earlier. And, as so often happens in times of stress, he picked the wrong answer.

"I was never there," he said.

"Sergeant Shea?" Donovan said again.

Yet again Shea set aside his spatula and got something for

the captain, in this case a manila folder. Shea handed it over, and Donovan waved it in front of Traks.

"When we invited you to bring us your tapes we had an ulterior motive," Donovan said.

"We wanted you away from your camp so we could get a cast of your shoeprint," Mosko said.

"And guess what?" Donovan said. "You wear size nine sneakers. Cute little feet you got there, professor. You too, Severino."

"We found a size nine sneaker print at the murder scene," Mosko said.

"You just said that this man has small feet, too," Traks stammered, pointing at Severino.

"Yeah, but he has one big advantage—a dozen or more witnesses who can account for his movements the night of the killing. One of them, by the way, is Officer Rodriguez here, whose talent and honesty I can vouch for. Sorry, Traks . . . you're it. You killed Harvey Cozzens."

Traks stood, shaking visibly, and stepped away from the picnic table. Instinctively, the others at the table leaned away from him. Donovan reached down and touched his shoulder holster. The music was playing loud behind them and the commotion begun when the mayor and cardinal and their entourage began making their way toward the limousine as the driver of that vehicle started his engine.

Traks said, "Why would I want to kill him?"

"You didn't go there to kill Cozzens," Donovan said. "You went there to kill Francois."

The Lauriats—father and son—glared at the other scientist.

Donovan continued. "You came to New York not so much to study rats as to get revenge on the man who cuckolded you. You made trips to Burger Demon to set up your alibi, but also to swing by the old gazebo to spy on Francois and learn his habits. Which, we all know by now, include an early-morning constitutional to clean up the beer bottles left behind by these two."

Donovan smiled at the teenage lovers, then continued: "You bought a gun, but stumbled on something nastier—an antique Moorish dagger given by Tommy Hertig to Gabriel Allen Cohen and recently stolen from his daughter. When revenge is the motive, it's always more satisfying to kill up close and personal . . . like a tarsier pouncing on its victim. Before you found that knife, however, it resided, along with a tube of very distinctive and long-lasting oil, in the fanny pack of an inline skater. The oil got on the knife, where it remained when we fished the still-bloody weapon out of the drink. Unfortunately for you, your intended victim took his signature jacket to the cleaners and Harvey Cozzens, a poor creep who had become infatuated with a young performance artist, had the bad luck to show up wearing a jacket that resembled it. And so he died horribly, with mutilation resulting from the rage that you flew into after discovering you killed the wrong man. You dragged his wretched corpse into the pond, the way the Sionoyas do by way of disposing of unwanted cadavers, and there it was the following morning when the crows woke up hungry."

Donovan didn't hear a caw, but thought of one, and so looked up to spot the bird, Nevermore, perched on the topmost branch of an ancient and honorable oak. A few kin birds were perched nearby, but Nevermore sat highest and, in his black fashion, most regally. Once again, the captain was sure that the critter was watching him.

Donovan said, "We got you, Traks. You're under arrest."

The captain heard a voice, the mayor's voice, calling "Hey Bill," but before he could react Traks's hand flicked in and out of his shoulder bag and came up with the Ruger Bearcat pistol. What happened next did so in scant seconds.

Eyes alight with fury, Traks aimed the weapon at the captain, who went for his automatic, the Cyrcad automatic that Pilcrow had asked him to test, the one with the radio-control wristband that allowed it to be fired only by its owner.

In the back of his senses, Donovan heard policemen shouting, someone rushing up behind him, and there was a flash of fire from the muzzle of the Bearcat and a slender but lethal twenty-two caliber bullet whizzed by his ear; he pulled the trigger on the Cyrcad and nothing happened, just the soft feel of *nothing* as the weapon failed to fire. Traks was aiming his weapon again, more carefully this time, and then came a roar, the grotesque blast of a nine-millimeter Glock automatic going off almost close enough to Donovan's ear for him to feel the chill of the composite material the gun was made of. And as the shock wave of the sound knocked his head to one side and stunned him and he felt like he had been hit on the side of the head with a two-by-four, he was dimly aware of Traks being hit in the chest and thrown to the ground.

There was a voice, young and familiar but not familiar, really, which said "Dad!" as Donovan let the Cyrcad slip from his fingers, the better to clamp a hand over his ear and keep his balance. Donovan didn't hear that word spoken, just the tone of voice; he would be told about it later.

Traks was a bleeding pile on the ground not far from the barbecue grill. From all over, cops were converging on the scene, weapons drawn. The mayor and the cardinal had ducked behind a police cruiser at the sound of the shots but ventured out, timidly at first, then readily once the coast was clear and the guns were put away. Lewis slipped the Glock back into its belt holster and snapped the catch that held it there.

Donovan retrieved his Cyrcad and tore off the wristband and gave both objects to Deputy Inspector Pilcrow when he arrived a few steps ahead of the dignitaries.

"It doesn't work," Donovan said, angling his left ear, the good one, toward his boss.

"Are you all right?" Pilcrow asked. "Who is this man?" The deputy inspector looked at the body, then looked at Lewis.

"Bill!" the mayor said. "You okay?"

"You'll have to speak up," Donovan said, still holding his right ear with one hand.

"What happened?"

Donovan grabbed Lewis by the arm and pulled him up alongside. Then the captain said, "The man on the ground, Rudolf Traks, is the one who killed Harvey Cozzens at Fiddler's Pond earlier this week. Natasha Cohen and Frank Lauriat are innocent. I was about to arrest Traks when he opened fire and my gun wouldn't shoot. I'm alive because Officer Rodriguez here shot him. Officer Rodriguez also helped develop the information that led to Traks."

"Good work, son," the mayor said, grabbing the young man's hand and pumping it.

"Thank you, sir!" Lewis replied, proud but unable, for some reason, to let go of his father's arm.

"Are you sure you're okay, Bill?"

"What did you say?" Donovan asked, the pain in his ear subsiding but replaced by numbness; he found himself partly deaf.

"Do you want a doctor?"

Donovan angled his head again so his left ear faced the mayor. That left him talking to Hizzoner but staring at the picnic table and his wife, who was coming over, and the Cohens and Lauriats, who sat dumbfounded. "The gun went off next to my ear. I'm a little stunned. "You're gonna have to speak up."

"As long as you're all right," the mayor said, stepping back to let Marcy come around to her husband's other side and put an arm around him.

Donovan said, "Patrolman Rodriguez is Deputy Chief Pilcrow's man, so you have him to thank too."

"Good work, Paul," the Mayor said to Pilcrow, who, after a moment of surprise in which he appeared to be trying to figure out what Donovan was up to, smiled and accepted a handshake.

To the cardinal, Donovan said, "Once again we'll need your talents." And the man bent over the corpse, crucifix in hand, administering last rites.

"It's getting dangerous being around you," the mayor said, grasping Donovan's arm and giving it a squeeze.

"What?" Donovan replied.

"Can I give you a lift home?"

"What?"

"Want a ride home?" the man fairly shouted.

"I think I'll sit here for a while," Donovan said, and then let his wife and eldest son lead him over to the redwood picnic table and a spot on the bench. The Cohens and Lauriats thanked the captain even more profusely than did the mayor, then melted off into a group by themselves, under the tree but away from the man who could indeed be dangerous to be around. Then Mosko came over, pointedly, with something on his mind.

The sergeant eyeballed Lewis and Marcy and then moved in close to Donovan and, picking the good ear, said, "He called you 'Dad.'"

"Oh, *that*," Donovan replied.

"What gives?"

"Brian . . . Officer Rodriguez . . . Lewis . . . is my son."

Mosko pointedly and silently mouthed the words "my son." Then he asked, "When did this happen?"

"Nearly twenty years ago. It's a long story for another day."

"You have a lot of those stories, don't you?"

"Not as important as this," Donovan said.

Mosko gave Lewis a peculiar look such as might suggest he was a space alien, then said, "You don't mind if I discuss business with your old man?"

"Have a ball," Lewis replied.

Mosko turned back to the captain and said, "I got to know . . . why did you stop me when I was about to accuse Frank Lauriat of planning to kill his father?"

"I wasn't sure he was guilty."

"He *looked* it."

"But we could have been wrong," Donovan said. "And if we were, I didn't want to plant the thought in Lauriat's mind that his son might have been out to kill him, even if we disproved it a few minutes later. The guy had just reconciled with his son after a long estrangement. He deserved a break." Donovan cast a glance at Lewis, and said, "The both of them did. Can I have a beer and a hamburger?"

"I'll get it for you," Lewis said, and began to jump up but Donovan held him down.

"No, you stay. I'm not letting go of you. You saved my life."

"Well, I don't know. The guy probably couldn't have killed you with a twenty-two."

"You saved his life," Marcy said. She arched her long and lean body around the front of her husband and kissed his son on the cheek then, saying, quietly, "Thank you." Then she called Shea to come over with lunch.

Donovan smiled contentedly despite the feeling in his head, which he later described as "brain Novocain." He closed his eyes for a second then opened them and looked around the treetops. The old crow was gone again.

The hill was an old one from Donovan's childhood and young manhood. It was in Riverside Park, not Central Park, and was perfectly suited for sledding, sloping not quite dangerously from the pedestrian walkway down to a broad and flat lawn that culminated in a waist-high stone wall overlooking the Hudson River. If the hill was for sledders, the lawn and stone wall were for families and lovers who were in that part of their lives spent easing up to making a family. On another spring Sunday, this one in May and two weeks down the road from the events of Earth Day Megacelebration, Donovan, his hearing more or less returned to normal, was thinking very hard about family as he sat with his two sons and watched the clouds drift over the river that separated New York City from the saner balance of the world.

Daniel lay in his carriage, happily sucking a binky and watching a seagull that soared over the treetops along the river bank, looking free of care and with no particular place to go. Lewis shifted his gaze between the half-brother he had met but recently and the father he had despised for years but had come to accept. At least that was how it seemed to Donovan, who had enough evidence of the accuracy of his intuition to accept this feeling as true. He was in a confident, expansive mood, and thus he treated his first-born to an oral tour of his first case to make headlines, the successful pursuit of a serial killer who lurked in the subterranean storm drains and other tunnels beneath Riverside Park—which was not a natural area but built upon a platform erected over the old West Side railroad tracks—some twenty years earlier.

"I had a hand-to-hand with him in the dark halfway up

the hill," Donovan said, coming to the end of his tale and swiveling around to point to the exact spot, now overgrown with bushes. "I was pretty tough in those days but he was twice my size and hard as an old river barge. I remember getting him with a right to the gut, and that was a punch that worked well for me and would have put down most normal men. But it was like my fist bounced off him and then he caught me on the side of the head and the lights went out."

Donovan touched his fingertips to the spot, then continued: "Anyway, I lived through it and shortly thereafter shot the sonofabitch in one of the tunnels. Right about there." He pointed down and to the left. "That's where the railroad tracks lead north out of the city to Albany and Canada. The tracks were abandoned in those days, and a couple of dozen homeless folks called the Mole People lived in the tunnel full-time. But the railroad evicted them when they started running trains again. Back during the Reagan years."

"Does one of your childhood friends really work as an advisor to the President?" Lewis asked.

"Yeah. For another year until the guy leaves office. I get Christmas cards from the White House, which is kind of cool. Anyway, this lawn is where your mom and I used to play Frisbee."

"Mom . . . played Frisbee?" Lewis laughed.

"No more?" Donovan asked.

"She's kind of put on weight."

"Haven't we all?"

"You look in shape," Lewis said.

"I'm a hundred eighty-three," Donovan replied. "I should be one seventy-five. I work out every day . . . well, to be honest, three times a week. Nothing too strenuous . . . I do a few Nautilus routines and some free weights."

"You seem happy. I mean, what do I know? I know you mainly . . . by reputation."

"As the Great Satan of your childhood," Donovan said.

"Or as New York's most brilliant detective."

"Not 'most unorthodox'?"

"Maybe. It's a little weird, being your kid."

"How so?"

"First everybody knew you as being a tough guy who fought and drank with both hands. Now you're a self-taught intellectual who appears on *Nightline*."

"Which one do you like better?" Donovan asked.

"This one," Lewis replied.

"I grew up and realized you could be more effective with your brain than with your fists. I think all guys go through that; maybe it was a bit more dramatic in my case. Anyway, I haven't done any *Nightline* since the O. J. trial ended."

"It's like starting out life the kid of Bruce Willis and winding up the son of . . . I don't know, give me the name of a really intelligent man you admire."

"Lewis Rodriguez," Donovan said.

Lewis smiled, then looked embarrassed, then looked away and down. A train was rumbling northward beneath them, and the ground shook faintly. "Where did you say you shot that guy?"

"Down there. Right in the middle of the tracks. Like I said, he was tough—it took three shots to bring him down. And if you look over there, halfway across the grass . . . see the jogging trail?"

Lewis said that he saw it.

"That's where Marcy was shot while working on the same case. Took a bullet in the stomach and had half of it removed. That's why she can eat so much without gaining weight. She can be really irritating that way."

"Marcy is still gorgeous. How old is she? Can you say?"

"Not if I value my life," Donovan replied.

"I think she's the reason mom doesn't want to get together with you. Look, there's something I want to ask."

"Sure," Donovan said.

"How did you know Traks was guilty?"

"He was the only one with a powerful enough motive. The motives for the rest of them were what-ifs and maybes. As for Natasha and Frank, two kids don't kill someone for no good reason, unless they're seriously psychotic to begin with or whacked out on something."

"Frank couldn't have killed Cozzens because he was stalking her?" Lewis asked.

"Maybe he could have, but Cozzens wasn't an aggressive stalker," Donovan said. "It wasn't like he was following her around with a gun or something. He just wanted to *see* her and get off. That's sleazy but not something a guy deserves to be killed for. Maybe Frank would have beaten him up, or tried to. But stab him however many times? No."

"What did that turn out to be in Frank's fanny pack?"

"I mentioned that a vendor was selling CDs of the waves breaking over the seashore in New Patagonia? He bought a rock from that beach. Seven dollars."

"What about Severino as a suspect?" Lewis asked.

"There were too many witnesses to the contrary."

"Lauriat? Your friend?"

"To protect his son he might have assaulted the guy . . . or tried to," Donovan said. "But killed him, no. I don't think he'd know how."

"Cohen?"

"He would have called the cops on his cell phone," Donovan said. "Poets aren't murderers, generally speaking, unless there's an overriding psychosis. Cohen may have led an apparently chaotic life and said a lot of radical things, but keep in mind that he lived a pretty nice life—great apartment, pretty young wife, etc. Now, some murderers may become poets, but that's mainly while killing time on death row."

"What about me?" Lewis asked, a bit coyly.

"To protect her? You're a cop, for God's sake. There are enough opportunities for inflicting pain of one kind or another without having to resort to murder. How is Natasha, by the way? I heard she's been in touch."

"Yeah," Lewis replied, his face sunnying up. "She e-mailed me. The way she sees it, you're her protector and I saved you so she's *very* grateful. We're getting together for coffee."

"She's underage," Donovan said.

"I know."

"Does the word 'jailbait' mean anything to you?"

"Stop fathering me," Lewis said.

"Never," Donovan said firmly.

"It's like we've only been speaking for five minutes and already you're hovering over me," Lewis objected.

"I've been doing it longer than five minutes. Remember when you were sixteen and those two crack dealers from Manhattan Avenue took a disliking to you and threatened you."

Lewis nodded.

"How do you think their paroles got revoked and they were sent back to jail?" Donovan said.

"That was you?"

Donovan nodded. "Guilty as charged."

"How did you know about them?" Lewis asked.

"Your mom and I talk on the phone from time to time."

"She never told me about calling you."

"Well, I'm sure it just slipped her mind," Donovan said.

After a thoughtful moment, Lewis said, "I'll never get rid of those records you gave me. Did you know that the monaural mix of the Hendrix album is worth a hundred and fifty bucks?"

Donovan hadn't known that.

"Where did you *get* that album?"

"It was nineteen sixty-seven. Who remembers?"

"Oh yeah, and I was talking to the lawyer, Irwin, while Traks's body was being hauled off. He said something about you having been active in the civil rights movement in the deep South when you were a kid. Something about a bridge?"

Donovan smiled, reached into the carriage, and stroked Daniel on the side of his cheek. Then the captain said, "To paraphrase Sam Spade, don't be fooled by the bad reputation. It makes it easier to deal with the enemy and get the job done."

Lewis made a funny face, then said, "You didn't answer me."

"Don't believe everything you hear," Donovan said. "And while we're on the subject of disbelief, how did Pilcrow take your not having gotten the goods on me?"

"Oh, that. Well, he was so grateful . . . I think he was stunned, actually . . . when you gave him credit for helping catch Traks . . . that he didn't say anything. I think he likes you now."

"As I said, don't believe everything you hear," Donovan said.

Daniel made a mewing sound and spit the pacifier out and then waved both arms in the air and said something like "uh uh."

"What's he want?" Lewis asked, a bit unnerved, as young single men will be, by an infant with needs.

"In the absence of his mom's breast, a bottle."

Donovan rummaged around in the carriage's carrying compartment and found a vinyl Teletubbies lunch box from which he extricated a six-ounce bottle filled with a slightly off-white fluid. Seeing Lewis's quizzical look, Donovan said, "Special formula for kids who can't drink cow's milk."

"He's got allergies?" Lewis asked.

342

"He's got a few things, allergies among them. It happens, I hear, when you have babies relatively late in life. Can you imagine a kid with Irish blood who can't drink milk?"

Lewis smiled and watched as Donovan slipped the bottle into the baby's mouth. "You're good at that," Lewis said.

"Want a bialy?" Donovan said, plucking one from a paper bag that he had tucked into the Teletubbies lunch box.

Lewis shook his head. "Tell me what I should do at the medal ceremony tomorrow."

"Shake everyone's hand and smile a lot," Donovan said. "The mayor and the police commissioner will do enough talking for everyone."

"I heard you keep your medals in a shoe box in the bottom of a closet."

"They're on the mantel now," Donovan replied, taking a bite and then leaning back on the bench, putting his feet up on one end of the carriage.

"I put in for transfer to Midtown," Lewis said. "I'd like to be in the thick of things. Enough walking around Central Park."

"Good for you. But you know there's a place for you on my squad should you ever want it."

"I need to find my own way for a while. But I may call you for advice from time to time."

"I'd like that," Donovan replied.

Then father and son . . . father and *sons* . . . fell silent, enjoying the splendid afternoon and listening to the low chugging of a Moran tug that was pushing a black barge, the cargo of which—Donovan couldn't tell what—made it lay deep in the water. The barge was heading upriver, against the tide, and shoving aside a wall of water that was white on the top foaming over onto the deck and blue and green on the sides spreading out to both banks of the Hudson. And in the sun and with the water and the waves, it was a good afternoon for them, a good time in general for Donovan and his boys.